ON THE EDGE

NEW YORK TIMES BESTSELLING AUTHOR

TESS GERRITSEN

Previously published as *Keeper of the Bride*
and *Undercover Avenger*

Recycling programs
for this product may
not exist in your area.

ISBN-13: 978-1-335-40638-5

On the Edge
First published as Keeper of the Bride in 1996.
This edition published in 2021.
Copyright © 1996 by Terry Gerritsen

Undercover Avenger
First published in 2004. This edition published in 2021.
Copyright © 2004 by Rita B. Herron

This edition published by arrangement with Harlequin Books S.A.

For questions and comments about the quality of this book, please contact us at CustomerService@Harlequin.com.

Harlequin Enterprises ULC
22 Adelaide St. West, 40th Floor
Toronto, Ontario M5H 4E3, Canada
www.Harlequin.com

Printed in U.S.A.

CONTENTS

KEEPER OF THE BRIDE 7
Tess Gerritsen

UNDERCOVER AVENGER 263
Rita Herron

Internationally bestselling author **Tess Gerritsen** is a graduate of Stanford University and went on to medical school at the University of California, San Francisco, where she was awarded her MD. Since 1987, her books have been translated into thirty-seven languages, and more than twenty-five million copies have been sold around the world. She has received the Nero Award and the RITA® Award, and she was a finalist for the Edgar Award. Now retired from medicine, she writes full-time. She lives in Maine.

Books by Tess Gerritsen

Call After Midnight
Under the Knife
Never Say Die
Whistleblower
Presumed Guilty
In Their Footsteps
Thief of Hearts
Keeper of the Bride

Visit the Author Profile page at Harlequin.com for more titles.

KEEPER OF THE BRIDE

Tess Gerritsen

Chapter 1

The wedding was off. Cancelled. Canned. Kaput.

Nina Cormier sat staring at herself in the church dressing room mirror and wondered why she couldn't seem to cry. She knew the pain was there, deep and terrible beneath the numbness, but she didn't feel it. Not yet. She could only sit dry-eyed, staring at her reflection. The picture-perfect image of a bride. Her veil floated in gossamer wisps about her face. The bodice of her ivory satin dress, embroidered with seed pearls, hung fetchingly off-shoulder. Her long black hair was gathered into a soft chignon. Everyone who'd seen her that morning in the dressing room—her mother, her sister Wendy, her stepmother Daniella—had declared her a beautiful bride.

And she *would* have been. Had the groom bothered to show up.

He didn't even have the courage to break the news to

her in person. After six months of planning and dreaming, she'd received his note just twenty minutes before the ceremony. Via the best man, no less.

Nina,
I need time to think about this. I'm sorry, I really am. I'm leaving town for a few days. I'll call you.
                                                    Robert

She forced herself to read the note again.
I need time.... I need time....
How much time does a man need? she wondered.

A year ago, she'd moved in with Dr. Robert Bledsoe. *It's the only way to know if we're compatible,* he'd told her. Marriage was such a major commitment, a permanent commitment, and he didn't want to make a mistake. At forty-one, Robert had known his share of disastrous relationships. He was determined not to make any more mistakes. He wanted to be sure that Nina was the one he'd been waiting for all his life.

She'd been certain Robert was the man *she'd* been waiting for. So certain that, on the very day he'd suggested they live together, she'd gone straight home and packed her bags....

"Nina? Nina, open the door!" It was her sister Wendy, rattling the knob. "Please let me in."

Nina dropped her head in her hands. "I don't want to see anyone right now."

"You need to be with someone."

"I just want to be alone."

"Look, the guests have all gone home. The church is empty. It's just me out here."

"I don't want to talk to anyone. Just go home, will you? Please, just go."

There was a long silence outside the door. Then Wendy said, "If I leave now, how're you going to get home? You'll need a ride."

"Then I'll call a cab. Or Reverend Sullivan can drive me. I need some time to think."

"You're sure you don't want to talk?"

"I'm sure. I'll call you later, okay?"

"If that's what you really want." Wendy paused, then added, with a note of venom that penetrated even through the oak door, "Robert's a jerk, you know. I might as well tell you. I've always thought he was."

Nina didn't answer. She sat at the dressing table, her head in her hands, wanting to cry, but unable to squeeze out a single tear. She heard Wendy's footsteps fade away, then heard only the silence of the empty church. Still no tears would come. She couldn't think about Robert right now. Instead, her mind seemed to focus stubbornly on the practical aspects of a cancelled wedding. The catered reception and all that uneaten food. The gifts she had to return. The nonrefundable airline tickets to St. John Island. Maybe she should go on that honeymoon anyway and forget Dr. Robert Bledsoe. She'd go by herself, just her and her bikini. Out of this whole heartbreaking affair, at least she'd come out with a tan.

Slowly she raised her head and once again looked at her reflection in the mirror. Not such a beautiful bride after all, she thought. Her lipstick was smeared and her chignon was coming apart. She was turning into a wreck.

With sudden rage she reached up and yanked off the veil. Hairpins flew in every direction, releasing a rebellious tumble of black hair. To hell with the veil; she tossed it in the trash can. She snatched up her bouquet of white lilies and pink sweetheart roses and slam-dunked it into the trash can as well. That felt good. Her anger was like some new and potent fuel flooding her veins. It propelled her to her feet.

She walked out of the church dressing room, the train of her gown dragging behind her, and entered the nave.

The pews were deserted. Garlands of white carnations draped the aisles, and the altar was adorned with airy sprays of pink roses and baby's breath. The stage had been beautifully set for a wedding that would never take place. But the lovely results of the florist's hard work was scarcely noticed by Nina as she strode past the altar and started up the aisle. Her attention was focused straight ahead on the front door. On escape. Even the concerned voice of Reverend Sullivan calling to her didn't slow her down. She walked past all the floral reminders of the day's fiasco and pushed through the double doors.

There, on the church steps, she halted. The July sunshine glared in her eyes, and she was suddenly, painfully aware of how conspicuous she must be, a lone woman in a wedding gown, trying to wave down a taxi. Only then, as she stood trapped in the brightness of afternoon, did she feel the first sting of tears.

Oh, no. Lord, no. She was going to break down and cry right here on the steps. In full view of every damn car driving past on Forest Avenue.

"Nina? Nina, dear."

She turned. Reverend Sullivan was standing on the step above her, a look of worry on his kind face.

"Is there anything I can do? Anything at all?" he asked. "If you'd like, we could go inside and talk."

Miserably she shook her head. "I want to get away from here. Please, I just want to get away."

"Of course. Of course." Gently, he took her arm. "I'll drive you home."

Reverend Sullivan led her down the steps and around the side of the building, to the staff parking lot. She gathered up her train, which by now was soiled from all that dragging, and climbed into his car. There she sat with all the satin piled high on her lap.

Reverend Sullivan slid in behind the wheel. The heat was stifling inside the car, but he didn't start the engine. Instead they sat for a moment in awkward silence.

"I know it's hard to understand what possible purpose the Lord may have for all this," he said quietly. "But surely there's a reason, Nina. It may not be apparent to you at the moment. In fact, it may seem to you that the Lord has turned His back."

"Robert's the one who turned his back," she said. Sniffling, she snatched up a clean corner of her train and wiped her face. "Turned his back and ran like hell."

"Ambivalence is common for bridegrooms. I'm sure Dr. Bledsoe felt this was a big step for him—"

"A big step for *him?* I suppose marriage is just a stroll in the park for me?"

"No, no, you misunderstand me."

"Oh, please." She gave a muffled sob. "Just take me home."

Shaking his head, he put the key in the ignition. "I only wanted to explain to you, dear, in my own clumsy way, that this isn't the end of the world. It's the nature of life. Fate is always throwing surprises at us, Nina. Crises we never expect. Things that seem to pop right out of the blue."

A deafening boom suddenly shook the church building. The explosion shattered the stained glass windows, and a hail of multicolored glass shards flew across the parking lot. Torn hymn books and fragments of church pews tumbled onto the blacktop.

As the white smoke slowly cleared, Nina saw a dusting of flower petals drift gently down from the sky and settle on the windshield right in front of Reverend Sullivan's shocked eyes.

"Right out of the blue," she murmured. "You couldn't have said it better."

"You two, without a doubt, are the biggest screwups of the year."

Portland police detective Sam Navarro, sitting directly across the table from the obviously upset Norm Liddell, didn't bat an eyelash. There were five of them sitting in the station conference room, and Sam wasn't about to give this prima donna D.A. the satisfaction of watching him flinch in public. Nor was Sam going to refute the charges, because they *had* screwed up. He and Gillis had screwed up big time, and now a cop was dead. An idiot cop, but a cop all the same. One of their own.

"In our defense," spoke up Sam's partner Gordon Gillis, "we never gave Marty Pickett permission to approach the site. We had no idea he'd crossed the police line—"

"You were in charge of the bomb scene," said Liddell. "That makes you responsible."

"Now, wait a minute," said Gillis. "Officer Pickett has to bear some of the blame."

"Pickett was just a rookie."

"He should've been following procedure. If he'd—"

"Shut up, Gillis," said Sam.

Gillis looked at his partner. "Sam, I'm only trying to defend our position."

"Won't do us a damn bit of good. Since we're obviously the designated fall guys." Sam leaned back in his chair and eyed Liddell across the conference table. "What do you want, Mr. D.A.? A public flogging? Our resignations?"

"No one's asking for your resignations," cut in Chief Abe Coopersmith. "And this discussion is getting us nowhere."

"*Some* disciplinary action is called for," said Liddell. "We have a dead police officer—"

"Don't you think I know that?" snapped Coopersmith. "*I'm* the one who had to answer to the widow. Not to mention all those bloodsucking reporters. Don't give me this *us* and *we* crap, Mr. D.A. It was one of *ours* who fell. A cop. *Not* a lawyer."

Sam looked in surprise at his chief. This was a new experience, having Coopersmith on his side. The Abe Coopersmith he knew was a man of few words, few of them complimentary. It was because Liddell was rubbing them all the wrong way. When under fire, cops always stuck together.

"Let's get back to the business at hand, okay?" said Coopersmith. "We have a bomber in town. And our first fatality. What do we know so far?" He looked at Sam, who was head of the newly re-formed Bomb Task Force. "Navarro?"

"Not a hell of a lot," admitted Sam. He opened a file folder and took out a sheaf of papers. He distributed copies to the other four men around the table—Liddell, Chief Coopersmith, Gillis, and Ernie Takeda, the explosives expert from the Maine State Crime Lab. "The first blast occurred around 2:15 a.m. The second blast around 2:30 a.m. It was the second one that pretty much levelled the R. S. Hancock warehouse. It also caused minor damage to two adjoining buildings. The night watchman was the one who found the first device. He noticed signs of breaking and entering, so he searched the building. The bomb was left on a desk in one of the offices. He put in the call at 1:30 a.m. Gillis got there around 1:50, I was there at 2:00 a.m. We had the blast area cordoned off and the top-vent container truck had just arrived when the first one went off. Then, fifteen minutes later—before we could search the building— the second device exploded. Killing Officer Pickett." Sam glanced at Liddell, but this time the D.A. chose to keep his mouth shut. "The dynamite was Dupont label."

There was a brief silence in the room. Then Coopersmith said, "Not the same Dupont lot number as those two bombs last year?"

"It's very likely," said Sam. "Since that missing lot number's the only reported large dynamite theft we've had up here in years."

"But the Spectre bombings were solved a year ago," said Liddell. "And we know Vincent Spectre's dead. So who's making *these* bombs?"

"We may be dealing with a Spectre apprentice. Someone who not only picked up the master's technique, but also has access to the master's dynamite supply. Which, I point out, we never located."

"You haven't confirmed the dynamite's from the same stolen lot number," said Liddell. "Maybe this has no connection at all with the Spectre bombings."

"I'm afraid we have other evidence," said Sam. "And you're not going to like it." He glanced at Ernie Takeda. "Go ahead, Ernie."

Takeda, never comfortable with public speaking, kept his gaze focused on the lab report in front of him. "Based on materials we gathered at the site," he said, "we can make a preliminary guess as to the makeup of the device. We believe the electrical action fuse was set off by an electronic delay circuit. This in turn ignited the dynamite via Prima detonating cord. The sticks were bundled together with two-inch-wide green electrical tape." Takeda cleared his throat and finally looked up. "It's the identical delay circuit that the late Vincent Spectre used in his bombings last year."

Liddell looked at Sam. "The same circuitry, the same dynamite lot? What the hell's going on?"

"Obviously," said Gillis, "Vincent Spectre passed on a few of his skills before he died. Now we've got a second-generation bomber on our hands."

"What we still have to piece together," said Sam, "is the psychological profile of this newcomer. Spectre's bombings were coldbloodedly financial. He was hired to do the jobs and he did them, *bam, bam, bam.* Efficient. Effective. This new bomber has to set a pattern."

"What you're saying," said Liddell, "is that you expect him to hit again."

Sam nodded wearily. "Unfortunately, that's exactly what I'm saying."

There was a knock on the door. A patrolwoman stuck her head into the conference room. "Excuse me, but there's a call for Navarro and Gillis."

"I'll take it," said Gillis. He rose heavily to his feet and went to the conference wall phone.

Liddell was still focused on Sam. "So this is all that Portland's finest can come up with? We wait for *another* bombing so that we can establish a *pattern?* And then maybe, just *maybe,* we'll have an idea of what the hell we're doing?"

"A bombing, Mr. Liddell," said Sam calmly, "is an act of cowardice. It's violence in the absence of the perpetrator. I repeat the word—*absence*. We have no ID, no fingerprints, no witnesses to the planting, no—"

"Chief," cut in Gillis. He hung up the phone. "They've just reported another one."

"What?" said Coopersmith.

Sam had already shot to his feet and was moving for the door.

"What was it this time?" called Liddell. "Another warehouse?"

"No," said Gillis. "A church."

The cops already had the area cordoned off by the time Sam and Gillis arrived at the Good Shepherd Church. A crowd was gathered up and down the street. Three patrol cars, two fire trucks and an ambulance were parked haphazardly along Forest Avenue. The bomb disposal truck and its boiler-shaped carrier in the flatbed stood idly near the church's front entrance— or what was left of the front entrance. The door had been blown clear off its hinges and had come to rest at the bottom of the front steps. Broken glass was everywhere. The wind scattered torn pages of hymn books like dead leaves along the sidewalk. Gillis swore. "This was a big one."

As they approached the police line, the officer in charge turned to them with a look of relief. "Navarro! Glad you could make it to the party."

"Any casualties?" asked Sam.

"None, as far as we know. The church was unoccupied at the time. Pure luck. There was a wedding scheduled for two, but it was cancelled at the last minute."

"Whose wedding?"

"Some doctor's. The bride's sitting over there in the

patrol car. She and the minister witnessed the blast from the parking lot."

"I'll talk to her later," said Sam. "Don't let her leave. Or the minister, either. I'm going to check the building for a second device."

"Better you than me."

Sam donned body armor made of overlapping steel plates encased in nylon. He also carried a protective mask, to be worn in case a second bomb was identified. A bomb tech, similarly garbed, stood by the front door awaiting orders to enter the building. Gillis would wait outside near the truck; his role this time around was to fetch tools and get the bomb carrier ready.

"Okay," Sam said to the technician. "Let's go."

They stepped through the gaping front entrance.

The first thing Sam noticed was the smell—strong and faintly sweet. Dynamite, he thought. He recognized the odor of its aftermath. The force of the blast had caused the pews at the rear to topple backward. At the front, near the altar, the pews had been reduced to splinters. All the stained glass panels were broken, and where the windows faced south, hazy sunlight shone in through the empty frames.

Without a word between them, Sam and the tech automatically split up and moved along opposite sides of the nave. The site would be more thoroughly searched later; this time around, their focus was only on locating any second bombs. The death of Marty Pickett still weighed heavily on Sam's conscience, and he wasn't about to let any other officers enter this building until he had cleared it.

Moving in parallel, the two men paced the nave, their eyes alert for anything resembling an explosive device. All the debris made it a slow search. As they moved forward, the damage visibly worsened, and the odor of exploded dynamite grew stronger. Getting closer, he thought. The bomb was planted somewhere around here...

In front of the altar, at a spot where the first row of pews would have stood, they found the crater. It was about three feet across and shallow; the blast had ripped through the carpet and pad, but had barely chipped the concrete slab below. A shallow crater was characteristic of a low-velocity blast—again, compatible with dynamite.

They would take a closer look at it later. They continued their search. They finished with the nave and progressed to the hallways, the dressing rooms, the restrooms. No bombs. They went into the annex and surveyed the church offices, the meeting rooms, the Sunday school classroom. No bombs. They exited through a rear door and searched the entire outside wall. No bombs.

Satisfied at last, Sam returned to the police line, where Gillis was waiting. There he took off the body armor. "Building's clean," Sam said. "We got the searchers assembled?"

Gillis gestured to the six men waiting near the bomb carrier truck. There were two patrolmen and four crime lab techs, each one clutching empty evidence bags. "They're just waiting for the word."

"Let's get the photographer in there first, then send the team in. The crater's up front, around the first row of pews on the right."

"Dynamite?"

Sam nodded. "If I can trust my nose." He turned and eyed the crowd of gawkers. "I'm going to talk to the witnesses. Where's the minister?"

"They just took him off to the ER. Chest pains. All that stress."

Sam gave an exasperated sigh. "Did anyone talk to him?"

"Patrolman did. We have his statement."

"Okay," said Sam. "I guess that leaves me with the bride."

"She's still waiting in the patrol car. Her name's Nina Cormier."

"Cormier. Gotcha." Sam ducked under the yellow police line and worked his way through the gathering of onlookers. Scanning the official vehicles, he spotted a silhouette in the front passenger seat of one of the cars. The woman didn't move as he approached; she was staring straight ahead like some wedding store mannequin. He leaned forward and tapped on the window.

The woman turned. Wide dark eyes stared at him through the glass. Despite the smudged mascara, the softly rounded feminine face was undeniably pretty. Sam motioned to her to roll down the window. She complied.

"Miss Cormier? I'm Detective Sam Navarro, Portland police."

"I want to go home," she said. "I've talked to so many cops already. Please, can't I just go home?"

"First I have to ask you a few questions."

"A few?"

"All right," he admitted. "It's more like a lot of questions."

She gave a sigh. Only then did he see the weariness in her face. "If I answer all your questions, Detective," she said, "will you let me go home?"

"I promise."

"Do you keep your promises?"

He nodded soberly. "Always."

She looked down at her hands, clasped in her lap. "Right," she muttered. "Men and their promises."

"Excuse me?"

"Oh, never mind."

He circled around the car, opened the door, and slid in behind the wheel. The woman next to him said nothing; she just sat there in resigned silence. She seemed almost swallowed up by those frothy layers of white satin. Her hairdo was coming undone and silky strands of black hair hung loose about her shoulders. Not at all the happy picture of a bride, he thought. She seemed stunned, and very much alone.

Where the hell was the groom?

Stifling an instinctive rush of sympathy, he reached for his notebook and flipped it open to a blank page. "Can I have your full name and address?"

The answer came out in a bare whisper. "Nina Margaret Cormier, 318 Ocean View Drive."

He wrote it down. Then he looked at her. She was still staring straight down at her lap. Not at him. "Okay, Miss Cormier," he said. "Why don't you tell me exactly what happened?"

She wanted to go home. She had been sitting in this patrol car for an hour and a half now, had talked to three different cops, had answered all their questions. Her wedding was a shambles, she'd barely escaped with her life, and those people out there on the street kept staring at her as though she were some sort of sideshow freak.

And this man, this cop with all the warmth of a codfish, expected her to go through it again?

"Miss Cormier," he sighed. "The sooner we get this

over with, the sooner you can leave. What, exactly, happened?"

"It blew up," she said. "Can I go home?"

"What do you mean by blew up?"

"There was a loud boom. Lots of smoke and broken windows. I'd say it was your typical exploding building."

"You mentioned smoke. What color was the smoke?"

"What?"

"Was it black? White?"

"Does it matter?"

"Just answer the question, please."

She gave an exasperated sigh. "It was white, I think."

"You think?"

"All right. I'm sure." She turned to look at him. For the first time she really focused on his face. If he'd been smiling, if there'd been even a trace of warmth, it would have been a pleasant enough face to look at. He was in his late thirties. He had dark brown hair that was about two weeks overdue for a trim. His face was thin, his teeth were perfect, and his deep-set green eyes had the penetrating gaze one expected of a romantic lead movie cop. Only this was no movie cop. This was an honest-to-goodness cop with a badge, and he wasn't in the least bit charming. He was studying her with a completely detached air, as though sizing up her reliability as a witness.

She gazed back at him, thinking, *Here I am, the rejected bride. He's probably wondering what's wrong with me. What terrible flaws I possess that led to my being stood up at the altar.*

She buried her fists in the white satin mounded on her lap. "I'm sure the smoke was white," she said tightly. "For whatever difference that makes."

"It makes a difference. It indicates a relative absence of carbon."

"Oh. I see." Whatever that told him.

"Were there any flames?"

"No. No flames."

"Did you smell anything?"

"You mean like gas?"

"Anything at all?"

She frowned. "Not that I remember. But I was outside the building."

"Where, exactly?"

"Reverend Sullivan and I were sitting in his car. In the parking lot around the side. So I wouldn't have smelled the gas. Anyway, natural gas is odorless. Isn't it?"

"It can be difficult to detect."

"So it doesn't mean anything. That I didn't smell it."

"Did you see anyone near the building prior to the explosion?"

"There was Reverend Sullivan. And some of my family. But they all left earlier."

"What about strangers? Anyone you don't know?"

"No one was inside when it happened."

"I'm referring to the time *prior* to the explosion, Miss Cormier."

"Prior?"

"Did you see anyone who shouldn't have been there?"

She stared at him. He gazed back at her, green eyes absolutely steady. "You mean—are you thinking—"

He didn't say anything.

"It wasn't a gas leak?" she said softly.

"No," he said. "It was a bomb."

She sank back, her breath escaping in a single

shocked rush. Not an accident, she thought. Not an accident at all....

"Miss Cormier?"

Wordlessly she looked at him. Something about the way he was watching her, that flat, emotionless gaze of his, made her frightened.

"I'm sorry to have to ask you this next question," he said. "But you understand, it's something I have to pursue."

She swallowed. "What...what question?"

"Do you know of anyone who might want you dead?"

Chapter 2

"This is crazy," she said. "This is absolutely nuts."

"I have to explore the possibility."

"*What* possibility? That the bomb was meant for *me*?"

"Your wedding was scheduled for two o'clock. The bomb went off at 2:40. It exploded near the front row of pews. Near the altar. There's no doubt in my mind, judging by the obvious force of the blast, that you and your entire wedding party would have been killed. Or, at the very least, seriously maimed. This *is* a bomb we're talking about, Miss Cormier. Not a gas leak. Not an accident. A bomb. It was meant to kill someone. What I have to find out is, who was the target?"

She didn't answer. The possibilities were too horrible to even contemplate.

"Who was in your wedding party?" he asked.

She swallowed. "There was...there was..."

"You and Reverend Sullivan. Who else?"

"Robert—my fiancé. And my sister Wendy. And Jeremy Wall, the best man…"

"Anyone else?"

"My father was going to give me away. And there was a flower girl and a ring bearer…"

"I'm only interested in the adults. Let's start with you."

Numbly she shook her head. "It—it wasn't me. It couldn't be me."

"Why couldn't it?"

"It's impossible."

"How can you be sure?"

"Because no one would want me dead!"

Her sharp cry seemed to take him by surprise. For a moment he was silent. Outside, on the street, a uniformed cop turned and glanced at them. Sam responded with an *everything's fine* wave of the hand, and the cop turned away again.

Nina sat clutching the rumpled hem of her gown. This man was horrid. Sam Spade without a trace of human warmth. Though it was getting hot in the car, she found herself shivering, chilled by the lack of obvious emotion displayed by the man sitting beside her.

"Can we explore this a little more?" he said.

She said nothing.

"Do you have any ex-boyfriends, Miss Cormier? Anyone who might be unhappy about your marriage?"

"No," she whispered.

"No ex-boyfriends at all?"

"Not—not in the last year."

"Is that how long you've been with your fiancé? A year?"

"Yes."

"His full name and address, please."

"Robert David Bledsoe, M.D., 318 Ocean View Drive."

"Same address?"

"We've been living together."

"Why was the wedding cancelled?"

"You'd have to ask Robert."

"So it was his decision? To call off the wedding?"

"As the expression goes, he left me at the altar."

"Do you know why?"

She gave a bitter laugh. "I've come to the earth-shattering conclusion, Detective, that the minds of men are a complete mystery to me."

"He gave you no warning at all?"

"It was just as unexpected as that…" She swallowed. "As that bomb. If that's what it was."

"What time was the wedding called off?"

"About one-thirty. I'd already arrived at the church, wedding gown and all. Then Jeremy—Robert's best man—showed up with the note. Robert didn't even have the nerve to tell me himself." She shook her head in disgust.

"What did the note say?"

"That he needed more time. And he was leaving town for a while. That's all."

"Is it possible Robert had any reason to—"

"No, it's *not* possible!" She looked him straight in the eye. "You're asking if Robert had something to do with it. Aren't you?"

"I keep an open mind, Miss Cormier."

"Robert's not capable of violence. For God's sake, he's a doctor!"

"All right. For the moment, we'll let that go. Let's look at other possibilities. I take it you're employed?"

"I'm a nurse at Maine Medical Center."

"Which department?"

"Emergency room."

"Any problems at work? Any conflicts with the rest of the staff?"

"No. We get along fine."

"Any threats? From your patients, for instance?"

She made a sound of exasperation. "Detective, wouldn't I know if I had enemies?"

"Not necessarily."

"You're trying your damn best to make me feel paranoid."

"I'm asking you to step back from yourself. Examine your personal life. Think of all the people who might not like you."

Nina sank back in the seat. *All the people who might not like me.* She thought of her family. Her older sister Wendy, with whom she'd never been close. Her mother Lydia, married to her wealthy snob of a husband. Her father George, now on his fourth wife, a blond trophy bride who considered her husband's offspring a nuisance. It was one big, dysfunctional family, but there were certainly no murderers among them.

She shook her head. "No one, Detective. There's no one."

After a moment he sighed and closed his notebook. "All right, Miss Cormier. I guess that's all for now."

"For now?"

"I'll probably have other questions. After I talk to the rest of the wedding party." He opened the car door, got out and pushed the door shut. Through the open window he said, "If you think of anything, anything at all, give me a call." He scribbled in his notebook and handed her the torn page with his name, Detective

Samuel I. Navarro, and a phone number. "It's my direct line," he said. "I can also be reached twenty-four hours a day through the police switchboard."

"Then... I can go home now?"

"Yes." He started to walk away.

"Detective Navarro?"

He turned back to her. She had not realized how tall he was. Now, seeing his lean frame at its full height, she wondered how he'd ever fit in the seat beside her. "Is there something else, Miss Cormier?" he asked.

"You said I could leave."

"That's right."

"I don't have a ride." She nodded toward the bombed-out church. "Or a phone either. Do you think you could give my mother a call? To come get me?"

"Your mother?" He glanced around, obviously anxious to palm off this latest annoyance. Finally, with a look of resignation, he circled around to her side of the car and opened the door. "Come on. We can go in my car. I'll drive you."

"Look, I was only asking you to make a call."

"It's no trouble." He extended his hand to help her out. "I'd have to go by your mother's house anyway."

"My mother's house? Why?"

"She was at the wedding. I'll need to talk to her, too. Might as well kill two birds with one stone."

What a gallant way to put it, she thought.

He was still reaching out to her. She ignored his outstretched hand. It was a struggle getting out of the car, since her train had wrapped itself around her legs, and she had to kick herself free of the hem. By the time she'd finally extricated herself from the car, he was regarding her with a look of amusement. She snatched up her train and whisked past him in a noisy rustle of satin.

"Uh, Miss Cormier?"

"What?" she snapped over her shoulder.

"My car's in the other direction."

She halted, her cheeks flushing. Mr. Detective was actually smiling now, a full-blown ate-the-canary grin.

"It's the blue Taurus," he pointed out. "The door's unlocked. I'll be right with you." He turned and headed away, toward the gathering of cops.

Nina flounced over to the blue Taurus. There she peered in disgust through the window. She was supposed to ride in *this* car? With that mess? She opened the door. A paper cup tumbled out. On the passenger floor was a crumpled McDonald's bag, more coffee cups and a two-day-old *Portland Press Herald.* The backseat was buried under more newspapers, file folders, a briefcase, a suit jacket and—of all things—a baseball mitt.

She scooped up the debris from the passenger side, tossed it into the back and climbed in. She only hoped the seat was clean.

Detective Cold Fish was walking toward the car. He looked hot and harassed. His shirtsleeves were rolled up now, his tie yanked loose. Even as he tried to leave the scene, cops were pulling him aside to ask questions.

At last he slid in behind the wheel and slammed the door. "Okay, where does your mother live?" he asked.

"Cape Elizabeth. Look, I can see you're busy—"

"My partner's holding the fort. I'll drop you off, talk to your mother and swing by the hospital to see Reverend Sullivan."

"Great. That way you can kill *three* birds with one stone."

"I do believe in efficiency."

They drove in silence. She saw no point in trying to dredge up polite talk. Politeness would go right over this man's head. Instead, she looked out the window and thought morosely about the wedding reception and all those finger sandwiches waiting for guests who'd never arrive. She'd have to call and ask for the food to be delivered to a soup kitchen before it all spoiled. And then there were the gifts, dozens of them, piled up at home. Correction—*Robert's* home. It had never really been *her* home. She had only been living there, a tenant. It had been her idea to pay half the mortgage. Robert used to point out how much he respected her independence, her insistence on a separate identity. In any good relationship, he'd say, privilege as well as responsibility was a fifty-fifty split. That's how they'd worked it from the start. First he'd paid for a date, then she had. In fact, she'd insisted, to show him that she was her own woman.

Now it all seemed so stupid.

I was never my own woman, she thought. *I was always dreaming, longing for the day I'd be Mrs. Robert Bledsoe.* It's what her family had hoped for, what her mother had expected of her: to marry well. They'd never understood Nina's going to nursing school, except as a way to meet a potential mate. A doctor. She'd met one, all right.

And all it's gotten me is a bunch of gifts I have to return, a wedding gown I can't return and a day I'll never, ever live down.

It was the humiliation that shook her the most. Not the fact that Robert had walked out. Not even the fact that she could have died in the wreckage of that church. The explosion itself seemed unreal to her, as remote as some TV melodramas. As remote as this man sitting beside her.

"You're handling this very well," he said.

Startled that Detective Cold Fish had spoken, she looked at him. "Excuse me?"

"You're taking this very calmly. Calmer than most."

"I don't know how else to take it."

"After a bombing, hysteria would not be out of line."

"I'm an E.R. nurse, Detective. I don't do hysteria."

"Still, this had to be a shock for you. There could well be an emotional aftermath."

"You're saying this is the calm before the storm?"

"Something like that." He glanced at her, his gaze meeting hers. Just as quickly, he looked back at the road and the connection was gone. "Why wasn't your family with you at the church?"

"I sent them all home."

"I would think you'd want them around for support, at least."

She looked out the window. "My family's not exactly the supportive type. And I guess I just…needed to be alone. When an animal gets hurt, Detective, it goes off by itself to lick its wounds. That's what I needed to do…" She blinked away an unexpected film of tears and fell silent.

"I know you don't feel much like talking right now," he said. "But maybe you can answer this question for me. Can you think of anyone else who might've been a target? Reverend Sullivan, for instance?"

She shook her head. "He's the last person anyone would hurt."

"It was his church building. He would've been near the blast center."

"Reverend Sullivan's the sweetest man in the world! Every winter, he's handing out blankets on the street. Or scrounging up beds at the shelter. In the E.R., when we see patients who have no home to go to, he's the one we call."

"I'm not questioning his character. I'm just asking about enemies."

"He has no enemies," she said flatly.

"What about the rest of the wedding party? Could any of them have been targets?"

"I can't imagine—"

"The best man, Jeremy Wall. Tell me about him."

"Jeremy? There's not much to say. He went to medical school with Robert. He's a doctor at Maine Med. A radiologist."

"Married?"

"Single. A confirmed bachelor."

"What about your sister, Wendy? She was your maid of honor?"

"Matron of honor. She's a happy homemaker."

"Any enemies?"

"Not unless there's someone out there who resents perfection."

"Meaning?"

"Let's just say she's the dream daughter every parent hopes for."

"As opposed to you?"

Nina gave a shrug. "How'd you guess?"

"All right, so that leaves one major player. The one who, coincidentally, decided not to show up at all."

Nina stared straight ahead. *What can I tell him about Robert,* she thought, *when I myself am completely in the dark?*

To her relief, he didn't pursue that line of questioning. Perhaps he'd realized how far he'd pushed her. How close to the emotional edge she was already tottering. As they drove the winding road into Cape Elizabeth, she felt her calm facade at last begin to crumble. Hadn't he warned her about it? The emotional aftermath. The pain creeping through the numbness. She had held together well, had weathered two devastating shocks with little more than a few spilt tears. Now her hands were beginning to shake, and she found that every breath she took was a struggle not to sob.

When at last they pulled up in front of her mother's house, Nina was barely holding herself together. She didn't wait for Sam to circle around and open her door. She pushed it open herself and scrambled out in a sloppy tangle of wedding gown. By the time he walked up the front steps, she was already leaning desperately on the doorbell, silently begging her mother to let her in before she fell apart completely.

The door swung open. Lydia, still elegantly coiffed and gowned, stood staring at her dishevelled daughter. "Nina? Oh, my poor Nina." She opened her arms.

Automatically Nina fell into her mother's embrace. So hungry was she for a hug, she didn't immediately register the fact that Lydia had drawn back to avoid wrinkling her green silk dress. But she did register her mother's first question.

"Have you heard from Robert yet?"

Nina stiffened. *Oh please,* she thought. *Please don't do this to me.*

"I'm sure this can all be worked out," said Lydia. "If you'd just sit down with Robert and have an honest discussion about what's bothering him—"

Nina pulled away. "I'm not going to sit down with Robert," she said. "And as for an honest discussion, I'm not sure we ever had one."

"Now, darling, it's natural to be angry—"

"But aren't you angry, Mother? Can't you be angry *for* me?"

"Well, yes. But I can't see tossing Robert aside just because—"

The sudden clearing of a male throat made Lydia glance up at Sam, who was standing outside the doorway.

"I'm Detective Navarro, Portland Police," he said. "You're Mrs. Cormier?"

"The name's now Warrenton." Lydia frowned at him. "What is this all about? What do the police have to do with this?"

"There was an incident at the church, ma'am. We're investigating.

"An incident?"

"The church was bombed."

Lydia stared at him. "You're not serious."

"I'm very serious. It went off at 2:40 this afternoon. Luckily no one was hurt. But if the wedding had been held…"

Lydia paled to a sickly white. She took a step back, her voice failing her.

"Mrs. Warrenton," said Sam, "I need to ask you a few questions."

Nina didn't stay to listen. She had heard too many questions already. She climbed upstairs to the spare bedroom, where she had left her suitcase—the suitcase she'd packed for St. John Island. Inside were her bathing suits and sundresses and tanning lotion. Everything she'd thought she needed for a week in paradise.

She took off the wedding dress and carefully draped it over an armchair where it lay white and lifeless. Useless. She looked at the contents of her suitcase, at the broken dreams packed neatly between layers of tissue paper. That's when the last vestiges of control failed her. Dressed only in her underwear, she sat down on the bed. Alone, in silence, she finally allowed the grief to sweep over her.

And she wept.

Lydia Warrenton was nothing like her daughter. Sam had seen it the moment the older woman opened the front door. Flawlessly made up, elegantly coiffed, her slender frame shown to full advantage by the green gown, Lydia looked like no mother of the bride he'd ever seen. There was a physical resemblance, of course. Both Lydia and Nina had the same black hair, the same dark, thickly lashed eyes. But while Nina had a softness about her, a vulnerability, Lydia was standoffish, as though surrounded by some protective force field that would zap anyone who ventured too close. She was definitely a looker, not only thin but also rich, judging by the room he was now standing in.

The house was a veritable museum of antiques. He had noticed a Mercedes parked in the driveway. And the living room, into which he'd just been ushered, had a spectacular ocean view. A million-dollar view. Lydia sat down primly on a brocade sofa and motioned him toward a wing chair. The needlepoint fabric was so pristine-looking he had the urge to inspect his clothes before sinking onto the cushion.

"A bomb," murmured Lydia, shaking her head. "I just can't believe it. Who would bomb a church?"

"It's not the first bombing we've had in town."

She looked at him, bewildered. "You mean the warehouse? The one last week? I read that had something to do with organized crime."

"That was the theory."

"This was a church. How can they possibly be connected?"

"We don't see the link either, Mrs. Warrenton. We're trying to find out if there is one. Maybe you can help us. Do you know of any reason someone would want to bomb the Good Shepherd Church?"

"I know nothing about that church. It's not one I attend. It was my daughter's choice to get married there."

"You sound as if you don't approve."

She shrugged. "Nina has her own odd way of doing things. I'd have chosen a more…established institution. And a longer guest list. But that's Nina. She wanted to keep it small and simple."

Simple was definitely not Lydia Warrenton's style, thought Sam, gazing around the room.

"So to answer your question, Detective, I can't think of any reason to bomb Good Shepherd."

"What time did you leave the church?"

"A little after two. When it became apparent there wasn't anything I could do for Nina."

"While you were waiting, did you happen to notice anyone who shouldn't have been there?"

"There were just the people you'd expect. The florists, the minister. The wedding party."

"Names?"

"There was me. My daughter Wendy. The best man—I don't remember his name. My ex-husband, George, and his latest wife."

"Latest."

She sniffed. "Daniella. His fourth so far."

"What about your husband?"

She paused. "Edward was delayed. His plane was two hours late leaving Chicago."

"So he hadn't even reached town yet?"

"No. But he planned to attend the reception."

Again, Sam glanced around the room, at the antiques. The view. "May I ask what your husband does for a living, Mrs. Warrenton?"

"He's president of Ridley-Warrenton."

"The logging company?"

"That's right."

That explained the house and the Mercedes, thought Sam. Ridley-Warrenton was one of the largest landowners in northern Maine. Their forest products, from raw lumber to fine paper, were shipped around the world.

His next question was unavoidable. "Mrs. Warrenton," he asked, "does your husband have any enemies?"

Her response surprised him. She laughed. "Anyone with money has enemies, Detective."

"Can you name anyone in particular?"

"You'd have to ask Edward."

"I will," said Sam, rising to his feet. "As soon as your husband's back in town, could you have him give me a call?"

"My husband's a busy man."

"So am I, ma'am," he answered. With a curt nod, he turned and left the house.

In the driveway, he sat in his Taurus for a moment, gazing up at the mansion. It was, without a doubt, one of the most impressive homes he'd ever been in. Not that he was all that familiar with mansions. Samuel Navarro was the son of a Boston cop who was himself the son of a Boston cop. At the age of twelve, he'd moved to Portland with his newly widowed mother. Nothing came easy for them, a fact of life which his mother resignedly accepted.

Sam had not been so accepting. His adolescence consisted of five long years of rebellion. Fistfights in the school yard. Sneaking cigarettes in the bathroom. Loitering with the rough-and-tumble crowd that hung out in Monument Square. There'd been no mansions in his childhood.

He started the car and drove away. The investigation was just beginning; he and Gillis had a long night ahead of them. There was still the minister to interview, as well as the florist, the best man, the matron of honor and the groom.

Most of all, the groom.

Dr. Robert Bledsoe, after all, was the one who'd called off the wedding. His decision, by accident or design, had saved the lives of dozens of people. That struck Sam as just a little bit too fortunate. Had Bledsoe received some kind of warning? Had he been the intended target?

Was that the real reason he'd left his bride at the altar?

Nina Cormier's image came vividly back to mind. Hers wasn't a face he'd be likely to forget. It was more than just those big brown eyes, that kissable mouth. It was her pride that impressed him the most. The sort of pride that kept her chin up, her jaw squared, even as the tears were falling. For that he admired her. No whining, no self-pity. The woman had been humiliated, abandoned and almost blown to smithereens. Yet she'd had enough spunk left to give Sam an occasional what-for. He found that both irritating and amusing. For a woman who'd probably grown up with everything handed to her on a silver platter, she was a tough little survivor.

Today she'd been handed a heaping dish of crow, and she'd eaten it just fine, thank you. Without a whimper.

Surprising, surprising woman.

He could hardly wait to hear what Dr. Robert Bledsoe had to say about her.

It was after five o'clock when Nina finally emerged from her mother's guest bedroom. Calm, composed, she was now wearing jeans and a T-shirt. She'd left her wedding dress hanging in the closet; she didn't even want to look at it again. Too many bad memories had attached themselves like burrs to the fabric.

Downstairs she found her mother sitting alone in the living room, nursing a highball. Detective Navarro was gone. Lydia raised the drink to her lips, and by the clinking of ice cubes in the glass, Nina could tell that Lydia's hands were shaking.

"Mother?" said Nina.

At the sound of her daughter's voice, Lydia's head jerked up. "You startled me."

"I think I'll be leaving now. Are you all right?"

"Yes. Yes, of course." Lydia gave a shudder. Then she added, almost as an afterthought, "How about you?"

"I'll be okay. I just need some time. Away from Robert."

Mother and daughter looked at each other for a moment, neither one speaking, neither one knowing what to say. This was the way things had always been between them. Nina had grown up hungry for affection. Her mother had always been too self-absorbed to grant it. And this was the result: the silence of two women who scarcely knew or understood each other. The distance between them couldn't be measured by years, but by universes.

Nina watched her mother take another deep swallow

of her drink. "How did it go?" she asked. "With you and that detective?"

Lydia shrugged. "What's there to say? He asked questions, I answered them."

"Did he tell you anything? About who might have done it?"

"No. He was tight as a clam. Not much in the way of charm."

Nina couldn't disagree. She'd known ice cubes that were warmer than Sam Navarro. But then, the man was just doing his job. He wasn't paid to be charming.

"You can stay for dinner, if you'd like," said Lydia. "Why don't you? I'll have the cook—"

"That's all right, Mother. Thank you, anyway."

Lydia looked up at her. "It's because of Edward, isn't it?"

"No, Mother. Really."

"That's why you hardly ever visit. Because of him. I wish you *could* get to like him." Lydia sighed and looked down at her drink. "He's been very good to me, very generous. You have to grant him that much."

When Nina thought of her stepfather, *generous* was not the first adjective that came to mind. No, *ruthless* would be the word she'd choose. Ruthless and controlling. She didn't want to talk about Edward Warrenton.

She turned and started toward the door. "I have to get home and pack my things. Since it's obvious I'll be moving out."

"Couldn't you and Robert patch things up somehow?"

"After today?" Nina shook her head.

"If you just tried harder? Maybe it's something you could talk about. Something you could change."

"Mother. Please."

Lydia sank back. "Anyway," she said, "you *are* invited to dinner. For what it's worth."

"Maybe some other time," Nina said softly. "Bye, Mother."

She heard no answer as she walked out the front door.

Her Honda was parked at the side of the house, where she'd left it that morning. The morning of what should have been her wedding. How proudly Lydia had smiled at her as they'd sat together in the limousine! It was the way a mother *should* look at her daughter. The way Lydia never had before.

And probably never would again.

That ride to the church, the smiles, the laughter, seemed a lifetime away. She started the Honda and pulled out of her mother's driveway.

In a daze she drove south, toward Hunts Point. Toward Robert's house. What had been *their* house. The road was winding, and she was functioning on automatic pilot, steering without thought along the curves. What if Robert hadn't really left town? she thought. What if he's home? What would they say to each other?

Try: goodbye.

She gripped the steering wheel and thought of all the things she'd *like* to tell him. All the ways she felt used and betrayed. *A whole year* kept going through her head. *One whole bloody year of my life.*

Only as she swung past Smugglers Cove did she happen to glance in the rearview mirror. A black Ford was behind her. The same Ford that had been there a few miles back, near Delano Park. At any other time, she would have thought nothing of it. But today, after the possibilities Detective Navarro had raised...

She shook off a vague sense of uneasiness and kept driving. She turned onto Ocean House Drive.

The Ford did too. There was no reason for alarm. Ocean House Drive was, after all, a main road in the neighborhood. Another driver might very well have reason to turn onto it as well.

Just to ease her anxiety, she took the left turnoff, toward Peabbles Point. It was a lonely road, not heavily traveled. Here's where she and the Ford would surely part company.

The Ford took the same turnoff.

Now she was getting frightened.

She pressed the accelerator. The Honda gained speed. At fifty miles per hour, she knew she was taking the curves too fast, but she was determined to lose the Ford. Only she wasn't losing him. He had sped up, too. In fact, he was gaining on her.

With a sudden burst of speed, the Ford roared up right beside her. They were neck and neck, taking the curves in parallel.

He's trying to run me off the road! she thought.

She glanced sideways, but all she could see through the other car's tinted window was the driver's silhouette. *Why are you doing this?* she wanted to scream at him. *Why?*

The Ford suddenly swerved toward her. The thump of the other car's impact almost sent the Honda spinning out of control. Nina fought to keep her car on course.

Her fingers clamped more tightly around the wheel. Damn this lunatic! She had to shake him off.

She hit the brakes.

The Ford shot ahead—only momentarily. It quickly slowed as well and was back beside her, swerving, bumping.

She managed another sideways glance. To her surprise, the Ford's passenger window had been rolled down. She caught a glimpse of the driver—a male. Dark hair. Sunglasses.

In the next instant her gaze shot forward to the road, which crested fifty yards ahead.

Another car had just cleared the crest and was barreling straight toward the Ford.

Tires screeched. Nina felt one last violent thump, felt the sting of shattering glass against her face. Then suddenly she was soaring sideways.

She never lost consciousness. Even as the Honda flew off the road. Even as it tumbled over and over across shrubbery and saplings.

It came to a rest, upright, against a maple tree.

Though fully awake, Nina could not move for a moment. She was too stunned to feel pain, or even fear. All she felt was amazement that she was still alive.

Then, gradually, an awareness of discomfort seeped through the layers of shock. Her chest hurt, and her shoulder. It was the seat belt. It had saved her life, but it had also bruised her ribs.

Groaning, she pressed the belt release and felt herself collapse forward, against the steering wheel.

"Hey! Hey, lady!"

Nina turned to see a face anxiously peering through the window. It was an elderly man. He yanked open her door. "Are you all right?" he asked.

"I'm— I think so."

"I'd better call an ambulance."

"No, I'm fine. Really, I am." She took a deep breath. Her chest was sore, but that seemed to be her only injury. With the old man's help, she climbed out of the car. Though a little unsteady, she was able to stand. She was shocked by the damage.

Her car was a mess. The driver's door had been

bashed in, the window was shattered and the front fender was peeled off entirely.

She turned and glanced toward the road. "There was another car," she said. "A black one—"

"You mean that damn fool who tried to pass you?"

"Where is it?"

"Took off. You oughta report that fella. Probably drunk as a skunk."

Drunk? Nina didn't think so. Shivering, she hugged herself and stared at the road, but she saw no sign of another car.

The black Ford had vanished.

Chapter 3

Gordon Gillis looked up from his burger and fries. "Anything interesting?" he asked.

"Not a damn thing." Sam hung his jacket up on the coatrack and sank into a chair behind his desk, where he sat wearily rubbing his face.

"How's the minister doing?"

"Fine, so far. Doctors doubt it's a heart attack. But they'll keep him in for a day, just to be sure."

"He didn't have any ideas about the bombing?"

"Claims he has no enemies. And everyone I talked to seems to agree that Reverend Sullivan is a certifiable saint." Groaning, Sam leaned back. "How 'bout you?"

Gillis peeled off the hamburger wrapper and began to eat as he talked. "I interviewed the best man, the matron of honor and the florist. No one saw anything."

"What about the church janitor?"

"We're still trying to locate him. His wife says he

usually gets home around six. I'll send Cooley over to talk to him."

"According to Reverend Sullivan, the janitor opens the front doors at 7:00 a.m. And the doors stay open all day. So anyone could've walked in and left a package."

"What about the night before?" asked Gillis. "What time did he lock the doors?"

"The church secretary usually locks up. She's a part-timer. Would've done it around 6:00 p.m. Unfortunately, she left for vacation this morning. Visiting family in Massachusetts. We're still trying to get hold of…" He paused.

Gillis's telephone was ringing. Gillis turned to answer it. "Yeah, what's up?"

Sam watched as his partner scribbled something on a notepad, then passed it across the desk. *Trundy Point Road* was written on the paper.

A moment later, Gillis said, "We'll be there," and hung up. He was frowning.

"What is it?" asked Sam.

"Report just came in from one of the mobile units. It's about the bride. The one at the church today."

"Nina Cormier?"

"Her car just went off the road near Trundy Point."

Sam sat up straight in alarm. "Is she all right?"

"She's fine. They wouldn't have called us at all, but she insisted they notify us."

"For an accident? Why?"

"She says it wasn't an accident. She says someone tried to run her off the road."

Her ribs hurt, her shoulder was sore and her face had a few cuts from flying glass. But at least her head was perfectly clear. Clear enough for her to recognize the man stepping out of that familiar blue Taurus that had just pulled up at the scene. It was that sullen detective, Sam Navarro. He didn't even glance in her direction.

Through the gathering dusk, Nina watched as he spoke to a patrolman. They conversed for a few moments. Then, together, the two men tramped through the underbrush to view the remains of her car. As Sam paced a slow circle around the battered Honda, Nina was reminded of a stalking cat. He moved with an easy, feline grace, his gaze focused in complete concentration. At one point he stopped and crouched to look at something on the ground. Then he rose to his feet and peered more closely at the driver's window. Or what was left of the window. He prodded the broken glass, then opened the door and climbed into the front seat. What on earth was he looking for? She could see his dark hair bobbing in and out of view. Now he seemed to be crawling all over the interior, and into the backseat. It was a good thing she had nothing to hide in there. She had no doubt that the sharp-eyed Detective Navarro could spot contraband a mile away.

At last he reemerged from her car, his hair tousled, his trousers wrinkled. He spoke again to the patrolman. Then he turned and looked in her direction.

And began to walk toward her.

At once she felt her pulse quickening. Something about this man both fascinated and frightened her. It was more than just his physical presence, which was impressive enough. It was also the way he looked at her, with a gaze that was completely neutral. That inscrutability unnerved her. Most men seemed to find Nina attractive, and they would at least make an attempt to be friendly.

This man seemed to regard her as just another homicide victim in the making. Worth his intellectual interest, but that was all.

She straightened her back and met his gaze without wavering as he approached.

"Are you all right?" he asked.

"A few bruises. A few cuts. That's all."

"You're sure you don't want to go to the E.R.? I can drive you."

"I'm fine. I'm a nurse, so I think I'd know."

"They say doctors and nurses make the worst patients. I'll drive you to the hospital. Just to be sure."

She gave a disbelieving laugh. "That sounds like an order."

"As a matter of fact, it is."

"Detective, I really think I'd know if I was…"

She was talking to his back. The man had actually turned his *back* to her. He was already walking away, toward his car. *"Detective!"* she called.

He glanced over his shoulder. "Yes?"

"I don't— This isn't—" She sighed. "Oh, never mind," she muttered, and followed him to his car. There was no point arguing with the man. He'd just turn his back on her again. As she slid into the passenger seat, she felt a sharp stab of pain in her chest. Maybe he was right after all. She knew it could take hours, or even days, for injuries to manifest themselves. She hated to admit it, but Mr. Personality was probably right about this trip to the E.R.

She was too uncomfortable to say much as they drove to the hospital. It was Sam who finally broke the silence.

"So, can you tell me what happened?" he asked.

"I already gave a statement. It's all in the police report. Someone ran me off the road."

"Yes, a black Ford, male driver. Maine license plate."

"Then you've been told the details."

"The other witness said he thought it was a drunk driver trying to pass you on the hill. He didn't think it was deliberate."

She shook her head. "I don't know what to think anymore."

"When did you first see the Ford?"

"Somewhere around Smugglers Cove, I guess. I noticed that it seemed to be following me."

"Was it weaving? Show any signs of driver impairment?"

"No. It was just…following me."

"Could it have been behind you earlier?"

"I'm not sure."

"Is it possible it was there when you left your mother's house?"

She frowned at him. He wasn't looking at her, but was staring straight ahead. The tenor of his questions had taken a subtle change of course. He had started out sounding noncommittal. Maybe even skeptical. But this last question told her he was considering a possibility other than a drunk driver. A possibility that left her suddenly chilled.

"Are you suggesting he was waiting for me?"

"I'm just exploring the possibilities."

"The other policeman thought it was a drunk driver."

"He has his opinion."

"What's your opinion?"

He didn't answer. He just kept driving in that maddeningly calm way of his. Did the man ever show any emotion? Once, just once, she'd like to see something get under that thick skin of his.

"Detective Navarro," she said. "I pay taxes. I pay

your salary. I think I deserve more than just a brush-off."

"Oh. The old civil servant line."

"I'll use whatever line it takes to get an answer out of you!"

"I'm not sure you want to hear my answer."

"Why wouldn't I?"

"I made a brief inspection of your car. What I found there backs up quite a bit of what you just told me. There were black paint chips on the driver's side, indicating that the vehicle that rammed yours was, indeed, black."

"So I'm not color blind."

"I also noticed that the driver's window was shattered. And that the breakage was in a starburst pattern. Not what I'd expect for a rollover accident."

"That's because the window was already broken when I went off the road."

"How do you know?"

"I remember I felt flying glass. That's how I cut my face. When the glass hit me. That was *before* I rolled over."

"Are you sure?" He glanced at her. "Absolutely sure?"

"Yes. Does it make a difference?"

He let out a breath. "It makes a lot of difference," he said softly. "It also goes along with what I found in your car."

"*In* my car?" Perplexed, she shook her head. "What, exactly, did you find?"

"It was in the right passenger door—the door that was jammed against the tree. The metal was pretty crumpled; that's why the other cops didn't notice it. But I knew it was there somewhere. And I found it."

"Found what?"

"A bullet hole."

Nina felt the blood drain from her face. She couldn't speak; she could only sit in shocked silence, her world rocked by the impact of his words.

He continued talking, his tone matter-of-fact. Chillingly so. *He's not human,* she thought. *He's a machine. A robot.*

"The bullet must have hit your window," he said, "just to the rear of your head. That's why the glass shattered. Then the bullet passed at a slightly forward angle, missed you completely and made a hole in the plastic molding of the opposite door, where it's probably still lodged. It'll be retrieved. By tonight, we'll know the caliber. And possibly the make of the gun. What I still don't know—what *you'll* have to tell me—is why someone's trying to kill you."

She shook her head. "It's a mistake."

"This guy's going to a lot of trouble. He's bombed a church. Tailed you. Shot at you. There's no mistake."

"There has to be!"

"Think of every possible person who might want to hurt you. Think, Nina."

"I told you, I don't have any enemies!"

"You must have."

"I don't! I don't…" She gave a sob and clutched her head in her hands. "I don't," she whispered.

After a long silence he said, gently, "I'm sorry. I know how hard it is to accept—"

"You *don't* know." She raised her head and looked at him. "You have no idea, Detective. I've always thought people liked me. Or—at least—they didn't *hate* me. I try so hard to get along with everyone. And now you're telling me there's someone out there—someone who wants to…" She swallowed and stared ahead, at the darkening road.

Sam let the silence stretch on between them. He knew she was in too fragile a state right now to press her with more questions. And he suspected she was hurting more, both physically and emotionally, than she was letting on. Judging by the condition of her car, her body had taken a brutal beating this afternoon.

In the E.R., he paced the waiting room while Nina was examined by the doctor on duty. A few X-rays later, she emerged looking even more pale than when she'd entered. It was reality sinking in, he thought. The danger was genuine, and she couldn't deny it any longer.

Back in his car, she sat in numb silence. He kept glancing sideways at her, waiting for her to burst into tears, into hysteria, but she remained unnervingly quiet. It concerned him. This wasn't healthy.

He said, "You shouldn't be alone tonight. Is there somewhere you can go?"

Her response was barely a shrug.

"Your mother's?" he suggested. "I'll take you home to pack a suitcase and—"

"No. Not my mother's," she murmured.

"Why not?"

"I…don't want to make things…uncomfortable for her."

"For *her*?" He frowned. "Pardon me for asking this, but isn't that what mothers are for? To pick us up and dust us off?"

"My mother's marriage isn't…the most supportive one around."

"She can't welcome her own daughter home?"

"It's not her home, Detective. It's her husband's. And he doesn't approve of me. To be honest, the feeling's mutual." She gazed straight ahead, and in that moment, she struck him as so very brave. And so very alone.

"Since the day they got married, Edward Warrenton has controlled every detail of my mother's life. He bullies her, and she takes it without a whimper. Because his money makes it all worthwhile for her. I just couldn't stand watching it any longer. So one day I told him off."

"Sounds like that's exactly what you should have done."

"It didn't do a thing for family harmony. I'm sure that's why he went on that business trip to Chicago. So he could conveniently skip my wedding." Sighing, she tilted her head back against the headrest. "I know I shouldn't be annoyed with my mother, but I am. I'm annoyed that she's never stood up to him."

"Okay. So I don't take you to your mother's house. What about dear old dad? Do you two get along?"

She gave a nod. A small one. "I suppose I could stay with him."

"Good. Because there's no way I'm going to let you be alone tonight." The sentence was scarcely out of his mouth when he realized he shouldn't have said it. It sounded too much as if he cared, as if feeling were getting mixed up with duty. He was too good a cop, too cautious a cop, to let that happen.

He could feel her surprised gaze through the darkness of the car.

In a tone colder than he'd intended, he said, "You may be my only link to this bombing. I need you alive and well for the investigation."

"Oh. Of course." She looked straight ahead again. And she didn't say another word until they'd reached her house on Ocean View Drive.

As soon as he'd parked, she started to get out of the

car. He reached for her arm and pulled her back inside. "Wait."

"What is it?"

"Just sit for a minute." He glanced up and down the road, scanning for other cars, other people. Anything at all suspicious. The street was deserted.

"Okay," he said. He got out and circled around to open her door. "Pack one suitcase. That's all we have time for."

"I wasn't planning to bring along the furniture."

"I'm just trying to keep this short and sweet. If someone's really looking for you, this is where they'll come. So let's not hang around, all right?"

That remark, meant to emphasize the danger, had its intended effect. She scooted out of the car and up the front walk in hyperspeed. He had to convince her to wait on the porch while he made a quick search of the house.

A moment later he poked his head out the door. "All clear."

While she packed a suitcase, Sam wandered about the living room. It was an old but spacious house, tastefully furnished, with a view of the sea. Just the sort of house one would expect a doctor to live in. He went over to the grand piano—a Steinway—and tapped out a few notes. "Who plays the piano?" he called out.

"Robert," came the answer from the bedroom. "Afraid I have a tin ear."

He focused on a framed photograph set on the piano. It was a shot of a couple, smiling. Nina and some blond, blue-eyed man. Undoubtedly Robert Bledsoe. The guy, it seemed, had everything: looks, money and a medical degree. And the woman. A woman he no longer wanted. Sam crossed the room to a display of diplomas, hanging on the wall. All of them Robert Bledsoe's. Groton prep. B.A. Dartmouth. M.D. Harvard. Dr. Bledsoe was Ivy League all the way. He was every mother's dream son-in-law. No wonder Lydia Warrenton had urged her daughter to patch things up.

The phone rang, the sound so abrupt and startling, Sam felt an instant rush of adrenaline.

"Should I get it?" Nina asked. She was standing in the doorway, her face drawn and tense.

He nodded. "Answer it."

She crossed to the telephone. After a second's hesitation, she picked up the receiver. He moved right beside her, listening, as she said, "Hello?"

No one answered.

"Hello?" Nina repeated. "Who is this? *Hello?*"

There was a click. Then, a moment later, the dial tone.

Nina looked up at Sam. She was standing so close to him, her hair, like black silk, brushed his face. He found himself staring straight into those wide eyes of hers, found himself reacting to her nearness with an unexpected surge of male longing.

This isn't supposed to happen. I can't let it happen.

He took a step back, just to put space between them. Even though they were now standing a good three feet apart, he could still feel the attraction. Not far enough apart, he thought. This woman was getting in the way of his thinking clearly, logically. And that was dangerous.

He looked down and suddenly noticed the telephone answering machine was blinking. He said, "You have messages."

"Pardon?"

"Your answering machine. It's recorded three messages."

Dazedly she looked down at the machine. Automatically she pressed the Play button.

There were three beeps, followed by three silences, and then dial tones.

Seemingly paralyzed, she stared at the machine. "Why?" she whispered. "Why do they call and hang up?"

"To see if you're home."

The implication of his statement at once struck her full force. She flinched away from the phone as if it had burned her. "I have to get out of here," she said, and hurried back into the bedroom.

He followed her. She was tossing clothes into a suitcase, not bothering to fold anything. Slacks and blouses and lingerie in one disorganized pile.

"Just the essentials," he said. "Let's leave."

"Yes. Yes, you're right." She whirled around and ran into the bathroom. He heard her rattling in the cabinets, collecting toiletries. A moment later she reemerged with a bulging makeup bag, which she tossed in the suitcase.

He closed and latched it for her. "Let's go."

In the car, she sat silent and huddled against the seat as he drove. He kept checking the rearview mirror, to see if they were being followed, but he saw no other headlights. No signs of pursuit.

"Relax, we're okay," he said. "I'll just get you to your dad's house, and you'll be fine."

"And then what?" she said softly. "How long do I hide there? For weeks, months?"

"As long as it takes for us to crack this case."

She shook her head, a sad gesture of bewilderment. "It doesn't make sense. None of this makes sense."

"Maybe it'll become clear when we talk to your fiancé. Do you have any idea where he might be?"

"It seems that I'm the last person Robert wanted to confide in…" Hugging herself, she stared out the window. "His note said he was leaving town for a while. I guess he just needed to get away. From me…"

"From you? Or from someone else?"

She shook her head. "There's so much I don't know. So much he never bothered to tell me. God, I wish I understood. I could handle this. I could handle anything. If only I understood."

What kind of man is Robert Bledsoe? Sam wondered. What kind of man would walk away from this woman? Leave her alone to face the danger left in his wake?

"Whoever made that hang-up call may pay a visit to your house," he said. "I'd like to keep an eye on it. See who turns up."

She nodded. "Yes. Of course."

"May I have access?"

"You mean…get inside?"

"If our suspect shows up, he may try to break in. I'd like to be waiting for him."

She stared at him. "You could get yourself killed."

"Believe me, Miss Cormier, I'm not the heroic type. I don't take chances."

"But if he does show up—"

"I'll be ready." He flashed her a quick grin for reassurance. She didn't look reassured. If anything, she looked more frightened than ever.

For me? he wondered. And that, inexplicably, lifted his spirits. Terrific. Next thing he knew, he'd be putting his neck in a noose, and all because of a pair of big brown eyes. This was just the kind of situation cops were warned to avoid: assuming the role of hero to some fetching female. It got men killed.

It could get *him* killed.

"You shouldn't do this by yourself," she said.

"I won't be alone. I'll have backup."

"You're sure?"

"Yeah, I'm sure."

"You promise? You won't take any chances?"

"What are you, my mother?" he snapped in exasperation.

She took her keys out of her purse and slapped them on the dashboard. "No, I'm not your mother," she retorted. "But you're the cop in charge. And I need you alive and well to crack this case."

He deserved that. She'd been concerned about his safety, and he'd responded with sarcasm. He didn't even know why. All he knew was, whenever he looked in her eyes, he had the overwhelming urge to turn tail and run. Before he was trapped.

Moments later, they drove past the wrought iron gates of her father's driveway. Nina didn't even wait for Sam to open her door. She got out of the car and started up the stone steps. Sam followed, carrying her suitcase. And ogling the house. It was huge—even more impressive than Lydia Warrenton's home, and it had the Rolls-Royce of security systems. Tonight, at least, Nina should be safe.

The doorbell chimed like a church bell; he could hear it echoing through what must be dozens of rooms. The door was opened by a blonde—and what a blonde! Not much older than thirty, she was wearing a shiny spandex leotard that hugged every taut curve. A healthy sweat sheened her face, and from some other room came the thumpy music of an exercise video.

"Hello, Daniella," Nina said quietly.

Daniella assumed a look of sympathy that struck Sam as too automatic to be genuine. "Oh Nina, I'm so *sorry* about what happened today! Wendy called and told us about the church. Was anyone hurt?"

"No. No, thank God." Nina paused, as though afraid to ask the next question. "Do you think I could spend the night with you?"

The expression of sympathy faded. Daniella looked askance at the suitcase Sam was carrying. "I, uh… let me talk to your dad. He's in the hot tub right now and—"

"Nina has no choice. She has to stay the night," said Sam. He stepped past Daniella, into the house. "It's not safe for her to be alone."

Daniella's gaze shifted to Sam, and he saw the vague spark of interest in those flat blue eyes. "I'm afraid I didn't catch your name," she said.

"This is Detective Navarro," said Nina. "He's with the Portland Bomb Squad. And this," she said to Sam, "is Daniella Cormier. My, uh…father's wife."

Stepmother was the appropriate term, but this stunning blonde didn't look like anybody's mother. And the look she was giving *him* was anything but maternal.

Daniella tilted her head, a gesture he recognized as both inquisitive and flirtatious. "So, you're a cop?"

"Yes, ma'am."

"Bomb Squad? Is that really what you think happened at the church? A bomb?"

"I'm not free to talk about it," he said. "Not while the investigation's underway." Smoothly he turned to Nina. "If you're okay for the night, I'll be leaving. Be sure to close those driveway gates. And activate the burglar alarm. I'll check back with you in the morning."

As he gave a nod of goodbye, his gaze locked with Nina's. It was only the briefest of looks, but once again he was taken by surprise at his instinctive response to this woman. It was an attraction so powerful he felt himself at once struggling to pull away.

He did. With a curt good-night, he walked out the front door.

Outside, in the darkness, he stood for a moment surveying the house. It seemed secure enough. With two other people inside, Nina should be safe. Still, he wondered whether those particular two people would be of much help in a crisis. A father soaking in a hot tub and a spandex-and-hormones stepmother didn't exactly inspire feelings of confidence. Nina, at least, was an intelligent woman; he knew she would be alert for signs of danger.

He drove back to Robert Bledsoe's house on Ocean View Drive and left the car on a side street around the corner.

With Nina's keys, he let himself in the front door and called Gillis to arrange for a surveillance team to patrol the area. Then he closed all the curtains and settled down to wait. It was nine o'clock.

At nine-thirty, he was already restless. He paced the living room, then roamed the kitchen, the dining room, the hallway. Any stalker watching the house would expect lights to go on and off in different rooms, at different times. Maybe their man was just waiting for the residents to go to bed.

Sam turned off the living room lights and went into the bedroom.

Nina had left the top dresser drawer hanging open. Sam, pacing the carpet, kept walking back and forth past that open drawer with its tempting glimpse of lingerie. Something black and silky lay on top, and one corner trailed partway out of the drawer. He couldn't resist the impulse. He halted by the dresser, picked up the item of lingerie and held it up.

It was a short little spaghetti-strap thing, edged with lace, and designed to show a lot. An awful lot. He tossed it back in and slammed the drawer shut.

He was getting distracted again. This shouldn't be happening. Something about Nina Cormier, and his reaction to her, had him behaving like a damn rookie.

Before, in the line of duty, he'd brushed up against other women, including the occasional stunner. Women like that spandex bimbo, Daniella Cormier, Nina's stepmother. He'd managed to keep his trousers zipped up and his head firmly screwed on. It was both a matter of self-control as well as self-preservation. The women he met on the job were usually in some sort of trouble, and it was too easy for them to consider Sam their white knight, the masculine answer to all their problems.

It was a fantasy that never lasted. Sooner or later the knight gets stripped of his armor and they'd see him for what he really was: just a cop. Not rich, not brilliant. Not much of anything, in fact, to recommend him.

It had happened to him once. Just once. She'd been an aspiring actress trying to escape an abusive boyfriend; he'd been a rookie assigned to watch over her. The chemistry was right. The situation was right. But the girl was all wrong. For a few heady weeks, he'd been in love, had thought *she* was in love.

Then she'd dropped Sam like a hot potato.

He'd learned a hard but lasting lesson: romance and police work did not mix. He had never again crossed that line while on the job, and he wasn't about to do it with Nina Cormier, either.

He turned away from the dresser and was crossing to the opposite end of the room when he heard a thump.

It came from somewhere near the front of the house.

Instantly he killed the bedroom lights and reached for his gun. He eased into the hallway. At the doorway to the living room he halted, his gaze quickly sweeping the darkness.

The streetlight shone in dimly through the windows. He saw no movement in the room, no suspicious shadows.

There was a scraping sound, a soft jingle. It came from the front porch.

Sam shifted his aim to the front door. He was crouched and ready to fire as the door swung open. The silhouette of a man loomed against the backlight of the streetlamp.

"Police!" Sam yelled. *"Freeze!"*

Chapter 4

The silhouette froze.

"Hands up," ordered Sam. "Come on, *hands up!*"

Both hands shot up. "Don't hurt me!" came a terrified plea.

Sam edged over to the light switch and flipped it on. The sudden glare left both men blinking. Sam took one look at the man standing in front of him and cursed.

Footsteps pounded up the porch steps and two uniformed cops burst through the doorway, pistols drawn. "We got him covered, Navarro!" one of them yelled.

"You're right on time," muttered Sam in disgust. "Forget it. This isn't the guy." He holstered his gun and looked at the tall blond man, who was still wearing a look of terror on his face. "I'm Detective Sam Navarro, Portland Police. I presume you're Dr. Robert Bledsoe?"

Nervously Robert cleared his throat. "Yeah, that's me. What's going on? Why are you people in my house?"

"Where've you been all day, Dr. Bledsoe?"

"I've been—uh, may I put my hands down?"

"Of course."

Robert lowered his hands and glanced cautiously over his shoulder at the two cops standing behind him. "Do they, uh, really need to keep pointing those guns at me?"

"You two can leave," Sam said to the cops. "I'm all right here."

"What about the surveillance?" one of them asked. "Want to call it off?"

"I doubt anything's coming down tonight. But hang around the neighborhood. Just until morning."

The two cops left. Sam said, again, "Where've you been, Dr. Bledsoe?"

With two guns no longer pointed at his back, Robert's terror had given way to righteous anger. He glared at Sam. "First, you tell me why you're in my house! What is this, a police state? Cops breaking in and threatening homeowners? You have no authority to be trespassing on my property. I'll have your ass in a sling if you don't produce a search warrant right now!"

"I don't have a warrant."

"You don't?" Robert gave an unpleasantly triumphant laugh. "You entered my house without a warrant? You break in here and threaten me with your macho cop act?"

"I didn't break in," Sam told him calmly. "I let myself in the front door."

"Oh, sure."

Sam pulled out Nina's keys and held them up in front of Robert. "With these."

"Those—those keys belong to my fiancé! How did you get them?"

"She lent them to me."

"She *what?*" Robert's voice had risen to a yelp of anger. "Where is Nina? She had no right to hand over the keys to my house."

"Correction, Doctor. Nina Cormier was living here with you. That makes her a legal resident of this house. It gives her the right to authorize police entry, which she did." Sam eyed the man squarely. "Now, I'll ask the question a third time. Where have you been, Doctor?"

"Away," snapped Robert.

"Could you be more specific?"

"All right, I went to Boston. I needed to get out of town for a while."

"Why?"

"What is this, an interrogation? I don't have to talk to you! In fact I *shouldn't* talk to you until I call my lawyer." He turned to the telephone and picked up the receiver.

"You don't need a lawyer. Unless you've committed a crime."

"A crime?" Robert spun around and stared at him. "Are you accusing me of something?"

"I'm not accusing you of anything. But I do need answers. Are you aware of what happened in the church today?"

Robert replaced the receiver. Soberly he nodded. "I... I heard there was some sort of explosion. It was on the news. That's why I came back early. I was worried someone might've been hurt."

"Luckily, no one was. The church was empty at the time it happened."

Robert gave a sigh of relief. "Thank God," he said softly. He stood with his hand still on the phone, as though debating whether to pick it up again. "Do the police—do you—know what caused it?"

"Yes. It was a bomb."

Robert's chin jerked up. He stared at Sam. Slowly he sank into the nearest chair. "All I'd heard was—the radio said—it was an explosion. There was nothing about a bomb."

"We haven't made a public statement yet."

Robert looked up at him. "Why the hell would anyone bomb a church?"

"That's what we're trying to find out. If the wedding had taken place, dozens of people might be dead right now. Nina told me you're the one who called it off. Why did you?"

"I just couldn't go through with it." Robert dropped his head in his hands. "I wasn't ready to get married."

"So your reason was entirely personal?"

"What else would it be?" Robert suddenly looked up with an expression of stunned comprehension. "Oh, my God. You didn't think the bomb had something to do with *me?*"

"It did cross my mind. Consider the circumstances. You cancelled the wedding without warning. And then you skipped town. Of course we wondered about your motives. Whether you'd received some kind of threat and decided to run."

"No, that's not at all what happened. I called it off because I didn't want to get married."

"Mind telling me why?"

Robert's face tightened. "Yes, as a matter of fact," he answered. Abruptly he rose from the chair and strode over to the liquor cabinet. There he poured himself a shot of Scotch and stood gulping it, not looking at Sam.

"I've met your fiancé," stated Sam. "She seems like a nice woman. Bright, attractive." *I'm sure as hell attracted to her,* he couldn't help adding to himself.

"You're asking why I left her at the altar, aren't you?" said Robert.

"Why did you?"

Robert finished off his drink and poured himself another.

"Did you two have an argument?"

"No."

"What was it, Dr. Bledsoe? Cold feet? Boredom?" Sam paused. "Another woman?"

Robert turned and glared at him. "This is none of your damn business. Get out of my house."

"If you insist. But I'll be talking to you again." Sam crossed to the front door, then stopped and turned back. "Do you know anyone who'd want to hurt your fiancé?"

"No."

"Anyone who'd want her dead?"

"What a ridiculous question."

"Someone tried to run her car off the road this afternoon."

Robert jerked around and stared at him. He looked genuinely startled. "*Nina?* Who did?"

"That's what I'm trying to find out. It may or may not be connected to the bombing. Do you have any idea at all what's going on? Who might try to hurt her?"

There was a split second's hesitation before Robert answered. "No. No one I can think of. Where is she?"

"She's in a safe place for tonight. But she can't stay in hiding forever. So if you think of anything, give me a call. If you still care about her."

Robert didn't say anything.

Sam turned and left the house.

Driving home, he used his car phone to dial Gillis. His partner, predictably, was still at his desk. "The bridegroom's back in town," Sam told him. "He claims he has no idea why the church was bombed."

"Why am I not surprised?" Gillis drawled.

"Anything new turn up?"

"Yeah. We're missing a janitor."

"What?"

"The church janitor. The one who unlocked the building this morning. We've been trying to track him down all evening. He never got home tonight."

Sam felt his pulse give a little gallop of excitement. "Interesting."

"We've already got an APB out. The man's name is Jimmy Brogan. And he has a record. Petty theft four years ago and two OUI's, that kind of stuff. Nothing major. I sent Cooley out to talk to the wife and check the house."

"Does Brogan have any explosives experience?"

"Not that we can determine. The wife swears up and down that he's clean. And he's always home for dinner."

"Give me more, Gillis. Give me more."

"That's all I have to give, unless you want me to slit open a vein. Right now I'm bushed and I'm going home."

"Okay, call it a day. I'll see you in the morning."

All the way home, Sam's mind was churning with facts. A cancelled wedding. A missing church janitor. An assassin in a black Ford.

And a bomb.

Where did Nina Cormier fit in this crazy thicket of events?

It was eleven-thirty when he finally arrived home. He let himself in the front door, stepped into the house and turned on the lights. The familiar clutter greeted him. What a god-awful mess. One of these days he'd have to clean up the place. Or maybe he should just move; that'd be easier.

He walked through the living room, picking up dirty laundry and dishes as he went. He left the dishes in the kitchen sink, threw the laundry in the washing machine and started the wash cycle. A Saturday night, and the swinging bachelor does his laundry. Wow. He stood in his kitchen, listening to the machine rumble, thinking about all the things he could do to make this house more of a home. Furniture, maybe? It was a good, sound little house, but he kept comparing it to Robert Bledsoe's house with its Steinway piano, the sort of house any woman would be delighted to call home.

Hell, Sam wouldn't know what to do with a woman even if one was crazy enough to move in with him. He'd been a bachelor too long, alone too long. There'd been the occasional woman, of course, but none of them had ever lasted. Too often, he had to admit, the fault lay with him. Or with his work. They couldn't understand why any man in his right mind would actually choose to stay with this insane job of bombs and bombers. They took it as a personal affront that he wouldn't quit the job and choose *them* instead.

Maybe he'd just never found a woman who made him *want* to quit.

And this is the result, he thought, gazing wearily at the basket of unfolded clothes. The swinging bachelor life.

He left the washing machine to finish its cycle and headed off to bed.

As usual, alone.

* * *

The lights were on at 318 Ocean View Drive. Some-one was home. The Cormier woman? Robert Bledsoe? Or both of them?

Driving slowly past the house in his green Jeep Cherokee, he took a good long look at the house. He noted the dense shrubbery near the windows, the shadow of pine and birch trees ringing both edges of the property. Plenty of cover. Plenty of concealment.

Then he noticed the unmarked car parked a block away. It was backlit by a streetlamp, and he could see the silhouettes of two men sitting inside. *Police,* he thought. They were watching the house.

Tonight was not the time to do it.

He rounded the corner and drove on.

This matter could wait. It was only a bit of cleanup, a loose end that he could attend to in his spare time.

He had other, more important work to complete, and only a week in which to do it.

He drove on, toward the city.

At 9:00 a.m., the guards came to escort Billy "The Snowman" Binford from his jail cell.

His attorney, Albert Darien, was waiting for him. Through the Plexiglas partition separating the two men, Billy could see Darien's grim expression and he knew that the news was not good. Billy sat down opposite his attorney. The guard wasn't standing close enough to catch their conversation, but Billy knew better than to speak freely. That stuff about attorney-client confidentiality was a bunch of bull. If the feds or the D.A. wanted you bad enough, they'd plant a bug on anyone, even your priest. It was outrageous, how they'd violate a citizen's rights.

"Hello, Billy," said Darien through the speaker phone. "How're they treating you?"

"Like a sultan. How the hell d'you *think* they're treating me? You gotta get me a few favors, Darien. A private TV. I'd like a private TV."

"Billy, we got problems."

Billy didn't like the tone of Darien's voice. "What problems?" he asked.

"Liddell's not even going to discuss a plea bargain. He's set on taking this to trial. Any other D.A.'d save himself the trouble, but I think Liddell's using you as a stepping stone to Blaine House."

"Liddell's running for governor?"

"He hasn't announced it. But if he puts you away, he'll be golden. And Billy, to be honest, he's got more than enough to put you away."

Billy leaned forward and glared through the Plexiglas at his attorney. "That's what I pay *you* for. So what the hell're you doing about the situation?"

"They've got too much. Hobart's turned state's witness."

"Hobart's a sleazeball. It'll be a piece of cake to discredit him."

"They've got your shipping records. It's all on paper, Billy."

"Okay, then let's try again with a plea bargain. Anything. Just keep my time in here short."

"I told you, Liddell's nixed a plea bargain."

Billy paused. Softly he said, "Liddell can be taken care of."

Darien stared at him. "What do you mean?"

"You just get me a deal. Don't worry about Liddell. I'm taking care of—"

"I don't want to know about it." Darien sat back, his

hands suddenly shaking. "I don't want to know a damn thing, okay?"

"You don't have to. I got it covered."

"Just don't get me involved."

"All I want from you, Darien, is to keep this from going to trial. And get me out of here soon. You got that?"

"Yeah. Yeah." Darien glanced nervously at the guard, who wasn't paying the least bit of attention to their conversation. "I'll try."

"Just watch," said Billy. A cocky grin spread on his lips. "Next week, things'll be different. D.A.'s office will be happy to talk plea bargain."

"Why? What happens next week?"

"You don't want to know."

Darien exhaled a deep sigh and nodded. "You're right," he muttered. "I don't want to know."

Nina awakened to the bass thump of aerobics dance music. Downstairs, she found Daniella stretched out on the polished oak floor of the exercise room. This morning Daniella was garbed in a shiny pink leotard, and her sleek legs knifed effortlessly through the air with every beat of the music. Nina stood watching in fascination for a moment, mesmerized by that display of taut muscles. Daniella worked hard at her body. In fact, she did little else. Since her marriage to George Cormier, Daniella's only goal in life seemed to be physical perfection.

The music ended. Daniella sprang to her feet with an easy grace. As she turned to reach for a towel, she noticed Nina standing in the doorway. "Oh. Good morning."

"Morning," said Nina. "I guess I overslept. Has Dad already left for work?"

"You know how he is. Likes to get started at the crack of dawn." With the towel, Daniella whisked away a delicate sheen of perspiration. A discomforting silence stretched between them. It always did. It was more than just the awkwardness of their relationship, the bizarre reality that this golden goddess was technically Nina's stepmother. It was also the fact that, except for their connection through George Cormier, the two women had absolutely nothing in common.

And never had that seemed more apparent to Nina than at this moment, as she stood gazing at the perfect face of this perfect blonde.

Daniella climbed onto an exercise bike and began pedaling away. Over the whir of the wheel, she said, "George had some board meeting. He'll be home for dinner. Oh, and you got two phone calls this morning. One was from that policeman. You know, the cute one."

"Detective Navarro?"

"Yeah. He was checking up on you."

So he's worried about me, thought Nina, feeling an unexpected lifting of her spirits. He'd cared enough to make sure she was alive and well. Then again, maybe he was just checking to make sure he didn't have a new corpse on his hands.

Yes, that was the likely reason he'd called.

Feeling suddenly glum, Nina turned to leave the room, then stopped. "What about the second call?" she asked. "You said there were two."

"Oh, right." Daniella, still pumping away, looked serenely over the handlebars. "The other call was from Robert."

Nina stared at her in shocked silence. "Robert called?"

"He wanted to know if you were here."

"Where is *he?*"

"At home."

Nina shook her head in disbelief. "You might have told me earlier."

"You were sound asleep. I didn't see the point of waking you." Daniella leaned into the handlebars and began to pedal with singleminded concentration. "Besides, he'll call back later."

I'm not waiting till later, thought Nina. *I want answers now. And I want them face-to-face.*

Heart thudding, she left the house. She borrowed her father's Mercedes to drive to Ocean View Drive. He'd never miss it; after all, he kept a spare Jaguar and a BMW in the garage.

By the time she pulled into Robert's driveway, she was shaking from both anger and dread. What on earth was she going to say to him?

What was he going to say to *her?*

She climbed the porch steps and rang the doorbell. She didn't have her house keys. Sam Navarro did. Anyway, this wasn't her house any longer. It never had been.

The door swung open and Robert stood looking at her in surprise. He was wearing running shorts and a T-shirt, and his face had the healthy flush of recent exercise. Not exactly the picture of a man pining for his fiancée.

"Uh, Nina," he said. "I—I was worried about you."

"Somehow I have a hard time believing that."

"I even called your father's house—"

"What happened, Robert?" Her breath rushed out in a bewildered sigh. "Why did you walk out on me?"

He looked away. That alone told her how far apart they'd drifted. "It's not easy to explain."

"It wasn't easy for me, either. Telling everyone to go

home. Not knowing why it fell apart. You could have told me. A week before. A *day* before. Instead you leave me there, holding the damn bouquet! Wondering if it was all *my* fault. Something *I* did wrong."

"It wasn't you, Nina."

"What was it, then?"

He didn't answer. He just kept looking away, unwilling to face her. Maybe afraid to face her.

"I lived with you for a whole year," she said with sad wonder. "And I don't have the faintest idea who you are." With a stifled sob, she pushed past him, into the house, and headed straight for the bedroom.

"What are you doing?" he yelled.

"Packing the rest of my things. And getting the hell out of your life."

"Nina, there's no need to be uncivilized about this. We tried to make it. It just didn't work out. Why can't we still be friends?"

"Is that what we are? Friends?"

"I like to think so. I don't see why we can't be."

She shook her head and laughed. A bitter sound. "*Friends* don't twist the knife after they stab you." She stalked into the bedroom and began yanking open drawers. She pulled out clothes and tossed them on the bed. She was beyond caring about neatness; all she wanted was to get out of this house and never see it again. Or him again. Up until a moment ago, she'd thought it still possible to salvage their relationship, to pick up the pieces and work toward some sort of life together. Now she knew there wasn't a chance of it. She didn't want *him*. She couldn't even recall what it was about Robert Bledsoe that had attracted her. His looks, his medical degree—those were things she'd considered nice but not that important. No, what she'd seen in Robert—or imagined she'd seen—was intelligence and wit and caring. He'd shown her all those things.

What an act.

Robert was watching her with a look of wounded nobility. As if this was all her fault. She ignored him and went to the closet, raked out an armful of dresses, and dumped them on the bed. The pile was so high it was starting to topple.

"Does it all have to be done right now?" he asked.

"Yes."

"There aren't enough suitcases."

"Then I'll use trash bags. And I need to take my books, too."

"Today? But you've got tons of them!"

"This week I've got tons of time. Since I skipped the honeymoon."

"You're being unreasonable. Look, I know you're angry. You have a right to be. But don't go flying off the damn handle."

"I'll fly off the handle if I *want* to!" she yelled.

The sound of a throat being cleared made them both turn in surprise. Sam Navarro stood in the bedroom doorway, looking at them with an expression of quiet bemusement.

"Don't you cops *ever* bother to knock?" snapped Robert.

"I did knock," said Sam. "No one answered. And you left the front door wide open."

"You're trespassing," said Robert. "*Again* without a warrant."

"He doesn't need a warrant," said Nina.

"The law says he does."

"Not if I invite him in!"

"You didn't invite him in. He *walked* in."

"The door was open," said Sam. "I was concerned." He looked at Nina. "That wasn't smart, Miss Cormier, driving here alone. You should have told me you were leaving your father's house."

"What am I, your prisoner?" she muttered and crossed back to the closet for another armload of clothes. "How did you track me down, anyway?"

"I called your stepmother right after you left the house. She thought you'd be here."

"Well, I am. And I happen to be busy."

"Yeah," muttered Robert. "She's really good at being busy."

Nina spun around to confront her ex-fiancé. "What's that supposed to mean?"

"I'm not the only one to blame in all this! It takes two people to screw up a relationship."

"I didn't leave *you* at the church!"

"No, but you left me. Every night, for months on end."

"What? *What?*"

"Every damn night, I was here on my own! I would have enjoyed coming home to a nice meal. But you were never here."

"They needed me on the evening shift. I couldn't change that!"

"You could've quit."

"Quit my *job?* To do what? Play happy homemaker to a man who couldn't even decide if he wanted to marry me?"

"If you loved me, you would have."

"Oh, my God. I can't believe you're turning this into my fault. I didn't *love* you enough."

Sam said, "Nina, I need to talk to you."

"Not now!" Nina and Robert both snapped at him.

Robert said to her, "I just think you should know I had my reasons for not going through with it. A guy has only so much patience. And then it's natural to start looking elsewhere."

"Elsewhere?" She stared at him with new comprehension. Softly she said, "So there was someone else."

"What do you think?"

"Do I know her?"

"It hardly makes a difference now."

"It does to *me*. When did you meet her?"

He looked away. "A while ago."

"How long?"

"Look, this is irrelevant—"

"For six months, we planned that wedding. Both of us. And you never bothered to tell me the minor detail that you were seeing another woman?"

"It's clear to me you're not rational at the moment. Until you are, I'm not discussing this." Robert turned and left the room.

"Not *rational?*" she yelled. "I'm more rational now than I was six months ago!"

She was answered by the thud of the front door as it slammed shut.

Another woman, she thought. *I never knew. I never even suspected.*

Suddenly feeling sick to her stomach, she sank down on the bed. The pile of clothes tumbled onto the floor, but she didn't even notice. Nor did she realize that she was crying, that the tears were dribbling down her cheeks and onto her shirt. She was both sick and numb at the same time, and oblivious to everything but her own pain.

She scarcely noticed that Sam had sat down beside

her. "He's not worth it, Nina," he soothed quietly. "He's not worth grieving over."

Only when his hand closed warmly over hers did she look up. She found his gaze focused steadily on her face. "I'm not grieving," she said.

Gently he brushed his fingers across her cheek, which was wet with tears. "I think you are."

"I'm not. I'm *not*." She gave a sob and sagged against him, burying her face in his shirt. "I'm not," she whispered against his chest.

Only vaguely did she sense his arms folding around her back, gathering her against him. Suddenly those arms were holding her close, wrapping tightly around her. He didn't say a thing. As always, the laconic cop. But she felt his breath warming her hair, felt his lips brush the top of her head, and she heard the quickening of his heartbeat.

Just as she felt the quickening of her own.

It means nothing, she thought. He was being kind to her. Comforting her the way he would any hurt citizen. It was what she did every day in the E.R. It was her job. It was his job.

Oh, but this felt so good.

It took a ruthless act of pure will to pull out of his arms. When she looked up, she found his expression calm, his green eyes unreadable. No passion, no desire. Just the public servant, in full control of his emotions.

Quickly she wiped away her tears. She felt stupid now, embarrassed by what he'd just witnessed between her and Robert. He knew it all, every humiliating detail, and she could scarcely bear to look him in the eye.

She stood up and began to gather the fallen clothes from the floor.

"You want to talk about it?" he asked.

"No."

"I think you need to. The man you loved leaves you for another woman. That must hurt pretty bad."

"Okay, I *do* need to talk about it!" She threw a handful of clothes on the bed and looked at him. "But not with some stone-faced cop who couldn't care less!"

There was a long silence. Though he looked at her without a flicker of emotion, she sensed that she'd just delivered a body blow. And he was too proud to show it.

She shook her head. "I'm sorry. Oh God, Navarro, I'm so sorry. You didn't deserve that."

"Actually," he said, "I think I did."

"You're just doing your job. And then I go and lash out at you." Thoroughly disgusted with herself, she sat down beside him on the bed. "I was just taking it out on you. I'm so—so angry at myself for letting him make me feel guilty."

"Why guilty?"

"That's the crazy part about it! I don't know why I should feel guilty! He makes it sound as if I neglected him. But I could never quit my job, even for him. I love my job."

"He's a doctor. He must've had long hours as well. Nights, weekends."

"He worked a lot of weekends."

"Did you complain?"

"Of course not. That's his job."

"Well?" He regarded her with a raised eyebrow.

"Oh." She sighed. "The old double standard."

"Exactly. I wouldn't expect my wife to quit a job she loved, just to make dinner and wait on me every night."

She stared down at her hands, clasped in her lap. "You wouldn't?"

"That's not love. That's possession."

"I think your wife's a very lucky woman," she said softly.

"I was only speaking theoretically."

She frowned at him. "You mean...it was just a theoretical wife?"

He nodded.

So he wasn't married. That piece of information made her flush with a strange and unexpected gladness. What on earth was the matter with her?

She looked away, afraid that he might see the confusion in her eyes. "You, uh, said you needed to talk to me."

"It's about the case."

"It must be pretty important if you went to all the trouble of tracking me down."

"I'm afraid we have a new development. Not a pleasant one."

She went very still. "Something's happened?"

"Tell me what you know about the church janitor."

She shook her head in bewilderment. "I don't know him at all. I don't even know his name."

"His name was Jimmy Brogan. We spent all yesterday evening trying to track Brogan down. We know he unlocked the church door yesterday. That he was in and out of the building all morning. But no one seems to know where he went after the explosion. We know he didn't turn up at the neighborhood bar where he usually goes every afternoon."

"You said *was*. That his name *was* Jimmy Brogan. Does that mean..."

Sam nodded. "We found his body this morning. He was in his car, parked in a field in Scarborough. He died from a gunshot wound to the head. The gun was in the car with him. It had his fingerprints on it."

"A suicide?" she asked softly.

"That's the way it looks."

She was silent, too shocked to say a thing.

"We're still waiting for the crime lab report. There are a number of details that bother me. It feels too neat, too packaged. It ties up every single loose end we've got."

"Including the bombing?"

"Including the bombing. There were several items in the car trunk that would seem to link Brogan to the bomb. Detonating cord. Green electrical tape. It's all pretty convincing evidence."

"You don't sound convinced."

"The problem is, Brogan had no explosives experience that we know of. Also, we can't come up with a motive for any bombing. Or for the attack on you. Can you help us out?"

She shook her head. "I don't know anything about the man."

"Are you familiar with the name Brogan?"

"No."

"He was familiar with *you*. There was a slip of paper with your address in his car."

She stared at him. His gaze was impenetrable. It frightened her, how little she could read in his eyes. How deeply the man was buried inside the cop. "Why would he have my address?" she asked.

"You must have some link to him."

"I don't know anyone named Brogan."

"Why would he try to kill you? Run you off the road?"

"How do you know *he* did it?"

"Because of his car. The one we found his body in."
She swallowed hard. "It was black?"
He nodded. "A black Ford."

Chapter 5

Sam drove her to the morgue. Neither one of them said much. He was being guarded about what information he told her, and she was too chilled to ask for the details. All the way there, she kept thinking, *Who was Jimmy Brogan and why did he want to kill me?*

In the morgue, Sam maintained a firm grip on her arm as they walked the corridor to the cold room. He was right beside her when the attendant led them to the bank of body drawers. As the drawer was pulled out she involuntarily flinched. Sam's arm came around her waist, a steady support against the terrible sight she was about to face.

"It ain't pretty," said the attendant. "Are you ready?"

Nina nodded.

He pulled aside the shroud and stepped back.

As an E.R. nurse, Nina had seen more than her share of grisly sights. This was by far the worst. She took one look at the man's face—what was left of it—and quickly turned away. "I don't know him," she whispered.

"Are you sure?" Sam asked.

She nodded and suddenly felt herself swaying. At once he was supporting her, his arm guiding her away from the drawers. Away from the cold room.

In the coroner's office she sat nursing a cup of hot tea while Sam talked on the phone to his partner. Only vaguely did she register his conversation. His tone was as matter-of-fact as always, betraying no hint of the horror he'd just witnessed.

"...doesn't recognize him. Or the name either. Are you sure we don't have an alias?" Sam was saying.

Nina cupped the tea in both hands but didn't sip. Her stomach was still too queasy. On the desk beside her was the file for Jimmy Brogan, open to the ID information sheet. Most of what she saw there didn't stir any memories. Not his address nor the name of his wife. Only the name of the employer was familiar: the Good Shepherd Church. She wondered if Father Sullivan had been told, wondered how he was faring in the hospital. It would be a double shock to the elderly man. First, the bombing of his church, and then the death of the janitor. She should visit him today and make sure he was doing all right...

"Thanks, Gillis. I'll be back at three. Yeah, set it up, will you?" Sam hung up and turned to her. Seeing her face, he frowned in concern. "You all right?"

"I'm fine." She shuddered and clutched the mug more tightly.

"You don't look fine. I think you need some recovery time. Come on." He offered his hand. "It's lunchtime. There's a café up the street."

"You can think about lunch?"

"I make it a point never to skip a chance at a meal. Or would you rather I take you home?"

"Anything," she said, rising from the chair. "Just get me out of this place."

Nina picked listlessly at a salad while Sam wolfed down a hamburger.

"I don't know how you do it," she said. "How you go straight from the morgue to a big lunch."

"Necessity." He shrugged. "In this job, a guy can get skinny real fast."

"You must see so many awful things as a cop."

"You're an E.R. nurse. I would think you've seen your share."

"Yes. But they usually come to us still alive."

He wiped his hands on a napkin and slid his empty plate aside. "True. If it's a bomb, by the time I get to the scene, we're lucky to find anyone alive. If we find much of them at all."

"How do you live with it? How do you stand a job like yours?"

"The challenge."

"Really, Navarro. How do you deal with the horror?"

"My name's Sam, okay? And as for how I deal with it, it's more a question of *why* I do it. The truth is, the challenge is a lot of it. People who make bombs are a unique breed of criminal. They're not like the guy who holds up your neighborhood liquor store. Bombers are craftier. A few of them are truly geniuses. But they're also cowards. Killers at a distance. It's that combination that makes those guys especially dangerous. And it makes my job all the more satisfying when I can nail them."

"So you actually enjoy it."

"*Enjoy* isn't the right word. It's more that I can't set the puzzle aside. I keep looking at the pieces and turning them around. Trying to understand the sort of mind that could do such a thing." He shook his head. "Maybe that makes me just as much a monster. That I find it so satisfying to match wits with these guys."

"Or maybe it means you're an outstanding cop."

He laughed. "Either that or I'm as screwy as the bombers are."

She gazed across the table at his smiling face and suddenly wondered why she'd ever considered those eyes of his so forbidding. One laugh and Sam Navarro transformed from a cop into an actual human being. And a very attractive man.

I'm not going to let this happen, she thought with sudden determination. *It would be such a mistake to rebound from Robert, straight into some crazy infatuation with a cop.*

She forced herself to look away, at anything but his face, and ended up focusing on his hands. At the long, tanned fingers. She said, "If Brogan was the bomber, then I guess I have nothing to worry about now."

"If he was the bomber."

"The evidence seems pretty strong. Why don't you sound convinced?"

"I can't explain it. It's just…a feeling. Instinct, I guess. That's why I still want you to be careful."

She lifted her gaze to meet his and found his smile was gone. The cop was back.

"You don't think it's over yet," she said.

"No. I don't."

Sam drove Nina back to Ocean View Drive, helped her load up the Mercedes with a few armloads of books and clothes and made sure she was safely on her way back to her father's house.

Then he returned to the station.

At three o'clock, they held a catch-up meeting. Sam, Gillis, Tanaka from the crime lab and a third detective on the Bomb Task Force, Francis Cooley, were in attendance. Everyone laid their puzzle pieces on the table.

Cooley spoke first. "I've checked and rechecked the records on Jimmy Brogan. There's no alias for the guy. That's his real name. Forty-five years old, born and raised in South Portland, minor criminal record. Married ten years, no kids. He was hired by Reverend Sullivan eight years ago. Worked as a janitor and handyman around the church. Never any problems, except for a few times when he showed up late and hung over after falling off the wagon. No military service, no education beyond the eleventh grade. Wife says he was dyslexic. I just can't see this guy putting together a bomb."

"Did Mrs. Brogan have any idea why Nina Cormier's address was in his car?" Sam asked.

"Nope. She'd never heard the name before. And she said the handwriting wasn't her husband's."

"Were they having any marital troubles?"

"Happy as clams, from what she told me. She's pretty devastated."

"So we've got a happily married, uneducated, dyslexic janitor as our prime suspect?"

"Afraid so, Navarro."

Sam shook his head. "This gets worse every minute." He looked at Tanaka. "Eddie, give us some answers. Please."

Tanaka, nervous as usual, cleared his throat. "You're not going to like what I have."

"Hit me anyway."

"Okay. First, the gun in the car was reported stolen a year ago from its registered owner in Miami. We don't know how Brogan got the gun. His wife says he didn't know the first thing about firearms. Second, Brogan's car *was* the black Ford that forced Miss Cormier's Honda off the road. Paint chips match, both ways. Third, the items in the trunk are the same elements used in the church bombing. Two-inch-wide green electrical tape. Identical detonator cord."

"That's Vincent Spectre's signature," said Gillis. "Green electrical tape."

"Which means we're probably dealing with an apprentice of Spectre's. Now here's something else you're not going to like. We just got back the preliminary report from the coroner. The corpse had no traces of gunpowder on his hand. Now, that's not necessarily conclusive, since powder can rub off, but it does argue against a self-inflicted wound. What clinches it, though, is the skull fracture."

"What?" Sam and Gillis said it simultaneously.

"A depressed skull fracture, right parietal bone. Because of all the tissue damage from the bullet wound, it wasn't immediately obvious. But it did show up on X-ray. Jimmy Brogan was hit on the head. *Before* he was shot."

The silence in the room stretched for a good ten seconds. Then Gillis said, "And I almost bought it. Lock, stock and barrel."

"He's good," said Sam. "But not good enough." He looked at Cooley. "I want more on Brogan. I want you and your team to get the names of every friend, every acquaintance Brogan had. Talk to them all. It looks like our janitor got mixed up with the wrong guy. Maybe someone knows something, saw something."

"Won't the boys in Homicide be beating those bushes?"

"We'll beat 'em as well. They may miss something. And don't get into any turf battles, okay? We're not trying to steal their glory. We just want the bomber."

Cooley sighed and rose to his feet. "Guess it's back to the ol' widow Brogan."

"Gillis," said Sam, "I need you to talk to the best man and the matron of honor again. See if they have any links to Brogan. Or recognize his photo. I'll go back to the hospital and talk to Reverend Sullivan. And I'll talk to Dr. Bledsoe as well."

"What about the bride?" asked Gillis.

"I've pressed the questions a couple times already. She denies knowing anything about him."

"She seems to be the center of it all."

"I know. And she hasn't the foggiest idea why. But maybe her ex-bridegroom does."

The meeting broke up and everyone headed off to their respective tasks. It would take teamwork to find this bomber, and although he had good people working with him, Sam knew they were stretched thin. Since that rookie cop's death in the warehouse blast a week ago, Homicide had stepped into the investigation, and they were sucking up men and resources like crazy. As far as Homicide was concerned, the Bomb Task Force was little more than a squad of "techies"—the guys you called in when you didn't want your own head blown off.

The boys in Homicide were smart enough.

But the boys in Bombs were smarter.

That's why Sam himself drove out to Maine Medical Center to reinterview Reverend Sullivan. This latest information on Jimmy Brogan's death had opened up a whole new range of possibilities. Perhaps Brogan had been a completely innocent patsy. Perhaps he'd witnessed something—and had mentioned it to the minister.

At the hospital, Sam learned that Reverend Sullivan had been transferred out of Intensive Care that morning. A heart attack had been ruled out, and Sullivan was now on a regular ward.

When Sam walked in the man's room, he found the minister sitting up in bed, looking glum. There was a visitor there already—Dick Yeats of Homicide. Not one of Sam's favorite people.

"Hey, Navarro," said Yeats in that cocky tone of his. "No need to spin your wheels here. We're on the Brogan case."

"I'd like to talk to Reverend Sullivan myself."

"He doesn't know anything helpful."

"Nevertheless," said Sam, "I'd like to ask my own questions."

"Suit yourself," Yeats said as he headed out the door. "Seems to me, though, that you boys in Bombs could make better use of your time if you'd let Homicide do its job."

Sam turned to the elderly minister, who was looking very unhappy about talking to yet another cop.

"I'm sorry, Reverend," said Sam. "But I'm afraid I'm going to have to ask you some more questions."

Reverend Sullivan sighed, the weariness evident in his lined face. "I can't tell you more than I already have."

"You've been told about Brogan's death?"

"Yes. That policeman—that Homicide person—"

"Detective Yeats."

"He was far more graphic than necessary. I didn't need all the…details."

Sam sat down in a chair. The minister's color was

better today, but he still looked frail. The events of the last twenty-four hours must be devastating for him. First the destruction of his church building, and then the violent death of his handyman. Sam hated to flog the old man with yet more questions, but he had no choice.

Unfortunately, he could elicit no new answers. Reverend Sullivan knew nothing about Jimmy Brogan's private life. Nor could he think of a single reason why Brogan, or anyone else for that matter, would attack the Good Shepherd Church. There had been minor incidents, of course. A few acts of vandalism and petty theft. That's why he had started locking the church doors at night, a move that grieved him deeply as he felt churches should be open to those in need, day or night. But the insurance company had insisted, and so Reverend Sullivan had instructed his staff to lock up every evening at 6:00 p.m., and reopen every morning at 7:00 a.m.

"And there've been no acts of vandalism since?" asked Sam.

"None whatsoever," affirmed the minister. "That is, until the bomb."

This was a dead end, thought Sam. Yeats was right. He was just spinning his wheels.

As he rose to leave, there was a knock on the door. A heavyset woman poked her head in the room.

"Reverend Sullivan?" she said. "Is this a good time to visit?"

The gloom on the minister's face instantly transformed to a look of relief. Thankfulness. "Helen! I'm so glad you're back! Did you hear what happened?"

"On the television, this morning. As soon as I saw it, I packed my things and started straight back for home." The woman, carrying a bundle of carnations, crossed to the bed and gave Reverend Sullivan a tear-ful hug. "I just saw the church. I drove right past it. Oh, what a mess."

"You don't know the worst of it," said Reverend Sullivan. He swallowed. "Jimmy's dead."

"Dear God." Helen pulled back in horror. "Was it... in the explosion?"

"No. They're saying he shot himself. I didn't even know he had a gun."

Helen took an unsteady step backward. At once Sam grasped her ample arm and guided her into the chair from which he'd just risen. She sat quivering, her face white with shock.

"Excuse me, ma'am," said Sam gently. "I'm Detective Navarro, Portland Police. May I ask your full name?"

She swallowed. "Helen Whipple."

"You're the church secretary?"

She looked up at him with dazed eyes. "Yes. Yes."

"We've been trying to contact you, Miss Whipple."

"I was—I was at my sister's house. In Amherst." She sat twisting her hands together, shaking her head. "I can't believe this. I saw Jimmy only yesterday. I can't believe he's gone."

"You saw Brogan? What time?"

"It was in the morning. Just before I left town." She began digging in her purse, desperately fishing for tissues. "I stopped in to pay a few bills before I left."

"Did you two speak?"

"Naturally. Jimmy's such..." She gave a soft sob. "*Was* such...a friendly man. He was always coming up to the office to chat. Since I was leaving on vacation, and Reverend Sullivan wasn't in yet. I asked Jimmy to do a few things for me."

"What things?"

"Oh, there was so much confusion. The wedding, you know. The florist kept popping in to use the phone. The men's bathroom sink was leaking and we needed some plumbing done quick. I had to give Jimmy some last minute instructions. Everything from where to put the wedding gifts to which plumber to call. I was so relieved when Reverend Sullivan arrived, and I could leave."

"Excuse me, ma'am," Sam cut in. "You said something about wedding gifts."

"Yes. It's a nuisance, how some people have gifts delivered to the church instead of the bride's home."

"How many gifts arrived at the church?"

"There was only one. Jimmy—oh, poor Jimmy. It's so unfair. A wife and all…"

Sam fought to maintain his patience. "What about the gift?"

"Oh. That. Jimmy said a man brought it by. He showed it to me. Very nicely wrapped, with all these pretty silver bells and foil ribbons."

"Mrs. Whipple," Sam interrupted again. "What happened to that gift?"

"Oh, I don't know. I told Jimmy to give it to the bride's mother. I assume that's what he did."

"But the bride's mother hadn't arrived yet, right? So what would Jimmy do with it?"

Helplessly Helen Whipple shrugged her shoulders. "I suppose he'd leave it where she'd be sure to find it. In the front pew."

The front pew. The center of the blast.

Sam said, sharply, "Who was the gift addressed to?"

"The bride and groom, of course."

"Dr. Bledsoe and his fiancée?"

"Yes. That was on the card. Dr. and Mrs. Robert Bledsoe."

* * *

It was starting to come together now, Sam thought as he got back in his car. The method of delivery. The time of planting. But the target wasn't quite clear yet. Was Nina Cormier or Robert Bledsoe supposed to die? Or was it both of them?

Nina, he knew, had no answers, no knowledge of any enemies. She couldn't help him.

So Sam drove to Ocean View Drive, to Robert Bledsoe's house. This time Bledsoe was damn well going to answer some questions, the first two being: Who was the other woman he'd been seeing, and was she jealous enough to sabotage her lover's wedding—and kill off a dozen people in the process?

Two blocks before he got there, he knew something was wrong. There were police lights flashing ahead and spectators gathered on the sidewalks.

Sam parked the car and quickly pushed his way through the crowd. At the edge of Bledsoe's driveway, a yellow police tape had been strung between wooden stakes. He flashed his badge to the patrolman standing guard and stepped across the line.

Homicide Detective Dick Yeats greeted him in the driveway with his usual I'm-in-charge tone of superiority.

"Hello again, Navarro. We have it all under control."

"You have *what* under control? What happened?"

Yeats nodded toward the BMW in the driveway.

Slowly Sam circled around the rear bumper. Only then did he see the blood. It was all over the steering wheel and the front seat. A small pool of it had congealed on the driveway pavement.

"Robert Bledsoe," said Yeats. "Shot once in the temple. The ambulance just left. He's still alive, but I don't expect he'll make it. He'd just pulled into his driveway and was getting out of his car. There's a sack of groceries in the trunk. Ice cream barely melted. The neighbor saw a green Jeep take off, just before she noticed Bledsoe's body. She thinks it was a man behind the wheel, but she didn't see his face."

"A man?" Sam's head snapped up. "Dark hair?"

"Yeah."

"Oh, God." Sam turned and started toward his car. *Nina,* he thought, and suddenly he was running. A dark-haired man had forced Nina off the road. Now Bledsoe was dead. Was Nina next?

Sam heard Yeats yell, "Navarro!" By then, he was already scrambling into his car. He made a screeching U-turn and headed away from Ocean View Drive.

He drove with his emergency lights flashing all the way to George Cormier's house.

It seemed he was ringing the bell forever before anyone answered the door. Finally it swung open and Daniella appeared, her flawless face arranged in a smile. "Why, hello, Detective."

"Where's Nina?" he demanded, pushing past her into the house.

"She's upstairs. Why?"

"I need to talk to her. *Now.*" He started for the stairway, then halted when he heard footsteps creak on the landing above. Glancing up, he saw Nina standing on the steps, her hair a tumble of black silk.

She's okay, he thought with relief. *She's still okay.*

She was dressed casually in jeans and a T-shirt, and she had a purse slung over her shoulder, as if she were just about to leave the house.

As she came down the stairs, she brought with her the elusive fragrance of soap and shampoo. Nina's scent, he thought with a pleasurable thrill of recognition. Since when had he committed her fragrance to memory?

By the time she reached the bottom step, she was frowning at him. "Has something happened?" she asked.

"Then no one's called you?"

"About what?"

"Robert."

She went very still, her dark eyes focused with sudden intensity on his face. He could see the questions in her eyes, and knew she was too afraid to ask them.

He reached for her hand. It was cold. "You'd better come with me."

"Where?"

"The hospital. That's where they took him." Gently he led her to the door.

"Wait!" called Daniella.

Sam glanced back. Daniella stood frozen, staring after them in panic. "What about Robert? What happened?"

"He's been shot. It happened a short while ago, just outside his house. I'm afraid it doesn't look good."

Daniella took a step backward, as though slapped. It was her reaction, that expression of horror in her eyes, that told Sam what he needed to know. *So she was the other woman,* he thought. *This blonde with her sculpted body and her perfect face.*

He could feel Nina's arm trembling in his grasp. He turned her toward the door. "We'd better go," he said. "There may not be much time."

Chapter 6

They spent the next four hours in a hospital waiting room.

Though Nina wasn't part of the medical team now battling to save Robert's life, she could picture only too vividly what was going on at that moment in the trauma suite. The massive infusions of blood and saline. The scramble to control the patient's bleeding, to keep his pressure up, his heart beating. She knew it all well because, at other times, on other patients, she had been part of the team. Now she was relegated to this useless task of waiting and worrying. Though her relationship with Robert was irrevocably broken, though she hadn't forgiven him for the way he'd betrayed her, she certainly didn't want him hurt.

Or dead.

It was only Sam's presence that kept her calm and sane during that long evening. Other cops came and went. As the hours stretched on, only Sam stayed next to her on the couch, his hand clasping hers in a silent gesture of support. She could see that he was tired, but he didn't leave her. He stayed right beside her as the night wore on toward ten o'clock.

And he was there when the neurosurgeon came out to inform them that Robert had died on the operating table.

Nina took the blow in numb silence. She was too stunned to shed any tears, to say much more than "Thank you for trying." She scarcely realized Sam had his arm around her. Only when she sagged against him did she feel his support, steadying her.

"I'm going to take you home," he said softly. "There's nothing more you can do here."

Mutely she nodded. He helped her to her feet and guided her toward the exit. They were halfway across the room when a voice called, "Miss Cormier? I need to ask you some more questions."

Nina turned and looked at the rodent-faced man who'd just spoken to her. She couldn't remember his name, but she knew he was a cop; he'd been in and out of the waiting room all evening. Now he was studying her closely, and she didn't like the look in his eyes.

"Not now, Yeats," said Sam, nudging her to the exit. "It's a bad time."

"It's the best time to ask questions," said the other cop. "Right after the event."

"She's already told me she knew nothing about it."

"She hasn't told *me*." Yeats turned his gaze back to Nina. "Miss Cormier, I'm with Homicide. Your fiancé never regained consciousness, so we couldn't question him. That's why I need to talk to you. Where were you this afternoon?"

Bewildered, Nina shook her head. "I was at my father's house. I didn't know about it until…"

"Until I told her," filled in Sam.

"*You* did, Navarro?"

"I went straight from the crime scene to her father's house. Nina was there. You can ask Daniella Cormier to confirm it."

"I will." Yeats's gaze was still fixed on Nina. "I understand you and Dr. Bledsoe just called off the engagement. And you were in the process of moving out of his house."

Softly Nina said, "Yes."

"I imagine you must have been pretty hurt. Did you ever consider, oh…getting back at him?"

Horrified by his implication, she gave a violent shake of her head. "You don't really think that—that I had something to do with this?"

"Did you?"

Sam stepped between them. "That's enough, Yeats."

"What are you, Navarro? Her lawyer?"

"She doesn't have to answer these questions."

"Yes, she does. Maybe not tonight. But she does have to answer questions."

Sam took Nina's arm and propelled her toward the exit.

"Watch it, Navarro!" Yeats yelled as they left the room. "You're on thin ice!"

Though Sam didn't answer, Nina could sense his fury just by the way he gripped her arm all the way to the parking lot.

When they were back in his car, she said, quietly, "Thank you, Sam."

"For what?"

"For getting me away from that awful man."

"Eventually, you *will* have to talk to him. Yeats may be a pain in the butt, but he has a job to do."

And so do you, she thought with a twinge of sadness. She turned to look out the window. He was the cop again, always the cop, trying to solve the puzzle. She was merely one of the pieces.

"You're going to have to talk to him tomorrow," said Sam. "Just a warning—he can be a tough interrogator."

"There's nothing I have to tell him. I was at my father's house. You know that. And Daniella will confirm it."

"No one can knock your alibi. But murder doesn't have to be done in person. Killers can be hired."

She turned to him with a look of disbelief. "You don't think I'd—"

"I'm just saying that's the logic Yeats will use. When someone gets murdered, the number one suspect is always the spouse or lover. You and Bledsoe just broke up. And it happened in the most public and painful way possible. It doesn't take a giant leap of logic to come up with murderous intent on your part."

"I'm not a murderer. You know I'm not!"

He didn't answer. He just went on driving as though he had not registered a word.

"Navarro, did you hear me? I'm not a murderer!"

"I heard you."

"Then why aren't you saying anything?"

"Because I think something else just came up."

Only then did she notice that he was frowning at the rearview mirror. He picked up his car phone and dialed. "Gillis?" he said. "Do me a favor. Find out if Yeats has a tail on Nina Cormier. Yeah, right now. I'm in the car. Call me back." He hung up.

Nina turned and looked out the rear window, at a pair of headlights behind them. "Is someone following us?"

"I'm not sure. I do know that car pulled out behind ours when we left the hospital. And it's been there ever since."

"Your buddy in Homicide must really think I'm dangerous if he's having me followed."

"He's just keeping tabs on his suspect."

Me, she thought, and sank back against the seat, grateful that the darkness hid her face. *Am I your suspect as well?*

He drove calmly, making no sudden moves to alarm whoever was in the car behind them. In that tense stillness, the ringing of the phone was startling.

He picked up the receiver. "Navarro." There was a pause, then he said, "You're sure?" Again he glanced in the mirror. "I'm at Congress and Braeburn, heading west. There's a dark truck—looks like a Jeep Cherokee—right behind me. I'll swing around, make a pass by Houlton. If you can be ready and waiting, we'll sandwich this guy. Don't scare him off. For now, just move in close enough to get a good look. Okay, I'm making my turn now. I'll be there in five minutes." He hung up and shot Nina a tense glance. "You pick up what's happening?"

"What *is* happening?"

"That's not a cop behind us."

She looked back at the headlights. Not a cop. "Then who is it?"

"We're going to find out. Now listen good. In a minute I'll want you down near the floor. Not yet—I don't want to make him suspicious. But when Gillis pulls in behind him, things could get exciting. Are you ready for this?"

"I don't think I have much of a choice..."

He made his turn. Not too fast—a casual change of direction to make it seem as if he'd just decided on a different route.

The other car made the turn as well.

Sam turned again, back onto Congress Street. They were headed east now, going back the way they'd come. The pair of headlights was still behind them. At 10:30 on a Sunday, traffic was light and it was easy to spot their pursuer.

"There's Gillis," Sam stated. "Right on schedule." He nodded at the blue Toyota idling near the curb. They drove past it.

A moment later, the Toyota pulled into traffic, right behind the Jeep.

"Perp sandwich," said Sam with a note of triumph. They were coming on a traffic light, just turning yellow. Purposely he slowed down, to keep the other two cars on his tail.

Without warning, the Cherokee suddenly screeched around them and sped straight through the intersection just as the light turned red.

Sam uttered an oath and hit the accelerator. They, too, lurched through the intersection just as a pickup truck barreled in from a side street. Sam swerved around it and took off after the sedan.

A block ahead, the Cherokee screeched around a corner.

"This guy's smart," muttered Sam. "He knew we were moving in on him."

"Watch out!" cried Nina as a car pulled out of a parking space, right in front of them.

Sam leaned on his horn and shot past.

This is crazy, she thought. *I'm riding with a maniac cop at the wheel.*

They spun around the corner into an alley. Nina, clutching the dashboard, caught a dizzying view of trash cans and Dumpsters as they raced through.

At the other end of the alley, Sam screeched to a halt.

There was no sign of the Cherokee. In either direction.

Gillis's Toyota squealed to a stop just behind them. "Which way?" they heard Gillis call.

"I don't know!" Sam yelled back. "I'll head east."

He turned right. Nina glanced back and saw Gillis turn left, in the other direction. A two-pronged search. Surely one of them would spot the quarry.

Four blocks later, there was still no sign of the Cherokee. Sam reached for the car phone and dialed Gillis.

"No luck here," he said. "How about you?" At the answer, he gave a grunt of disappointment. "Okay. At least you got the license number. I'll check back with you later." He hung up.

"So he did catch the number?" Nina asked.

"Massachusetts plate. APB's going out now. With any luck, they'll pick him up." He glanced at Nina. "I'm not so sure you should go back to your father's house."

Their gazes locked. What she saw, in his eyes, confirmed her fears.

"You think he was following me," she said softly.

"What I want to know is, why? There's something weird going on here, something that involves both you and Robert. You must have *some* idea what it is."

She shook her head. "It's a mistake," she whispered. "It must be."

"Someone's gone to a lot of trouble to ensure your

deaths. I don't think he—or she—would mistake the target."

"She? Do you really think…"

"As I said before, murder needn't be done in person. It can be bought and paid for. And that could be what we're dealing with. I'm more and more certain of it. A professional."

Nina was shaking now, unable to answer him. Unable to argue. The man next to her was talking so matter-of-factly. *His* life didn't hang in the balance.

"I know it's hard to accept any of this yet," he added. "But in your case, denial could be fatal. So let me lay it out for you. The brutal facts. Robert's already dead. And you could be next."

But I'm not worth killing! she thought. *I'm no threat to anyone.*

"We can't pin the blame on Jimmy Brogan," said Sam. "I think he's the innocent in all this. He saw something he shouldn't have, so he was disposed of. And then his death was set up to look like a suicide, to throw us off the track. Deflect our bomb investigation. Our killer's very clever. And very specific about his targets." He glanced at her, and she heard, in his voice, pure, passionless logic. "There's something else I learned today," he told her. "The morning of your wedding, a gift was delivered to the church. Jimmy Brogan may have seen the man who left it. We think Brogan put the parcel somewhere near the front pews. Right near the blast center. The gift was addressed specifically to you and Robert." He paused, as though daring her to argue that away.

She couldn't. The information was coming too fast, and she was having trouble dealing with the terrifying implications.

"Help me out, Nina," he urged. "Give me a name. A motive."

"I told you," she said, her voice breaking to a sob. "I don't know!"

"Robert admitted there was another woman. Do you know who that might be?"

She was hugging herself, huddling into a self-protective ball against the seat. "No."

"Did it ever seem to you that Daniella and Robert were particularly close?"

Nina went still. *Daniella?* Her father's wife? She thought back over the past six months. Remembered the evenings she and Robert had spent at her father's house. All the invitations, the dinners. She'd been pleased that her fiancé had been so quickly accepted by her father and Daniella, pleased that, for once, harmony had been achieved in the Cormier family. Daniella, who'd never been particularly warm toward her stepdaughter, had suddenly started including Nina and Robert in every social function.

Daniella and Robert.

"That's another reason," he said, "why I don't think you should go back to your father's house tonight."

She turned to him. "You think Daniella…"

"We'll be questioning her again."

"But why would she kill Robert? If she loved him?"

"Jealousy? If she couldn't have him, no one could?"

"But he'd already broken off our engagement! It was over between us!"

"Was it really?"

Though the question was asked softly, she sensed at once an underlying tension in his voice.

She said, "You were there, Sam. You heard our argument. He didn't love me. Sometimes I think he never did." Her head dropped. "For him it was definitely over."

"And for you?"

Tears pricked her eyes. All evening she'd managed not to cry, not to fall apart. During those endless hours in the hospital waiting room, she'd withdrawn so completely into numbness that when they'd told her Robert was dead, she'd registered that fact in some distant corner of her mind, but she hadn't *felt* it. Not the shock, nor the grief. She knew she *should* be grieving. No matter how much Robert had hurt her, how bitterly their affair had ended, he was still the man with whom she'd spent the last year of her life.

Now it all seemed like a different life. Not hers. Not Robert's. Just a dream, with no basis in reality.

She began to cry. Softly. Wearily. Not tears of grief, but tears of exhaustion.

Sam said nothing. He just kept driving while the woman beside him shed soundless tears. There was plenty he *wanted* to say. He wanted to point out that Robert Bledsoe had been a first-class rat, that he was scarcely worth grieving over. But women in love weren't creatures you could deal with on a logical level. And he was sure she did love Bledsoe; it was the obvious explanation for those tears.

He tightened his grip on the steering wheel as frustration surged through him. Frustration at his own inability to comfort her, to assuage her grief. The Roberts of the world didn't deserve any woman's tears. Yet they were the men whom women always seemed to cry over. The golden boys. He glanced at Nina, huddled against the door, and he felt a rush of sympathy. And something more, something that surprised him. Longing.

At once he quelled the feeling. It was yet another

sign that he should not be in this situation. It was fine for a cop to sympathize, but when the feelings crossed that invisible line into more dangerous emotions, it was time to pull back.

But I can't pull back. Not tonight. Not until I make sure she's safe.

Without looking at her, he said, "You can't go to your father's. Or your mother's for that matter—her house isn't secure. No alarm system, no gate. And it's too easy for the killer to find you."

"I—I signed a lease on a new apartment today. It doesn't have any furniture yet, but—"

"I assume Daniella knows about it?"

She paused, then replied, "Yes. She does."

"Then that's out. What about friends?"

"They all have children. If they knew a killer was trying to find me…" She took a deep breath. "I'll go to a hotel."

He glanced at her and saw that her spine was suddenly stiff and straight. And he knew she was fighting to put on a brave front. That's all it was, a front. God, what was he supposed to do now? She was scared and she had a right to be. They were both exhausted. He couldn't just dump her at some hotel at this hour. Nor could he leave her alone. Whoever was stalking her had done an efficient job of dispatching both Jimmy Brogan and Robert Bledsoe. For such a killer, tracking down Nina would be no trouble at all.

The turnoff to Route 1 north was just ahead. He took it.

Twenty minutes later they were driving past thick stands of trees. Here the houses were few and far between, all the lots heavily forested. It was the trees that had first attracted Sam to this neighborhood. As a boy, first in Boston, then in Portland, he'd always lived in the heart of the city. He'd grown up around concrete and asphalt, but he'd always felt the lure of the woods. Every summer, he'd head north to fish at his lakeside camp.

The rest of the year, he had to be content with his home in this quiet neighborhood of birch and pine.

He turned onto his private dirt road, which wound a short way into the woods before widening into his gravel driveway. Only as he turned off the engine and looked at his house did the first doubts assail him. The place wasn't much to brag about. It was just a two-bedroom cottage of precut cedar hammered together three summers ago. And as for the interior, he wasn't exactly certain how presentable he'd left it.

Oh, well. There was no changing plans now.

He got out and circled around to open her door. She stepped out, her gaze fixed in bewilderment on the small house in the woods.

"Where are we?" she asked.

"A safe place. Safer than a hotel anyway." He gestured toward the front porch. "It's just for tonight. Until we can make other arrangements."

"Who lives here?"

"I do."

If that fact disturbed her, she didn't show it. Maybe she was too tired and frightened to care. In silence she waited while he unlocked the door. He stepped inside after her and turned on the lights.

At his first glimpse of the living room, he gave a silent prayer of thanks. No clothes on the couch, no dirty dishes on the coffee table. Not that the place was pristine. With newspapers scattered about and dust bunnies in the corners, the room had that unmistakable look of a sloppy bachelor. But at least it wasn't a major disaster area. A minor one, maybe.

He locked the door and turned the dead bolt.

She was just standing there, looking dazed. Maybe by the condition of his house? He touched her shoulder and she flinched.

"You okay?" he asked.

"I'm fine."

"You don't look so fine."

In fact she looked pretty pitiful, her eyes red from crying, her cheeks a bloodless white. He had the sudden urge to take her face in his hands and warm it with his touch. Not a good idea. He was turning into a sucker for women in distress, and this woman was most certainly in distress.

Instead he turned and went into the spare bedroom. One glance at the mess and he nixed that idea. It was no place to put up a guest. Or an enemy, for that matter. There was only one solution. He'd sleep on the couch and let her have his room.

Sheets. Oh Lord, did he have any clean sheets?

Frantically he rummaged in the linen closet and found a fresh set. He was on top of things after all. Turning, he found himself face-to-face with Nina.

She held out her arms for the sheets. "I'll make up the couch."

"These are for the bed. I'm putting you in my room."

"No, Sam. I feel guilty enough as it is. Let me take the couch."

Something in the way she looked at him—that upward tilt of her chin—told him she'd had enough of playing the object of pity.

He gave her the sheets and added a blanket. "It's a lumpy couch. You don't mind?"

"I've taken a lot of lumps lately. I'll hardly notice a few more."

Almost a joke. That was good. She was pulling herself together—an act of will he found impressive.

While she made up the couch, he went to the kitchen and called Gillis at home.

"We got the info on that Massachusetts plate," Gillis told him. "It was stolen two weeks ago. APB hasn't netted the Cherokee yet. Man, this guy's quick."

"And dangerous."

"You think he's our bomber?"

"Our shooter, too. It's all tangled together, Gillis. It has to be."

"How does last week's warehouse bombing fit in? We figured that was a mob hit."

"Yeah. A nasty message to Billy Binford's rivals."

"Binford's in jail. His future's not looking so bright. Why would he order a church bombed?"

"The church wasn't the target, Gillis. I'm almost certain the target was Bledsoe or Nina Cormier. Or both."

"How does that tie in with Binford?"

"I don't know. Nina's never heard of Binford." Sam rubbed his face and felt the stubble of beard. God, he was tired. Too tired to figure anything out tonight. He said, "There's one other angle we haven't ruled out. The old crime of passion. You interviewed Daniella Cormier."

"Yeah. Right after the bombing. What a looker."

"You pick up anything odd about her?"

"What do you mean?"

"Anything that didn't sit right? Her reactions, her answers?"

"Not that I recall. She seemed appropriately stunned. What are you thinking?"

"I'm thinking Homicide should get their boys over there to question her tonight."

"I'll pass that message along to Yeats. What's your hunch?"

"She and Robert Bledsoe had a little thing going on the side."

"And she blew up the church out of jealousy?" Gillis laughed. "She didn't seem the type."

"Remember what they say about the female of the species."

"Yeah, but I can't imagine that gorgeous blonde—"

"Watch the hormones, Gillis."

His partner snorted. "If anyone better watch his hormones, it's you."

That's what I keep telling myself, thought Sam as he hung up. He paused for a moment in the kitchen, giving himself the same old lecture he'd given himself a dozen times since meeting Nina. *I'm a cop, I'm here to serve and protect. Not seduce.*

Not fall in love.

He went into the living room. At his first sight of Nina, he felt his resolve crumble. She was standing at the window, peering out at the darkness. He'd hung no curtains; here in the woods, he'd never felt the need for them. But now he realized just how open and vulnerable she was. And that worried him—more than he cared to admit.

He said, "I'd feel better if you came away from those windows."

She turned, a startled look in her eyes. "You don't think someone could have followed us?"

"No. But I'd like you to stay away from the windows all the same."

Shuddering, she moved to the couch and sat down.

She'd already made the couch into a bed, and only now did he realize how tattered the blanket was. Tattered furniture, tattered linens. Those were details that had never bothered him before. So many things about his life as a bachelor had not bothered him, simply because he'd never stopped to think how much better, sweeter, his life could be. Only now, as he saw Nina sitting on his couch, did it occur to him how stark the room was. It was only the presence of this woman that gave it any life. Any warmth.

Too soon, she'd be gone again.

The sooner the better, he told himself. Before she grew on him. Before she slipped too deeply into his life.

He paced over to the fireplace, paced back toward the kitchen door, his feet restless, his instincts telling him to say something.

"You must be hungry," he said.

She shook her head. "I can't think about food. I can't think about anything except…"

"Robert?"

She lowered her head and didn't answer. Was she crying again? She had a right to. But she just sat very still and silent, as though struggling to hold her emotions in check.

He sat down in the chair across from her. "Tell me about Robert," he prompted. "Tell me everything you know about him."

She took a shaky breath, then said softly, "I don't know what to say. We lived together a year. And now I feel as if I never knew him at all."

"You met at work?"

She nodded. "The Emergency Room. Evening shift. I'd been working there for three years. Then Robert joined the E.R. staff. He was a good doctor. One of the

best I'd ever worked with. And he was so fun to talk to.
He'd traveled everywhere, done everything. I remember how surprised I was to learn he wasn't married."

"Never?"

"Never. He told me he was holding out for the best. That he just hadn't found the woman he wanted to spend his life with."

"At forty-one, he must've been more than a little picky."

Her glance held a trace of amusement. "*You're* not married, Detective. Does that make you more than a little picky?"

"Guilty as charged. But then, I haven't really been looking."

"Not interested?"

"Not enough time for romance. It's the nature of the job."

She gave a sigh. "No, it's the nature of the beast. Men don't really want to be married."

"Did I say that?"

"It's something I've finally figured out after years of spinsterhood."

"We're all rats, that kind of thing? Let's get back to one specific rat. Robert. You were telling me you two met in the E.R. Was it love at first sight?"

She leaned back, and he could clearly see the remembered pain on her face. "No. No, it wasn't. At least, not for me. I thought he was attractive, of course."

Of course, thought Sam with an undeniable twinge of cynicism.

"But when he asked me out, that first time, I didn't really think it would go anywhere. It wasn't until I introduced him to my mother that I began to realize what a catch he was. Mom was thrilled with Robert. All these years, I'd been dating guys she considered losers. And here I show up with a doctor. It was more than she'd ever expected of me, and she was already hearing wedding bells."

"What about your father?"

"I think he was just plain relieved I was dating someone who wouldn't marry me for *his* money. That's always been Dad's preoccupation. His money. And his wives. Or rather, whichever wife he happens to be married to at the time."

Sam shook his head. "After what you've seen of your parents' marriages, I'm surprised you wanted to take the plunge at all."

"But that's exactly why I *did* want to be married!" She looked at him. "To make it *work*. I never had that stability in my family. My parents were divorced when I was eight, and after that it was a steady parade of stepmothers and Mother's boyfriends. I didn't want to live my own life that way." Sighing, she looked down at her ringless left hand. "Now I wonder if it's just another urban myth. A stable marriage."

"My parents had one. A good one."

"Had?"

"Before my dad died. He was a cop, in Boston. Didn't make it to his twentieth year on the force." Now Sam was the one who wasn't looking at *her*. He was gazing, instead, at some distant point in the room, avoiding her look of sympathy. He didn't feel he particularly needed her sympathy. One's parents died, and one went on with life. There was no other choice.

"After my dad died, Mom and I moved to Portland," he continued. "She wanted a safer town. A town where she wouldn't have to worry about her kid being shot on the street." He gave a rueful smile. "She wasn't too happy when I became a cop."

"Why did you become a cop?"

"I guess it was in the genes. Why did you become a nurse?"

"It was definitely *not* in the genes." She sat back, thinking it over for a moment. "I guess I wanted that one-on-one sense of helping someone. I like the contact. The touching. That was important to me, that it be hands-on. Not some vague idea of service to humanity." She gave a wry smile. "You said your mother didn't want you to be a cop. Well, my mother wasn't too happy about *my* career choice, either."

"What does she have against nursing?"

"Nothing. Just that it's not an appropriate profession for her daughter. She thinks of it as manual labor, something other women do. I was expected to marry well, entertain with flair and help humanity by hosting benefits. That's why she was so happy about my engagement. She thought I was finally on the right track. She was actually...*proud* of me for the first time."

"That's not why you wanted to marry Robert, was it? To please your mother?"

"I don't know." She looked at him with genuine puzzlement. "I don't know anymore."

"What about love? You must have loved him."

"How can I be sure of anything? I've just found out he was seeing someone else. And now it seems as if I were caught up in some fantasy. In love with a man I made up." She leaned back and closed her eyes. "I don't want to talk about him anymore."

"It's important you tell me everything you know. That you consider all the possible reasons someone wanted him dead. A man doesn't just walk up to a stranger and shoot him in the head. The killer had a reason."

"Maybe he didn't. Maybe he was crazy. Or high on drugs. Robert could have been in the wrong place at the wrong time."

"You don't really believe that. Do you?"

She paused. Then, softly, she said, "No, I guess I don't."

He watched her for a moment, thinking how very vulnerable she looked. Had he been any other man, he would be taking her in his arms, offering her comfort and warmth.

Suddenly he felt disgusted with himself. This was the wrong time to be pressing for answers, the wrong time to be doing the cop act. Yet that act was the only thing that kept him comfortably at a distance. It protected him, insulated him. From her.

He rose from the chair. "I think we both need to get some sleep."

Her response was a silent nod.

"If you need anything, my room's at the end of the hall. Sure you wouldn't rather take my bed? Give me the couch?"

"I'll be fine here. Good night."

That was his cue to retreat. He did.

In his bedroom, he paced between the closet and the dresser, unbuttoning his shirt. He felt more restless than tired, his brain moving a mile a minute. In the last two days, a church had been bombed, a man shot to death and a woman run off the road in an apparent murder attempt. He felt certain it was all linked, perhaps even linked to that warehouse bombing a week ago, but he couldn't see the connection. Maybe he was too dense.

Maybe his brain was too drunk on hormones to think straight.

It was all her fault. He didn't need or want this complication. But he couldn't seem to think about this case without lingering on thoughts of her.

And now she was in his house.

He hadn't had a woman sleeping under his roof since...well, it was longer than he cared to admit. His last fling had amounted to little more than a few weeks of lust with a woman he'd met at some party. Then, by mutual agreement, it was over. No complications, no broken hearts.

Not much satisfaction, either.

These days, what satisfaction he got came from the challenge of his work. That was one thing he could count on: the world would never run out of perps.

He turned off the lights and stretched out on the bed, but still he wasn't ready to sleep. He thought of Nina, just down the hall. Thought of what a mismatch they'd be together. And how horrified her mother would be if a cop started squiring around her daughter. If a cop even had a chance.

What a mistake, bringing her here. Lately it seemed he was making a lot of mistakes. He wasn't going to compound this one by falling in love or lust or whatever it was he felt himself teetering toward.

Tomorrow, he thought, *she's out of here.*

And I'm back in control.

Chapter 7

Nina knew she ought to be crying, but she couldn't. In darkness she lay on the couch and thought about those months she'd lived with Robert. The months she'd thought of as stepping stones to their marriage. When had it fallen apart? When had he stopped telling her the truth? She should have noticed the signs. The avoided looks, the silences.

She remembered that two weeks ago, he'd suggested the wedding be postponed. She'd assumed it was merely bridegroom jitters. By then, the arrangements were all made, the date set in stone.

How trapped he must have felt.

Oh, Robert. If only you'd come out and told me.

She could have dealt with the truth. The pain, the rejection. She was strong enough and adult enough. What she couldn't deal with was the fact that, all these months, she'd been living with a man she scarcely knew.

Now she'd never know what he really felt about her. His death had cut off any chance she had to make peace with him.

At last she did fall asleep, but the couch was lumpy and the dreams kept waking her up.

Dreams not of Robert, but of Sam Navarro.

He was standing before her, silent and unsmiling. She saw no emotion in his eyes, just that flat, unreadable gaze of a stranger. He reached out to her, as though to take her hand. But when she looked down, there were handcuffs circling her wrists.

"You're guilty," he said. And he kept repeating the word. *Guilty. Guilty.*

She awakened with tears in her eyes. Never had she felt so alone. And she *was* alone, reduced to the pitiful state of seeking refuge in the home of a cop who cared nothing at all about her. Who considered her little more than an added responsibility. An added bother.

It was a flicker of shadow across the window that drew her attention. She would not have noticed it at all, save for the fact it had passed just to the right of her, a patch of darkness moving across her line of vision. Suddenly her heart was thudding. She stared at the curtainless squares of moonlight, watching for signs of movement.

There it was again. A shadow, flitting past.

In an instant she was off the couch and running blindly up the hallway to Sam's room. She didn't stop to knock, but pushed right inside.

"Sam?" she whispered. He didn't answer. Frantic to wake him, she reached down to give him a shake, and her hands met warm, bare flesh. "Sam?"

At her touch, he awoke with such a violent start she jerked away in fright. "What?" he said. "What is it?"

"I think there's someone outside!"

At once he seemed to snap fully awake. He rolled off the bed and grabbed his trousers from a chair. "Stay here," he whispered. "Don't leave the room."

"What are you going to do?"

She was answered by a metallic click. A gun. Of course he had a gun. He was a cop.

"Just stay here," he ordered, and slipped out of the room.

She wasn't crazy; she wasn't going to go wandering around a dark house when there was a cop with a loaded gun nearby. Chilled and shivering, she stood by the door and listened. She heard Sam's footsteps creak down the hall toward the living room. Then there was silence, a silence so deep it made every breath she took seem like a roar. Surely he hadn't left the house? He wouldn't go outside, would he?

The creak of returning footsteps made her back away from the door. She scurried to the far side of the bed. At the first glimpse of a figure entering the room, she ducked behind the mattress. Only when she heard Sam say, "Nina?" did she dare raise her head.

"Here," she whispered, suddenly feeling ridiculous as she emerged from her hiding place.

"There's no one out there."

"But I saw someone. Something."

"It could have been a deer. An owl flying past." He set his gun down on the nightstand. The solid clunk of metal on wood made her flinch. She hated guns. She wasn't sure she wanted to be anywhere near a man who owned one. Tonight, though, she didn't have a choice.

"Nina, I know you're scared. You have a right to be. But I've checked, and there's no one out there." He reached toward her. At the first touch of his hand on her arm, he gave a murmur of alarm. "You're freezing."

"I'm scared. Oh God, Sam. I'm so scared…"

He took her by the shoulders. By now she was shaking so hard she could barely form any words. Awkwardly, he drew her against him, and she settled, trembling, against his chest. If only he'd hold her. If only he'd put his arms around her. When at last he did, it was like being welcomed home. Enclosed in warmth and safety. This was not the man she'd dreamed about, not the cold, unsmiling cop. This was a man who held her and murmured comforting sounds. A man whose face nuzzled her hair, whose lips, even now, were lowering toward hers.

The kiss was gentle. Sweet. Not the sort of kiss she ever imagined Sam Navarro capable of. Certainly she never imagined being hugged by him, comforted by him. But here she was, in his arms, and she had never felt so protected.

He coaxed her, still shivering, to the bed. He pulled the covers over them both. Again, he kissed her. Again the kiss was gently undemanding. The heat of the bed, of their bodies, banished her chill. And she became aware of so many other things: the scent of his bare skin, the bristly plane of his chest. And most of all, the touch of his lips, lingering against hers.

They had their arms wrapped around each other now, and their legs were slowly twining together. The kiss had gone beyond sweetness, beyond comfort. This was transforming to lust, pure and simple, and she was responding with such a rush of eagerness it astonished her. Her lips parted, welcoming the thrust of his tongue. Through the tangle of sheets, the barrier of her clothes, she felt the undeniable evidence of his arousal burgeoning against her.

She had not meant for this to happen, had not expected this to happen. But as their kiss deepened, as his hand slid hungrily down the curve of her waist, the flare of her hips, she knew that this had been inevitable. That for all his cool, unreadable looks, Sam Navarro harbored more passion than any man she'd ever known.

He regained control first. Without warning, he broke off the kiss. She heard his breathing, harsh and rapid, in the darkness.

"Sam?" she whispered.

He pulled away from her and sat up on the side of the bed. She watched his silhouette in the darkness, running his hands through his hair. "God," he murmured. "What am I doing?"

She reached out toward the dark expanse of his back. As her fingers brushed his skin, she felt his shudder of pleasure. He wanted her—that much she was certain of. But he was right, this was a mistake, and they both knew it. She'd been afraid and in need of a protector. He was a man alone, in need of no one, but still a man with needs. It was natural they'd seek each other's arms for comfort, however temporary it might be.

Staring at him now, at the shadow huddled at the side of the bed, she knew she still wanted him. The longing was so intense it was a physical ache.

She said, "It's not so awful, is it? What just happened between us?"

"I'm not getting sucked into this again. I can't."

"It doesn't have to mean anything, Sam. Not if you don't want it to."

"Is that how you see it? Quick and meaningless?"

"No. No, that's not at all what I said."

"But that's how it'd end up." He gave a snort of self-disgust. "This is the classic trap, you know. I want to keep you safe. You want a white knight. It's good only as long as that lasts. And then it falls apart." He rose from the bed and moved to the door. "I'll sleep on the couch."

He left the room.

She lay alone in his bed, trying to sort out the confusing whirl of emotions. Nothing made sense to her. Nothing was under her control. She tried to remember a time when her life was in perfect order. It was before Robert. Before she'd let herself get caught up in those fantasies of the perfect marriage. That was where she'd gone wrong. Believing in fantasies.

Her reality was growing up in a broken home, living with a succession of faceless stepparents, having a mother and father who despised each other. Until she'd met Robert, she hadn't expected to marry at all. She'd been content enough with her life, her job. That's what had always sustained her: her work.

She could go back to that. She *would* go back to that.

That dream of a happy marriage, that fantasy, was dead.

Sam was up at dawn. The couch had been even more uncomfortable than he'd expected. His sleep had been fitful, his shoulder ached, and at 7:00 a.m., he was unfit for human companionship. So when the phone rang, he was hard-pressed to answer with a civil "Hello."

"Navarro, you've got some explaining to do," said Abe Coopersmith.

Sam sighed. "Good morning, Chief."

"I just got an earful from Yeats in Homicide. I

shouldn't have to tell you this, Sam. Back off the Cormier woman."

"You're right. You shouldn't have to tell me. But you did."

"Anything going on between you two?"

"I felt she was in danger. So I stepped in."

"Where is she right now?"

Sam paused. He couldn't avoid this question; he had to answer it. "She's here," he admitted. "My house."

"Damn."

"Someone was following us last night. I didn't think it was prudent to leave her alone. Or unprotected."

"So you brought her to *your* house? Where, exactly, did you happen to park your common sense?"

I don't know, thought Sam. *I lost track of it when I looked into Nina Cormier's big brown eyes.*

"Don't tell me you two are involved. Please don't tell me that," said Coopersmith.

"We're not involved."

"I hope to God you're not. Because Yeats wants her in here for questioning."

"For Robert Bledsoe's murder? Yeats is fishing. She doesn't know anything about it."

"He wants to question her. Bring her in. One hour."

"She has an airtight alibi—"

"*Bring her in,* Navarro." Coopersmith hung up.

There was no way around this. Much as he hated to do it, he'd have to hand Nina over to the boys in Homicide. Their questioning might be brutal, but they had their job to do. As a cop, he could hardly stand in their way.

He went up the hall to the bedroom door and knocked. When she didn't answer, he cautiously cracked open the door and peeked inside.

She was sound asleep, her hair spread across the pillow in a luxurious fan of black. Just the sight of her, lying so peacefully in his bed, in his house, sent a rush of yearning through him. It was so intense he had to grip the doorknob just to steady himself. Only when it had passed, when he had ruthlessly suppressed it, did he dare enter the room.

She awakened with one gentle shake of the shoulder. Dazed by sleep, she looked at him with an expression of utter vulnerability, and he cleared his throat just to keep his voice steady.

"You'll have to get up," he told her. "The detectives in Homicide want to see you downtown."

"When?"

"One hour. You have time to take a shower. I've already got coffee made."

She didn't say anything. She just looked at him with an expression of bewilderment. And no wonder. Last night they had held each other like lovers.

This morning, he was behaving like a stranger.

This was a mistake, coming into her room. Approaching the bed. At once he put distance between them and went to the door. "I'm sure it'll just be routine questions," he said. "But if you feel you need a lawyer—"

"Why should I need a lawyer?"

"It's not a bad idea."

"I don't need one. I didn't do anything." Her gaze was direct and defiant. He'd only been trying to protect her rights, but she had taken his suggestion the wrong way, had interpreted it as an accusation.

He didn't have the patience right now to set her straight. "They'll be waiting for us" was all he said, and he left the room.

While she showered, he tried to scrounge together a breakfast, but could come up with only frozen French bread and a months-old box of cornflakes. Both the pantry and the refrigerator looked pretty pathetic; bachelorhood was showing, and he wasn't at all proud of it.

In disgust, he went outside to fetch the newspaper, which had been delivered to its usual spot at the end of the driveway. He was walking back toward the house when he abruptly halted and stared at the ground.

There was a footprint.

Or, rather, a series of footprints. They tracked through the soft dirt, past the living room window, and headed off among the trees. A man's shoes, thick soled. Size eleven at least.

He glanced toward the house and thought about what the man who'd made those prints could have seen last night, through the windows. Only darkness? Or had he seen Nina, a moving target as she walked around the living room?

He went to his car, parked near the front porch. Slowly, methodically, he examined it from bumper to bumper. He found no signs of tampering.

Maybe I'm paranoid. Maybe those footprints mean nothing.

He went back inside, into the kitchen, and found Nina finishing up her cup of coffee. Her face was flushed, her hair still damp from the shower. At her first look at him, she frowned. "Is something wrong?" she asked.

"No, everything's fine." He carried his cup to the sink. There he looked out the window and thought about how isolated this house was. How open those windows were to the sight of a gunman.

He turned to her and said, "I think it's time to leave."

* * *

I should have taken Sam's advice. I should have hired a lawyer.

That was the thought that now crossed Nina's mind as she sat in an office at the police station and faced the three Homicide detectives seated across the table from her. They were polite enough, but she sensed their barely restrained eagerness. Detective Yeats in particular made her think of an attack dog—leashed, but only for the moment.

She glanced at Sam, hoping for moral support. He gave her none. Throughout the questioning, he hadn't even looked at her. He stood at the window, his shoulders rigid, his gaze focused outside. He'd brought her here, and now he was abandoning her. The cop, of course, had his duty to perform. And at this moment, he was playing the cop role to the hilt.

She said to Yeats, "I've told you everything I know. There's nothing else I can think of."

"You were his fiancé. If anyone would know, you would."

"I don't. I wasn't even there. If you'd just talk to Daniella—"

"We have. She confirms your alibi," Yeats admitted.

"Then why do you keep asking me these questions?"

"Because murder doesn't have to be done in person," one of the other cops said.

Now Yeats leaned forward, his gaze sympathetic, his voice quietly coaxing. "It must have been pretty humiliating for you," he persisted. "To be left at the altar. To have the whole world know he didn't want you."

She said nothing.

"Here's a man you trusted. A man you loved. And for weeks, maybe months, he was cheating on you. Probably laughing at you behind your back. A man like that doesn't deserve a woman like you. But you loved him anyway. And all you got for it was pain."

She lowered her head. She still didn't speak.

"Come on, Nina. Didn't you want to hurt him back? Just a little?"

"Not—not that way," she whispered.

"Even when you found out he was seeing someone else? Even when you learned it was your own step-mother?"

She looked up sharply at Yeats.

"It's true. We spoke to Daniella and she admitted it. They'd been meeting on the sly for some time. While you were at work. You didn't know?"

Nina swallowed. In silence she shook her head.

"I think maybe you *did* know. Maybe you found out on your own. Maybe he told you."

"No."

"And how did it make you feel? Hurt? Angry?"

"I didn't know."

"Angry enough to strike back? To find someone who'd strike back *for* you?"

"I didn't know!"

"That's simply not believable, Nina. You expect us to accept your word that you knew nothing about it?"

"I didn't!"

"You *did*. You—"

"That's *enough*." It was Sam's voice that cut in. "What the hell do you think you're doing, Yeats?"

"My job," Yeats shot back.

"You're badgering her. Interrogating without benefit of counsel."

"Why should she need a lawyer? She claims she's innocent."

"She *is* innocent."

Yeats glanced smugly at the other Homicide detectives. "I think it's pretty obvious, Navarro, that you no longer belong on this investigation."

"You don't have the authority."

"Abe Coopersmith's given me the authority."

"Yeats, I don't give a flying—"

Sam's retort was cut off by the beeping of his pocket pager. Irritably he pressed the Silence button. "I'm not through here," he snapped. Then he turned and left the room.

Yeats turned back to Nina. "Now, Miss Cormier," he said. All trace of sympathy was gone from his expression. In its place was the razor-tooth smile of a pit bull. "Let's get back to the questions."

The page was from Ernie Takeda in the crime lab, and the code on the beeper readout told Sam it was an urgent message. He made the call from his own desk.

It took a few dialings to get through; the line was busy. When the usually low-key Takeda finally answered, there was an uncharacteristic tone of excitement in his voice.

"We've got something for you, Sam," said Takeda. "Something that'll make you happy."

"Okay. Make me happy."

"It's a fingerprint. A partial, from one of the device fragments from the warehouse bomb. It could be enough to ID our bomber. I've sent the print off to NCIC. It'll take a few days to run it through the system. So be patient. And let's hope our bomber is on file somewhere."

"You're right, Ernie. You've made me a happy man."

"Oh, one more thing. About that church bomb."

"Yes?"

"Based on the debris, I'd say the device had some sort of gift wrapping around it. Also, since it had no timing elements, my guess is, it was designed to be triggered on opening. But it went off prematurely. Probably a short circuit of some kind."

"You mentioned gift wrapping."

"Yeah. Silver-and-white paper."

Wedding wrap, thought Sam, remembering the gift that had been delivered that morning to the church. If the bomb was meant to explode on opening, then there was no longer any doubt who the intended victims were.

But why kill Nina? he wondered as he headed back to the conference room. Could this whole mess be attributed to another woman's jealousy? Daniella Cormier had a motive, but would she have gone so far as to hire a bomber?

What was he missing here?

He opened the office door and halted. The three homicide detectives were still sitting at the table. Nina wasn't. She was gone.

"Where is she?" Sam asked.

Yeats shrugged. "She left."

"What?"

"She got fed up with our questions, so she walked out."

"You *let* her leave?"

"We haven't charged her with anything. Are you saying we should have, Navarro?"

Sam's reply was unrepeatable. With a sudden sense of anxiety, he left Yeats and headed out the front entrance of police headquarters. He stood on the sidewalk, looking up and down the street.

Nina was nowhere in sight.

Someone was trying to kill her, he thought as he headed for his car. *I have to reach her first.*

From his car phone, he called Nina's father's house. She wasn't there. He called Robert Bledsoe's house. No answer. He called Lydia Warrenton's house. Nina wasn't there either.

On a hunch, he drove to Lydia's Cape Elizabeth home anyway. People in distress often flee home for comfort, he reasoned. Eventually, Nina might wind up at her mother's.

He found Lydia at home. But no Nina—not yet, at least.

"I haven't spoken to her since yesterday morning," said Lydia, ushering Sam into the seaview room. "I'm not sure she *would* come here."

"Do you know where she might go?" Sam asked. "Someone she might turn to?"

Lydia shook her head. "I'm afraid my daughter and I aren't very close. We never were. The truth is, she wasn't the easiest child."

"What do you mean, Mrs. Warrenton?"

Lydia seated herself on the white couch. Her silk pantsuit was a startling slash of purple against the pale cushions. "What I mean to say—I know it sounds awful—is that Nina was something of a disappointment to me. We offered her so many opportunities. To study abroad, for instance. At a boarding school in Switzerland. Her sister Wendy went and benefited wonderfully. But Nina refused to go. She insisted on staying home. Then there were the other things. The boys she brought home. The ridiculous outfits she'd wear. She could be doing so much with her life, but she never achieved much."

"She earned a nursing degree."

Lydia gave a shrug. "So do thousands of other girls."

"She's not any other girl, Mrs. Warrenton. She's your daughter."

"That's why I expected more. Her sister speaks three languages and plays the piano and cello. She's married to an attorney who's in line for a judicial seat. While Nina…" Lydia sighed. "I can't imagine how sisters could be so different."

"Maybe the real difference," said Sam, rising to his feet, "was in how you loved them." He turned and walked out of the room.

"Mr. Navarro!" he heard Lydia call as he reached the front door.

He looked back. She was standing in the hallway, a woman of such perfectly groomed elegance that she didn't seem real or alive. Or touchable.

Not like Nina at all.

"I think you have entirely the wrong idea about me and my daughter," Lydia said.

"Does it really matter what I think?"

"I just want you to understand that I did the best I could, under the circumstances."

"Under the circumstances," replied Sam, "so did she." And he left the house.

Back in his car, he debated which way to head next. Another round of phone calls came up empty. Where the hell was she?

The only place he hadn't checked was her new apartment. She'd told him it was on Taylor Street. There was probably no phone in yet; he'd have to drive there to check it out.

On his way over, he kept thinking about what Lydia Warrenton had just told him. He thought about what it must have been like for Nina to grow up the black sheep, the unfavored child. Always doing the wrong thing, never meeting Mommy's approval. Sam had been fortunate to have a mother who'd instilled in him a sense of his own competence.

I understand now, he thought, *why you wanted to marry Robert.* Marrying Robert Bledsoe was the one sure way to gain her mother's approval. And even that had collapsed in failure.

By the time he pulled up at Nina's new apartment building, he was angry. At Lydia, at George Cormier and his parade of wives, at the entire Cormier family for its battering of a little girl's sense of self-worth.

He knocked harder at the apartment door than he had to.

There was no response. She wasn't here, either.

Where are you, Nina?

He was about to leave when he impulsively gave the knob a turn. It was unlocked.

He pushed the door open. "Nina?" he called.

Then his gaze focused on the wire. It was almost invisible, a tiny line of silver that traced along the doorframe and threaded toward the ceiling.

Oh, my God...

In one fluid movement he pivoted away and dived sideways, down the hallway.

The force of the explosion blasted straight through the open door and ripped through the wall in a flying cloud of wood and plaster.

Deafened, stunned by the blast, Sam lay facedown in the hallway as debris rained onto his back.

Chapter 8

"Man, oh man," said Gillis. "You sure did bring down the house."

They were standing outside, behind the yellow police line, waiting for the rest of the search team to assemble. The apartment house—what was left of it—had been cleared of any second devices, and now it was Ernie Takeda's show. Takeda was, at that moment, diagramming the search grid, handing out evidence bags and assigning his lab crew to their individual tasks.

Sam already knew what they'd find. Residue of Dupont label dynamite. Scraps of green two-inch-wide electrical tape. And Prima detonating cord. The same three components as the church bomb and the warehouse bomb.

And every other bomb put together by the late Vincent Spectre.

Who's your heir apparent, Spectre? Sam wondered.

To whom did you bequeath your tricks of the trade? And why is Nina Cormier the target?

Just trying to reason it through made his head pound. He was still covered in dust, his cheek was bruised and swollen, and he could barely hear out of his left ear. But he had nothing to complain about. He was alive.

Nina would not have been so fortunate.

"I've got to find her," he said. "Before he does."

"We've checked with the family again," said Gillis. "Father, mother, sister. She hasn't turned up anywhere."

"Where the hell could she have gone?" Sam began to pace along the police line, his worry turning to agitation. "She walks out of headquarters, maybe she catches a cab or a bus. Then what? What would she do?"

"Whenever my wife gets mad, she goes shopping," Gillis offered helpfully.

"I'm going to call the family again." Sam turned to his car. "Maybe she's finally shown up somewhere."

He was about to reach inside the Taurus for the car phone when he froze, his gaze focused on the edge of the crowd. A small, dark-haired figure stood at the far end of the street. Even from that distance, Sam could read the fear, the shock, in her pale face.

"Nina," he murmured. At once he began to move toward her, began to push, then shove his way through the crowd. "Nina!"

She caught sight of him, struggling to reach her. Now she was moving as well, frantically plunging into the gathering of onlookers. They found each other, fell into each other's embrace. And at that moment, there was no one else in the world for Sam, no one but the woman he was holding. She felt so very precious in his arms, so easily taken from him.

With a sudden start, he became acutely aware of the

crowd. All these people, pressing in on them. "I'm getting you out of here," he said. Hugging her close to his side, he guided her toward his car. The whole time, he was scanning faces, watching for any sudden movements.

Only when he'd bundled her safely into the Taurus did he allow himself a deep breath of relief.

"Gillis!" he called. "You're in charge here!"

"Where you going?"

"I'm taking her somewhere safe."

"But—"

Sam didn't finish the conversation. He steered the car out of the crowd and they drove away.

Drove north.

Nina was staring at him. At the bruise on his cheek, the plaster dust coating his hair. "My God, Sam," she murmured. "You've been hurt—"

"A little deaf in one ear, but otherwise I'm okay." He glanced at her and saw that she didn't quite believe him. "I ducked out just before it blew. It was a five-second delay detonator. Set off by opening the door." He paused, then added quietly, "It was meant for you."

She said nothing. She didn't have to; he could read the comprehension in her gaze. This bombing was no mistake, no random attack. She was the target and she could no longer deny it.

"We're chasing down every lead we have," he said. "Yeats is going to question Daniella again, but I think that's a dead end. We did get a partial fingerprint off the warehouse bomb, and we're waiting for an ID. Until then, we've just got to keep you alive. And that means you have to cooperate. Do exactly what I tell you to do." He gave an exasperated sigh and clutched the steering wheel tighter. "That was *not* smart, Nina. What you did today."

"I was angry. I needed to get away from all you cops."

"So you storm out of headquarters? Without telling me where you're going?"

"You threw me to the wolves, Sam. I expected Yeats to clap the handcuffs on me. And you delivered me to him."

"I had no choice. One way or the other, he was going to question you."

"Yeats thinks I'm guilty. And since *he* was so sure of it, I thought... I thought you must have your doubts as well."

"I have no doubts," he said, his voice absolutely steady. "Not about you. And after this latest bomb, I don't think Yeats'll have any doubts either. You're the target."

The turnoff to Route 95—the Interstate—was just ahead. Sam took it.

"Where are we going?" she asked.

"I'm getting you out of town. Portland isn't a safe place for you. So I have another spot in mind. A fishing camp on Coleman Pond. I've had it for a few years. You'll be roughing it there, but you can stay as long as you need to."

"You won't be staying with me?"

"I have a job to do, Nina. It's the only way we'll get the answers. If I do my job."

"Of course, you're right." And she looked straight ahead at the road. "I forget sometimes," she said softly, "that you're a cop."

Across the street from the police line, he stood in the thick of the crowd, watching the bomb investigators scurry about with their evidence bags and their notebooks. Judging by the shattered glass, the debris in the street, the blast had been quite impressive. But of course he'd planned it that way.

Too bad Nina Cormier was still alive.

He'd spotted her just moments before, being escorted through the crowd by Detective Sam Navarro. He'd recognized Navarro at once. For years he'd followed the man's career, had read every news article ever written about the Bomb Squad. He knew about Gordon Gillis and Ernie Takeda as well. It was his business to know. They were the enemy, and a good soldier must know his enemy.

Navarro helped the woman into a car. He seemed unusually protective—not like Navarro at all, to be succumbing to romance on the job. Cops like him were supposed to be professionals. What had happened to the quality of civil servants these days?

Navarro and the woman drove away.

There was no point trying to follow them; another opportunity would arise.

Right now he had a job to do. And only two days in which to finish it.

He gave his gloves a little tug. And he walked away, unnoticed, through the crowd.

Billy "The Showman" Binford was happy today. He was even grinning at his attorney, seated on the other side of the Plexiglas barrier.

"It's gonna be all right, Darien," said Billy. "I got everything taken care of. You just get ready to negotiate that plea bargain. And get me out of here, quick."

Darien shook his head. "I told you, Liddell's not in a

mood to cut any deals. He's out to score big with your conviction."

"Darien, Darien. You got no faith."

"What I got is a good grip on reality. Liddell's aiming for a higher office. For that, he's got to put you away."

"He won't be putting anyone away. Not after Saturday."

"What?"

"You didn't hear me say nothing, okay? I didn't say nothing. Just believe me, Liddell won't be a problem."

"I don't want to know. Don't tell me about it."

Billy regarded his attorney with a look of both pity and amusement. "You know what? You're like that monkey with his paws over his ears. Hear no evil. That's you."

"Yeah," Darien agreed. And he nodded miserably. "That's me exactly."

A fire crackled in the hearth, but Nina felt chilled to the bone. Outside, dusk had deepened, and the last light was fading behind the dense silhouettes of pine trees. The cry of a loon echoed, ghostlike, across the lake. She'd never been afraid of the woods, or the darkness, or of being alone. Tonight, though, she *was* afraid, and she didn't want Sam to leave.

She also knew he had to.

He came tramping back into the cottage, carrying an armload of firewood, and began to stack it by the hearth. "This should do you for a few days," he said. "I just spoke to Henry Pearl and his wife. Their camp's up the road. They said they'd check up on you a few times a day. I've known them for years, so I know you can count on them. If you need anything at all, just knock on their door."

He finished stacking the wood and clapped the dirt from his hands. With his shirtsleeves rolled up and sawdust clinging to his trousers, he looked more like a woodsman than a city cop. He threw another birch log on the fire and the flames shot up in a crackle of sparks. He turned to look at her, his expression hidden against the backlight of fire.

"You'll be safe here, Nina. I wouldn't leave you alone if I had even the slightest doubt."

She nodded. And smiled. "I'll be fine."

"There's a fishing pole and tackle box in the kitchen, if you feel like wrestling with a trout. And feel free to wear anything you find in the closet. None of it'll fit, but at least you'll be warm. Henry's wife'll drop by some, uh, women's wear tomorrow." He paused and laughed. "Those probably won't fit either. Since she's twice *my* size."

"I'll manage, Sam. Don't worry about me."

There was a long silence. They both knew there was nothing more to say, but he didn't move. He glanced around the room, as though reluctant to leave. Almost as reluctant as she was to see him go.

"It's a long drive back to the city," she said. "You should eat before you go. Can I interest you in dinner? Say, a gourmet repast of macaroni and cheese?"

He grinned. "Make it anything else and I'll say yes."

In the kitchen, they rummaged through the groceries they'd bought at a supermarket on the way. Mushroom omelets, a loaf of French bread and a bottle of wine soon graced the tiny camp table. Electricity had not yet made it to this part of the lake, so they ate by the light of a hurricane lamp. Outside, dusk gave way to a darkness alive with the chirp of crickets.

She gazed across the table at him, watching the way

his face gleamed in the lantern light. She kept focusing on that bruise on his cheek, thinking about how close he'd come to dying that afternoon. But that was exactly the sort of work he did, the sort of risk he took all the time. Bombs. Death. It was insane, and she didn't know why any man in his right mind would take those risks. *Crazy cop,* she thought. *And I must be just as insane, because I think I'm falling for this guy.*

She took a sip of wine, the whole time intensely, almost painfully aware of his presence. And of her attraction toward him, an attraction so strong she was having trouble remembering to eat.

She had to remind herself that he was just doing his job, that to him, she was nothing more than a piece of the puzzle he was trying to solve, but she couldn't help picturing other meals, other nights they might spend together. Here, on the lake. Candlelight, laughter. Children. She thought he'd be good with children. He'd be patient and kind, just as he was with her.

How would I know that? I'm dreaming. Fantasizing again.

She reached across to pour him more wine.

He put his hand over the glass. "I have to be driving back."

"Oh. Of course." Nervously she set the bottle down again. She folded and refolded her napkin. For a whole minute they didn't speak, didn't look at each other. At least, she didn't look at him.

But when she finally raised her eyes, she saw that he was watching her. Not the way a cop looks at a witness, at a piece of a puzzle.

He was watching her the way a man watches a woman he wants.

He said, quickly, "I should leave now—"

"I know."

"—before it gets too late."

"It's still early."

"They'll need me, back in the city."

She bit her lip and said nothing. Of course he was right. The city did need him. Everyone needed him. She was just one detail that required attending to. Now she was safely tucked away and he could go back to his real business, his real concerns.

But he didn't seem at all eager to leave. He hadn't moved from the chair, hadn't broken eye contact. She was the one who looked away, who nervously snatched up her wineglass.

She was startled when he reached over and gently caught her hand. Without a word he took the glass and set it down. He raised her hand, palm side up, and pressed a kiss, ever so light, to her wrist. The lingering of lips, the tickle of his breath, was the sweetest torture. If he could wreak such havoc kissing that one square inch of skin, what could he do with the rest of her?

She closed her eyes and gave a small, soft moan. "I don't want you to leave," she whispered.

"It's a bad idea. For me to stay."

"Why?"

"Because of this." He kissed her wrist again. "And this." His lips skimmed up her arm, his beard delightfully rough against her sensitive skin. "It's a mistake. You know it. I know it."

"I make mistakes all the time," she replied. "I don't always regret them."

His gaze lifted to hers. He saw both her fear and her fearlessness. She was hiding nothing now, letting him read all. Her hunger was too powerful to hide.

He rose from the table. So did she.

He pulled her toward him, cupped her face in his hands and pressed his lips to hers. The kiss, sweet with the taste of wine and desire, left her legs unsteady. She swayed against him, her arms reaching up to clutch his shoulders. Before she could catch her breath, he was kissing her again, deeper. As their mouths joined, so did their bodies. His hands slid down her waist, to her hips. He didn't need to pull her against him; she could already feel him, hard and aroused. And that excited her even more.

"If we're going to stop," he breathed, "it had better be now…"

She responded with a kiss that drowned out any more words between them. Their bodies did all the talking, all the communicating.

They were tugging at each other's clothes, feverish for the touch of bare skin. First her sweater came off, then his shirt. They kissed their way into the next room, where the fire had quieted to a warm glow. Still kissing her, he pulled the afghan off the couch and let it fall onto the floor by the hearth.

Facing each other, they knelt before the dying fire. His bare shoulders gleamed in the flickering light. She was eager, starved for his touch, but he moved slowly, savoring every moment, every new experience of her. He watched with longing as she unhooked her bra and shrugged the straps off her shoulders. When he reached out to cup her breast, to tug at her nipple, she let her head sag back with a moan. His touch was ever so gentle, yet it left her feeling weak. Conquered. He tipped her back and lowered her onto the afghan.

Her body was pure liquid now, melting under his touch. He unzipped her jeans, eased them off her hips.

Her underwear slid off with the hiss of silk. She lay unshielded to his gaze now, her skin rosy in the firelight.

"I've had so many dreams about you," he whispered as his hand slid exploringly down her belly, toward the dark triangle of hair. "Last night, when you were in my house, I dreamed of holding you. Touching you just the way I am now. But when I woke up, I told myself it could never happen. That it was all fantasy. All longing. And here we are…" He bent forward, his kiss tender on her lips. "I shouldn't be doing this."

"I want you to. I want us to."

"I want it just as much. More. But I'm afraid we're going to regret it."

"Then we'll regret it later. Tonight, let's just be you and me. Let's pretend there's nothing else, no one else."

He kissed her again. And this time his hand slipped between her thighs, his finger dipping into her wetness, sliding deep into her warmth. She groaned, helpless with delight. He slid another finger in, and felt her trembling, tightening around him. She was ready, so ready for him, but he wanted to take his time, to make this last.

He withdrew his hand, just long enough to remove the rest of his clothes. As he knelt beside her, she couldn't help drawing in a sharp breath of admiration. What a beautiful man he was. Not just his body, but his soul. She could see it in his eyes: the caring, the warmth. Before it had been hidden from her, concealed behind that tough-cop mask of his. Now he was hiding nothing. Revealing everything.

As she was revealing everything to him.

She was too lost in pleasure to feel any modesty, any shame. She lay back, whimpering, as his fingers found her again, withdrew, teased, plunged back in. Already she was slick with sweat and desire, her hips arching against him.

"Please," she murmured. "Oh, Sam. I—"

He kissed her, cutting off any protest. And he continued his torment, his fingers dipping, sliding, until she was wound so tight she thought she'd shatter.

Only then, only as she reached the very edge, did he take away his hand, fit his hips to hers and thrust deep inside her.

She gripped him, crying out as he swept her, and himself, toward climax. And when it came, when she felt herself tumbling into that wondrous free fall, they clung to each other and they tumbled together, to a soft and ever-so-gentle landing.

She fell asleep, warm and safe, in his arms.

It was later, much later, when she awakened in the deepest chill of night.

The fire had died out. Although she was cocooned in the afghan, she found herself shivering.

And alone.

Hugging the afghan to her shoulders, she went into the kitchen and peered out the window. By the light of the moon, she could see that Sam's car was gone. He had returned to the city.

Already I miss him, she thought. Already his absence was like a deep, dark gulf in her life.

She went into the bedroom, climbed under the blankets, and tried to stop shivering, but she could not. When Sam had left, he had taken with him all the warmth. All the joy.

It scared her, how much she felt his absence. She was not going to fall in love with him; she could not afford to. What they'd experienced tonight was pleasure. The enjoyment of each other's bodies. As a lover, he was superb.

But as a man to love, he was clearly wrong for her.

No wonder he'd stolen away like a thief in the night. He'd known it was a mistake, just as she did. At this moment, he was probably regretting what they'd done.

She burrowed deeper under the blankets and waited for sleep, for dawn—whichever came first. Anything to ease the ache of Sam's departure.

But the night, cold and lonely, stretched on.

It was a mistake. A stupid, crazy mistake.

All the way back to Portland, on the drive down that long, dark highway, Sam kept asking himself how he could have let it happen.

No, he *knew* how it happened. The attraction between them was just too strong. It had been pulling them together from the first day they'd met. He'd fought it, had never stopped reminding himself that he was a cop, and she was an important element in his investigation. Good cops did not fall into this trap.

He used to think he was a good cop. Now he knew he was far too human, that Nina was a temptation he couldn't resist and that the whole investigation would probably suffer because he'd lost his sense of objectivity.

All because she'd come to mean too much to him.

Not only would the investigation suffer, *he* would as well, and he had only himself to blame. Nina was scared and vulnerable; naturally she'd turn to her protector for comfort. He should have kept her at arm's length, should have kept his own urges in check. Instead he'd succumbed, and now she was all he could think about.

He gripped the steering wheel and forced himself to focus on the road. On the case.

By 1:00 a.m., he was back in the city. By 1:30, he was at his desk, catching up on the preliminary reports from Ernie Takeda. As he'd expected, the bomb in Nina's apartment was similar to the devices that blew up the church and the warehouse. The difference between the three was in the method of detonation. The warehouse device had had a simple timer. The church device was a package bomb, designed to explode on opening. Nina's apartment had been wired to blow after the door opened. This bomber was a versatile fellow. He could trigger a blast in any number of ways. He varied his device according to the situation, and that made him both clever and extremely dangerous.

He went home at 5:00 a.m., caught a few hours of sleep and was back at headquarters for an eight o'clock meeting.

With three bombings in two weeks, the pressure was on, and the tension showed in the faces around the conference table. Gillis looked beat, Chief Coopersmith was testy and even the normally unemotional Ernie Takeda was showing flashes of irritation. Part of that irritation was due to the presence of two federal agents from Alcohol, Tobacco and Firearms. Both the men from ATF wore expressions of big-time experts visiting Hicksville.

But the most annoying source of irritation was the presence of their esteemed D.A. and perpetual pain in the neck, Norm Liddell.

Liddell was waving the morning edition of the *New York Times*. "Look at the headline," he said. "'Portland, Maine, the new bombing capital?' New York's saying that about us? *Us?*" He threw the newspaper down on the table. "What the hell is going on in this town? Who *is* this bomber?"

"We can give you a likely psychological profile," said one of the ATF agents. "He's a white male, intelligent—"

"I already know he's intelligent!" snapped Liddell. "A hell of a lot more intelligent than we are. I don't want some psychological profile. I want to know who he *is*. Does anyone have any idea about his identity?"

There was a silence at the table. Then Sam said, "We know who he's trying to kill."

"You mean the Cormier woman?" Liddell snorted. "So far, no one's come up with a single good reason why she's the target."

"But we know she is. She's our one link to the bomber."

"What about the warehouse bomb?" said Coopersmith. "How's that connect to Nina Cormier?"

Sam paused. "That I don't know," he admitted.

"I'd lay ten-to-one odds that Billy Binford's people ordered that warehouse bombing," said Liddell. "It was a logical move on his part. Scare off a prosecution witness. Does the Cormier woman have any connection to Binford?"

"All she knows about him is what she's read in the newspapers," said Sam. "There's no link."

"What about her family? Are they linked at all to Binford?"

"No link there, either," spoke up Gillis. "We've checked into the finances of the whole family. Nina Cormier's father, mother, stepfather, stepmother. No connection to Binford. Her ex-fiancé was just as clean."

Liddell sat back. "Something's coming. I can feel it. Binford's got something big planned."

"How do you know?" asked Coopersmith.

"I have sources." Liddell shook his head in disgust. "Here I finally get The Snowman behind bars, and he's still pulling strings, still making mincemeat of the court system. I'm convinced that warehouse bomb was an intimidation tactic. He's trying to scare all my witnesses. If I don't get a conviction, he'll be a free man in a few months. And he'll be scaring them in person."

"But chances are good you'll get that conviction," Coopersmith reassured him. "You've got credible witnesses, financial records. And you've drawn a law-and-order judge."

"Even so," countered Liddell, "Binford's not finished maneuvering. He's got something up his sleeve. I just wish I knew what it was." He looked at Sam. "Where are you hiding Nina Cormier?"

"A safe place," said Sam.

"You keeping it top secret or something?"

"Under the circumstances, I'd prefer to keep it known only to myself and Gillis. If you have questions to ask her, I can ask them for you."

"I just want to know what her connection is to these bombings. Why The Snowman wants her dead."

"Maybe this has nothing to do with Binford," suggested Sam. "He's in jail, and there's another party involved here. The bomber."

"Right. So find him for me," snapped Liddell. "Before Portland gets known as the American Beirut." He rose from his chair, his signal that the meeting was over. "Binford goes to trial in a month. I don't want my witnesses scared off by any more bombs. So *get* this guy, before he destroys my case." With that, Liddell stalked out.

"Man, election year is hell," muttered Gillis.

As the others filed out of the room, Coopersmith said, "Navarro, a word with you."

Sam waited, knowing full well what was coming. Coopersmith shut the door and turned to look at him.

"You and Nina Cormier. What's going on?"

"She needs protection. So I'm looking out for her."

"Is that all you're doing?"

Sam let out a weary sigh. "I…may be more involved than I should be."

"That's what I figured." Coopersmith shook his head. "You're too smart for this, Sam. This is the sort of mistake rookies make. Not you."

"I know."

"It could put you both in a dangerous situation. I ought to yank you off the case."

"I need to stay on it."

"Because of the woman?"

"Because I want to nail this guy. I'm *going* to nail him."

"Fine. Just keep your distance from Nina Cormier. I shouldn't have to tell you this. This kind of thing happens, someone always gets hurt. Right now she thinks you're John Wayne. But when this is all over, she's gonna see you're human like the rest of us. Don't set yourself up for this, Sam. She's got looks, she's got a daddy with lots of money. She doesn't want a cop."

I know he's right, thought Sam. *I know it from personal experience. Someone's going to get hurt. And it'll be me.*

The conference room door suddenly swung open and an excited Ernie Takeda stuck his head in the room. "You're not gonna believe this," he said, waving a sheet of fax paper.

"What is it?" asked Coopersmith.

"From NCIC. They just identified that fingerprint off the bomb fragment."

"And?"

"It's a match. With Vincent Spectre."

"That's impossible!" exclaimed Sam. He snatched the sheet from Ernie's grasp and stared at the faxed report. What he read there left no doubt that the ID was definite.

"There has to be a mistake," said Coopersmith. "They found his body. Spectre's been dead and buried for months."

Sam looked up. "Obviously not," he growled.

Chapter 9

The rowboat was old and well used, but the hull was sound. At least, it didn't leak as Nina rowed it out into the lake. It was late afternoon and a pair of loons were paddling lazily through the water, neither one alarmed by the presence of a lone rower. The day was utter stillness, utter peace, as warm as a summer day should be.

Nina guided the boat to the center of the pond, where sunlight rippled on the water, and there she let the boat drift. As it turned lazy circles, she lay back and stared up at the sky. She saw birds winging overhead, saw a dragonfly hover, iridescent in the slanting light.

And then she heard a voice, calling her name.

She sat up so sharply the boat rocked. She saw him then, standing at the water's edge, waving to her.

As she rowed the boat back to shore, her heart was galloping, more from anticipation than exertion. Why had he returned so soon? Last night he'd left without a word of goodbye, the way a man leaves a woman he never intends to see again.

Now here he was, standing silent and still on the shore, his gaze as unreadable as ever. She couldn't figure him out. She'd never be able to figure him out. He was a man designed to drive her crazy, and as she glided across the last yards of water, she could already feel that lovely insanity take hold of her. It required all her willpower to suppress it.

She tossed him the painter rope. He hauled the rowboat up onto the shore and helped her step out. Just the pressure of his hand grasping her arm gave her a thrill of delight. But one look at his face quelled any hopes that he was here as a lover. This was the cop, impersonal, businesslike. Not at all the man who'd held her in his arms.

"There's been a new development," he said.

Just as coolly, she met his gaze. "What development?"

"We think we know who the bomber is. I want you to take a look at some photographs."

On the couch by the fireplace—the same fireplace that had warmed them when they'd made love the night before—Nina sat flipping through a book of mug shots. The hearth was now cold, and so was she, both in body and in spirit. Sam sat a good foot away, not touching her, not saying a word. But he was watching her expectantly, waiting for some sign that she recognized a face in that book.

She forced herself to concentrate on the photos. One by one she scanned the faces, carefully taking in the features of each man pictured there. She reached the last page. Shaking her head, she closed the cover.

"I don't recognize anyone," she declared.

"Are you certain?"

"I'm certain. Why? Who am I supposed to recognize?"

His disappointment was apparent. He opened the book to the fourth page and handed it back to her. "Look at this face. Third one down, first column. Have you ever seen this man?"

She spent a long time studying the photo. Then she said, "No. I don't know him."

With a sigh of frustration, Sam sank back against the couch. "This doesn't make any sense at all."

Nina was still focused on the photograph. The man in the picture appeared to be in his forties, with sandy hair, blue eyes, and hollow, almost gaunt, cheeks. It was the eyes that held her attention. They stared straight at her, a look of intimidation that burned, lifelike, from a mere two-dimensional image. Nina gave an involuntary shiver.

"Who is he?" she asked.

"His name is—or was—Vincent Spectre. He's five foot eleven, 180 pounds, forty-six years old. At least, that's what he would be now. If he's still alive."

"You mean you don't know if he is?"

"We thought he was dead."

"You're not sure?"

"Not any longer." Sam rose from the couch. It was getting chilly in the cabin; he crouched at the hearth and began to arrange kindling in the fireplace.

"For twelve years," he said, "Vincent Spectre was an army demolitions expert. Then he got booted out of the service. Dishonorable discharge, petty theft. It didn't take him long to launch a second career. He became what we call a specialist. Big bangs, big bucks. Hired himself out to anyone who'd pay for his expertise. He worked for terrorist governments. For the mob. For crime bosses all over the country.

"For years he raked in the money. Then his luck ran out. He was recognized on a bank security camera. Arrested, convicted, served only a year. Then he escaped."

Sam struck a match and lit the kindling. It caught fire in a crackle of sparks and flames. He lay a log on top and turned to look at her.

"Six months ago," he continued, "Spectre's remains were found in the rubble after one of his bombs blew up a warehouse. That is, authorities *thought* it was his body. Now we think it might have been someone else's. And Spectre's still alive."

"How do you know that?"

"Because his fingerprint just turned up. On a fragment of the warehouse bomb."

She stared at him. "You think he also blew up the church?"

"Almost certainly. Vincent Spectre's trying to kill you."

"But I don't know any Vincent Spectre! I've never even heard his name before!"

"And you don't recognize his photo."

"No."

Sam stood up. Behind him, the flames were now crackling, consuming the log. "We've shown Spectre's photo to the rest of your family. They don't recognize him, either."

"It must be a mistake. Even if the man's alive, he has no reason to kill me."

"Someone else could have hired him."

"You've already explored that. And all you came up with was Daniella."

"That's still a possibility. She denies it, of course. And she passed the polygraph test."

"She let you hook her up to a *polygraph?*"

"She consented. So we did it."

Nina shook her head in amazement. "She must have been royally ticked off."

"As a matter of fact, I think she rather enjoyed giving the performance. She turned every male head in the department."

"Yes, she's good at that. She certainly turned my father's head. And Robert's, too," Nina added softly.

Sam was moving around the room now, pacing a slow circle around the couch. "So we're back to the question of Vincent Spectre," he said. "And what his connection is to you. Or Robert."

"I told you, I've never heard his name before. I don't remember Robert ever mentioning the name, either."

Sam paced around the couch, returned to stand by the fireplace. Against the background of flames, his face was unreadable. "Spectre *is* alive. And he built a bomb intended for you and Robert. Why?"

She looked down again at the photo of Vincent Spectre. Try as she might, she could conjure up no memory of that face. The eyes, perhaps, seemed vaguely familiar. That stare was one she might have seen before. But not the face.

"Tell me more about him," she suggested.

Sam went to the couch and sat down beside her. Not quite close enough to touch her, but close enough to make her very aware of his presence.

"Vincent Spectre was born and raised in California. Joined the army at age nineteen. Quickly showed an aptitude for explosives work, and was trained in demolitions. Saw action in Grenada and Panama. That's where he lost his finger—trying to disarm a terrorist explosive. At that point, he could have retired on disability but—"

"Wait. Did you just say he was missing a finger?"

"That's right."

"Which hand?"

"The left. Why?"

Nina went very still. Thinking, remembering. A missing finger. Why did that image seem so vividly familiar?

Softly she said, "Was it the left middle finger?"

Frowning, Sam reached for his briefcase and took out a file folder. He flipped through the papers contained inside. "Yes," he said. "It was the middle finger."

"No stump at all? Just...missing entirely."

"That's right. They had to amputate all the way back to the knuckle." He was watching her, his eyes alert, his voice quiet with tension. "So you *do* know him."

"I—I'm not sure. There was a man with an amputated finger—the left middle finger—"

"What? Where?"

"The Emergency Room. It was a few weeks ago. I remember he was wearing gloves, and he didn't want to take them off. But I had to check his pulse. So I pulled off the left glove. And I was so startled to see he was missing a finger. He'd stuffed the glove finger with cotton. I think I... I must have stared. I remember I asked him how he lost it. He told me he'd caught it in some machinery."

"Why was he in the E.R.?"

"It was—I think an accident. Oh, I remember. He was knocked down by a bicycle. He'd cut his arm and needed stitches put in. The strange part about it all was the way he vanished afterward. Right after the cut was sutured, I left the room to get something. When I came back, he was gone. No thank you, nothing. Just—disappeared. I thought he was trying to get away without paying his bill. But I found out later that he did pay the clerk. In cash."

"Do you remember his name?"

"No." She gave a shrug. "I'm terrible with names."

"Describe him for me. Everything you remember."

She was silent for a moment, struggling to conjure up the face of a man she'd seen weeks ago, and only once. "I remember he was fairly tall. When he lay down on the treatment table, his feet hung over the edge." She looked at Sam. "He'd be about your height."

"I'm six feet. Vincent Spectre's five-eleven. What about his face? Hair, eyes?"

"He had dark hair. Almost black. And his eyes..." She sat back, frowning in concentration. Remembered how startled she'd been by the missing finger. That she'd looked up and met the patient's gaze. "I think they were blue."

"The blue eyes would match Spectre's. The black hair doesn't. He could've dyed it."

"But the face was different. It didn't look like this photo."

"Spectre has resources. He could've paid for plastic surgery, completely changed his appearance. For six months we assumed he was dead. During that time he could've remade himself into an entirely different man."

"All right, what if it *was* Spectre I saw in the E.R. that day? Why does that make me a target? Why would he want to kill me?"

"You saw his face. You could identify him."

"A lot of people must have seen his face!"

"You're the only one who could connect that face

with a man who was missing a finger. You said he was wearing gloves, that he didn't want to remove them."

"Yes, but it was part of his uniform. Maybe the only reason for the gloves was—"

"What uniform?"

"Some sort of long-sleeved jacket with brass buttons. White gloves. Pants with this side stripe. You know, like an elevator operator. Or a bellhop."

"Was there a logo embroidered on the jacket? A building or hotel name?"

"No."

Sam was on his feet now, pacing back and forth with new excitement. "Okay. Okay, he has a minor accident. Cuts his arm, has to go to the E.R. for stitches. You see that he's missing a finger. You see his face. And you see he's wearing some sort of uniform..."

"It's not enough to make me a threat."

"Maybe it is. Right now, he's operating under a completely new identity. The authorities have no idea what he looks like. But that missing finger is a giveaway. You saw it. And his face. You could identify him for us."

"I didn't know anything about Vincent Spectre. I wouldn't have thought to go to the police."

"We were already raising questions about his so-called death. Wondering if he was still alive and operating. Another bombing, and we might have figured out the truth. All we had to do was tell the public we were looking for a man missing his left middle finger. You would have come forward. Wouldn't you?"

She nodded. "Of course."

"That may be what he was afraid of. That you'd tell us the one thing we didn't know. What he looks like."

For a long moment she was silent. She was staring down at the book of mug shots, thinking about that day in the E.R. Trying to remember the patients, the crises. Sore throats and sprained ankles. She'd been a nurse for eight years, had treated so many patients, that the days all seemed to blend together. But she did remember one more detail about that visit from the man with the gloves. A detail that left her suddenly chilled.

"The doctor," she said softly. "The doctor who sutured the cut—"

"Yes? Who was it?"

"Robert. It was Robert."

Sam stared at her. In that instant, he understood. They both did. Robert had been in the same room as well. He'd seen the patient's face, had seen the mutilated left hand. He, like Nina, could have identified Vincent Spectre.

Now Robert was dead.

Sam reached down to take Nina's hand. "Come on." He pulled her to her feet.

They were standing face-to-face now, and she felt her body respond immediately to his nearness, felt her stomach dance that little dance of excitement. Arousal.

"I'm driving you back to Portland," he said.

"Tonight?"

"I want you to meet with our police artist. See if you two can come up with a sketch of Spectre's face."

"I'm not sure I can. If I saw him, I'd recognize him. But just to describe his face—"

"The artist will walk you through it. The important thing is that we have something to work with. Also, I need you to help me go through the E.R. records. Maybe there's some information you've forgotten."

"We keep a copy of all the encounter forms. I can find his record for you." *I'll do anything you want me to do,* she thought, *if only you'll stop this tough-cop act.*

As they stood gazing at each other, she thought she saw a ripple of longing in his eyes. Too quickly, he turned away to get a jacket from the closet. He draped it over her shoulders. Just the brushing of his fingers against her skin made her quiver.

She shifted around to face him. To confront him.

"Has something happened between us?" she asked softly.

"What do you mean?"

"Last night. I didn't imagine it, Sam. We made love, right here in this room. Now I'm wondering what I did wrong. Why you seem so…indifferent."

He sighed, a sound of weariness. And perhaps regret. "Last night," he began, "shouldn't have happened. It was a mistake."

"I didn't think so."

"Nina, it's always a mistake to fall in love with the investigating cop. You're scared, you're looking for a hero. I happen to fall into the role."

"But you're not playing a role! Neither am I. Sam, I care about you. I think I'm falling in love with you."

He just looked at her without speaking, his silence as cutting as any words.

She turned away, so that she wouldn't have to see that flat, emotionless gaze of his. With a forced laugh she said, "God, I feel like such an idiot. Of course, this must happen to you all the time. Women throwing themselves at you."

"It's not like that."

"Isn't it? The hero cop. Who could resist?" She turned back to him. "So, how do I compare with all the others?"

"There aren't any others! Nina, I'm not trying to shove you away. I just want you to understand that it's the situation that's pulled us together. The danger. The intensity. You look at me and you completely miss all the flaws. All the reasons I'm not the right guy for you. You were engaged to Robert Bledsoe. Ivy League. Medical degree. House on the water. What the hell am I but a civil servant?"

She shook her head, tears suddenly filling her eyes. "Do you really think that's how I see you? As just a civil servant? Just a cop?"

"It's what I am."

"You're so much more." She reached up to touch his face. He flinched, but didn't pull away as her fingers caressed the roughness of his jaw. "Oh, Sam. You're kind. And gentle. And brave. I haven't met any other man like you. Okay, so you're a cop. It's just part of who you are. You've kept me alive. You've watched over me..."

"It was my job."

"Is that all it was?"

He didn't answer right away. He just looked at her, as though reluctant to tell the truth.

"Is it, Sam? Just a part of your job?"

He sighed. "No," he admitted. "It was more than that. You're more than that."

Pure joy made her smile. Last night she'd felt it— his warmth, his caring. For all his denials, there was a living, breathing man under that mask of indifference. She wanted so badly to fall into his arms, to coax the real Sam Navarro out from his hiding place.

He reached up for her hand and gently but firmly lowered it from his face. "Please, Nina," he said. "Don't make this hard for both of us. I have a job to do, and I can't be distracted. It's dangerous. For you and for me."

"But you do care. That's all I need to know. That you care."

He nodded. It was the most she could hope for.

"It's getting late. We should leave," he mumbled. And he turned toward the door. "I'll be waiting for you in the car."

Nina frowned at the computer-generated sketch of the suspect's face. "It's not quite right," she said.

"What's not right about it?" asked Sam.

"I don't know. It's not easy to conjure up a man's face. I saw him only that one time. I didn't consciously register the shape of his nose or jaw."

"Does he look anything like this picture?"

She studied the image on the computer screen. For an hour, they'd played with different hairlines, noses, shapes of jaws and chins. What they'd come up with seemed generic, lifeless. Like every other police sketch she'd ever seen.

"To be honest," she admitted with a sigh, "I can't be sure this is what he looks like. If you put the real man in a lineup, I think I'd be able to identify him. But I'm not very good at re-creating what I saw."

Sam, obviously disappointed, turned to the computer technician. "Print it up anyway. Send copies to the news stations and wire services."

"Sure thing, Navarro," the tech replied and he flipped on the printer switch.

As Sam led Nina away, she said miserably, "I'm sorry. I guess I wasn't much help."

"You did fine. And you're right, it's not easy to re-create a face. Especially one you saw only once. You really think you'd know him if you saw him?"

"Yes. I'm pretty sure of it."

He gave her arm a squeeze. "That may be all we'll

need from you. Assuming we ever get our hands on him. Which leads to the next item on our agenda."

"What's that?"

"Gillis is already at the hospital, pulling those treatment records. He'll need you to interpret a few things on the encounter form."

She nodded. "*That* I know I can do."

They found Gillis sitting in a back room of the E.R., papers piled up on the table in front of him. His face was pasty with fatigue under the fluorescent lights. It was nearly midnight, and he'd been on the job since 7:00 a.m. So had Sam.

For both of them, the night was just beginning.

"I pulled what I think is the right encounter form," said Gillis. "May 29, 5:00 p.m. Sound about right, Miss Cormier?"

"It could be."

Gillis handed her the sheet. It was the one-page record of an E.R. visit. On top was the name Lawrence Foley, his address and billing information. On the line Chief Complaint, she recognized her own handwriting: Laceration, left forearm. Below that, she had written: forty-six-year-old white male hit by bicycle in crosswalk. Fell, cut arm on fender. No loss of consciousness."

She nodded. "This is the one. Here's Robert's signature, on the bottom. Treating physician. He sutured the cut—four stitches, according to his notes."

"Have we checked out this name, Lawrence Foley?" Sam asked Gillis.

"No one by that name living at that address," Gillis informed him. "And that's a nonexistent phone number."

"Bingo," said Sam. "False address, false identity. This is our man."

"But we're no closer to catching him," stressed Gillis. "He left no trail, no clues. Where are we supposed to look?"

"We have a sketch of his face circulating. We know he was wearing some sort of uniform, possibly a bellhop's. So we check all the hotels. Try to match the sketch with any of their employees." Sam paused, frowning. "A hotel. Why would he be working at a hotel?"

"He needed a job?" Gillis offered.

"As a bellhop?" Sam shook his head. "If this is really Vincent Spectre, he had a reason to be there. A contract. A target..." He sat back and rubbed his eyes. The late hour, the stress, was showing in his face. All those shadows, all those lines of weariness. Nina longed to reach out to him, to stroke away the worry she saw there, but she didn't dare. Not in front of Gillis. Maybe not ever. He'd made it perfectly clear she was a distraction to him, to his work, and that distractions were dangerous. That much she accepted.

Yet how she ached to touch him.

Sam rose to his feet and began to move about, as though forcing himself to stay awake. "We need to check all the hotels. Set up a lineup of bellhops. And we need to check police reports. Maybe someone called in that bicycle accident."

"Okay, I'll get Cooley on it."

"What we really need to know is—who is he after? Who's the target?"

"We're not going to figure that out tonight," said Gillis. "We need more to go on." He yawned, and added, "And we need some sleep. Both of us."

"He's right," said Nina. "You can't function without rest, Sam. You need to sleep on this."

"In the meantime, Spectre's at work on God knows what catastrophe. So far we've been lucky. Only one bombing casualty. But the next time…" Sam stopped pacing. Stopped because he'd simply run out of steam. He was standing in one spot, his shoulders slumped, his whole body drooping.

Gillis looked at Nina. "Get him home, will ya? Before he keels over and I have to drag him."

Nina rose from her chair. "Come on, Sam," she said softly. "I'll drive you home."

Heading out to the car, he kept insisting he could drive, that he was in perfectly good shape to take the wheel. She, just as insistently, pointed out that he was a menace on the road.

He let her drive.

Scarcely after she'd pulled out of the hospital parking lot, he was sound asleep.

At his house, she roused him just long enough to climb out of the car and walk in the front door. In his bedroom, he shrugged off his gun holster, pulled off his shoes and collapsed on the bed. His last words were some sort of apology. Then he was fast asleep.

Smiling, she pulled the covers over him and went out to check the windows and doors. Everything was locked tight; the house was secure—as secure as it could be.

Back in Sam's room, she undressed in the dark and climbed into bed beside him. He didn't stir. Gently she stroked her fingers through his hair and thought, *My poor, exhausted Sam. Tonight, I'll watch over you.*

Sighing, he turned toward her, his arm reaching out to hug her against him. Even in his sleep, he was trying to protect her.

Like no other man I've ever known.

Nothing could hurt her. Not tonight, not in his arms. She'd stake her life on it.

* * *

They were showing his picture on the morning news.

Vincent Spectre took one look at the police sketch on the TV screen and he laughed softly. What a joke. The picture looked nothing like him. The ears were too big, the jaw was too wide and the eyes looked beady. He did not have beady eyes. How had they gotten it so wrong? What had happened to the quality of law enforcement?

"Can't catch me, I'm the gingerbread man," he murmured.

Sam Navarro was slipping, if that drawing was the best he could come up with. A pity. Navarro had seemed such a clever man, a truly worthy opponent. Now it appeared he was as dumb a cop as all the others. Though he *had* managed to draw one correct conclusion.

Vincent Spectre was alive and back in the game.

"Just wait till you see how alive I am," he said.

That Cormier woman must have described his face to the police artist. Although the sketch wasn't anything for him to worry about, Nina Cormier did concern him. Chances were, she'd recognize him in a room of anonymous strangers. She was the only one who could link his face to his identity, the only one who could ruin his plan. She would have to be disposed of.

Eventually.

He turned off the TV and went into the apartment bedroom, where the woman was still asleep. He'd met Marilyn Dukoff three weeks ago at the Stop Light Club, where he'd gone to watch the topless dance revue. Marilyn had been the blonde in the purple-sequined G-string. Her face was coarse, her IQ a joke, but her figure was a marvel of nature and silicone. Like so many other women on the exotic dance circuit, she was in desperate need of money and affection.

He'd offered her both, in abundance.

She'd accepted his gifts with true gratitude. She was like a puppy who'd been neglected too long, loyal and hungry for approval. Best of all, she asked no questions. She knew enough not to.

He sat down beside her on the bed and nudged her awake. "Marilyn?"

She opened one sleepy eye and smiled at him. "Good morning."

He returned her smile. And followed it with a kiss. As usual, she responded eagerly. Gratefully. He removed his clothes and climbed under the sheets, next to that architecturally astonishing body. It took no coaxing at all to get her into the mood.

When they had finished, and she lay smiling and satisfied beside him, he knew it was the right time to ask.

And he said, "I need another favor from you."

Two hours later, a blond woman in a gray suit presented her ID to the prison official. "I'm an attorney with Frick and Darien," she said. "Here to see our client, Billy Binford."

Moments later she was escorted to the visiting room. Billy "The Snowman" took a seat on the other side of the Plexiglas. He regarded her for a moment, then said, "I been watching the news on TV. What the hell's all this other stuff going on?"

"He says it's all necessary," said the blonde.

"Look, I just wanted the job done like he promised."

"It's being taken care of. Everything's on schedule. All you have to do is sit back and wait."

Billy glanced at the prison guard, who was standing off to the side and obviously bored. "I got everything riding on this," he muttered.

"It will happen. But he wants to make sure you keep up your end of the bargain. Payment, by the end of the week."

"Not yet. Not till I'm sure it's done. I got a court date coming up fast—too fast. I'm counting on this."

The blonde merely smiled. "It'll happen," she said. "He guarantees it."

Chapter 10

Sam woke up to the smell of coffee and the aroma of something cooking, something delicious. It was Saturday. He was alone in the bed, but there was no question that someone else was in the house. He could hear the bustle in the kitchen, the soft clink of dishes. For the first time in months, he found himself smiling as he rose from bed and headed to the shower. There was a woman in the kitchen, a woman who was actually cooking breakfast. Amazing how different that made the whole house feel. Warm. Welcoming.

He came out of the shower and stood in front of the mirror to shave. That's when his smile faded. He suddenly wondered how long he'd been asleep. He'd slept so heavily he hadn't heard Nina get out of bed this morning, hadn't even heard her take a shower. But she'd been in here; the shower curtain had already been damp when he stepped in.

Last night someone could have broken into the house, and he would have slept right through it.

I'm useless to her, he thought. He couldn't track down Spectre and keep Nina safe at the same time. He didn't have the stamina or the objectivity. He was worse than useless; he was endangering her life.

This was exactly what he'd been afraid would happen.

He finished shaving, got dressed, and went into the kitchen.

Just the sight of her standing at the stove was enough to shake his determination. She turned and smiled at him.

"Good morning," she murmured, and wrapped her arms around him in a sweetly scented hug. Lord, this was every man's fantasy. Or, at least, it was *his* fantasy: a gorgeous woman in his kitchen. The good morning smile. Pancakes cooking in the skillet.

A woman in the house.

Not just any woman. Nina. Already he felt his resistance weakening, felt the masculine urges taking over again. This was what always happened when he got too close to her.

He took her by the shoulders and stepped away. "Nina, we have to talk."

"You mean…about the case?"

"No. I mean about you. And me."

All at once that radiant smile was gone from her face. She'd sensed that a blow was about to fall, a blow that would be delivered by *him*. Mutely she turned, lifted the pancake from the skillet, and slid it onto a plate. Then she just stood there, looking at it lying on the countertop.

He hated himself at that moment. At the same time

he knew there was no other way to handle this—not if he really cared about her.

"Last night shouldn't have happened," he said.

"But nothing *did* happen between us. I just brought you home and put you to bed."

"That's exactly what I'm talking about. Nina, I was so exhausted last night, someone could've driven a damn train through my bedroom and I wouldn't have moved a muscle. How am I supposed to keep you safe when I can't even keep my eyes open?"

"Oh, Sam." She stepped toward him, her hands rising to caress his face. "I don't expect you to be my guardian. Last night, I wanted to take care of *you.* I was so happy to do it."

"I'm the cop, Nina. I'm responsible for your safety."

"For once, can't you stop being a cop? Can't you let me take care of *you?* I'm not so helpless. And you're not so tough that you don't need someone. When I was scared, you were there for me. And I want to be here for *you.*"

"I'm not the one who could get killed." He took both her hands and firmly lowered them from his face. "This isn't a good idea, getting involved, and we both know it. I can't watch out for you the way I should. Any other cop could do a better job."

"I don't trust any other cop. I trust you."

"And that could be a fatal mistake." He pulled away, gaining himself some breathing space. Anything to put distance between them. He couldn't think clearly when she was so near; her scent, her touch, were too distracting. He turned and matter-of-factly poured himself a cup of coffee, noting as he did it that his hand wasn't quite steady. Her effect, again. Not looking at her, he said, "It's time to focus on the case, Nina. On finding

Spectre. That's the best way to ensure your safety. By doing my job and doing it right."

She said nothing.

He turned and saw that she was gazing listlessly at the table. It had already been set with silverware and napkins, glasses of juice and a small crock of maple syrup. Again he felt that stab of regret. *I've finally found a woman I care about, a woman I could love, and I'm doing my best to push her away.*

"So," she said softly. "What do you propose, Sam?"

"I think another man should be assigned to protect you. Someone who has no personal involvement with you."

"Is that what we have? A personal involvement?"

"What else would you call it?"

She shook her head. "I'm beginning to think we have no involvement at all."

"For God's sake, Nina. We slept with each other! How can two people get more involved than that?"

"For some people, sex is purely a physical act. And that's all it is." Her chin tilted up in silent inquiry. *For some people.*

Meaning me?

Damn it, he refused to get caught up in this hopeless conversation. She was baiting him, trying to get him to admit there was more to that act of lovemaking than just sex. He was not about to admit the truth, not about to let her know how terrified he was of losing her.

He knew what had to be done.

He crossed the kitchen to the telephone. He'd call Coopersmith, ask him to assign a man to pull guard duty. He was about to pick up the receiver when the phone suddenly rang.

He answered it with a curt "Navarro."

"Sam, it's me."

"Morning, Gillis."

"Morning? It's nearly noon. I've already put in a full day here."

"Yeah, I'm hanging my head in shame."

"You should. We've got that lineup scheduled for one o'clock. Bellhops from five different hotels. You think you can bring Nina Cormier down here to take a look? That is, if she's there with you."

"She's here," admitted Sam.

"That's what I figured. Be here at one o'clock, got it?"

"We'll be there." He hung up and ran his hand through his damp hair. God. Nearly noon? He was getting lazy. Careless. All this agonizing over him and Nina, over a relationship that really had nowhere to go, was cutting into his effectiveness as a cop. If he didn't do his job right, *she* was the one who'd suffer.

"What did Gillis say?" he heard her ask.

He turned to her. "They've scheduled a lineup at one o'clock. Want you to look at a few hotel bellhops. You up to it?"

"Of course. I want this over with as much as you do."

"Good."

"And you're right about turning me over to another cop. It's all for the best." She met his gaze with a look of clear-eyed determination. "You have more important things to do than baby-sit me."

He didn't try to argue with her. In fact, he didn't say a thing. But as she walked out of the kitchen, leaving him standing alone by that cozily set breakfast table, he thought, *You're wrong. There's no more important job in the world to me than watching over you.*

* * *

Eight men stood on the other side of the one-way mirror. All of them were facing forward. All of them looked a little sheepish about being there.

Nina carefully regarded each man's uniform in turn, searching for any hint of familiarity. Any detail at all that might trip a memory.

She shook her head. "I don't see the right uniform."

"You're absolutely certain?" asked Gillis.

"I'm certain. It wasn't any of those."

She heard an undisguised snort of disappointment. It came from Norm Liddell, the D.A. who was standing next to Gillis. Sam, poker-faced, said nothing.

"Well, this was a big waste of my time," muttered Liddell. "Is this all you've come up with, Navarro? A bellhop roundup?"

"We know Spectre was wearing some sort of uniform similar to a bellhop's," said Sam. "We just wanted her to look over a few."

"We did track down a police report of that bike accident," said Gillis. "The bicyclist himself called it in. I think he was worried about a lawsuit, so he made a point of stating that he hit the man outside a crosswalk. Apparently, Spectre was jaywalking when he was hit on Congress Street."

"Congress?" Liddell frowned.

"Right near the Pioneer Hotel," said Sam. "Which, we've found out, is where the Governor plans to stay day after tomorrow. He's the guest speaker at some small business seminar."

"You think Spectre's target is the Governor?"

"It's a possibility. We're having the Pioneer checked and double-checked. Especially the Governor's room."

"What about the Pioneer's bellhops?"

"We eliminated all of them, just based on height and age. No one's missing any fingers. That one there—number three—is the closest to Spectre's description. But he has all his fingers, too. We just wanted Nina to take a look at the uniform, see if it jogged a memory."

"But no one in that lineup is Spectre."

"No. We've looked at everyone's hands. No missing fingers."

Nina's gaze turned to number three in the lineup. He was dressed in a bellhop's red jacket and black pants. "Is that what all the Pioneer's bellhops wear?" she asked.

"Yeah," said Gillis. "Why?"

"I don't think that's the uniform I saw."

"What's different about it?"

"The man I saw in the E.R.—I'm just remembering it—his jacket was green. Sort of a forest green. It was definitely not red."

Gillis shook his head. "We got us a problem then. The Holiday Inn's uniform is red, too. Marriott's green, but it's not located anywhere near the bicycle accident."

"Check out their staff anyway," Liddell ordered. "If you have to interview every bellhop in town, I want this guy caught. And I sure as hell want him caught before he blows up some high-muck-a-muck. When's the Governor arriving tomorrow?"

"Sometime in the afternoon," said Gillis.

Liddell glanced at his watch. "We have a full twenty-four hours. If anything comes up, I get called. Got it?"

"Yes, sir, your highness," muttered Gillis.

Liddell glanced sharply at him, but obviously decided to drop it. "My wife and I'll be at the Brant Theater tonight. I'll have my beeper with me, just in case."

"You'll be first on our list to call," said Sam.

"We're in the spotlight on this. So let's not screw

up." It was Liddell's parting shot, and the two cops took it in silence.

Only after Liddell had left the room did Gillis growl, "I'm gonna get that guy. I swear, I'm gonna get him."

"Cool it, Gillis. He may be governor someday."

"In which case, I'll help Spectre plant the damn bomb myself."

Sam took Nina's arm and walked her out of the room. "Come on. I have my hands full today. I'll introduce you to your new watchdog."

Passing me off already, she thought. Was she such a nuisance to him?

"For now, we're keeping you in a hotel," he said. "Officer Pressler's been assigned to watch over you. He's a sharp cop. I trust him."

"Meaning I should, too?"

"Absolutely. I'll call you if we turn up any suspects. We'll need you to identify them."

"So I may not be seeing you for a while."

He stopped in the hallway and looked at her. "No. It may be a while."

They faced each other for a moment. The hallway was hardly private; certainly this wasn't the time or the place to confess how she felt about him. *She* wasn't even sure how she felt about him. All she knew was that it hurt to say goodbye. What hurt even worse was to look in his eyes and see no regret, no distress. Just that flat, unemotional gaze.

So it was back to Mr. Civil Servant. She could deal with that. After the trauma of this last week, she could deal with anything, including the realization that she had, once again, gotten involved with the wrong man.

She met his gaze with one just as cool and said, "You

find Spectre. I'll identify him. Just do it soon, okay? So I can get on with my life."

"We're working on it round the clock. We'll keep you informed."

"Can I count on that?"

He answered with a curt dip of the head. "It's part of my job."

Officer Leon Pressler was not a conversationalist. In fact, whether he could converse at all was in question. For the past three hours, the muscular young cop had done a terrific sphinx imitation, saying nary a word as he roamed the hotel room, alternately checking the door and glancing out the third floor window. The most he would say was "Yes, ma'am," or "No, ma'am," and that was only in response to a direct question. Was the strong, silent bit some kind of cop thing? Nina wondered. Or was he under orders not to get too chatty with the witness?

She tried to read a novel she'd picked up in the hotel gift shop, but after a few chapters she gave up. His silence made her too nervous. It was simply not natural to spend a day in a hotel room with another person and not, at the very least, talk to each other. Lord knew, she tried to draw him out.

"Have you been a cop a long time, Leon?" she asked.

"Yes, ma'am."

"Do you enjoy it?"

"Yes, ma'am."

"Does it ever scare you?"

"No, ma'am."

"Never?"

"Sometimes."

Now they were getting somewhere, she thought.

But then Officer Pressler crossed the room and peered out the window, ignoring her.

She put her book aside and launched another attempt at conversation.

"Does this sort of assignment bore you?" she asked.

"No, ma'am."

"It would bore me. Spending all day in a hotel room doing nothing."

"Things could happen."

"And I'm sure you'll be ready for it." Sighing, she reached for the remote and clicked on the TV. Five minutes of channel surfing turned up nothing of interest. She clicked it off again. "Can I make a phone call?" she asked.

"Sorry."

"I just want to call my nursing supervisor at Maine Medical. To tell her I won't be coming in next week."

"Detective Navarro said no phone calls. It's necessary for your safety. He was very specific on that."

"What else did the good detective tell you?"

"I'm to keep a close eye. Not let my guard down for a minute. Because if anything happened to you..." He paused and gave a nervous cough.

"What?"

"He'd, uh, have my hide."

"That's quite an incentive."

"He wanted to make sure I took special care. Not that I'd let anything happen. I owe him that much."

She frowned at him. He was at the window again, peering down at the street. "What do you mean, you owe him?"

Officer Pressler didn't move from the window. He stood looking out, as though unwilling to meet her gaze. "It was a few years back. I was on this domestic call.

Husband didn't much like me sticking my nose into his business. So he shot me."

"My god."

"I radioed for help. Navarro was first to respond." Pressler turned and looked at her. "So you see, I do owe him." Calmly he turned back to the window.

"How well do you know him?" she asked softly.

Pressler shrugged. "He's a good cop. But real private. I'm not sure anyone knows him very well."

Including me, she thought. Sighing, she clicked on the boob tube again and channel surfed past a jumble of daytime soaps, a TV court show and a golf tournament. She could almost feel another few brain cells collapse into mush.

What was Sam doing right now? she wondered.

And ruthlessly suppressed the thought. Sam Navarro was his own man. That much was perfectly clear.

She would have to be her own woman.

I wonder what Nina's doing right now. At once Sam tried to suppress the thought, tried to concentrate instead on what was being said at the meeting, but his mind kept drifting back to the subject of Nina. Specifically, her safety. He had every reason to trust Leon Pressler. The young cop was sharp and reliable, and he owed his life to Sam. If anyone could be trusted to keep Nina out of harm's way, it would be Pressler.

Still, he couldn't shake that lingering sense of uneasiness. And fear. It was one more indication that he'd lost his objectivity, that his feelings were way out of control. To the point of affecting his work...

"...the best we can do? Sam?"

Sam suddenly focused on Abe Coopersmith. "Excuse me?"

Coopersmith sighed. "Where the hell are you, Navarro?"

"I'm sorry. I let my attention drift for a moment."

Gillis said, "Chief asked if we're following any other leads."

"We're following every lead we have," Sam informed him. "The sketch of Spectre is circulating. We've checked all the hotels in Portland. So far, no employees with a missing finger. Problem is, we're operating blind. We don't know Spectre's target, when he plans to strike or where he plans to strike. All we have is a witness who's seen his face."

"And this bit about the bellhop's uniform."

"That's right."

"Have you shown all those uniforms to Miss Cormier? To help us identify which hotel we're talking about?"

"We're getting together a few more samples for her to look at," said Gillis. "Also, we've interviewed that bicyclist. He doesn't remember much about the man he hit. It happened so fast, he didn't really pay attention to the face. But he does back up Miss Cormier's recollection that the uniform jacket was green. Some shade of it, anyway. And he confirms that it happened on Congress Street, near Franklin Avenue."

"We've combed that whole area," said Sam. "Showed the sketch to every shopkeeper and clerk within a five-block radius. No one recognized the face."

Coopersmith gave a grunt of frustration. "We've got the Governor arriving tomorrow afternoon. And a bomber somewhere in the city."

"We don't know if there's a connection. Spectre could be targeting someone else entirely. It all depends on who hired him."

"He may not even plan a hit at all," suggested Gillis. "Maybe he's finished his job. Maybe he's left town."

"We have to assume he's still here," cautioned Coopersmith. "And up to no good."

Sam nodded in agreement. "We have twenty-four hours before the Governor's meeting. By then, something's bound to turn up."

"God, I hope so," said Coopersmith, and he rose to leave. "If there's one thing we don't need, it's another bomb going off. And a dead Governor."

"Let's take it from the top. Measure 36." The conductor raised his baton, brought it down again. Four beats later, the trumpets blared out the opening notes of "Wrong Side of the Track Blues," to be joined seconds later by woodwinds and bass. Then the sax slid in, its plaintive whine picking up the melody.

"Never did understand jazz," complained the Brant Theater manager, watching the rehearsal from the middle aisle. "Lotta sour notes if you ask me. All the instruments fighting with each other."

"I like jazz," said the head usher.

"Yeah, well, you like rap, too. So I don't think much of your taste." The manager glanced around the theater, surveying the empty seats. He noted that everything was clean, that there was no litter in the aisles. The audience tonight would be a discriminating crowd. Bunch of lawyer types. They wouldn't appreciate sticky floors or wadded-up programs in the chairs.

Just a year ago, this building had been a porn palace, showing X-rated films to an audience of nameless, faceless men. The new owner had changed all that. Now, with a little private money from a local benefactor, the Brant Theater had been rehabilitated into a live perfor-

mance center, featuring stage plays and musical art-
ists. Unfortunately, the live performances brought in
fewer crowds than the porn had. The manager wasn't
surprised.

Tonight, at least, a big audience was assured—
five hundred paid and reserved seats, with additional
walk-ins expected, to benefit the local Legal Aid office. Imagine that. All those lawyers actually paying to
hear jazz. He didn't get it. But he was glad these seats
would be filled.

"Looks like we may be short a man tonight," said
the head usher.

"Who?"

"That new guy you hired. You know, the one from
the agency. Showed up for work two days ago. Haven't
heard from him since. I tried calling him, but no luck."

The manager cursed. "Can't rely on these agency
hires."

"That's for sure."

"You just gotta work the crowd with four men tonight."

"Gonna be a bear. Five hundred reserved seats and all."

"Let some of 'em find their own seats. They're lawyers. They're supposed to have brains." The manager
glanced at his watch. It was six-thirty. He'd have just
enough time to wolf down that corned beef sandwich
in his office. "Doors open in an hour," he said. "Better
get your supper now."

"Sure thing," replied the head usher. He swept up
the green uniform jacket from the seat where he'd left
it. And, whistling, he headed up the aisle for his dinner.

At seven-thirty, Officer Pressler escorted Nina back
to police headquarters. The building was quieter than it

had been that afternoon, most of the desks deserted, and only an occasional clerk circulating in the halls. Pressler brought Nina upstairs and ushered her into an office.

Sam was there.

He gave her only the most noncommittal of greetings: a nod, a quiet hello. She responded in kind. Pressler was in the room too, as were Gillis and another man in plainclothes, no doubt a cop as well. With an audience watching, she was not about to let her feelings show. Obviously Sam wasn't, either.

"We wanted you to take a look at these uniforms," Sam said, gesturing to the long conference table. Laid out on the table were a half dozen uniform jackets of various colors. "We've got bellhops, an elevator operator, and an usher's uniform from the downtown Cineplex. Do any of them strike you as familiar?"

Nina approached the table. Thoughtfully she eyed each one, examining the fabrics, the buttons. Some of them had embroidered hotel logos. Some were trimmed with gold braid or nametags.

She shook her head. "It wasn't one of these."

"What about that green one, on the end?"

"It has gold braid. The jacket I remember had black braid, sort of coiled up here, on the shoulder."

"Geez," murmured Gillis. "Women remember the weirdest things."

"Okay," Sam said with a sigh. "That's it for this session. Thanks, everyone. Pressler, why don't you take a break and get some supper. I'll bring Miss Cormier back to her hotel. You can meet us there in an hour or so."

The room emptied out. All except Sam and Nina.

For a moment, they didn't speak to each other. They didn't even look at each other. Nina almost wished that the earnest Officer Pressler was back with her again;

at least *he* didn't make her feel like turning tail and running.

"I hope your hotel room's all right," he finally said.

"It's fine. But I'll be going stir crazy in another day. I have to get out of there."

"It's not safe yet."

"When will it be safe?"

"When we have Spectre."

"That could be never." She shook her head. "I can't live this way. I have a job. I have a life. I can't stay in a hotel room with some cop who drives me up a wall."

Sam frowned. "What's Pressler done?"

"He won't sit still! He never stops checking the windows. He won't let me touch the phone. And he can't carry on a decent conversation."

"Oh." Sam's frown evaporated. "That's just Leon doing his job. He's good."

"Maybe he is. But he still drives me crazy." Sighing, she took a step toward him. "Sam, I can't stay cooped up. I have to get on with my life."

"You will. But we have to get you through this part alive."

"What if I left town? Went somewhere else for a while—"

"We might need you here, Nina."

"You don't. You have his prints. You know he's missing a finger. You could identify him without any question—"

"But we need to spot him first. And for that, we might need you to pick him out of a crowd. So you have to stay in town. Available. We'll keep you safe, I promise."

"I suppose you'll have to. If you want to catch your man."

He took her by the shoulders. "That's not the only reason, and you know it."

"Do I?"

He leaned closer. For one astonishing moment she thought he was going to kiss her. Then a rap on the door made them both jerk apart.

Gillis, looking distinctly ill at ease, stood in the door-way. "Uh… I'm heading over to get a burger. You want I should get you something, Sam?"

"No. We'll pick something up at her hotel."

"Okay." Gillis gave an apologetic wave. "I'll be back here in an hour." He departed, leaving Sam and Nina alone once again.

But the moment was gone forever. If he'd intended to kiss her, she saw no hint of it in his face.

He said, simply, "I'll drive you back now."

In Sam's car, she felt as if they'd reverted right back to the very first day they'd met, to the time when he'd been the stone-faced detective and she'd been the be-wildered citizen. It was as if all the events of the past week—their nights together, their lovemaking—had never happened. He seemed determined to avoid any talk of feelings tonight, and she was just as determined not to broach the subject.

The only safe topic was the case. And even on that topic, he was not very forthcoming.

"I notice you've circulated the police sketch," she said.

"It's been everywhere. TV, the papers."

"Any response?"

"We've been inundated by calls. We've spent all day chasing them down. So far, nothing's panned out."

"I'm afraid my description wasn't very helpful."

"You did the best you could."

She looked out the window, at the streets of down-town Portland. It was already eight o'clock, the summer dusk just slipping into night. "If I saw him again, I'd know him. I'm sure I would."

"That's all we need from you, Nina."

All you want from me, too, she thought sadly. She asked, "What happens tomorrow?"

"More of the same. Chase down leads. Hope someone recognizes that sketch."

"Do you know if Spectre's even in the city?"

"No. He may be long gone. In which case we're just spinning our wheels. But my instincts are telling me he's still here somewhere. And he's got something planned, something big." He glanced at her. "*You* could be the wrench in the works. The one person who can recognize him. That's why we have to keep you under wraps."

"I can't stand much more of this. I'm not even allowed to make a phone call."

"We don't want people to know your whereabouts."

"I won't tell anyone. I promise. It's just that I feel so cut off from everyone."

"Okay." He sighed. "Who do you want to call?"

"I could start with my sister Wendy."

"I thought you two didn't get along."

"We don't. But she's still my sister. And she can tell the rest of the family I'm okay."

He thought it over for a moment, then said, "All right, go ahead and call her. You can use the car phone. But don't—"

"I know, I know. Don't tell her where I am." She picked up the receiver and dialed Wendy's number. She heard three rings, and then a woman's voice answered—a voice she didn't recognize.

"Hayward residence."

"Hello, this is Nina. I'm Wendy's sister. Is she there?"

"I'm sorry, but Mr. and Mrs. Hayward are out for the evening. I'm the baby-sitter."

That's how worried she is about me, thought Nina with an irrational sense of abandonment.

"Would you like her to call you back?" asked the baby-sitter.

"No, I, uh, won't be available. But maybe I can call her later. Do you know what time she'll be home?"

"They're at the Brant Theater for that Legal Aid benefit. I think it runs till ten-thirty. And then they usually go out for coffee and dessert, so I'd expect them home around midnight."

"Oh. That's too late. I'll call tomorrow, thanks." She hung up and gave a sigh of disappointment.

"Not home?"

"No. I should have guessed they'd be out. In Jake's law firm, the business day doesn't end at five. The evenings are taken up by business affairs, too."

"Your brother-in-law's an attorney?"

"With ambitions of being a judge. And he's only thirty years old."

"Sounds like a fast-tracker."

"He is. Which means he needs a fast-track wife. Wendy's perfect that way. I'll bet you that right at this moment, she's at the theater charming the socks off some judge. And she can do it without even trying. She's the politician in the family." She glanced at Sam and saw that he was frowning. "Is something wrong?" she asked.

"What theater? Where did they go tonight?"

"The Brant Theater. That's where the benefit is."

"Benefit?"

"The baby-sitter said it was for Legal Aid. Why?"

Sam stared ahead at the road. "The Brant Theater. Didn't it just reopen?"

"A month ago. It was a disgrace before. All those porn flicks."

"Damn. Why didn't I think of it?"

Without warning, he made a screeching U-turn and headed the car the way they'd come, back toward the downtown district.

"What are you doing?" she demanded.

"The Brant Theater. A Legal Aid benefit. Who do you suppose'll be there?"

"A bunch of lawyers?"

"Right. As well as our esteemed D.A., Norm Liddell. Now, I'm not particularly fond of lawyers, but I'm not crazy about picking up their dead bodies, either."

She stared at him. "You think that's the target? The Brant Theater?"

"They'll need ushers tonight. Think about it. What does an usher wear?"

"Sometimes it's just black pants and a white shirt."

"But in a grand old theater like the Brant? They just might be dressed in green jackets with black braid...."

"That's where we're going?"

He nodded. "I want you to take a look. Tell me if we're warm. Tell me if that uniform you saw could've been a theater usher's."

By the time they pulled up across the street from the Brant Theater, it was 8:20. Sam didn't waste his time looking for a parking space; he left the car angled against the red-painted curb. As he and Nina climbed out, they heard a doorman yell, "Hey, you can't park there!"

"Police!" Sam answered, waving his badge. "We need to get in the theater."

The doorman stepped aside and waved them in.

The lobby was deserted. Through the closed aisle doors, they could hear the bluesy wail of clarinets, the syncopated beats of a snare drum. No ushers were in sight.

Sam yanked open an aisle door and slipped into the theater. Seconds later, he reemerged with a short and loudly protesting usher in tow. "Look at the uniform," he said to Nina. "Look familiar?"

Nina took one glance at the short green jacket, the black braid and brass buttons, and she nodded. "That's it. That's the one I saw."

"*What's* the one?" demanded the usher, yanking himself free.

"How many ushers working here tonight?" snapped Sam.

"Who are you, anyway?"

Again Sam whipped out his badge. "Police. There's a chance you have a bomb somewhere in there. So tell me quick. How many ushers?"

"A bomb?" The man's gaze darted nervously toward the lobby exit. "Uh, we got four working tonight."

"That's it?"

"Yeah. One didn't show up."

"Did he have a missing finger?"

"Hell, I don't know. We all wear gloves." The usher looked again toward the exit. "You really think there could be a bomb in there?"

"We can't afford to make a wrong guess. I'm evacuating the building." He glanced at Nina. "Get out of here. Wait in the car."

"But you'll need help—"

He was already pushing through the door, into the darkened theater. From the open doorway, she watched him walk swiftly down the aisle. He climbed up to the stage and crossed to the conductor, who regarded him with a look of startled outrage.

The musicians, just as startled, stopped playing.

Sam grabbed the conductor's microphone. "Ladies and gentlemen," he said curtly. "This is the Portland Police. We have had a bomb threat. Calmly, but without delay, will everyone please evacuate the building. I repeat, stay calm, but please evacuate the building."

Almost immediately the exodus began. Nina had to scramble backward out of the doorway to avoid the first rush of people heading up the aisle. In the confusion, she lost sight of Sam, but she could still hear his voice over the speaker system.

"Please remain calm. There is no immediate danger. Exit the building in an orderly fashion."

He's going to be the last one out, she thought. *The one most likely hurt if a bomb does go off.*

The exodus was in full force now, a rush of frightened men and women in evening clothes. The first hint of disaster happened so quickly Nina didn't even see it. Perhaps someone had tripped over a long hem; perhaps there were simply too many feet storming the doorway. Suddenly people were stumbling, falling over each other. A woman screamed. Those still backed up in the aisle instantly panicked.

And rushed for the door.

Chapter 11

Nina watched in horror as a woman in a long evening gown fell beneath the stampede. Struggling to reach her, Nina shoved through the crowd, only to be swept along with them and forced out the lobby doors and into the street. To get back inside the building was impossible; she'd be moving against the crowd, against the full force of panic.

Already the street was filling up with evacuees, everyone milling about looking dazed. To her relief, she caught sight of Wendy and Jake among the crowd; at least her sister was safe and out of the building. The flood of people out the doors gradually began to ebb.

But where was Sam? Had he made it out yet?

Then, through the crowd, she spotted him emerging from the lobby door. He had his arm around an elderly man, whom he hauled to the sidewalk and set down against the lamppost.

As Nina started toward him, Sam spotted her and yelled, "This one needs attention. Take care of him!"

"Where are you going?"

"Back inside. There are a few more in there."

"I can help you—"

"Help me by staying *out* of the building. And see to that man."

He has his job to do, she thought, watching Sam head back into the theater. *So do I.*

She turned her attention to the elderly man propped up against the lamppost. Kneeling beside him she asked, "Sir, are you all right?"

"My chest. It hurts…"

Oh, no. A coronary. And no ambulance in sight. At once she lowered his head onto the sidewalk, checked his pulse and unbuttoned his shirt. She was so busy attending to her patient she scarcely noticed when the first patrol car pulled up in front of the theater. By then the crowd was a mass of confusion, everyone demanding to know what was going on.

She looked up to see Sam push out the lobby door again, this time carrying the woman in the evening dress. He lay the woman down beside Nina.

"One more inside," he said, turning back to the building. "Check the lady out."

"Navarro!" yelled a voice.

Sam glanced back as a man in a tuxedo approached. "What the hell is going on?"

"Can't talk, Liddell. I've got work to do."

"Was there a bomb call or not?"

"Not a call."

"Then why'd you order an evacuation?"

"The usher's uniform." Again Sam turned toward the building.

"Navarro!" Liddell yelled. "I want an explanation! People have been hurt because of this! Unless you can justify it—"

Sam had vanished through the lobby doors.

Liddell paced the sidewalk, waiting to resume his harangue. At last, in frustration, he shouted, "I'm going to have your ass for this, Navarro!"

Those were the last words out of Liddell's mouth before the bomb exploded.

The force of the blast threw Nina backward, onto the street. She landed hard, her elbows scraping across the pavement, but she felt no pain. The shock of the impact left her too stunned to feel anything at all except a strange sense of unreality. She saw broken glass pelt the cars in the street. Saw smoke curl through the air and scores of people lying on the road, all of them just as stunned as she was. And she saw that the lobby door of the Brant Theater was tilted at a crazy angle and hanging by one hinge.

Through the pall of silence, she heard the first moan. Then another. Then came sobs, cries from the injured. Slowly she struggled to sit up. Only then did she feel the pain. Her elbows were torn and bleeding. Her head ached so badly she had to clutch it just to keep from throwing up. But as the awareness of pain crept into her consciousness, so too did the memory of what had happened just before the blast.

Sam. Sam had gone into the building.

Where was he? She scanned the road, the sidewalk, but her vision was blurry. She saw Liddell, sitting up now and groaning by the lamppost. Next to him was the elderly man whom Sam had dragged out of the theater. He, too, was conscious and moving. But there was no Sam.

She stumbled to her feet. A wave of dizziness almost sent her back down to her knees. Fighting it, she forced herself to move toward that open door and stepped inside.

It was dark, too dark to see anything. The only light was the faint glow from the street, shining through the doorway. She stumbled across debris and landed on her knees. Quickly she rose back to her feet, but she knew it was hopeless. It was impossible to navigate, much less find anyone in this darkness.

"Sam?" she cried, moving deeper into the shadows. *"Sam?"*

Her own voice, thick with despair, echoed back at her.

She remembered that he'd stepped into the lobby a moment before the blast. He could be anywhere in the building, or he could be somewhere nearby. Somewhere she could reach him.

Again she cried out, "Sam!"

This time, faintly, she heard a reply. "Nina?" It didn't come from inside the building. It came from the outside. From the street.

She turned and felt her way back toward the exit, guided by the glow of the doorway. Even before she reached it, she saw him standing there, silhouetted in the light from the street.

"Nina?"

"I'm here. I'm here...." She stumbled through the last stretch of darkness dividing them and was instantly swept into an embrace that was too fierce to be gentle, too terrified to be comforting.

"What the hell were you doing in *there?*" he demanded.

"Looking for you."

"You were supposed to stay outside. Away from the building. When I couldn't find you…" His arms tightened around her, drawing her so close she felt as though it were his heart hammering in her chest. "Next time, you *listen* to me."

"I thought you were inside—"

"I came out the other door."

"I didn't see you!"

"I was dragging the last man out. I'd just got out when the bomb went off. It blew us both out onto the sidewalk." He pulled back and looked at her. Only then did she see the blood trickling down his temple.

"Sam, you need to see a doctor—"

"We have a lot of people here who need a doctor." He glanced around at the street. "I can wait."

Nina, too, focused on the chaos surrounding them. "We've got to get people triaged for the ambulances. I'll get to work."

"You feeling up to it?"

She gave him a nod. And a quick smile. "This is my forte, Detective. Disasters." She waded off into the crowd.

Now that she knew Sam was alive and safe, she could concentrate on what needed to be done. And one glance at the scene told her this was the start of a busy night. Not just here, in the street, but in the E.R. as well. All the area hospitals would need to call in every E.R. nurse they had to attend to these people.

Her head was starting to ache worse than ever, her scraped elbows stung every time she bent her arms. But at this moment, as far as she knew, she was the only nurse on the scene.

She focused on the nearest victim, a woman whose leg was cut and bleeding. Nina knelt down, ripped a strip of fabric from the victim's hem and quickly wrapped a makeshift pressure bandage around the bleeding limb. When she'd finished tying it off, she noted to her satisfaction that the flow of blood had stopped.

That was only the first, she thought, and she looked around for the next patient. There were dozens more to go....

Across the street, his face hidden in the shadows, Vincent Spectre watched the chaos and muttered a curse. Both Judge Stanley Dalton and Norm Liddell were still alive. Spectre could see the young D.A. sitting against the lamppost, clutching his head. The blond woman sitting beside him must be Liddell's wife. They were right in the thick of things, surrounded by dozens of other injured theater patrons. Spectre couldn't just walk right over and dispatch Liddell, not without being seen by a score of witnesses. Sam Navarro was just a few yards from Liddell, and Navarro would certainly be armed.

Another humiliation. This would destroy his reputation, not to mention his back account. The Snowman had promised four hundred thousand dollars for the deaths of Dalton and Liddell. Spectre had thought this an elegant solution: to kill both of them at once. With so many other victims, the identity of the targets might never be pinpointed.

But the targets were still alive, and there'd be no payment forthcoming.

The job had become too risky to complete, especially with Navarro on the scent. Thanks to Navarro, Spectre would have to bow out. And kiss his four hundred thousand goodbye.

He shifted his gaze, refocusing on another figure in

the crowd. It was that nurse, Nina Cormier, bandaging one of the injured. This fiasco was her fault, too; he was sure of it. She must've given the police just enough info to tip them off to the bomb. The usher's uniform, no doubt, had been the vital clue.

She was another detail he hadn't bothered to clean up, and look at the result. No hit, no money. Plus, she could identify him. Though that police sketch was hopelessly generic, Spectre had a feeling that, if Nina Cormier ever saw his face, she would remember him. That made her a threat he could no longer ignore.

But now was not the opportunity. Not in this crowd, in this street. The ambulances were arriving, siren after siren whooping to a stop. And the police had cordoned off the street from stray vehicles.

Time to leave.

Spectre turned and walked away, his frustration mounting with every step he took. He'd always prided himself on paying attention to the little things. Anyone who worked with explosives had to have a fetish for details, or they didn't last long. Spectre intended to hang around in this business, which meant he would continue to fuss over the details.

And the next detail to attend to was Nina Cormier.

She was magnificent. Sam paused wearily amid the broken glass and shouting voices and he gazed in Nina's direction. It was ten-thirty, an hour and a half since the explosion, and the street was still a scene of confusion. Police cars and ambulances were parked haphazardly up and down the block, their lights flashing like a dozen strobes. Emergency personnel were everywhere, picking through the wreckage, sorting through the victims. The most seriously injured had already been evacuated, but there were dozens more still to be transported to hospitals.

In the midst of all that wreckage, Nina seemed an island of calm efficiency. As Sam watched, she knelt down beside a groaning man and dressed his bleeding arm with a makeshift bandage. Then, with a reassuring pat and a soft word, she moved on to the next patient. As though sensing she was being watched, she suddenly glanced in Sam's direction. Just for a moment their gazes locked across the chaos, and she read the question in his eyes: *Are you holding up okay?*

She gave him a wave, a nod of reassurance. Then she turned back to her patient.

They both had their work cut out for them tonight. He focused his attention, once again, on the bomb scene investigation.

Gillis had arrived forty-five minutes ago with the personal body armor and mask. The rest of the team had straggled in one by one—three techs, Ernie Takeda, Detective Cooley. Even Abe Coopersmith had appeared, his presence more symbolic than practical. This was Sam's show, and everyone knew it. The bomb disposal truck was in place and parked nearby. Everyone was waiting.

It was time to go in the building. Time to search for any second device.

Sam and Gillis, both of them wearing headlamps, entered the theater.

The darkness made the search slow and difficult. Stepping gingerly over debris, Sam headed down the left aisle, Gillis the right. The back rows of seats had sustained damage only to the upholstery—shredded fabric and stuffing. The farther they advanced the more severe the damage.

"Dynamite," Gillis noted, sniffing the air.

"Looks like the blast center's near the front."

Sam moved slowly toward the orchestra pit, the beam of his headlamp slicing the darkness left and right as he scanned the area around the stage—or what had once been the stage. A few splintered boards was all that remained.

"Crater's right here," observed Gillis.

Sam joined him. The two men knelt down for a closer inspection. Like the church bomb a week before, this one was shallow—a low-velocity blast. Dynamite.

"Looks like the third row, center stage," said Sam. "Wonder who was sitting here."

"Assigned seating, you figure?"

"If so, then we'll have ourselves a convenient list of potential targets."

"Looks all clear to me," Gillis declared.

"We can call in the searchers." Sam rose to his feet and at once felt a little dizzy. The aftereffects of the blast. He'd been in so many bombs lately, his brain must be getting scrambled. Maybe some fresh air would clear his head.

"You okay?" asked Gillis.

"Yeah. I just need to get out of here for a moment." He stumbled back up the aisle and through the lobby doors. Outside he leaned against a lamppost, breathing gulps of night air. His dizziness faded and he became aware, once again, of the activity in the street. He noticed that the crowds had thinned, and that the injured had all been evacuated. Only one ambulance was still parked in the road.

Where was Nina?

That one thought instantly cleared his head. He

glanced up and down the street, but caught no glimpse of her. Had she left the scene? Or was she taken from it?

A young cop manning the police line glanced up as Sam approached. "Yes, sir?"

"There was a woman—a nurse in street clothes—working out here. Where'd she go?"

"You mean the dark-haired lady? The pretty one?"

"That's her."

"She left in one of the ambulances, about twenty minutes ago. I think she was helping with a patient."

"Thanks." Sam went to his car and reached inside for his cellular phone. He was not taking any chances; he had to be sure she was safe. He dialed Maine Med E.R.

The line was busy.

In frustration he climbed in the car. "I'm heading to the hospital!" he yelled to Gillis. "Be right back."

Ignoring his partner's look of puzzlement, Sam lurched away from the curb and steered through the obstacle course of police vehicles. Fifteen minutes later, he pulled into a parking stall near the hospital's emergency entrance.

Even before he walked in the doors, he could hear the sounds of frantic activity inside. The waiting area was mobbed. He pushed his way through the crowd until he'd reached the triage desk, manned by a clearly embattled nurse.

"I'm Detective Navarro, Portland Police," he said. "Is Nina Cormier working here?"

"Nina? Not tonight, as far as I know."

"She came in with one of the ambulances."

"I might have missed her. Let me check." She punched the intercom button and said, "There's a policeman out here. Wants to speak to Nina. If she's back there, can you ask her to come out?"

For a good ten minutes, he waited with growing impatience. Nina didn't appear. The crowd in the E.R. seemed to grow even larger, packing into every available square inch of the waiting area. Even worse, the reporters had shown up, TV cameras and all. The triage nurse had her hands full; she'd forgotten entirely about Sam.

Unable to wait any longer, he pushed past the front desk. The nurse was calming down a hysterical family member; she didn't even notice Sam had crossed into the inner sanctum and was heading up the E.R. corridor.

Treatment rooms lined both sides of the halls. He glanced in each one as he passed. All were occupied and overflowing with victims from the bombing. He saw stunned faces, bloodied clothes. But no Nina.

He turned, retraced his steps down the hall, and paused outside a closed door. It was the trauma room. From beyond the door came the sound of voices, the clang of cabinets. He knew that a crisis was in full swing, and he was reluctant to intrude, but he had no alternative. He had to confirm that Nina was here, that she'd made it safely to the E.R.

He pushed open the door.

A patient—a man—was lying on the table, his body white and flaccid under the lights. Half a dozen medical personnel were laboring over him, one performing CPR, the others scurrying about with IVs and drugs. Sam paused, momentarily stunned by the horror of the scene.

"Sam?"

Only then did he notice Nina moving toward him from the other side of the room. Like all the other nurses, she was dressed in scrub clothes. He hadn't even noticed her in that first glimpse of blue-clad personnel.

She took his arm and quickly tugged him out of the room. "What are you doing here?" she whispered.

"You left the blast site. I wasn't sure what happened to you."

"I rode here in one of the ambulances. I figured they needed me." She glanced back at the door to the trauma room. "I was right."

"Nina, you can't just take off without telling me! I had no idea if you were all right."

She regarded him with an expression of quiet wonder, but didn't say a thing.

"Are you listening to me?" he said.

"Yes," she replied softly. "But I don't believe what I'm hearing. You actually sound scared."

"I wasn't scared. I was just—I mean—" He shook his head in frustration. "Okay, I was worried. I didn't want something to happen to you."

"Because I'm your witness?"

He looked into her eyes, those beautiful, thoughtful eyes. Never in his life had he felt so vulnerable. This was a new feeling for him and he didn't like it. He was not a man who was easily frightened, and the fact that he had experienced such fear at the thought of losing her told him he was far more deeply involved than he'd ever intended to be.

"Sam?" She reached up and touched his face.

He grasped her hand and gently lowered it. "Next time," he instructed, "I want you to tell me where you're going. It's *your* life at stake. If you want to risk it, that's your business. But until Spectre's under arrest, your safety's my concern. Do you understand?"

She withdrew her hand from his. The retreat was more than physical; he could feel her pulling away emotionally as well, and it hurt him. It was a pain of his own choosing, and that made it even worse.

She said, tightly, "I understand perfectly well."

"Good. Now, I think you should go back to the hotel where we can keep an eye on you tonight."

"I can't leave. They need me here."

"I need you, too. Alive."

"Look at this place!" She waved toward the waiting area, crowded with the injured. "These people all have to be examined and treated. I can't walk out now."

"Nina, I have a job to do. And your safety is part of that job."

"I have a job to do, too!" she asserted.

They faced each other for a moment, neither one willing to back down.

Then Nina snapped, "I don't have time for this," and she turned back toward the trauma room.

"Nina!"

"I'll do my job, Sam. You do yours."

"Then I'm sending a man over to keep an eye on you."

"Do whatever you want."

"When will you be finished here?"

She stopped and glanced at the waiting patients. "My guess? Not till morning."

"Then I'll be back to get you at 6:00 a.m."

"Whatever you say, Detective," she retorted and pushed into the trauma room. He caught a fleeting glimpse of her as she rejoined the surgical team, and then the door closed behind her.

I'll do my job. You do yours, she'd told him.

She's right, he thought. *That's exactly what I should be focusing on. My job.*

From his car phone, he put in a call to Officer Pressler

and told him to send his relief officer down to Maine
Med E.R., where he'd be the official baby-sitting service for the night. Then, satisfied that Nina was in good
hands, he headed back to the bomb scene.

It was eleven-thirty. The night was just beginning.

Nina made it through the next seven hours on sheer
nerve. Her conversation with Sam had left her hurt and
angry, and she had to force herself to concentrate on the
work at hand—tending to the dozens of patients who
now filled the waiting area. Their injuries, their discomfort, had to take priority. But every so often, when she'd
pause to collect her thoughts or catch her breath, she'd
find herself thinking about Sam, about what he'd said.

I have a job to do. And your safety is part of that job.

Is that all I am to you? she wondered as she signed
her name to yet another patient instruction sheet. A job,
a burden? And what had she expected, anyway? From
the beginning, he'd been the unflappable public official,
Mr. Cool himself. There'd been flashes of warmth, of
course, even the occasional glimpse of the man inside,
a man of genuine kindness. But every time she thought
she'd touched the real Sam Navarro, he'd pull away from
her as though scalded by the contact.

What am I to do with you, Sam? she wondered sadly.
And what was she to do with all the feelings she had
for him?

Work was all that kept her going that night. She never
even noticed when the sun came up.

By the time 6:00 a.m. rolled around, she was so tired
she could scarcely walk without weaving, but at last the
waiting room was empty and the patients all sent home.
Most of the E.R. staff had gathered, shell-shocked, in
the employee lounge for a well-deserved coffee break.

Nina was about to join them when she heard her name called.

She turned. Sam was standing in the waiting room.

He looked every bit as exhausted as she felt, his eyes bleary, his jaw dark with a day's growth of beard. At her first sight of his face, all the anger she'd felt the night before instantly evaporated.

My poor, poor Sam, she thought. *You give so much of yourself. And what comfort do you have at the end of the day?*

She went to him. He didn't speak; he just looked at her with that expression of weariness. She put her arms around him. For a moment they held each other, their bodies trembling with fatigue. Then she heard him say, softly, "Let's go home."

"I'd like that," she said. And smiled.

She didn't know how he managed to pilot the car to his house. All she knew was that a moment after she dozed off, they were in his driveway, and he was gently prodding her awake. Together they dragged themselves into the house, into his bedroom. No thoughts of lust crossed her mind, even as they undressed and crawled into bed together, even as she felt his lips brush her face, felt his breath warm her hair.

She fell asleep in his arms.

She felt so warm, so perfect, lying beside him. As if she belonged here, in his bed.

Sam gazed through drowsy eyes at Nina, who was still sound asleep. It was already afternoon. He should have been up and dressed hours ago, but sheer exhaustion had taken its toll.

He was getting too old for this job. For the past eighteen years, he'd been a cop through and through.

Though there were times when he hated the work, when the ugly side of it seemed to overwhelm his love for the job, he'd never once doubted that a cop was exactly what he was meant to be. And so it dismayed him now that, at this moment, being a cop was the furthest thing from his mind.

What he wanted, really wanted, was to spend eternity in this bed, gazing at this woman. Studying her face, enjoying the view. Only when Nina was asleep did he feel it was safe to really look at her. When she was awake, he felt too vulnerable, as though she could read his thoughts, could see past his barriers, straight to his heart. He was afraid to admit, even to himself, the feelings he harbored there.

As he studied her now, he realized there was no point denying it to himself: he couldn't bear the thought of her walking out of his life. Did that mean he loved her? He didn't know.

He did know this was not the turn of events he'd wanted or expected.

But last night he'd watched her at work in the wreckage of the bomb site, and he'd admired a new dimension of Nina, one he saw for the first time. A woman with both compassion and strength.

It would be so easy to fall in love with her. It would be such a mistake.

In a month, a year, she'd come to see him for what he was: no hero with a badge, but an everyday guy doing his job the best way he knew how. And there she'd be in that hospital, working side by side with men like Robert Bledsoe. Men with medical degrees and houses on the water. How long would it take for her to grow weary of the cop who just happened to love her?

He sat up on the side of the bed and ran his hands

through his hair, trying to shake off the last vestiges of sleep. His brain wasn't feeling alert yet. He needed coffee, food, anything to snap him back into gear. There were so many details to follow up on, so many leads still to check out.

Then he felt a touch, soft as silk, caress his bare back. All at once, work was the last thing on his mind.

He turned and met her gaze. She was looking drowsily at him, her smile relaxed and contented. "What time is it?" she murmured.

"Almost three."

"We slept that long?"

"We needed it. Both of us. It was okay to let our guard down. Pressler was watching the house."

"You mean he was outside all day?"

"I made the arrangements last night. Before he went off duty. I knew I wanted to bring you home with me."

She opened her arms to him. That gesture of invitation was too tempting to resist. With a groan of surrender, he lay down beside her and met her lips with a kiss. At once his body was responding, and so was she. Their arms were entwined now, their warmth mingling. He couldn't stop, couldn't turn back; he wanted her too badly. He wanted to feel their bodies join, just one last time. If he couldn't have her for the rest of his life, at least he would have her for this moment. And he'd remember, always, her face, her smile, her sweet moans of desire as he thrust, hard and deep, inside her.

They both took. They both gave.

But even as he reached his climax, even as he felt the first glorious release, he thought, *This is not enough. This could never be enough.* He wanted to know more than just her body; he wanted to know her soul.

His passion was temporarily sated, yet he felt both

unsatisfied and depressed as he lay beside her afterward. Not at all what the carefree bachelor should expect to feel after a conquest. If anything, he was angry at himself for sliding into this situation. For allowing this woman to become so important to him.

And here she was, smiling, working her way even deeper into his life.

His response was to pull away, to rise from the bed and head into the shower. When he reemerged, clean and still damp, she was sitting up on the side of the bed, watching him with a look of bewilderment.

"I have to get back to work," he said, pulling on a clean shirt. "I'll invite Pressler inside to sit with you."

"The bombing's over and done with. Spectre's probably a thousand miles away by now."

"I can't take that chance."

"There are others who know his face. The theater ushers. They could identify him."

"One of them hit his head on the sidewalk. He's still in and out of consciousness. The other one can't even decide on the color of Spectre's eyes. That's how helpful the ushers are."

"Nevertheless, you've got other witnesses and Spectre knows it." She paused. "I'd say that lets both of us off the hook."

"What do you mean?"

"I can stop worrying about being a target. And you can stop worrying about keeping me alive. And go back to your real job."

"This is part of my job."

"So you've told me." She tilted her chin up, and he saw the brief gleam of tears in her eyes. "I wish I was more than that. God, I wish..."

"Nina, please. This doesn't help either one of us."

Her head drooped. The sight of her, hurt, silent, was almost more than he could stand. He knelt down before her and took her hands in his. "You know I'm attracted to you."

She gave a softly ironic laugh. "That much, I guess, is obvious to us both."

"And you also know that I think you're a terrific woman. If I ever get hauled to the E.R .in an ambulance, I hope you're the nurse who takes care of me."

"But?"

"But…" He sighed. "I just don't see us together. Not for the long haul."

She looked down again, and he could sense her struggle for composure. He'd hurt her, and he hated himself for it, hated his own cowardice. That's what it was, of course. He didn't believe hard enough in their chances. He didn't believe in *her*.

All he was certain of was that he'd never, ever get over her.

He rose to his feet. She didn't react, but just sat on the bed, staring down. "It's not you, Nina," he said. "It's *me*. It's something that happened to me years ago. It convinced me that this situation we're in—it doesn't last. It's artificial. A scared woman. And a cop. It's a setup for all kinds of unrealistic expectations."

"Don't give me the old psychology lecture, Sam. I don't need to hear about transference and misplaced affections."

"You have to hear it. And understand it. Because the effect goes both ways. How you feel about me, and how I feel about you. My wanting to take care of you, protect you. It's something I can't help, either." He sighed, a sound of both frustration and despair. *It's too late,* he thought. *We both feel things we shouldn't be feeling. And it's impossible to turn back the clock.*

"You were saying something happened to you. Years ago," she said. "Was it…another woman?"

He nodded.

"The same situation? Scared woman, protective cop?"

Again he nodded.

"Oh." She shook her head and murmured in a tone of self-disgust, "I guess I fell right into it."

"We both did."

"So who left whom, Sam? The last time this happened?"

"It was the only time it happened. Except for you." He turned away, began to move around the room. "I was just a rookie patrolman. Twenty-two years old. Assigned to protect a woman being stalked. She was twenty-eight going on forty when it came to sophistication. It's not surprising I got a little infatuated. The surprising part was that she seemed to return the sentiment. At least, until the crisis was over. Then she decided I wasn't so impressive after all. And she was right." He stopped and looked at her. "It's that damn thing called reality. It has a way of stripping us all down to what we really are. And in my case, I'm just a hardworking cop. Honest for the most part. Brighter than some, dumber than others. In short, I'm not anyone's hero. And when she finally saw that, she turned right around and walked out, leaving behind one sadder but wiser rookie."

"And you think that's what I'm going to do."

"It's what you should do. Because you deserve so much, Nina. More than I can ever give you."

She shook her head. "What I really want, Sam, has nothing to do with what a man can *give* me."

"Think about Robert. What you could have had with him."

"Robert was the perfect example! He had it all. Everything except what I wanted from him."

"What did you want, Nina?"

"Love. Loyalty." She met his gaze. "Honesty."

What he saw in her eyes left him shaken. Those were the things he wanted to give her. The very things he was afraid to give her.

"Right now you think it's enough," he remarked. "But maybe you'll find out it's not."

"It's more than I ever got from Robert." *More than I'll ever get from you, too,* was what her eyes said.

He didn't try to convince her otherwise. Instead, he turned toward the door.

"I'm going to call Pressler inside," he told her. "Have him stay with you all day today."

"There's no need."

"You shouldn't be alone, Nina."

"I won't be." She looked up at him. "I can go back to my father's house. He has that fancy security system. Not to mention a few dogs. Now that we know Daniella isn't the one running around planting bombs, I should be perfectly safe there." She glanced around the room. "I shouldn't be staying here, anyway. Not in your house."

"You can. As long as you need to."

"No." She met his gaze. "I don't really see the point, Sam. Since it's so apparent to us both that this is a hopeless relationship."

He didn't argue with her. And that, more than anything else, was what hurt her. He could see it in her face.

He simply said, "I'll drive you there." Then he turned and left the room. He had to.

He couldn't bear to see the look in her eyes.

Chapter 12

"We think we know who the target was," reported Sam. "It was our wonderful D.A., Liddell."

Chief Coopersmith stared across the conference table at Sam and Gillis. "Are you certain?"

"Everything points that way. We pinpointed the bomb placement to somewhere in Row Three, Seats G through J. The seating last night was reserved weeks in advance. We've gone over the list of people sitting in that row and section. And Liddell and his wife were right smack in the center. They would've been killed instantly."

"Who else was in that row?"

"Judge Dalton was about six seats away," said Gillis. "Chances are, he would've been killed, too. Or at least seriously maimed."

"And the other people in that row?"

"We've checked them all out. A visiting law professor from California. A few relatives of Judge Dalton's. A pair of law clerks. We doubt any of them would've attracted the interest of a hired killer. Oh, and you may be interested to hear Ernie Takeda's latest report. He called it in from the lab this afternoon. It was dynamite, Dupont label. Prima detonating cord. Green electrical tape."

"Spectre," said Coopersmith. He leaned back and exhaled a loud sigh of weariness. They were all tired. Every one of them had worked straight through the night, caught a few hours of sleep, and then returned to the job. Now it was 5:00 p.m., and another night was just beginning. "God, the man is back with a vengeance."

"Yeah, but he's not having much luck," commented Gillis. "His targets keep surviving. Liddell. Judge Dalton. Nina Cormier. I'd say that the legendary Vincent Spectre must be feeling pretty frustrated about now."

"Embarrassed, too," added Sam. "His reputation's on the line, if it isn't already shot. After this fiasco, he's washed up as a contract man. Anyone with the money to hire will go elsewhere."

"Do we know who *did* hire him?"

Sam and Gillis glanced at each other. "We can make a wild guess," said Gillis.

"Billy Binford?"

Sam nodded. "The Snowman's trial is coming up in a month. And Liddell was dead set against any plea bargains. Rumor has it, he was going to use a conviction as a jumping-off place for some political campaign. I think The Snowman knows he's in for a long stay in jail. I think he wants Liddell off the prosecution team. Permanently."

"If Sam hadn't cleared that theater," added Gillis, "we could have lost half our prosecutors. The courts would've been backed up for months. In that situation, Binford's lawyers could've written the plea bargain for him."

"Any way we can pin this down with proof?"

"Not yet. Binford's attorney, Albert Darien, denies any knowledge of this. We're not going to be able to shake a word out of him. ATF's going over the video-tapes from the prison surveillance cameras, looking over all the visitors that Binford had. We may be able to identify a go-between."

"You think it's someone other than his attorney?"

"Possibly. If we can identify that go-between, we may have a link to Spectre."

"Go for it," said Coopersmith. "I want this guy, and I want him bad."

At five-thirty, the meeting broke up and Sam headed for the coffee machine in search of a caffeine boost that would keep him going for the next eight hours. He was just taking his first sip when Norm Liddell walked into the station. Sam couldn't help feeling a prick of satis-faction at the sight of the bruises and scrapes on Lid-dell's face. The injuries were minor, but last night, after the bomb, Liddell had been among those screaming the loudest for medical assistance. His own wife, who'd sustained a broken arm, had finally told her husband to shut up and act like a man.

Now here he was, sporting a few nasty scrapes on his face as well as a look of—could it be? Contrition?

"Afternoon, Navarro," said Liddell, his voice sub-dued.

"Afternoon."

"I, uh…" Liddell cleared his throat and glanced around the hall, as though to check if anyone was lis-tening. No one was.

"How's the wife doing?" asked Sam.

"Fine. She'll be in a cast for a while. Luckily, it was just a closed fracture."

"She handled herself pretty well last night, considering her injury," Sam commented. *Unlike you.*

"Yes, well, my wife's got a spine of steel. In fact, that's sort of why I want to talk to you."

"Oh?"

"Look, Navarro. Last night… I guess I jumped on you prematurely. I mean, I didn't realize you had information about any bomb."

Sam didn't say a word. He didn't want to interrupt this enjoyable performance.

"So when I got on your case last night—about evacuating the building—I should've realized you had your reasons. But damn it, Navarro, all I could see was all those people hurt in the stampede. I thought you'd gotten them panicked for nothing, and I—" He paused, obviously struggling to bite back his words. "Anyway, I apologize."

"Apology accepted."

Liddell gave a curt nod of relief.

"Now you can tell your wife you're off the hook."

The look on Liddell's face was all Sam needed to know that he'd guessed right. This apology had been Mrs. Liddell's idea, bless her steely spine. He couldn't help grinning as he watched the other man turn and walk stiffly toward Chief Coopersmith's office. The good D.A., it appeared, was not the one wearing the pants in the family.

"Hey, Sam!" Gillis was heading toward him, pulling on his jacket. "Let's go."

"Where?"

"Prison's got a surveillance videotape they want us

to look at. It's The Snowman and some unknown visitor from a few days ago."

Sam felt a sudden adrenaline rush. "Was it Spectre?"

"No. It was a woman."

"There. The blonde," said Detective Cooley.

Sam and Gillis leaned toward the TV screen, their gazes fixed on the black-and-white image of the woman. The view of her face was intermittently blocked by other visitors moving in the foreground, but from what they could see, the woman was indeed a blonde, twenties to thirties, and built like a showgirl.

"Okay, freeze it there," Cooley said to the video tech. "That's a good view of her."

The woman was caught in a still frame, her face turned to the surveillance camera, her figure momentarily visible between two passersby. She was dressed in a skirt suit, and she appeared to be carrying a briefcase. Judging by her attire, she might be an attorney or some other professional. But two details didn't fit.

One was her shoes. The camera's angle, facing downward, captured a view of her right foot, perched atop a sexy spike-heeled sandal with a delicate ankle strap.

"Not the kind of shoes you wear to court," noted Sam.

"Not unless you're out to give the judge a thrill," Gillis said. "And look at that makeup."

It was the second detail that didn't fit. This woman was made up like no lawyer Sam had ever seen. Obviously false eyelashes. Eyeshadow like some tropical fish. Lipstick painted on in bold, broad smears.

"Man, she sure ain't the girl next door," Gillis observed.

"What's the name on the visitor log?" asked Sam.

Cooley glanced at a sheet of paper. "She signed in as Marilyn Dukoff. Identified her purpose for visiting The Snowman as attorney-client consultation."

Gillis laughed. "If she's an attorney, then I'm applying to law school."

"Which law firm did she say she was with?" asked Sam.

"Frick and Darien."

"Not true?"

Cooley shook his head. "She's not on the firm's list of partners, associates or clerks. But…" He leaned forward, a grin on his face. "We think we know where she *did* work."

"Where?"

"The Stop Light."

Gillis shot Sam a look of *Didn't I tell ya?* No one had to explain a thing. They knew all about the Stop Light and its stage shows, pasties optional.

"Let me guess," said Sam. "Exotic dancer."

"You got it," affirmed Cooley.

"Are we sure we're talking about the right Marilyn Dukoff?"

"I think we are," Cooley answered. "See, all visitors to the prison have to present ID, and that's the name she gave, backed up by a Maine driver's license. We've pulled the license file. And here's the photo." Cooley passed a copy of the photo to Sam and Gillis.

"It's her," said Gillis.

"Which means we're talking about the right Marilyn Dukoff," said Cooley. "I think she just waltzed in under her own name and didn't bother with fake IDs. All she faked was her profession."

"Which is obviously not in the legal field," Gillis drawled.

Sam gave a nod to Cooley. "Good work."

"Unfortunately," added the younger detective, "I can't seem to locate the woman herself. We know where she *was* employed, but she left the job two weeks ago. I sent a man to the address listed on her license. She doesn't answer the door. And her phone's just been disconnected." He paused. "I think it's time for a search warrant."

"Let's get it." Sam rose to his feet and glanced at Gillis. "Meet you in the car, ten minutes."

"The blonde's?"

"Unless you've got somewhere better to go."

Gillis looked back at the video screen. At that still shot of a slim ankle, a sexy shoe. "Better than *that?*" He laughed. "I don't think so."

The police were getting too close for comfort.

Spectre slouched in the doorway of an apartment building half a block away and watched the cops come out of Marilyn's old building. Only moments before, Spectre had been inside that apartment, checking to make sure Marilyn hadn't left behind any clues to her current whereabouts. Luckily for him, he'd slipped out just ahead of Navarro's arrival.

They'd been inside almost an hour. They were good, all right—but Spectre was cleverer. Hours after the theater bombing, he'd hustled Marilyn into a different apartment across town. He'd known that his target might become apparent once they'd pinpointed the bomb placement in the theater. And that Marilyn would inevitably come under their scrutiny. Luckily, she'd been cooperative.

Unfortunately, her usefulness was just about over,

and the time had come to end their association. But first, he needed her for one more task.

His face tightened as he spotted a familiar figure emerge from the building. Navarro again. The detective had come to represent all the failures that Spectre had suffered over the past week. Navarro was the brains behind the investigation, the one man responsible for Liddell still being alive.

No hit. No fee. Navarro had cost him money—a lot of it.

Spectre watched the cops confer on the sidewalk. There were five of them, three in plain clothes, two in uniform, but it was Navarro on whom he focused his rage. This had turned into a battle of wits between them, a test of determination. In all his years as a "fuse" man, Spectre had never matched skills with such a wily opponent.

The safe thing to do was merely to slip away from this town and seek out contracts elsewhere. Miami or New Orleans. But his reputation had suffered a serious blow here; he wasn't sure he could land a job in Miami. And he had the feeling Navarro wouldn't give up the pursuit, that, wherever Spectre went, the detective would be dogging his trail.

And then, there was the matter of getting even. Spectre wasn't going to walk away without exacting some kind of payback.

The three plainclothes cops climbed into an unmarked car and drove away. A moment later, the uniformed cops were gone as well. They had found nothing in Marilyn's apartment; Spectre had seen to it.

Catch me if you can, Navarro, he thought. *Or will I catch you first?*

He straightened and stamped his feet, feeling the

blood return to his legs. Then he left the doorway and walked around the corner, to his car.

Navarro. Once and for all, he had to take care of Navarro. And he had the perfect plan. It would require Marilyn's help. One little phone call—that's all he'd ask. And then he'd ask no more of her.

Ever again.

The dinner was excellent. The company was wretched.

Daniella, dressed in an iridescent green leotard and a slinky wraparound skirt, sullenly picked at her salad, ignoring the platter of roast duckling and wild rice. She was not speaking to her husband, and he was not speaking to her, and Nina was too uncomfortable to speak to either one of them.

After all those questions by the police, the matter of Daniella's affair with Robert had come to light. While Nina would never forgive Daniella for that betrayal, at least she could manage to pull off a civil evening with the woman.

Nina's father could not. He was still in a state of shock from the revelation. His showpiece wife, the stunning blonde thirty years his junior, had not been satisfied with marrying mere wealth. She'd wanted a younger man. After four marriages, George Cormier still didn't know how to choose the right wife.

Now it looks like this will be his fourth divorce, Nina thought. She glanced at her father, then at Daniella. Though she loved her father, she couldn't help feeling that he and Daniella deserved each other. In the worst possible way.

Daniella set down her fork. "If you'll excuse me," she

said, "I don't really have much of an appetite. I think I'll skip out for a movie."

"What about me?" snapped George. "I know I'm just your husband, but a few evenings a week with your boring old spouse isn't too much to ask, is it? Considering all the benefits you get in exchange."

"Benefits? *Benefits?*" Daniella drew herself to her feet in anger. "All the money in the world can't make up for being married to an old goat like you."

"Goat?"

"An old goat. Do you hear me? *Old.*" She leaned across the table. "In every sense of the word."

He, too, rose to his feet. "Why, you bitch..."

"Go ahead. Call me names. I can think of just as many to call you back." With a whisk of her blond hair, she turned and walked out of the dining room.

George stared after her for a moment. Slowly, he sank back in his chair. "God," he whispered. "What was I thinking when I married her?"

You weren't thinking at all, Nina felt like saying. She touched her father's arm. "Seems like neither one of us is any good at picking spouses. Are we, Dad?"

He regarded his daughter with a look of shared misery. "I sincerely hope you haven't inherited my bad luck with love, sweetheart."

They sat for a moment without speaking. Their supper lay, almost untouched, on the table. In another room, music had started up, the fast and thumping rhythm of an aerobics tape. Daniella was at it again, working off her anger by sculpting a new and better body. Smart girl; she was going to come out of a divorce looking like a million bucks.

Nina sighed and leaned back. "Whether it's bad luck

or character flaws, Dad, maybe some people are just meant to be single."

"Not you, Nina. You *need* to love someone. You always have. And that's what makes you so easy to love."

She gave a sad laugh but said nothing. *Easy to love, easy to leave,* she thought.

Once again, she found herself wondering what Sam was doing. What he was thinking. Not about her, surely; he was too much the cop to be bothered by minor distractions.

Yet when the phone rang, she couldn't suppress the sudden hope that he was calling. She sat at the table, heart thumping hard as she listened to Daniella's voice in the next room talking on the phone.

A moment later, Daniella appeared in the doorway and said, "It's for you, Nina. The hospital. They said they've been trying to reach you."

Disappointed, Nina rose to take the call. "Hello?"

"Hi, this is Gladys Power, the night nursing supervisor. Sorry to bother you—we got your phone number from your mother. We have a number of staff out sick tonight, and we were wondering if you could come in to cover for the E.R."

"Night shift?"

"Yes. We could really use you."

Nina glanced toward Daniella's exercise room, where the music was playing louder than ever. She had to get out of this house. Away from this emotional battleground.

She said, "Okay, I'll take the shift."

"See you at eleven o'clock."

"Eleven?" Nina frowned. The night shift usually started at midnight. "You want me there an hour early?"

"If you could manage it. We're shorthanded on the evening shift as well."

"Right. I'll be there, eleven o'clock." She hung up and breathed a soft sigh of relief. Work was exactly what she needed. Maybe eight hours of crises, major and minor, would get her mind back on track.

And off the subject of Sam Navarro.

Marilyn hung up the phone. "She said she'd be there."

Spectre gave a nod of approval. "You handled it well."

"Of course." Marilyn favored him with that satisfied smile of hers. A smile that said, *I'm worth every penny you pay me.*

"Did she seem at all suspicious?" he asked.

"Not a bit. I'm telling you, she'll be there. Eleven o'clock, just like you wanted." Marilyn tilted back her head and gave her lips a predatory lick. "Now, do I get what I want?"

He smiled. "What *do* you want?"

"You know." She sidled toward him and unbuckled his belt. His breath caught in an involuntary gasp as that hot little hand slid inside his trousers. Her touch was delicious, expert, her technique designed to reduce a man to begging. Oh yes, he knew exactly what she was asking for.

And it wasn't sex.

Why not enjoy the moment? he thought. She was willing, and he still had the time to spare. Three hours until Nina Cormier showed up for her shift at the hospital. Some quick amusement with Marilyn, and then on to more serious business.

She dropped to her knees before him. "You said you'd pay me what I was worth," she whispered.

He groaned. "I promised…"

"I'm worth a lot. Don't you think?"

"Absolutely."

"I can be worth even more to you."

He gave a jerk of pleasure and grasped her face. Breathing heavily, he stroked down her cheek, her jaw, to her neck. Such a long, slender neck. How easy it should be to finish it. First, though, he'd let *her* finish…

"Oh, yes," she murmured. "You're ready for me."

He pulled her, hard, against him. And he thought, *A pity you won't be ready for me.*

It was ten-thirty by the time a weary Sam stepped through his front door. The first thing he noticed was the silence. The emptiness. It was a house that had somehow lost its soul.

He turned on the lights, but even the glow of all those lamps couldn't seem to dispel the shadows. For the past three years, this was the house he'd called home, the house he'd returned to every evening after work. Now the place felt cold to him, like the house of a stranger. Not a home at all.

He poured himself a glass of milk and drank it in a few thirsty gulps. So much for supper; he didn't have the energy to cook. He poured a second glass and carried it over to the telephone. All evening, he'd been itching to make this call, but something had always interrupted him. Now that he had a few blessed moments of peace, he was going to call Nina. He was going to tell her what he'd been afraid to tell her, what he could no longer deny to her, or to himself.

It had come to him this afternoon, a realization that had struck him, oddly enough, in the midst of searching

Marilyn Dukoff's apartment. He'd stood in the woman's bedroom and gazed at the empty bureau drawers, the stripped mattress. And without warning, he'd been struck by a sense of loneliness so intense it made his chest ache. Because that abandoned room had suddenly come to represent his life. It had a purpose, a function, but it was nevertheless empty.

I've been a cop too long, he'd thought. *I've let it take over my life.* Only at that moment, standing in that empty bedroom, did it occur to him how little of his own life he really had. No wife, no kids, no family.

Nina had opened his eyes to the possibilities. Yes, he was scared. Yes, he knew just how much, how deeply, he would be hurt if she ever left him. But the alternative was just as bleak; that he would never even give it a chance.

He'd been a coward. But no longer.

He picked up the phone and dialed Nina's father's house.

A few rings later, the call was answered by a bland "Hello?" Not Nina but Daniella, the fitness freak.

"This is Sam Navarro," he said. "Sorry to call so late. May I speak to Nina?"

"She's not here."

His immediate pang of disappointment was quickly followed by a cop's sense of dismay. How could she not be there? She was supposed to stay in a safe place tonight, not run around unprotected.

"Mind telling me where she went?" he asked.

"The hospital. They called her in to work the night shift."

"The Emergency Room?"

"I guess so."

"Thanks." He hung up, his disappointment so heavy

it felt like a physical weight on his shoulders. What the hell. He was not going to hold off any longer. He was going to tell her now. Tonight.

He dialed Maine Medical E.R.

"Emergency Room."

"This is Detective Sam Navarro, Portland Police. May I speak with Nina Cormier?"

"Nina's not here tonight."

"Well, when she gets there, could you ask her to call me at home?"

"She's not scheduled to come in."

"Excuse me?"

"I have the time sheet right in front of me. Her name's not down here for tonight."

"I was told someone called her in to work the night shift."

"I don't know anything about that."

"Well, can you find out? This is urgent."

"Let me check with the supervisor. Can you hold?"

In the silence that followed, Sam could hear his own blood rushing through his ears. Something was wrong. That old instinct of his was tingling.

The woman came back on the line. "Detective? I've checked with the supervisor. She says she doesn't know anything about it, either. According to her schedule, Nina isn't listed for any shifts until next week."

"Thank you," said Sam softly.

For a moment he sat thinking about that phone call from the hospital. Someone had known enough to locate Nina at her father's house. Someone had talked her into leaving those protective gates at an hour of night when there'd be few witnesses to see what was about to happen.

Not just someone. Spectre.

It was 10:45.

In a heartbeat, he was out the door and running to his car. Even as he roared out of his driveway, he knew he might already be too late. Racing for the freeway, he steered with one hand and dialed his car phone with the other.

"Gillis here," answered a weary voice.

"I'm on my way to Maine Med," Sam said. "Spectre's there."

"What?"

"Nina got a bogus call asking her to come in to work. I'm sure it was him. She's already left the house—"

Gillis replied, "I'll meet you there," and hung up.

Sam turned his full attention to the road. The speedometer hit seventy. Eighty.

Don't let me be too late, he prayed.

He floored the accelerator.

The hospital parking garage was deserted, a fact that scarcely concerned Nina as she drove through the automatic gate. She had often been in this garage late at night, either coming to, or leaving from, her shifts in the E.R., and she'd never encountered any problems. Portland, after all, was one of the safest towns in America.

Provided you're not on someone's hit list, she reminded herself.

She pulled into a parking stall and sat there for a moment, trying to calm her nerves. She wanted to start her shift with her mind focused clearly on the job. Not on death threats. Not on Sam Navarro. Once she walked in those doors, she was first and foremost a professional. Peoples' lives depended on it.

She opened the door and stepped out of the car.

It was still an hour before the usual shift change. Come midnight, this garage would be busy with hospital staff coming or going. But at this moment, no one else was around. She quickened her pace. The hospital elevator was just ahead; the way was clear. Only a dozen yards to go.

She never saw the man step out from behind the parked car.

But she felt a hand grasp her arm, felt the bite of a gun barrel pressed against her temple. Her scream was cut off by the first words he uttered.

"Not a sound or you're dead." The gun at her head was all the emphasis needed to keep her silent.

He yanked her away from the elevator, shoved her toward a row of parked cars. She caught a fleeting glimpse of his face as she was spun around. *Spectre.* They were moving now, Nina sobbing as she stumbled forward, the man gripping her arm with terrifying strength.

He's going to kill me now, here, where no one will see it....

The pounding of her own pulse was so loud at first, she didn't hear the faint squeal of tires across pavement.

But her captor did. Spectre froze, his grip still around her arm.

Now Nina heard it too: car tires, screeching up the garage ramp.

With savage force, Spectre wrenched her sideways, toward the cover of a parked car. *This is my only chance to escape,* she thought.

In an instant she was fighting back, struggling against his grip. He was going to shoot her anyway. Whether it happened in some dark corner or out here, in the open, she would not go down without a fight. She kicked, flailed, clawed at his face.

He swung at her, a swift, ugly blow that slammed against her chin. The pain was blinding. She staggered, felt herself falling. He grasped her arm and began dragging her across the pavement. She was too stunned to fight now, to save herself.

Light suddenly glared in her eyes, a light so bright it seemed to stab straight through her aching head. She heard tires screech and realized she was staring at a pair of headlights.

A voice yelled, *"Freeze!"*

Sam. It was Sam.

"Let her go, Spectre!" Sam shouted.

The gun barrel was back at Nina's head, pressing harder than ever. "What superb timing, Navarro," Spectre drawled without a trace of panic in his voice.

"I said, *let her go.*"

"Is that a command, Detective? I certainly hope not. Because, considering the young woman's situation—" Spectre grabbed her by the chin and turned her face toward Sam "—offending me could prove hazardous to her health."

"I know your face. So do the ushers at the Brant Theater. You have no reason to kill her now!"

"No reason? Think again." Spectre, still holding the gun to Nina's head, nudged her forward. Toward Sam. "Move out of the way, Navarro."

"She's worthless to you—"

"But not to you."

Nina caught a glimpse of Sam's face, saw his look of helpless panic. He was gripping his gun in both hands, the barrel aimed, but he didn't dare shoot. Not with her in the line of fire.

She tried to go limp, tried to slump to the ground. No good; Spectre was too strong and he had too firm a grip around her neck. He simply dragged her beside him, his arm like a vise around her throat.

"Back off!" Spectre yelled.

"You don't want her!"

"Back off or it ends here, with her brains all over the ground!"

Sam took a step back, then another. Though his gun was still raised, it was useless to him. In that instant, Nina's gaze locked with his, and she saw more than fear, more than panic in his eyes. She saw despair.

"Nina," he said. "Nina—"

It was her last glimpse of Sam before Spectre pulled her into Sam's car. He slammed the door shut and threw the car in Reverse. Suddenly they were screeching backward down the ramp. She caught a fast-moving view of parked cars and concrete pillars, and then they crashed through the arm of the security gate.

Spectre spun the car around to face forward and hit the accelerator. They roared out of the driveway and onto the road.

Before she could recover her wits, the gun was back at her head. She looked at him, and saw a face that was frighteningly calm. The face of a man who knew he was in complete control.

"I have nothing to lose by killing you," he said.

"Then why don't you?" she whispered.

"I have plans. Plans that happen to include you."

"What plans?"

He gave a low, amused laugh. "Let's just say they involve Detective Navarro, his Bomb Squad and a rather large amount of dynamite. I like spectacular endings, don't you?" He smiled at her.

That's when she realized whom she was looking at. What she was looking at.

A monster.

Chapter 13

Sam raced down the parking garage ramp, his legs pumping with desperate speed. He emerged from the building just in time to see his car, Spectre at the wheel, careening out of the driveway and taking off down the road.

I've lost her, he thought as the taillights winked into the night. *My God. Nina...*

He sprinted to the sidewalk and ran halfway down the block before he finally came to a stop. The taillights had vanished.

The car was gone.

He gave a shout of rage, of despair, and heard his voice echo in the darkness. Too late. He was too late.

A flash of light made him spin around. A pair of headlights had just rounded the corner. Another car was approaching—one he recognized.

"Gillis!" he shouted.

The car braked to a stop near the curb. Sam dashed to the passenger door and scrambled inside.

"Go. *Go!*" he barked.

A perplexed Gillis stared at him. "What?"

"Spectre's got Nina! Move it!"

Gillis threw the car into gear. They screeched away from the curb. "Which way?"

"Left. Here!"

Gillis swerved around the corner.

Sam caught a glimpse of his own car, two blocks ahead, as it moved into an intersection and turned right.

"There!"

"I see it," Gillis said, and made the same turn.

Spectre must have spotted them, too. A moment later he accelerated and shot through a red light. Cars skidded to a stop in the intersection.

As Gillis steered through the maze of vehicles and pressed his pursuit, Sam picked up the car phone and called for assistance from all available patrol cars. With a little help, they could have Spectre boxed in.

For now, they just had to keep him in sight.

"This guy's a maniac," Gillis muttered.

"Don't lose her."

"He's gonna get us all killed. Look!"

Up ahead, Spectre swerved into the left lane, passed a car, and swerved back to the right just as a truck barreled down on him.

"Stay with them!" Sam ordered.

"I'm trying, I'm trying." Gillis, too, swerved left to pass. Too much traffic was heading toward them; he swerved back.

Seconds were lost. Seconds that Spectre pushed to his advantage.

Gillis tried again, this time managing to scoot back

into his lane before colliding head-on with an oncoming van.

Spectre was nowhere in sight.

"What the hell?" muttered Gillis.

They stared at the road, saw stray taillights here and there, but otherwise it was an empty street. They drove on, through intersection after intersection, scanning the side roads. With every block they passed, Sam's panic swelled.

A half mile later, he was forced to accept the obvious. They had lost Spectre.

He had lost Nina.

Gillis was driving in grim silence now. Sam's despair had rubbed off on him as well. Neither one said it, but both of them knew. Nina was as good as dead.

"I'm sorry, Sam," murmured Gillis. "God, I'm sorry."

Sam could only stare ahead, wordless, his view blurring in a haze of tears. Moments passed. An eternity.

Patrol cars reported in. No trace of the car. Or Spectre.

Finally, at midnight, Gillis pulled over and parked at the curb. Both men sat in silence.

Gillis said, "There's still a chance."

Sam dropped his head in his hands. *A chance.* Spectre could be fifty miles away by now. Or he could be right around the corner. *What I would give for one, small chance....*

His gaze fell and he focused on Gillis's car phone. *One small chance.*

He picked up the phone and dialed.

"Who're you calling?" asked Gillis.

"Spectre."

"What?"

"I'm calling my car phone." He listened as it rang. Five, six times.

Spectre answered, his voice raised in a bizarre falsetto. "Hello, you have reached the Portland Bomb Squad. No one's available to answer your call, as we seem to have misplaced our damn telephone."

"This is Navarro," growled Sam.

"Why, hello, Detective Navarro. How *are* you?"

"Is she all right?"

"Who?"

"Is she all right?"

"Ah, you must be referring to the young lady. Perhaps I'll let her speak for herself."

There was a pause. He heard muffled voices, some sort of scraping sound. A soft, distant whine. Then Nina's voice came on, quiet, frightened. "Sam?"

"Are you hurt?"

"No. No, I'm fine."

"Where are you? Where's he taken you?"

"Oops," cut in Spectre. "Forbidden topic, Detective. Afraid I must abort this phone call."

"Wait. *Wait!*" cried Sam.

"Any parting words?"

"If you hurt her, Spectre—if anything happens to her—I swear I'll kill you."

"Is this a *law* enforcement officer I'm speaking to?"

"I mean it. I'll *kill* you."

"I'm shocked. *Shocked,* I tell you."

"Spectre!"

He was answered by laughter, soft and mocking. And then, abruptly, the line went dead.

Frantically Sam redialed and got a busy signal. He hung up, counted to ten, and dialed once more.

Another busy signal. Spectre had taken the phone off the hook.

Sam slammed the receiver down. "She's still alive."

"Where are they?"

"She never got the chance to tell me."

"It's been an hour. They could be anywhere within a fifty-mile radius."

"I know, I know." Sam sat back, trying to think through his swirl of panic. During his years as a cop, he'd always managed to keep his head cool, his thoughts focused. But tonight, for the first time in his career, he felt paralyzed by fear. By the knowledge that, with every moment that passed, every moment he did nothing, Nina's chances for survival faded.

"Why hasn't he killed her?" murmured Gillis. "Why is she still alive?"

Sam looked at his partner. At least Gillis still had a functioning brain. And he was thinking. Puzzling over a question that should've been obvious to them both.

"He's keeping her alive for a reason," said Gillis.

"A trump card. Insurance in case he's trapped."

"No, he's already home free. Right now, she's more of a liability than a help. Hostages slow you down. Complicate things. But he's allowed her to live."

So far, thought Sam with a wave of helpless rage. *I'm losing it, losing my ability to think straight. Her life depends on me. I can't afford to blow it.*

He looked at the phone again, and a memory echoed in his head. Something he'd heard over the phone during that brief pause between hearing Spectre's voice and Nina's. That distant wail, rising and falling.

A siren.

He reached for the phone again and dialed 911.

"Emergency operator," answered a voice.

"This is Detective Sam Navarro, Portland Police. I need a list of all emergency dispatches made in the last twenty minutes. Anywhere in the Portland-South Portland area."

"Which vehicles, sir?"

"Everything. Ambulance, fire, police. All of them."

There was a brief silence, then another voice came on the line. Sam had his notepad ready.

"This is the supervisor, Detective Navarro," a woman said. "I've checked with the South Portland dispatcher. Combined, we've had three dispatches in the last twenty minutes. At 11:55, an ambulance was sent to 2203 Green Street in Portland. At 12:10, the police were dispatched to a burglar alarm at 751 Bickford Street in South Portland. And at 12:13, a squad car was called to the vicinity of Munjoy Hill for a report of some disturbance of the peace. There were no fire trucks dispatched during that period."

"Okay, thanks." Sam hung up and rifled through the glove compartment for a map. Quickly he circled the three dispatch locations.

"What now?" asked Gillis.

"I heard a siren over the phone, when I was talking to Spectre. Which means he had to be within hearing distance of some emergency vehicle. And these are the only three locations vehicles were dispatched to."

Gillis glanced at the map and shook his head. "We've got dozens of city blocks covered there! From point of dispatch to destination."

"But these are starting points."

"Like a haystack's a starting point."

"It's all we have to go on. Let's start at Munjoy Hill."

"This is crazy. The APB's out on your car. We've got people looking for it already. We'd be running ourselves ragged trying to chase sirens."

"Munjoy Hill, Gillis. Go."

"You're beat. I'm beat. We should go back to HQ and wait for things to develop."

"You want me to drive? Then move the hell over."

"Sam, are you *hearing* me?"

"Yes, damn you!" Sam shouted back in a sudden outburst of rage. Then, with a groan, he dropped his head in his hands. Quietly he said, "It's my fault. My fault she's going to die. They were right there in front of me. And I couldn't think of any way to save her. Any way to keep her alive."

Gillis gave a sigh of comprehension. "She means that much to you?"

"And Spectre knows it. Somehow he knows it. That's why he's keeping her alive. To torment me. Manipulate me. He has the winning hand and he's using it." He looked at Gillis. "We have to find her."

"Right now, he has the advantage. He has someone who means a lot to you. And *you're* the cop he seems to be focused on. The cop he wants to get back at." He glanced down at his car phone. It was ringing.

He answered it. "Gillis here." A moment later he hung up and started the car. "Jackman Avenue," he said, pulling into the road. "It could be our break."

"What's on Jackman Avenue?"

"An apartment, unit 338-D. They just found a body there."

Sam went very still. A sense of dread had clamped down on his chest, making it difficult to breathe. He asked, softly, "Whose body?"

"Marilyn Dukoff's."

* * *

He was singing "Dixie!" as he worked, stringing out wire in multicolored lengths along the floor. Nina, hands and feet bound to a heavy chair, could only sit and watch helplessly. Next to Spectre was a toolbox, a soldering iron and two dozen dynamite sticks.

"In Dixieland where I was born, early on a frosty mornin'…"

Spectre finished laying out the wire and turned his attention to the dynamite. With green electrical tape, he neatly bundled the sticks together in groups of three and set the bundles in a cardboard box.

"In Dixieland we'll make our stand, to live and die in Dixie. Away, away, away down south, in DIXIE!" he boomed out, and his voice echoed in the far reaches of the vast and empty warehouse. Then, turning to Nina, he dipped his head in a bow.

"You're crazy," whispered Nina.

"But what is madness? Who's to say?" Spectre wound green tape around the last three dynamite sticks. Then he gazed at the bundles, admiring his work. "What's that saying? 'Don't get mad, get even'? Well, I'm not mad, in any sense of the word. But I *am* going to get even."

He picked up the box of dynamite and was carrying it toward Nina when he seemed to stumble. Nina's heart almost stopped as the box of explosives tilted toward the floor. Toward her.

Spectre gave a loud gasp of horror just before he caught the box. To Nina's astonishment, he suddenly burst out laughing. "Just an old joke," he admitted. "But it never fails to get a reaction."

He really was crazy, she thought, her heart thudding.

Carrying the box of dynamite, he moved about the

warehouse, laying bundles of explosives at measured intervals around the perimeter. "It's a shame, really," he said, "to waste so much quality dynamite on one building. But I do want to leave a good impression. A lasting impression. And I've had quite enough of Sam Navarro and his nine lives. This should take care of any extra lives he still has."

"You're laying a trap."

"You're so clever."

"Why? Why do you want to kill him?"

"Because."

"He's just a policeman doing his job."

"*Just* a policeman?" Spectre turned to her, but his expression remained hidden in the shadows of the warehouse. "Navarro is more than that. He's a challenge. My nemesis. To think, after all these years of success in cities like Boston and Miami, I should find my match in a small town like this. Not even Portland, Oregon, but Portland, *Maine*." He gave a laugh of self-disgust. "It ends here, in this warehouse. Between Navarro and me."

Spectre crossed toward her, carrying the final bundle of dynamite. He knelt beside the rocking chair where Nina sat with hands and ankles bound. "I saved the last blast for you, Miss Cormier," he said. And he taped the bundle under Nina's chair. "You won't feel a thing," he assured her. "It will happen so fast, why, the next thing you know, you'll be sprouting angel's wings. So will Navarro. If he gets his wings at all."

"He's not stupid. He'll know you've set a trap."

Spectre began stringing out more color-coded wire now, yards and yards of it. "Yes, it should be quite obvious this isn't any run-of-the-mill bomb. All this wire, tangled up to confuse him. Circuitry that makes no sense…" He snipped a white wire, then a red one. With his soldering iron, he connected the ends. "And the time ticking away. Minutes, then seconds. Which is the detonator wire? Which wire should he cut? The wrong one, and it all goes up in smoke. The warehouse. You. And him—if he has nerve enough to see it to the end. It's a hopeless dilemma, you see. He stays to disarm it and you could both die. He chickens out and runs, and *you* die, leaving him with guilt he'll never forget. Either way, Sam Navarro suffers. And I win."

"You can't win."

"Spare me the moralistic warnings. I have work to do. And not much time to do it." He strung the wires out to the other dynamite bundles, crisscrossing colors, splicing ends to blasting caps.

Not much time to do it, he had said. How much time was he talking about?

She glanced down at the other items laid out on the floor. A digital timer. A radio transmitter. It was to be a timed device, she realized, the countdown triggered by that transmitter. Spectre would be safely out of the building when he armed the bomb. Out of harm's way when it exploded.

Stay away, Sam, she thought. *Please stay away. And live.*

Spectre rose to his feet and glanced at his watch. "Another hour and I should be ready to make the call." He looked at her and smiled. "Three in the morning, Miss Cormier. That seems as good an hour as any to die, don't you think?"

The woman was nude from the waist down, her body crumpled on the wood floor. She had been shot once, in the head.

"The report came in at 10:45," said Yeats from Homicide. "Tenant below us noticed bloodstains seeping across the ceiling and called the landlady. She opened the door, saw the body and called us. We found the victim's ID in her purse. That's why we called you."

"Any witnesses? Anyone see anything, hear anything?" asked Gillis.

"No. He must've used a silencer. Then slipped out without being seen."

Sam gazed around at the sparsely furnished room. The walls were bare, the closets half empty, and there were boxes of clothes on the floor—all signs that Marilyn Dukoff had not yet settled into this apartment.

Yeats confirmed it. "She moved in a day ago, under the name Marilyn Brown. Paid the deposit and first month's rent in cash. That's all the landlady could tell me."

"She have any visitors?" asked Gillis.

"Next-door tenant heard a man's voice in here yesterday. But never saw him."

"Spectre," said Sam. He focused once again on the body. The criminalists were already combing the room, dusting for prints, searching for evidence. They would find none, Sam already knew; Spectre would've seen to it.

There was no point hanging around here; they'd be better off trying to chase sirens. He turned to the door, then paused as he heard one of the detectives say, "Not much in the purse. Wallet, keys, a few bills—"

"What bills?" asked Sam.

"Electric, phone. Water. Look like they're to the old apartment. The name Dukoff's on them. Delivered to a P.O. box."

"Let me see the phone bill."

At his first glance at the bill, Sam almost uttered a

groan of frustration. It was two sheets long and covered with long distance calls, most of them to Bangor numbers, a few to Massachusetts and Florida. It would take hours to track all those numbers down, and the chances were it would simply lead them to Marilyn Dukoff's bewildered friends or family.

Then he focused on one number, at the bottom of the bill. It was a collect call charge, from a South Portland prefix, dated a week and a half ago at 10:17 p.m. Someone had called collect and Marilyn Dukoff had accepted the charges.

"This could be something," Sam noted. "I need the location of this number."

"We can call the operator from my car," said Gillis. "but I don't know what it's going to get you."

"A hunch. That's what I'm going on," Sam admitted.

Back in Gillis's car, Sam called the Directory Assistance supervisor.

After checking her computer, she confirmed it was a pay phone. "It's near the corner of Calderwood and Hardwick, in South Portland."

"Isn't there a gas station on that corner?" asked Sam. "I seem to remember one there."

"There may be, Detective. I can't tell you for certain."

Sam hung up and reached for the South Portland map. Under the dome light, he pinpointed the location of the pay phone. "Here it is," he said to Gillis.

"There's just some industrial buildings out there."

"Yeah, which makes a collect call at 10:17 p.m. all the more interesting."

"Could've been anyone calling her. Friends, family. For all we know—"

"It was Spectre," Sam said. His head jerked up in sudden excitement. "South Portland. Let's *go*."

"What?"

Sam thrust the map toward Gillis. "Here's Bickford Street. A squad car was dispatched there at 12:10. And here's Calderwood and Hardwick. The squad car would've gone right through this area."

"You think Spectre's holed up around there?"

Sam scrawled a circle on the map, a three-block radius around Calderwood and Hardwick. "He's here. He's got to be around here."

Gillis started the car. "I think our haystack just got a hell of a lot smaller."

Twenty minutes later, they were at the corner of Hardwick and Calderwood. There was, indeed, a gas station there, but it had been closed down and a For Sale—Commercial Property sign was posted in the scraggly strip of a garden near the road. Sam and Gillis sat in their idling car for a moment, scanning the street. There was no other traffic in sight.

Gillis began to drive up Hardwick. The neighborhood was mostly industrial. Vacant lots, a boating supply outlet. A lumber wholesaler. A furniture maker. Everything was closed for the night, the parking lots empty, the buildings dark. They turned onto Calderwood.

A few hundred yards later, Sam spotted the light. It was faint, no more than a yellowish glow from a small window—the only window in the building. As they pulled closer, Gillis cut his headlights. They stopped half a block away.

"It's the old Stimson warehouse," said Sam.

"No cars in the lot," Gillis noted. "But it looks like someone's home."

"Didn't the Stimson cannery close down last year?"

Sam didn't answer; he was already stepping out of the car.

"Hey!" whispered Gillis. "Shouldn't we call for backup?"

"You call. I'm checking it out."

"Sam!" Gillis hissed. "Sam!"

Adrenaline pumping, Sam ignored his partner's warnings and started toward the warehouse. The darkness was in his favor; whoever was inside wouldn't be able to spot his approach. Through the cracks in the truck bay doors, he saw more light, vertical slivers of yellow.

He circled the building, but spotted no ground floor windows, no way to look inside. There was a back door and a front door, but both were locked.

At the front of the building, he met up with Gillis.

"Backup's on the way," Gillis informed him.

"I have to get in there."

"We don't know what we'll find in there—" Gillis suddenly paused and glanced at his car.

The phone was ringing.

Both men scurried back to answer it.

Sam grabbed the receiver. "Navarro here."

"Detective Navarro," said the police operator. "We have an outside phone call for you. The man says it's urgent. I'll put it through."

There was a pause, a few clicks, and then a man's voice said, "I'm so glad to reach you, Detective. This car phone of yours is coming in handy."

"Spectre?"

"I'd like to issue a personal invitation, Detective. To you and you alone. A reunion, with a certain someone who's right here beside me."

"Is she all right?"

"She's perfectly fine." Spectre paused and added with a soft tone of threat. "For the moment."

"What do you want from me?"

"Nothing at all. I'd just like you to come and take Miss Cormier off my hands. She's becoming an inconvenience. And I have other places to go to."

"Where is she?"

"I'll give you a clue. Herring."

"What?"

"Maybe the name *Stimson* rings a bell? You can look up the address. Sorry I won't be here to greet you, but I really *must* be going."

Spectre hung up the phone and smiled at Nina. "Time for me to go. Lover boy should be here any minute." He picked up his toolbox and set it in the car, which he'd driven through the loading bay to keep it out of sight.

He's leaving, she thought. *Leaving me as bait for the trap.*

It was cool in the warehouse, but she felt a drop of sweat slide down her temple as she watched Spectre reach down for the radio transmitter. All he had to do was flick one switch on that radio device, and the bomb would be armed, the countdown started.

Ten minutes later, it would explode.

Her heart gave a painful thud as she saw him reach for the radio switch. Then he smiled at her.

"Not yet," he said. "I wouldn't want things to happen prematurely."

Turning, he walked toward the truck bay door. He gave Nina a farewell salute. "Say goodbye to Navarro for me. Tell him I'm so sorry to miss the big kaboom." He unlatched the bay door and gave the handle a yank.

It slid up with the sound of grating metal. It was almost open when Spectre suddenly froze.

Right in front of him, a pair of headlights came on.

"Freeze, Spectre!" came a command from somewhere in the darkness. "Hands over your head!"

Sam, thought Nina. *You found me....*

"Hands up!" yelled Sam. "Do it!"

Silhouetted against the headlights, Spectre seemed to hesitate for a few seconds. Then, slowly, he raised his hands over his head.

He was still holding the transmitter.

"Sam!" cried Nina. "There's a bomb! He's got a transmitter!"

"Put it down," Sam ordered. "Put it down or I shoot!"

"Certainly," agreed Spectre. Slowly he dropped to a crouch and lowered the transmitter toward the floor. But as he lay it down, there was a distinct *click* that echoed through the warehouse.

My God, he's armed the bomb, thought Nina.

"Better run," said Spectre. And he dived sideways, toward a stack of crates.

He wasn't fast enough. In the next instant, Sam squeezed off two shots. Both bullets found their target.

Spectre seemed to stumble. He dropped to his knees and began to crawl forward, but his limbs were moving drunkenly, like a swimmer trying to paddle across land. He was making gurgling sounds now, gasping out curses with his last few breaths.

"Dead," wheezed Spectre, and it was almost a laugh. "You're all dead…"

Sam stepped over Spectre's motionless body and started straight toward Nina.

"No!" she cried. "Stay away!"

He stopped dead, staring at her with a look of bewilderment. "What is it?"

"He's wired a bomb to my chair," sobbed Nina. "If you try to cut me loose it'll go off!"

At once Sam's gaze shot to the coils of wire ringing her chair, then followed the trail of wire to the warehouse wall, to the first bundle of dynamite, lying in plain view.

"He has eighteen sticks planted all around the building," she said. "Three are under my chair. It's set to go off in ten minutes. Less, now."

Their gazes met. And in that one glance she saw his look of panic. It was quickly suppressed. He stepped across the wire and crouched by her chair.

"I'm getting you out of here," he vowed.

"There's not enough time!"

"Ten minutes?" He gave a terse laugh. "That's loads of time." He knelt down and peered under the seat. He didn't say a thing, but when he rose again, his expression was grim. He turned and called, "Gillis?"

"Right here," Gillis answered, stepping gingerly over the wires. "I got the toolbox. What do we have?"

"Three sticks under the chair, and a digital timer." Sam gently slid out the timing device, bristling with wires, and set it carefully on the floor. "It looks like a simple series-parallel circuit. I'll need time to analyze it."

"How long do we have?"

"Eight minutes and forty-five seconds and counting."

Gillis cursed. "No time to get the bomb truck."

A wail of a siren suddenly cut through the night. Two police cruisers pulled up outside the bay door.

"Backup's here," Gillis said. He hurried over to the doors, waving at the other cops. "Stay back!" he yelled.

"We got a bomb in here! I want a perimeter evac *now!* And get an ambulance here on standby."

I won't need an ambulance, thought Nina. *If this bomb goes off, there'll be nothing left of me to pick up.*

She tried to calm her racing heart, tried to stop her slide toward hysteria, but sheer terror was making it hard for her to breathe. There was nothing she could do to save herself. Her wrists were tightly bound; so were her ankles. If she so much as shifted too far in her chair, the bomb could be triggered.

It was all up to Sam.

Chapter 14

Sam's jaw was taut as he studied the tangle of wires and circuitry. There were so many wires! It would take an hour just to sort them all out. But all they had were minutes. Though he didn't say a word, she could read the urgency in his face, could see the first droplets of sweat forming on his forehead.

Gillis returned to his partner's side. "I checked the perimeter. Spectre's got the building wired with fifteen or more sticks. No other action fuses as far as I can see. The brain to this whole device is right there in your hands."

"It's too easy," muttered Sam, scanning the circuitry. "He *wants* me to cut this wire."

"Could it be a double feint? He knew we'd be suspicious. So he made it simple on purpose—just to throw us?"

Sam swallowed. "This looks like the arming switch

right here. But over here, he's got the cover soldered shut. He could have a completely different switch inside. Magnetic reed or a Castle-Robins device. If I pry off that cap, it could fire."

Gillis glanced at the digital timer. "Five minutes left."

"I know, I know." Sam's voice was hoarse with tension, but his hands were absolutely steady as he traced the circuitry. One tug on the wrong wire, and all three of them could be instantly vaporized.

Outside, more sirens whined to a stop. Nina could hear voices, the sounds of confusion.

But inside, there was silence.

Sam took a breath and glanced up at her. "You okay?"

She gave a tense nod. And she saw, in his face, the first glimpse of panic. *He won't figure this out in time, and he knows it.*

This was just what Spectre had planned. The hopeless dilemma. The fatal choice. Which wire to cut? One? None? Does he gamble with his own life? Or does he make the rational choice to abandon the building—and her?

She knew the choice he would make. She could see it in his eyes.

They were both going to die.

"Two and a half minutes," said Gillis.

"Go on, get out of here," Sam ordered.

"You need an extra pair of hands."

"And your kids need a father. Get the hell out."

Gillis didn't budge.

Sam picked up the wire cutters and isolated a white wire.

"You're guessing, Sam. You don't know."

"Instinct, buddy. I've always had good instincts. Better leave. We're down to two minutes. And you're not doing me any good."

Gillis rose to his feet, but lingered there, torn between leaving and staying. "Sam—"

"Move."

Gillis said, softly, "I'll have a bottle of Scotch waiting for you, buddy."

"You do that. Now get out of here."

Without another word, Gillis left the building.

Only Sam and Nina remained. *He doesn't have to stay,* she thought. *He doesn't have to die.*

"Sam," she whispered.

He didn't seem to hear her; he was concentrating too hard on the circuit board, his wire cutters hovering between a life-and-death choice.

"Leave, Sam," she begged.

"This is my job, Nina."

"It's not your job to die!"

"We're not going to die."

"You're right. *We* aren't. *You* aren't. If you leave now—"

"I'm not leaving. You understand? I'm *not*." His gaze rose to meet hers. And she saw, in those steady eyes, that he had made up his mind. He'd made the choice to live—or die—with her. This was not the cop looking at her, but the man who loved her. The man *she* loved.

She felt tears trickle down her face. Only then did she realize she was crying.

"We're down to a minute. I'm going to make a guess here," he said. "If I'm right, cutting this wire should do the trick. If I'm wrong..." He let out a breath. "We'll know pretty quick one way or the other." He slipped the teeth of the cutter around the white wire. "Okay, I'm going with this one."

"Wait."

"What is it?"

"When Spectre was putting it together, he soldered a white wire to a red one, then he covered it all up with green tape. Does that make a difference?"

Sam stared down at the wire he'd been about to cut. "It does," he said softly. "It makes a hell of a lot of difference."

"Sam!" came Gillis's shout through a megaphone. "You've got ten seconds left!"

Ten seconds to run.

Sam didn't run. He moved the wire cutter to a black wire and positioned the jaws to cut. Then he stopped and looked up at Nina.

They stared at each other one last time.

"I love you," he said.

She nodded, the tears streaming down her face. "I love you too," she whispered.

Their gazes remained locked, unwavering, as he slowly closed the cutter over the wire. Even as the jaws came together, even as the teeth bit into the plastic coating, Sam was looking at her, and she at him.

The wire snapped in two.

For a moment neither one of them moved. They were still frozen in place, still paralyzed by the certainty of death.

Then, outside, Gillis yelled, "Sam? You're past countdown! *Sam!*"

All at once, Sam was cutting the bonds from her hands, her ankles. She was too numb to stand, but she didn't need to. He gathered her up into his arms and carried her out of the warehouse, into the night.

Outside, the street was ablaze with the flashing lights of emergency vehicles: squad cars, ambulances, fire trucks. Sam carried her safely past the yellow police tape and set her down on her feet.

Instantly they were surrounded by a mob of officials, Chief Coopersmith and Liddell among them, all clamoring to know the bomb's status. Sam ignored them all. He just stood there with his arms around Nina, shielding her from the chaos.

"Everyone back!" shouted Gillis, waving the crowd away. "Give 'em some breathing space!" He turned to Sam. "What about the device?"

"It's disarmed," said Sam. "But be careful. Spectre may have left us one last surprise."

"I'll take care of it." Gillis started toward the warehouse, then turned back. "Hey, Sam?"

"Yeah?"

"I'd say you just earned your retirement." Gillis grinned. And then he walked away.

Nina looked up at Sam. Though the danger was over, she could still feel his heart pounding, could feel her own heart beating just as wildly.

"You didn't leave me," she whispered, new tears sliding down her face. "You could have—"

"No, I couldn't."

"I told you to go! I *wanted* you to go."

"And I wanted to stay." He took her face in his hands. Firmly, insistently. "There was no other place I'd be but right there beside you, Nina. There's no other place I ever want to be."

She knew a dozen pairs of eyes were watching them. Already the news media had arrived with their camera flashbulbs and their shouted questions. The night was alive with voices and multicolored lights. But at that moment, as he held her, as they kissed, there was no one else but Sam.

When dawn broke, he would still be holding her.

Epilogue

The wedding was on. No doubt about it.

Accompanied by a lilting Irish melody played by flute and harp, Nina and her father walked arm in arm into the forest glade. There, beneath the fiery brilliance of autumn foliage, stood Sam. Just as she knew he would be.

He was grinning, as nervous as a rookie cop on his first beat. Beside him stood his best man, Gillis, and Reverend Sullivan, both wearing smiles. A small circle of friends and family stood gathered under the trees: Wendy and her husband. Chief Coopersmith. Nina's colleagues from the hospital. Also among the guests was Lydia, looking quietly resigned to the fact her daughter was marrying a mere cop.

Some things in life, thought Nina, cannot be changed. She had accepted that. Perhaps Lydia, some day, would learn to be as accepting.

The music faded, and the leaves of autumn drifted down in a soft rain of red and orange. Sam reached out to her. His smile told her all she needed to know. This was right; this was meant to be.

She took his hand.

* * * * *

USA TODAY bestselling author **Rita Herron** wrote her first book when she was twelve but didn't think real people grew up to be writers. Now she writes so she doesn't have to get a real job. A former kindergarten teacher and workshop leader, she traded storytelling to kids for writing romance, and now she writes romantic comedies and romantic suspense. Rita lives in Georgia with her family. She loves to hear from readers, so please visit her website, ritaherron.com.

Books by Rita Herron

Harlequin Intrigue

A Badge of Honor Mystery

Mysterious Abduction
Left to Die
Protective Order
Suspicious Circumstances

The Heroes of Horseshoe Creek

Lock, Stock and McCullen
McCullen's Secret Son
Roping Ray McCullen
Warrior Son
The Missing McCullen
The Last McCullen

Cold Case at Camden Crossing
Cold Case at Carlton's Canyon
Cold Case at Cobra Creek
Cold Case in Cherokee Crossing

Visit the Author Profile page at Harlequin.com for more titles.

UNDERCOVER AVENGER

Rita Herron

To Melissa Endlich for all your support!

And to the Georgia Romance Writers for being the greatest chapter ever! Thanks a bunch for turning out at the signings.

Prologue

Eric Caldwell walked a fine line with the law, but he didn't care. He had trusted the Feds before and people had died. He didn't intend to let it happen to this witness.

Even if he and his brother, Cain, fought again. Cain, always the good guy, the one on the right side of the law. The man who never saw the grays.

The only color Eric did see.

"Come on, Eric, where's the witness in the Bronsky case?" Cain asked.

"What?" Sarcasm laced Eric's voice. "Did the police lose another witness?"

"We do the best we can," his brother said. "Do you know where he is?"

Eric grabbed a Marlboro and pushed it into the corner of his mouth. "Sorry, can't help you, bro."

Cain hissed, his message ringing loud and clear. Eric

was lying, but Cain knew better than to push it. Eric would do whatever he could to keep the witness alive. "You can't go around undermining the cops and the FBI, Eric, or killing every criminal who escapes the system."

He glared at Cain over the duffel bag he'd been packing. "I didn't kill anyone."

Cain's gaze turned deadly. "I don't want to see your vigilante ways get you in trouble. It's like you're on a death mission, taking everything into your own hands." Cain's voice thickened. "One day you're going to cross the wrong people."

Eric ignored the concern in Cain's warning, zipped his bag, then threw it over his shoulder, grabbed his keys and strode toward the door. "Like you don't cross the wrong kind all the time."

"It's not the same thing," Cain argued. "I have people covering me. You're on your own."

Eric hesitated. "You could quit the force and help me. Make it your New Year's resolution."

"New Year's has come and gone," Cain said. Their gazes locked briefly and Eric's stomach clenched. His brother was serious. "Join the force, Eric, and work with the law, not against us."

But Eric could not fit the mold. "I guess we hit that impasse again." He snagged his laptop off the counter.

Cain's jaw tightened. "Watch your back. If you get into trouble—"

"Then you'll be there to help me." A cocky grin slid onto Eric's face. "Now, I'd love to stay and talk politics but I gotta go."

Cain caught his arm before he could fly past. "Where are you going?"

Eric stared him down hard, the way he had when

they were boys and they'd argued over whether or not to interfere when things had gone sour at home. When their father had taken his rage out on their mother and them. "I have business to finish," he said between clenched teeth. "Legitimate business at the ranch."

His brother studied him, didn't believe him. Eric didn't care.

Or maybe he did, but he would do what he had to do anyway.

Mottled storm clouds rolled across the sky as he headed outside, thunder rumbling above the trees. The wind howled off the lake, a haunting reminder of the bleakness that had become his life.

He didn't have time for self-analysis, though. He had to get the witness to a safe house, then meet that woman his friend Polenta had sent his way. She'd sounded desperate, as if she was in trouble. And there was a kid involved. Some baby named Simon. The woman hadn't made sense. She claimed they were after the baby, that he was the product of a research experiment.

He'd known then he had to help her and the child. He'd even considered confiding in Cain, but she had turned to him for a reason. Because she couldn't trust the cops.

The reason he did what he did.

Eric could never say no to a woman or child in trouble. Not when his own past haunted him, when memories of his mother's suicide still sent sweat trickling down his spine. Years ago, he'd started working with an underground organization to help women escape abusive homes so they didn't meet the same fate, and their children didn't suffer from abuse themselves. Someone had to help them break the cycle.

He jogged down the front-porch steps two at a time,

heading toward the lean-to where he'd parked the Jeep. Thankfully, his brother followed him to the porch. The witness was hiding in the back room, waiting to escape out the side door, then slip through the woods to the SUV.

Rocks and gravel sprayed beneath his boots as he walked, the sting of his brother's disapproval burning his back. He shrugged it off, tossed his duffel bag into the back seat along with his computer and saw the witness crawl into the passenger seat. He waited until Cain turned before he went to retrieve the cash he kept stashed in the shed for emergencies.

Shaded by the thick forest of trees between his property and the road, he stepped toward the knotty pines. But a sudden explosion rent the air, the impact throwing him against a tree. Glass shards and flying metal assaulted him. He banged his head and tasted dirt, then jerked around on his knees in shock. His Jeep had exploded. A fireball rolled off it toward the sky. Ignoring the blinding pain that seared him, he lurched forward to rescue the witness, but another explosion rocked the ground and sent him hurling backward again into the woods.

Fire breathed against his skin, catching his clothes and singeing his arms and legs. A jagged rock pierced his skull.

The world went momentarily dark, the crackle of fire eating into the night. Eric pulled himself from the haze and tried to yell for help, but his vocal cords shut down. The smoke and fire robbed him of air. He coughed, inhaling the acrid odor of his own burning flesh. Pain, intense and raw, seared him. Flames clawed at his face, and pieces of hot metal stabbed his thigh. Then dizziness swept over him.

He released a silent scream into the night, welcoming death and telling his brother goodbye.

Chapter 1

Three Months Later

"Did you find my birth parents?" Melissa Fagan asked.

Larry Dormer, a local Atlanta private investigator she'd hired, hesitated before answering. "I hit a lot of dead ends."

He was stalling. Melissa steadied her voice to hide the disappointment. She wanted a name, just a name. At least for starters. "So, why did you call me in, Mr. Dormer?"

"You told me to let you know if I found anything. I have a lead." Anxiety emanated from him in the uneven breaths that rasped through the air, along with the scent of his perspiration. He'd cracked his knuckles more than once, as well, reaching for cigarettes, then fighting the urge, a definite sign of nerves.

Instead, he drummed a pencil on his desk. How bad could it be? Had he located her parents and been told they didn't want to be found? Were they shady people?

"You know most records are sealed—"

"Just tell me," she said, growing impatient. She could feel his pity, hear the disapproval in his voice, sense he was holding back. He didn't think she should search for people who might not want to be found. She should respect their privacy. She'd heard it all before. But she had to know the truth. "Look, I understand how difficult it is to hack into confidential files. Believe me, I've tried several sources. But I want to know everything you learned."

"You're sure? You registered in the national database for adopted children, so if your parents were looking for you, they'd be able to contact you."

"Maybe they're not certain I'd welcome them."

He still hesitated. "All right. But you may not like what you discover."

"I'm well aware of that." All those years of foster care, she'd prayed she'd be adopted. Or that her mother or father would suddenly appear and rescue her from a life of being shuffled from one place to another. That hadn't happened.

Now at twenty-six, she had no such illusions that her life would be so idyllic.

Her mother had left her on the doorstep of a church with no note, nothing except a tiny handmade crocheted bonnet with a pink ribbon. She had no idea why she'd been deserted. If she did, maybe she could overcome this dreadful sense of abandonment.

Besides, it would be nice to feel connected to someone else in the world. Not to feel so alone. To at least know the truth about the woman who'd given birth to her.

He still hesitated, studying her over square glasses, giving her time to contemplate her options.

What if her mother or father had searched for her but had encountered the same brick walls she had? Or what if her parents had given her away because they couldn't handle parenting an imperfect child?

She massaged her temple, fighting an agitation-induced headache. The one that indicated the onslaught of a seizure. Her medication helped immensely, but occasionally she still experienced the episodes. They were mild, not epileptic in nature, and her symptoms mimicked a bad migraine—she became disoriented, slipped into a trancelike state for a few minutes—but they still embarrassed her and made her feel flawed. Besides, the attacks always left her physically exhausted and slightly depressed.

Other questions assailed her. What if her mother had never told her father about her existence? What if one of her parents could accept her and be proud that she'd become an independent young woman? A physical therapist, when so many people hadn't believed she'd succeed.

What if your parents are happily married to other people and have families of their own? What if they're ashamed of you, the bastard child?

What if you weren't born out of a night of passion? Are you prepared for an ugly truth like that?

How could she go on not knowing, though? She'd lived in darkness all her life, her past an empty vacuum—at least this was one door she could open, look through, then close it if need be.

She braced herself for the worst. "Tell me what you discovered."

He sighed and reached for a cigarette, this time relenting and lighting up. The stench of smoke filled the air, his shaky rasp of contentment following. "Your mother's name was Candace Latone."

Candace? She savored the name for a moment. "Was Latone her maiden name or married name?"

"She wasn't married."

"What else can you tell me?"

"She was young. Gave birth to you in Savannah, Georgia." He hesitated, his reluctancy to answer her palpable.

"What?" Anger tightened her throat. "I'm paying you for the truth, not to sugarcoat it."

"All right." He wheezed, his cheap suit coat rattling as he swiped at the perspiration on his face. "She spent some time in a hospital down there."

"You mean she worked at one? Was she a nurse, an aide, a doctor? What?"

"She was a patient, Miss Fagan. She attended college in Savannah and got involved in some kind of research experiment at the hospital where she volunteered."

"What kind of experiment?"

"I haven't been able to find that out. Records are sealed. No one is talking."

"And my father?"

"Nothing so far."

Her mind veered off on a tangent—could the research experiment have caused her seizure disorder? The doctors hadn't been able to explain the exact cause, but suggested it was genetic. And though not life threatening, the disorder deterred people from adopting her. Worse, she was afraid she might pass it on to a child.

Maybe if she discovered the cause, the doctors could prevent her offspring from inheriting the condition.

"If I were you, I'd forget the search." He stood, inhaling smoke and shuffling papers, his demeanor indicating an end to their meeting.

"Can you keep looking?" Melissa asked.

"I told you everything, Miss Fagan. Now, I'd let sleeping dogs lie."

Melissa shivered and gripped the chair edge. She didn't believe him. He was hiding something.

Still, learning her mother's name should have been enough. Melissa had been born in Savannah; she had a place to start. But the fact that Candace had been involved in a research project, and that Melissa suffered from seizures no one could explain, triggered more questions. "All right, thank you for your help."

He snapped the file closed as if glad to be finished with it. "Goodbye, Miss Fagan."

Melissa headed to the door, still contemplating his odd behavior. The elevator dinged, and she waited for the people to exit, then stepped inside, fighting off the stench of body odors, stifling perfumes and smoke lingering inside.

Frustration clawed at her as the doors closed, claustrophobia choking her. She pulled at her collar and inhaled, wrestling with bitter memories of being locked in a small room by her foster parents. They'd claimed they wanted to prevent her from wandering around at night, had been afraid she'd stumble into something. Instead, they'd confined her like a prisoner.

The elevator whirled to a stop, the doors buzzed open, and she stepped outside, breathing in the fresh air. A warm spring breeze brushed her neck, the scents of freshly baked bread and Italian cuisine floating from the neighborhood restaurant. The hum of Atlanta traffic whizzed around her—a horn blowing, a siren wailing, pedestrians passing. A homeless man in ratty clothes reeking of booze and filth hugged a bottle of wine to his chest, his glassy eyes staring up at her, glazed and disoriented. Compassion filled her. She understood how it felt to be homeless, unwanted.

She slipped inside a neighboring bagel shop, bought a bagful of bagels and a cup of hot coffee, then hurried out and handed them to him. Then she hailed a cab. At least she had more information than she'd had the day before.

Tomorrow, she would check out the research park in Savannah and get a job there. Once she located her parents, she could put the past to rest.

Eric still couldn't believe he was alive.

Although the pain he had endured for the past few months had been excruciating, the doctors had claimed his strong will had brought him through.

Eric knew differently. He had survived so he could get revenge.

So he could find the person responsible for killing his witness and make him pay. And when he'd learned that the killer had also tried to murder his brother, an innocent woman and baby, he'd decided to do whatever was necessary to catch him.

Even work with the FBI.

"You can't go undercover, Eric. For God's sake, you're in a wheelchair. You're too vulnerable."

Eric rubbed a hand along his jaw, ignoring the distress on Cain's face. "I don't want your damn pity, Cain. And I won't be in this chair long."

Still uncomfortable with the chair and his new

image, Eric gripped the metal arms. But his new face beat the hideous one he'd awakened to three months before. And he would walk again, no matter how much physical therapy he had to endure.

"Hell, Cain, I thought you'd be glad I finally hooked up with the Feds."

"But working undercover at the Coastal Island Research Park is too risky," Cain argued. "What if someone realizes who you are?"

Eric pointed to the hospital mirror. "Look at me, bro. You didn't even recognize me. How will anyone at CIRP, when they've never seen me?" He wheeled the chair toward the door. "I'm the last person they'd expect to show up as a patient."

"I don't like that, either," Cain said. "Damn. If it weren't for Alanna and Simon, I'd take the job."

"No, they need you," Eric said. "Besides, the people at CIRP would recognize you."

His brother couldn't argue with that point. "If Hughes has resurfaced, and they discover you're with the Feds, there's no telling what they'll do to you. Do you have any idea the lengths some of those scientists have resorted to in order to cover themselves?"

His brother was right. The Feds had already briefed him on earlier questionable events at the center.

Eric's mind ticked back to what he knew so far. Arnold Hughes had co-founded the research park, but years ago, he'd tried to sell research to a foreign source, then committed murder to cover his actions. When the police tried to arrest him, he'd escaped. His boat had exploded, but his body had never been found. Recent rumors suggested he'd resurfaced. That he'd not only supported a memory transplant experiment in which a former Savannah cop, Clayton Fox, had had his memory erased and been made to believe he was a man named Cole Turner, but he'd spearheaded an experiment to explore creating the perfect child. The child had been Simon—the baby his brother's wife had protected by kidnapping him from the center.

Hughes was Simon's father, only he didn't know it.

And now a manhunt was on for Hughes.

The fact that the Feds suspected Hughes had resurfaced with a new identity had sparked the idea for Eric to capitalize on his own new face and work undercover. Ironic, but cunning—he'd use their own game to trap them. He'd even adopted a fake last name, Collier, to cover himself.

"The doctors are going to patch up my body," Eric said with a wry grin. "It's the least they can do after destroying it."

"That's just it, you're not physically strong enough to defend yourself right now."

Cain's comment cut to the bone. "Another reason I'm having therapy. Besides, I need time to heal before the doctors can perform more skin grafts. I might as well be useful in the meantime." The rehab arrangement at CIRP offered private bungalows on-site for recovery, which would allow him mobility and a beach view, a helluva lot better setup than another god-awful hospital, or having to arrange transportation from his own cabin to a rehab facility on a daily basis. He refused to be dependent on his brother.

Cain caught his arm just as Eric reached for the doorknob. Déjà vu flooded him. Another time when his brother had tried to stop him. If he'd listened to him then, the witness might still be alive.

But one look at the wheelchair, and he had to follow

through. After all, it was spring. Cain had a new wife and a baby. A life to live.

Eric's future was bleak. No spring roses or kids or lovers in his future. He had nothing but a battered, scarred body. And a dark soul, to boot.

One no woman would want.

All he had to live for was his revenge.

A week later, Melissa had landed a job at the Coastal Island Research Park Hospital, and moved into one of the small cottages on Skidaway Island CIRP had built for employees. But she'd hit a brick wall in Savannah when she tried to locate Candace Latone. Apparently, there weren't any Latones living in the area, either that or they weren't listed in the phone book. It was possible her mother had come to Savannah as a student from another city. Although Melissa's funds were limited, her investigative skills were even more so. She would have to hire another P.I. to search for Candace.

Unless she discovered information at the school or hospital that would lead her to her mother.

People were funny about keeping secrets, even ones over twenty years old. She had to pursue her search slowly, so as not to upset the tide should someone object to her jimmying the closed doors of their lives. Last year, she'd read an article about an adopted child who'd been murdered because she'd unearthed the truth about her parentage. Her father had been a well-known politician who'd wanted to cover his mistakes.

Mistake—was that what she had been?

Shaking off the troubling reminder that she'd been unwanted, she considered the possibilities. But she doubted she'd discover anything quite so newsworthy or dramatic in her past. Still, Dormer's warning had unnerved her, as had the stories she'd heard about the research park since she'd arrived—unethical research experiments, the death of the former director, the disappearance of another, Arnold Hughes, the murder attempt on a scientist and his wife when they had defied the institute. All too scary.

Deciding to lie low the first few days, make friends, acquaint herself with the patient load and staff, she focused on meeting the nurses, doctors and other therapists. She had just finished with her first patient, a child who'd suffered two broken legs in a car accident, when Nancy, one of the college-age girls who volunteered at the center, nudged her. Melissa's gaze veered toward the door, where a broad-shouldered man with dark brown hair rolled toward them in a wheelchair. Masculinity and sex appeal oozed from him, along with the anguish evident in his tightly set jaw and black expression. He hated the wheelchair, that was obvious. Hated his weakness, that was obvious, too.

She didn't blame him. She hated her own weaknesses.

"Not bad for an old guy," Nancy murmured.

Melissa winced. He was only thirty-four. His name, Eric Collier. His chart revealed he was over six feet tall, weighed two hundred pounds. He didn't have to stand up for her to see that his body was muscular. His face was nice looking, too, a broad jaw, angular with a firm nose and deep-set dark eyes.

"What's his story?" Nancy asked.

Melissa explained his injuries. "He also suffered burns over twenty-five percent of his body, he's had some skin grafts, waiting for more."

Nancy shivered. "What happened?"

"Some kind of car accident. Apparently there was a gas leak and his car exploded."

Nancy backed away, stricken. "Poor man. He was probably even better-looking before."

He's gorgeous anyway, Melissa wanted to say, but she didn't. She had to remain professional. She never got involved with patients. And she wouldn't make an exception here.

But the injuries and scars didn't faze her as they did the young girl beside her. The courage the patients possessed did—everyone she worked with had a story. Dreams lost, shattered bodies and bruised self-esteem. Some gave in to pity, others fought hard not to succumb to the depression. To regain those dreams and their lives. With every failure and setback, she felt their frustration. With every success, their joy. And for those who tried to give up, she rallied harder to encourage them to fight back.

This one looked like a fighter.

The wheelchair rolled to a stop, the man's hard gaze pinning her as he looked up into her eyes. His were a muddy brown, almost black. Angry. Full of pride. Challenge. Pain.

"Eric Cal... Collier," he said. "I'm here for my session."

She extended her hand, ignoring the fact that he was as handsome as sin. Anger radiated from his every pore in palpable waves, an attitude of aloofness surrounding him that would have been off-putting had she not seen it before. This man was not only scarred on the outside but on the inside, as well. Old wounds hadn't healed, had festered instead, maybe all the way to his soul. She understood about those kinds of wounds too. She'd lived with them all her life. "Melissa Fagan."

His mouth twitched as if he was trying for a smile but couldn't force his lips to form one. She smiled for him instead. She'd seen tough men before and understood their difficulty in accepting help, as well as their own imperfections.

Especially when they had to depend on a woman.

Male pride and all that. This guy possessed it in spades.

"We'll start over here, Mr. Collier." She directed him to a desk in the corner for their first consultation. As soon as she sat, he relaxed slightly, although for a fleeting second his gaze skittered over her in an almost appreciative way, as if he'd noticed her as a man notices a woman. Good, some part of him wasn't dead.

She'd wondered at first.

As a therapist, in the past, a few patients had been attracted to her. At first. But once they started the sessions, they usually wound up hating her. Hating her for pushing them. For punishing their bodies. For reminding them she could walk without help and they couldn't.

She didn't let their attitudes affect her, either. In the end, when they stood and walked out on their own two feet, free of their crutches, tolerating their temper outbursts was worth it.

Thankfully, putting herself more on his level helped dissipate some of his tension. She'd seen that reaction before, too. Men despised women towering over them. Control issues.

"Well," she said, inflecting a cheerfulness in her voice she used with her patients. "It looks like we have our work cut out for us, Mr. Collier." She reviewed his injuries and described the strategy for getting him back in shape, outlining basic exercise routines to be performed at the center and at home. "Remember, it takes time to regain your strength. You have to be patient."

His curt nod warned her not to count on it.

She gestured toward the workout area. "Are you ready to get out of that chair, Eric?"

He seemed momentarily startled she'd used his first name, but he dismissed it quickly, then nodded, somber but determined.

"Good, but remember, you'll have to take it one step at a time, one day at a time." She smiled, hoping to temper her comment. "If you overdo, you can damage yourself further and cause a setback, so remember when I tell you to stop, it's for a reason."

"Right." His sarcastic reply wasn't lost on her. She'd have to stay on top of him or he'd ignore caution.

She pointed to the locker room and watched him wheel toward it, his broad shoulders stiff, his head held high. She hoped he would maintain the attitude.

He would need it to survive the long grueling sessions ahead of him.

Eric steeled himself against the instant attraction he felt for Melissa Fagan while he changed into workout shorts and a T-shirt. He should have worn them to the session, but pride had made him stall in revealing his scars. Especially when he'd heard his therapist was going to be female.

Disgust filled him for even momentarily noticing her beauty. This woman had read his chart. She knew the extent of his injuries. She would have to help him stand, help him learn to walk again.

She would have to touch his ugly marred flesh.

He could not think of her as a woman.

Still, he sucked in a sharp breath at the thought of

exposing himself to her, though after all he'd endured in the hospital the last three months, he should be accustomed to it. The baths, the skin grafts, the constant poking and prodding. But somehow revealing his wounds to Melissa made him feel even more naked and raw.

Focus on the job. On catching Hughes.

His resolve set, he wheeled through the doors to the locker room, but the young blond candy striper winced as her gaze landed on his scarred thigh. He gritted his teeth and rolled past her, stopping directly in front of Melissa Fagan, daring her to do the same. She didn't. She simply offered him a smile and gestured for him to follow as if his injuries didn't faze her.

He gave her credit for not flinching, when he had almost gagged the first time the doctor had removed the bandages and he'd seen the mounds of discolored, purplish-red mangled flesh that had once been his solid, slick muscular thighs and arms and chest.

Of course, she was simply doing a job. Maybe she'd become immune to reacting to patients the way he'd forced himself to be impersonal when he dealt with victims. God knows, he'd seen some horrors in the past few years.

He remembered the courage the brutalized women he'd helped had shown as he gritted his teeth and endured the painful stretching and warm-up exercises she instructed him to do. He wouldn't complain. Wouldn't growl at her or curse even though he desperately needed to vent.

He would suffer through torture if it would make him whole again.

Damn it, his thigh completely cramped. The shooting pain radiated all the way from his upper leg down through his calf. Nausea gripped his stomach from the impact of the muscle spasm, but he sucked in air to control it.

"That's right, breathe in, out." Melissa gently kneaded the muscle, slowly stretching his leg and fitting his foot against her thigh. He focused on the deep-breathing exercises to stifle the rage of temper that attacked him at his helplessness.

Her silky hair swayed around her shoulders as she leaned forward to press her fingers into his leg, rubbing and massaging with long nimble strokes that felt like heaven.

He stared at her hands. He'd never quite appreciated the power of the pleasure they could offer a man. At least, not when the act wasn't sexual. Her fingers pressed harder as she leaned forward to continue her ministrations, and he glimpsed the perfect pale skin of her neck. But he didn't dwell on it or allow himself to enjoy the sweet fragrance of her soap and shampoo or the way her lips were the color of sun-ripened raspberries. And when images of her long dark hair cascading across his stomach intervened, he banished them, as well.

"That's the reason we start with those basic warm-up and stretching exercises," she said softly. "Although cramps are inevitable, especially in the early stages of therapy." She angled her face toward him and smiled. The light softened her already pale green eyes. "Feeling better?"

He nodded, reminding himself that her smile and the soft words she murmured in that thick, sultry voice were intended to encourage him to work harder. They were also filled with compassion that he didn't want to need or feel.

Because feeling only meant more pain. And he had reached his limit.

* * *

The sight of Eric's proud stubborn chin thrust high as he wheeled toward the locker room stirred Melissa's admiration even more, but the sensations she'd felt when she'd massaged the cramps in his legs had her heart pounding. When she'd helped him into the whirlpool, she had watched the bubbling water ooze over his flesh and had ached to soothe the tension from his strained face, the strain caused by working so hard to camouflage his agony.

She had never reacted this way to a patient before.

Touching and massaging body parts had become rote, impersonal. Yet, her stomach had fluttered when she'd placed Eric's foot against her leg and touched his thigh. He had struggled to contain his reaction, although she'd glimpsed the fine sheen of perspiration that had beaded his lip when her fingers had pressed against his sensitive skin.

Hating herself for allowing personal feelings to intervene during work, she justified her reaction as a product of loneliness. She'd moved to a new place. She felt isolated and wanted to connect with someone.

She had been lonely and isolated her entire life.

Dismissing the melancholy thought, she wiped the back of her neck with a gym towel and hurried toward the break room for coffee. She could not start lusting after her patients. Good grief, she would lose her job. Not that she planned to stay here long. No, as soon as she discovered her parents' identity and location, she'd hightail it to wherever they lived.

Eric Collier's tortured dark eyes rose to taunt her.

The sooner she left town, the better.

Deciding to forgo the coffee, she went to search for the old records. They would either be kept on microfiche or stored in the basement of the main facility, not in the rehab building, so she detoured through the breezeway that connected the rehab building to the main hospital. Confidential or not, she had to see if the hospital still had records on Candace Latone.

She checked over her shoulder as she hurried down the hallway to the restricted area, determined to keep a low profile so as not to arouse suspicion.

Every muscle and joint in Eric's body throbbed with pain. Even his teeth hurt.

It still hadn't kept him from noticing Melissa Fagan though, or reacting as a man would to a woman's touch.

Damn. He tossed the towel into the dirty-clothes bin and wheeled toward the exit. Forget the shower. He'd take one when he returned to his room. Where he had privacy and strangers didn't have to watch him drag his butt from the chair to another one to wash his battered body.

He hesitated, chastising himself for indulging in a pity party. He had noticed others suffering while they worked through their own therapy. A young boy, about twelve. What was his story? An elderly woman—did she have family? A tiny toddler with leg braces—God.

Seeing them had affected him. At least enough to jolt him out of his own depression and finish the reps Melissa had assigned him. She'd warned him not to overdo.

Hell, he'd barely been able to manage the exercises she'd asked of him.

He hated the weakness. Hated immobility. Hated that a beautiful woman like Melissa had to see his ugliness.

He'd told Cain he could do his job, but what if he couldn't?

Fighting the uncertainty over his recovery, he thrust

himself forward, pushing down the hall. Maybe he'd take a scenic tour of the hospital on the way out and study the layout. At least then he could say he'd started investigating. If anyone stopped him, he could always claim he'd gotten lost.

Play up the invalid bit.

Just as he rounded the corner near the bottom floor, he spotted Melissa. He wheeled to an abrupt stop, watching her from a distance. Breathing in her beauty and telling himself not to.

But a frown pulled at his mouth. She was checking over her shoulder as if she thought someone might be following her. He edged into the corner of the doorway behind the open doors so she wouldn't see him. She bit down on her lip as her gaze scanned the hall. Apparently deciding it was clear, she ducked into the doors and disappeared.

He inched the chair from behind the doorway and wheeled closer. The sign on the door said Restricted.

From the nervous look on her face, she wasn't supposed to be entering the area. So what exactly was she up to?

Chapter 2

Melissa eased down the long corridor, listening for voices or footsteps, peering at the frosted glass of the doors labeled to identify the areas. Several labs caught her attention, along with a hallway that led to another restricted area and a dark cavern of testing areas connected by steel slab doors that required special clearance and were designed with passkey codes. The entire wing felt alien and cold, the air stale. The absence of antiseptic odors or other chemical scents seemed odd in itself. Gray linoleum, light gray walls, reinforced-steel beams supported the forbidden structure. She felt as if she'd stepped into a tomb.

What exactly was going on behind those closed doors?

The sound of distant footsteps echoed from the neighboring wing, and she hesitated, planting herself in the corner as they passed. She held her breath while they crossed the opening, perspiration dotting her palms. Finally, when the footsteps faded into the distance, she veered to the right, bypassed a room marked X-rays, then spotted the file room. Wiping her damp hands on her slacks, she reached for the doorknob.

"Excuse me, what are you doing here?"

Melissa froze, possible excuses racing through her head. Taking a calming breath, she turned and forced a smile. "I'm new to the center and need to review some patient files."

"Your name?"

A security guard faced her, clad in a gray uniform, a name tag attached to the stiff pocket of his shirt. His posture indicated he meant business, his tone implied she was in trouble.

"Melissa Fagan. I'm a physical therapist working with the rehabilitation program."

He copied down her name, then checked it against a master list from his clipboard. His finger thumped onto the line where she must have been listed, because his gaze rose to meet hers. Still skeptical. "Do you have clearance to be in this area?"

Melissa played dumb. "Clearance?"

His puffy lips twitched in irritation. "Yes, this is a restricted area."

Melissa glanced around, pretending innocence. "Actually, it's only my first day here. I must have missed the sign and didn't realize."

"Any files you need for patients are housed in the computer system in the rehab area. Older ones are also kept in the basement of that area."

"Oh, I see." She offered him a watery smile. "I guess I got confused. But thanks for straightening that out. I've always been directionally impaired."

His eyes narrowed as if he thought she was lying or virtually incompetent. "I'll have to report you were in the area."

She turned to escape, but his gruff voice added, "CIRP is very careful of its restricted areas, so don't let it happen again, Miss Fagan. Snooping into confidential files and restricted areas could be dangerous."

A chill skittered up her spine. Had he meant the comment as a warning or a threat?

Eric had wheeled his chair to a corner and was studying the doors where Melissa had disappeared, wondering how difficult it would be to break CIRP's security codes. He wished like hell he could walk so he could delve into the case rather than speculate.

The doors suddenly opened and Melissa reappeared. Her green eyes flickered with panic as she stepped into the light, and her hands were trembling. Although earlier he'd sensed steely determination in the woman when she'd pushed him through his therapy, vulnerability shadowed her pale face now.

What was she up to?

Determined not to be caught watching her, he spun the chair around and wheeled to the nearest exit. Barreling down the handicap ramp, he cursed again when the chair caught in a piece of loose gravel and jolted forward. It took him a second to dislodge the stone before he could continue. He followed the concrete path to the bungalows, grateful CIRP had designed the facility to give patients as much mobility as possible. Being robbed of his independence hacked at his self-esteem, but it would be intolerable if he had to rely on his brother to drive him back and forth to a rehab facility, or if he was confined to a hospital room like the other facilities Cain had mentioned.

Another reason CIRP had appealed to him.

That and finding Hughes and getting revenge for the death of the witness his people had killed. This afternoon he'd review the list of employees, including every scientist at CIRP and the CEO who'd replaced Hughes and start trying to pinpoint which man might be Hughes in disguise.

Fishing the key from his pocket, he unlocked the door to the cabin, tossed his duffel bag inside, then rolled across the slick wood floor, his mind ticking back to Melissa Fagan. Why had she been snooping around in the restricted area? What was she looking for?

Could she possibly be an undercover detective posing as a physical therapist? If not, what other explanation could there be?

But if she was an undercover cop or agent, why hadn't he been informed?

A testament to his lack of faith and truth—one minute he'd been attracted to her, the next he suspected her of subterfuge.

Only one way to find out. The shower beckoned, but first he grabbed his cell phone and called his contact at the FBI, Luke Devlin a forty-something workaholic with a badass attitude. Eric normally despised the slick-suited agents, but he had connected with Devlin immediately. Something dark and edgy tainted the man's gray eyes, a haunted look Eric knew was mirrored in his own.

"Devlin here. What's up?"

"It's Eric. Is there another agent working at CIRP undercover?"

Devlin hesitated. "Why do you ask?"

Eric frowned. Devlin had a habit of answering a question with a question. "Would you tell me if someone else was working with you? If you guys are undermining me or working another angle, I need to know."

"Don't get so defensive. I simply wanted to know if you'd seen something suspicious. I assume you did or you wouldn't be asking."

Eric bottled his temper, and explained about Melissa Fagan's odd behavior.

"No, she's not one of ours. That doesn't mean she's not working for someone else though."

"The locals maybe?"

"Actually, we're coordinating with them, so no," Devlin said, "but I'll check her out and call you back."

"Thanks. I'll keep an eye on her. If she's not a cop or agent, maybe she's connected to Hughes's return," Eric suggested. "Or who knows, she might be here to steal research of some kind."

"Right, keep an eye on her." Devlin sighed. "Anything else to report?"

"Nothing yet. I...just had my first session today."

"It's going to take time to heal," Devlin said. "Be patient."

Eric ignored the comment. "I'll review the data you sent and see if I can narrow down the list of suspects fitting Hughes's profile." Eric agreed to report in a few days, then hung up, looked down at his battered body and tried to lift his leg. It weighed a ton and refused to move as he wanted. Damn it.

Be patient.

Easy for a mobile man to say, not so easy when you couldn't take a baby step. Instead of the shower, he dragged himself up on the bed and collapsed, unable to fight the lingering fatigue from his accident.

But even in his sleep, he couldn't rest.

He dreamed about the explosion. The witness he'd been protecting clawed at the inside of the car, screaming for help. His eyes were glassy with pain and horror. Blood gushed down his face.

Eric lay helpless on the ground, blazing metal trapping him. His body was on fire, burning, burning, burning.

Melissa was still a wreck when she returned to the rehab center for her next patient session. How would she ever bypass security and locate those files when CIRP had the entire place under lock and key?

She definitely hadn't started out well by getting caught and receiving a warning on her first day of the job.

Shaking off the anxiety that she might never find the answers she wanted, she pasted on a smile and focused on her patients. The first, a teenager who'd been in an alcohol-related accident and barely survived. Thankfully, he had been humbled by the experience. The second, a war veteran who'd lost a leg from diabetes. He'd been fitted with a prosthesis but had not handled the adjustment very well. The last was a salt-and-pepper-haired doctor in his early fifties who'd been injured in the terrorist attacks on 9/11.

When she finished charting the patient records for the day, she slipped into the employee lounge. Helen Anderson, one of the nurses she'd met when she arrived, waved her over. In her late fifties, she had a mop of curly brown hair dusted in gray. Padded with a few extra pounds, but not heavy, she mothered the other staff members.

"Sit down and put your feet up, honey. You've had a busy morning."

Melissa nodded, dumped a packet of sweetener in her coffee and plopped onto the love seat across from the woman. "How long have you worked here, Helen?"

Helen popped a powdered doughnut hole into her mouth, then dabbed at the corners. "Seems like forever," she said with a laugh. "But it's only been thirty years."

Since before Melissa was born. Maybe this woman did know something....

"I imagine the center's changed a lot."

"Changed and grown. When the hospital was first built, it was very small, everything was housed in one building. Now it's all spread out, and the research facilities have expanded. Whew, I can't keep up."

"I know, I've read about some of the cutting-edge techniques." Melissa had studied the layout. The psychiatric ward was actually in another building, which was attached by crosswalks, as were the rehab facility and the main hospital. Other buildings housed experimental-research centers and laboratories scattered across Catcall Island, with additional ones on the more remote Whistlestop and Nighthawk Islands.

Helen shook her head. "Hopefully, all the trouble's passed."

"But you're worried?"

"You hear things, you know, about questionable projects out on Nighthawk Island. Did you know they named the island after some mysterious nighthawk who preys on people, not just other animals?"

"No, but that's interesting." Melissa sipped her coffee. "They conduct government experiments on the island?"

"Yes, but everything's so danged secretive. One of the founders, Arnold Hughes, actually killed a scientist a long time ago because Hughes wanted to sell the man's research to a higher bidder. And when this cop named Clayton Fox started nosing around last year, they replaced his memory with another man's." She shuddered. "And then there was that poor baby…"

Melissa chewed her lip. So the things she'd read online had been true.

Helen twisted her hands. "Maybe I'm getting paranoid in my old age, but I worry they're doing chemical and biological warfare research," she admitted, her agitation growing. "With all this talk of terrorist attacks and war, it could be awful. And what if they release chemicals or germs on the people through the water?"

"It is scary. Since 9/11, I've had a few nightmares myself."

Helen rubbed her fingers together while Melissa struggled for a way to ask more questions without arousing suspicion. "Have you always worked with rehab patients, or did you ever work in other departments?"

"I moved around when I first came here, trying to find my place." Helen folded her arms across her plump belly. "Worked in labor and delivery awhile, the cardiac unit, the E.R., then I got my PT license."

"Delivering babies must have been exciting."

Helen shrugged, then stiffened and stood, dumping her coffee into the trash. An odd expression streaked her face. Panic? "I… Break's over. I have to get back to work now."

Without another word, she hurried from the room, looking agitated and eager to escape more questions.

Melissa frowned. What had triggered her reaction?

Two hours later, Eric finally dragged himself from bed to the shower. Even with the handicap rails, pulling his body from the chair into the tub and onto the customized seat took enormous effort and taxed his upper-body strength. The grueling morning session had taken its toll. Although he was tempted to add a few reps to the series of stretching exercises Melissa Fagan had assigned him, he worried he'd barely complete the basic ones.

At any rate, he wasn't supposed to tackle them until after dinner. Maybe he'd take a nice long stroll outside—in his chair—for some fresh air, scope out the facility.

Maybe he'd even run into his therapist. Not that he wanted to see her again...

And even if you did, he thought, what would she want with some scarred, crippled man?

Disgusted with himself, he toweled off, dressed in baggy sweats and a T-shirt, then wheeled outside to get some air. He couldn't let himself become obsessed with things he couldn't have. Like a woman.

But there she was.

Standing off the path, looking out at the ocean. A stiff wind flung her hair around her face. Her cheeks looked softer in the fading sunlight, but her eyes looked troubled. What exactly was her story? And why did he care if she was lonely? He wasn't anyone's hero, not anymore...

Unable to resist the forces drawing him to her, though, he wheeled over to her. The creak of his chair alerted her to his presence and she glanced his way. A small smile lifted the corner of her mouth.

"Hi, Eric."

God, he loved the way she murmured his name. He must be desperate. "Hi."

"How are you feeling tonight?"

He shrugged. "I hate to admit it, but you wore me out earlier."

A twinkle replaced the sadness in her eyes, and he grinned.

"It's always hard at first," she said softly. "It'll get easier."

But never quite back to normal. He knew it. But he didn't want to believe it.

"You like the ocean?" he asked.

She nodded and angled her face into the wind again, once again melancholy. "I haven't spent much time at the beach, though. The sea is so vast, it looks like it could go on forever."

There was that sadness in her voice again. "I know what you mean." Damn. He was bad at chit chat. Didn't know how to talk to a woman anymore. "Back home I have a cabin on the lake. At night, I like to sit outside, look at the stars and the moon. It's peaceful."

She tucked a strand of hair behind her ear and glanced down at him. Moonlight played off her hair, making him itch to touch it. Her lips parted, eliciting fantasies of long slow kisses that went on forever, just like the ocean.

But he couldn't even reach her, much less kiss her. Not sitting down.

A reminder of his condition.

Reality crashed over him, just like the waves breaking on the shore. "I guess I'd better go. Can I walk you to your cottage?" The minute the words came out, he realized how ridiculous they sounded.

But she didn't react. Probably out of pity.

"Sure." He wheeled beside her, the tension crackling as they crossed the path. When they reached her cottage, she turned to him. "Thanks, Eric. I'll see you tomorrow."

"Yeah."

"Get some rest."

Any illusion he might have harbored about her seeing him as a man was shattered. She saw him as a patient.

And he'd damn well better remember it.

Furious with himself, he wheeled back to his cabin. He'd do his job, learn to walk again and get the hell out of Savannah. Determined, he spread out the computer printout listing all the CIRP employees. He studied ages and basic body sizes, narrowing the field down to five potential men who might be Hughes. The new CEO of CIRP was a definite possibility. But claiming Hughes's original position would almost be too obvious. Another possibility was Dennis Hopkins, a scientist who'd recently transferred to CIRP from the Oakland facility in Tennessee, and a chemist, Wallace Thacker. Of course, the list might not be complete. With the classified projects on Nighthawk Island, CIRP might also have employees who weren't listed in the database the FBI had tapped into. Previously, the police had uncovered research on experiments to create a superhuman child and memory transplants.

What kind of projects were under way now?

"All right, do we have the team put together?"

"Yes." Dennis Hopkins shuffled through the latest data from his research study. "I'm ready to move ahead. Preliminary results of the drugs we're testing combined with hypnosis look good."

"Great. I have clearance to see the results."

"I'm grateful the government is being so cooperative." In fact, Hopkins had been amazed when the special agent had contacted him with a request for the type of research work he had already begun. Brainwashing techniques had always been used by secret government agencies, but most relied on torture. A smile lifted his lips.

His methods were definitely more advanced, civilized, ingenious.

"Are you kidding? With terrorism and the situation in the Middle East, we need your techniques yesterday."

Pride puffed up Hopkins's chest, along with sarcasm in his response. "I'm glad to do whatever I can for my country."

"Right." The special agent on the other end of the line didn't find him amusing. "Let me know if you have any problems, and we'll take care of them."

Hopkins chuckled. He understood the agent's implications. Problems, as in someone snooping around. Hell, if he discovered trouble, if anyone interfered, he'd simply turn the unwanted party into a live subject for his experiment.

And he wouldn't fail as they had with the memory transplant they'd performed on that cop Clayton Fox. No, his study of the brain exceeded their original piece of work.

And he had secret government clearance to do whatever was necessary to perfect it.

Now, all he needed was the human subjects. Willing or unwilling, it really didn't matter....

Chapter 3

Two weeks later, Eric woke from another haunting nightmare of the explosion, his breathing erratic, his body drenched in sweat. The incessant itching from his scars was driving him crazy. Early morning sunlight flowed through the blinds, streaking the discolored flesh on his chest. He muttered an oath and forced himself to look at the puckered skin anyway. To see himself the way he knew others did, a man branded by his disfigurement, a cicatrix, like a rock standing alone on the side of a mountain.

Half an hour later, he faced Melissa. She seemed tired, too, and distracted, as if she hadn't slept well either. But since that night by the ocean, he'd staunchly avoided any personal conversation.

Her perfect mouth parted in a smile. "Ready to get started?"

Damn. He wanted to kiss her. He grunted instead,

adopting his detached persona as the heat from her fingertips began to massage the ache in his calf.

The other part of him that ached would have to continue to do so.

The past two weeks had been a series of mindless, torturous exercises and grueling physical routines that had stolen the last vestiges of his pride and reminded him that he hadn't just lost skin and mobility in the accident, but endurance as well.

But he would walk again. He couldn't quit, or he'd never exact his revenge.

Admittedly, seeing Melissa Fagan's encouraging smile eased the pain.

She finished the warm-up exercises, then coached him through stretches. There were times during the sessions when he hated her. Times she pushed him to the limits. Times she forced him to continue when he wanted to succumb to the mind numbing pity and self-recrimination that snuck from the dark hiding places of his soul barking that he was a failure. That he should have died instead of that witness.

But in the black emptiness of his cabin at night, when the ceiling fan swirled lazily above him and he remembered the scent of Melissa's silky hair, he closed his eyes and ached to feel alive. To hold her.

He jerked upright, pulling away from her. "I can take it from here."

Her fingers paused on his upper thigh, and he gritted his teeth. "Are you sure?"

"Yes. I'm ready for the weights."

She nodded, her troubled gaze meeting his. But he had snapped at her enough over the last few days that she didn't argue. She simply offered him that damn sweet smile and gestured toward another patient.

"I'll be right over there if you need me."

He gave a clipped nod. Hell, he did need her. But not in the way she meant.

Only he'd never be able to have her.

By the time Eric got back to his cabin, he was exhausted. He had to finish this job so he could get out of Savannah. Away from Melissa.

He pulled out his notes and reviewed them. So far, he'd met each of the men he suspected to be Hughes and photographed them with the FBI's miniature camera, but he was still no closer to the truth than before. He'd heard hints of some secretive projects under way involving germ warfare, but he'd yet to access any specific information. Maybe the Feds had chosen the wrong guy for the job.

The phone rang. He stifled irritation as he swung his stiff body sideways to a sitting position to answer it. "Caldwell here."

"Eric, it's Luke Devlin."

"Yeah?"

"I discovered some interesting things about the woman you asked me to investigate."

Melissa? "Yeah?"

"Background is shady. She was an orphan, abandoned and left on the doorsteps of a church when she was a baby."

Eric's throat tightened. "Was she adopted?"

"No. Her file was dog-eared with a medical problem, some odd disorder, but the doctors couldn't pinpoint the cause. Must have scared people away."

Medical problem? Melissa Fagan appeared completely healthy, normal…no more, than normal. She had to be physically strong to perform her job.

"So, what happened to her?"

"Same old, same old. Apparently, she was juggled from one foster home to another, ended up in a group home outside Atlanta as a teen. Earned a scholarship and a degree, then attended PT school at Emory."

Impressive. But those foster homes—although the system tried, Eric had witnessed horror stories of failed results and homes that never should have been recommended for the foster care program, children battered and abused and traumatized from the results of misplacements. What was Melissa's story?

"What's she doing here at CIRP?"

Devlin's breath wheezed over the line, and Eric realized he was smoking. His hand automatically dropped to his bedside table, a self-deprecating chuckle following. He'd quit, not by choice, but during his hospital stay, he hadn't been able to smoke. The first time he'd smelled a cigarette afterwards, it had triggered memories of the scent of his own flesh burning.

"Miss Fagan recently hired a private investigator. Apparently she's trying to locate her birth parents."

"She believes they're here?"

"She was born in Savannah not long after the hospital was opened. In fact, shortly after Hughes came on board."

Eric sat up straighter, his anxiety level rising a notch. Too coincidental. The research experiments with baby Simon hadn't been the first, he was certain. One of the locals, Detective Black's sister Denise Harley, had researched methods to enhance cognitive growth, but she'd supposedly scratched the research, afraid it would fall into the wrong hands. Had the facility conducted questionable experiments back in the eighties? And if so, could Melissa be somehow connected?

No, he was jumping to conclusions, letting his imagination run away from him because of Simon. Hundreds of babies were born each year, abandoned, adopted, all normal deliveries.

Still, as he hung up, worry assaulted him. Even if there weren't any strange circumstances surrounding her birth, what would happen if she started asking questions?

Did her parents want to be found or would they rather their secrets be buried forever?

After her morning sessions, Melissa had tried to hack into the computer system again, but failed. Helen walked by the cafeteria and barely spared her a glance. So much for forging a friendship here. Melissa had definitely upset the woman that day when she'd asked about the labor and delivery wing. Helen had avoided her since.

Dreading her afternoon session with Eric, she finished her bagel, a slight headache pinching. To avoid a seizure, she seriously needed to destress, but how could she relax when questions from her past haunted her? Who was she? How sick had her mother been? Why hadn't one of the other family members possessed the ability to love her? What kind of people were the Latones?

They'd deserted a baby…

Unfortunately, she wouldn't find the answers in the cafeteria, so took a pain reliever and hurried back to the rehab wing. She'd been pushing Eric hard, and he'd made great strides.

But as he entered, she recognized anger and mounting despair in his eyes. He wasn't recovering as quickly as he wanted. And although he kept his emotions sealed in a steel vault, they had been bottled so long she sensed the door might blow open any minute.

When that happened—and she knew it would, because every patient experienced the boiling point—she would be there to push him further. She refused to let him give up. Even if he did hate her. And lately, it appeared that way. His behavior might not have hurt so much if she hadn't sensed heat between them that night he'd met her by the ocean. And when he'd escorted her back to her room, she'd thought he might kiss her.

But she couldn't allow herself to get involved, especially when she needed to focus on finding out the truth about her identity.

Besides, she had never trusted enough to allow anyone close before. Not after all the times she'd been rejected. The memory of her college boyfriend's reaction to her seizure had been burned into her brain as deeply as the physical scars on Eric's body.

A body that, in spite of its scars was taut and muscular and undeniably attractive.

Her cheeks flared with heat at the thought of being intimate with him. He would be the first…only he didn't seem to want her.

He rolled toward her, and she inhaled deeply to stymie her natural reaction. Fatigue shadowed his dark eyes, the remnants of lack of sleep evident in the tiny lines around his mouth.

She wondered what he'd look like if he actually smiled.

But she doubted she'd see it anytime soon.

"Afternoon, Eric."

He simply scowled, offering no more conversation than usual.

"Have a good break?"

"Yeah, I guess."

She dragged her gaze from his face to his chart. She'd added a few more exercises to the original regimen.

He parked the chair beside the exercise equipment and flattened his hands on his thighs, beginning the sequence of warm-up exercises that had become routine for both of them. He stretched and flexed while she massaged the cramped muscle in his lower calf. His right leg seemed stronger daily, but the left one had sustained more damage and was progressing slower.

His skin felt hot to the touch, the dark hairs on his leg brushing sensitive nerve endings as she stroked and applied pressure to the muscle. He gritted his teeth, his tight jaw masking any reaction to the pain.

"How are you sleeping?" she asked as she extended his left leg and nodded for him to push against her hand.

"Fine."

"Your eyes tell a different story."

He jerked his head up, a haunted hollow look his only reply.

"The doctor could give you something so you can rest. To help with the nightmares."

"Who said I have nightmares?"

She smiled, continuing her workout as she spoke. "You wouldn't be human if you didn't, not after what you've been through."

He gripped the chair edge. "I'm sure they'll fade with time."

"Probably." She gestured toward the bars. "But talking about them might help."

"So you're offering shrink services, too?"

Melissa hesitated, sensing his coiled emotions on the verge of exploding. "I'm not a shrink, just a friend."

"Friend?" A bitter-sounding laugh rumbled from his chest. "Well, honey, I've been short on those lately."

This time her head jerked up. It was the first time he'd called her anything but Miss Fagan.

As if he decided he'd made a huge faux pas, his mouth flattened into a tight line again, and he grabbed the bar to hoist himself up. Melissa reached out an arm to help him, but he pushed her hand away.

What the hell made him say a fool thing like that to his therapist? One minute she was suggesting he needed a shrink, the next minute he'd all but flirted with her. Eric Caldwell didn't know how to flirt anymore, or do anything but work.

Melissa Fagan felt sorry for him, nothing more.

How could she feel anything else when she saw his ugly body and touched his mangled flesh on a daily basis? When she of all people knew his limitations, that he was no longer a whole man?

As if to cement his feelings, the young candy striper watched from the corner, her gaze full of pity. Bitterness swelled inside him as he struggled to straighten his legs and put weight on them. He had to brace himself with his arms, the force causing his muscles to strain. Shoving any ideas of chitchat from his head, he ordered himself to focus. To concentrate on making his legs work the way they once had.

Until his body had forgotten.

They spent the next half hour in grueling silence, going through several reps of leg extensions and flexing exercises. Eric was tired of the tidbits of progress. He wanted to walk.

"You were in a hospital in Atlanta before this?" Melissa asked.

"Yes."

"What brought you all the way to Savannah for therapy? Atlanta has some great facilities."

"Yes, but the on-site living and ocean here appealed to me. Being confined to a hospital room was too suffocating."

Melissa smiled. "I understand the feeling. I get claustrophobic myself." She gestured for him to stop. "I think we can call it quits for today."

Eric glared at her. "No, not yet."

Melissa's gaze met his. "Remember my warning about not overdoing, Eric."

"I'm tired of this crap," Eric growled. "I want to do more. I *can* do more."

"No."

Anger fed him as he attempted to move his foot forward, but his leg refused to budge. Steeling his rage, he stared down at the appendage, willing it to move.

"Eric, you're exhausted, let's rest."

"No, damn it. I'm going to walk." Channeling every ounce of misery into determination, he pushed his foot a fraction of an inch, but his leg cramped and his knees buckled. He tried to catch himself before he went down, but his arms were shaking from the exertion, and he wound up landing on his butt, heaving for air. "Damn it, damn it, damn it." He scraped his hands through his hair, then grabbed his leg and rubbed the knotted muscle.

Melissa knelt, her soft hand on his back, angering him more. "Come on, you need to rest."

"Leave me alone." All his pent-up frustration snapped, exploding in jerky movements. He felt like a failure.

Melissa eased around in front of him, cradled his

calf between her hands and kneaded the muscle, applying pressure at the pinpoints of pain and smoothing them away. She had magic hands. He felt weak, relieved, indebted.

Out of the corner of his eye, he noticed the young candy striper's sympathetic look again. Still, he was helpless to refuse Melissa's ministrations. Worse, he despised himself for not wanting her to stop, for having to accept the role of victim when he had always been the one to lend help to the weaker.

"I might as well give up." He dropped his head forward, unable to believe he'd finally voiced his doubts.

Melissa's hands stilled. Her voice was quiet when she spoke, reassuring. "You will walk again, Eric, but you have to be patient."

"Patient?"

"Yes, you can't quit."

"Why not? It's been two weeks, and I still can't slide my foot a damn inch."

She gripped his hands in hers. "You are making progress, Eric. You can't expect damaged muscles to work without proper rest and retraining. Recovery is hard and slow, but time does heal things."

"How would you know?" His past with his family, the explosion, the cases with the women he'd worked with, all converged, blotting out any hope from the darkness. He felt as if he'd been thrown into a pit of endless gray and couldn't climb out. Ever.

She dropped her hands. "You're not the first patient I've worked with, nor will you be the last."

"That's right. I'm just a patient to you, nothing more." He fisted his hands. "You feel sorry for me—"

"I don't feel sorry for you, Eric. You've covered that yourself."

He knotted his fists. Her words hit home. Still, he was helpless to react, because all those lonely mornings of waking and wanting more from her than therapy flashed into his mind. God, he yearned to have her hands all over him, massaging more than his legs...

"I also know what it's like to overcome a physical problem," Melissa said so quietly he almost didn't hear her.

He flattened his hands in an effort to push himself up. He remembered the report from Devlin, but he couldn't believe she had medical issues. She was too beautiful, too tough, too compassionate and strong. Her condition must have been so minor, she'd overcome it long ago. "How can you possibly understand?"

"Because I have a seizure disorder," she said matter-of-factly.

His gaze met hers. For a brief second, he realized the pain in her confession.

"I'm not epileptic," Melissa said. "But occasionally I have mild seizures. I take medication for them daily." Her voice dropped to a thready whisper. "My condition has complicated my life."

Luke had mentioned that she'd been shuffled from one home to another, never been adopted. Eric had spent his entire life helping women in need, yet now he was taking his frustrations out on her.

Good God. He was no better than his father.

Shame replaced his anger. "I'm sorry. I..."

"Now you're feeling sorry for me." Her quick flash of temper was real. Eric had no idea how to rectify his blunder. He'd just insulted her by doing the very thing he'd accused her of, offering her pity.

"Now, let's get you off the floor."

He started to apologize, but her dark look warned

him to drop the subject. He gripped her arm and allowed her to help him stand.

"You want to try again?"

He nodded, more determined than ever.

The next few minutes, he forgot the darkness in his soul and his need for revenge as she murmured words of encouragement. Instead, he imagined stepping toward her, taking her in his arms and kissing those luscious pink lips. Finally, he managed to slide his foot forward a fraction of an inch.

"You did it!"

He glanced down and a ghost of a smile flitted on his mouth. Although the step had been minute, it gave him hope.

And he vowed not to unleash his rage on Melissa again.

Emotions ping-ponged in Melissa's chest as she finished her snack, the memory of Eric's first step still exhilarating her. He would progress much faster now—that one step would fuel his drive and confidence.

It was time she made progress with her own quest. She wrapped the crumbs of her snack in a paper towel and dabbed at her mouth. Nancy had hurried through her coffee to meet her boyfriend. Helen remained quiet, thumbing through a magazine. Two of the younger doctors breezed in for coffee. A third, a bone specialist, Steve Crayton, smiled at her.

"You're doing an excellent job, Miss Fagan. We're glad to have you on board."

"Thanks."

Although some of the other nurses found him attractive, something about his intense demeanor prickled at her nerves. Granted he was handsome, and well established for a man in his forties, but his eyes seemed too probing.

"I have surgery in a few minutes. I'll probably refer this patient to you afterward."

"Fine, let me know when you're ready for a consultation."

Hoping Helen would linger for a few minutes, Melissa hurried back to the center's office and slid up to the computer. Within seconds, she'd tapped into the main list of patient files, but couldn't gain access to the older records in the labor/delivery unit without a password. Hmm. She hated to be sneaky, but she had to have answers, so she searched through the drawer and found Helen's organizer. Helen had consulted it before, seemingly embarrassed that her memory sometimes failed her. She'd admitted she kept everything written down. Melissa scrolled down the list, located the woman's password and logged on. Several minutes later, she'd entered Candace Latone's name, along with the date of her own birth and had almost accessed the file, when a voice sounded behind her.

"What are you doing?"

Melissa froze. Helen's tone sounded cold. Suspicious.

Melissa scrambled for a lie, but decided to opt for the truth. She turned to her with imploring eyes. "I'm trying to find my birth parents," she said. "I know my mother's name. Maybe you remember her."

Helen's eyes darted around the room. "I can't remember every patient from years ago. And you have no right to sneak into my things. I should report you."

Melissa gave her a beseeching look. "Please don't, Helen. I wasn't trying to hurt anyone, just locate information on my mother. I have reason to believe a woman named Candace Latone gave birth to me here, and that she gave me up for adoption."

The woman's face blanched. "Candace Latone?"

"Yes. Apparently she was involved in some kind of research experiment." Melissa wondered exactly what type of experiment. "You knew her, didn't you?"

"I…" Helen's hand flew to her cheek, where she picked at a loose strand of hair. "I vaguely remember the name."

"What happened to her?" Melissa clutched Helen's hand. Had the scientist done something to hurt her? "Please tell me, I have to know."

"She wasn't quite right, you know…refused to leave Savannah." Her voice quavered. "I believe her family set her up in some kind of cabin nearby."

"Oh my gosh, you mean she's in Savannah? But I searched and didn't find any Latones."

"Her phone number may be unlisted. The last thing I heard she lived on the Isle of Hope."

"Do you know the address?" Melissa asked.

"No."

"Do you have any idea what kind of experiment she was involved in?"

"No. I wasn't aware she'd participated in anything like that." She fidgeted with her hands. "Rumor said she did drugs, that's what caused her mental instability."

Melissa frowned, then glanced up and noticed Nancy watching them. How much had she overheard? Nancy waved. "Your next patient is here, Melissa."

"Thanks, I'll be right there."

Helen closed the files, the conversation over. But excitement filled Melissa as she worked through the afternoon sessions. The minute she finished, she climbed in her car and drove toward the Isle of Hope. The name somehow fit the moment.

What would Candace Latone think when she showed up at her door, claiming to be her daughter?

After his afternoon session Eric had collapsed and dreamed about kissing Melissa. Long slow lazy kisses that had ended with them naked in his bed. Only he wasn't a scarred man, but the old Eric Caldwell, the confident man who protected others.

The dream still haunted him while he met with the plastic surgeon. Although he'd set up the consultation to discuss his own injuries, he had a secret agenda. Somehow, he had to gain access to the doctor's computer and locate files on Hughes. If he could verify that Hughes had resurfaced and locate a file with information regarding his new identity, catching him would be easier.

Dr. Crane greeted him with a handshake. "Nice to meet you, Mr. Collier. I've already reviewed your charts."

Eric nodded while Crane took a seat behind his massive desk. Eric's file was open, before-and-after photographs of his injured body spread out. Eric swallowed hard, reminding himself he looked better now than he had. At least the Atlanta doctors had repaired his face. They'd yet to complete skin grafts on his chest and left leg, though.

"You look like you're healing nicely."

Eric chuckled. "There's nothing nice about this body now."

The doctor ran long fingers through his thinning white hair. "It takes time."

"So everyone keeps telling me."

Crane nodded. "Are you satisfied with the face now,

or do you want more changes?" He stood and examined Eric, probing around his cheekbones and eyes, then lifted the scraggly hair that had grown back in patches around his forehead. A thin, jagged scar marred his hairline.

"I can take care of that."

Eric shrugged. "I'm more interested in repairing this." He lifted his T-shirt and indicated the most severe areas.

Crane studied the scarring. "We can take skin grafts and smooth over the skin. There'll be some residual scarring, but it'll look ten times more normal than now."

He nodded, and glanced at his watch just as the phone rang. Devlin was right on time. He was supposed to create a distraction to lure the doctor out of his office so Eric could search his computer.

"Yes." Crane angled his head to the earpiece. "My car is being towed? Whatever for?" He hesitated. "But I have an assigned spot." Another pause. "I can't believe they're repaving the parking lot during the week." He reached for his keys. "All right, I'll be right there." Crane slammed down the phone and stood. "This is ridiculous. Will you excuse me for a moment? I'll be right back."

Eric nodded. "I'd offer to move it for you, but hey, I brought my wheels with me."

The doctor's eyes narrowed, then an apologetic smile creased his lips. "Right, I shouldn't complain."

He rushed out the door, looking harried. Eric waited until the door closed, then wheeled around the desk and glanced at the computer.

He clicked on the keyboard to access patient files but footsteps quickly returned. Crane hadn't had time to walk downstairs. Damn it. Eric rolled back to the opposite side of the desk, pretending innocence when Crane strode back in.

"That was fast."

"I caught my assistant, had him move the car."

He should have known Crane wouldn't make it easy. He'd have to work on hacking into the system when he returned to his cabin.

An hour and a half later, Melissa was about to give up her search. She'd asked about Candace Latone at a local diner, at a craft shop and finally at a real estate agency, but the woman glared at her as if she suspected Melissa might be a stalker. Finally, Melissa drove up and down the island, checking mailboxes, but she didn't locate a single one labeled Latone. Her head was beginning to ache, and her muscles strained from fatigue. The gas gauge on her trusted Camry wobbled to the empty mark and she pulled off at a small gas station. Weary and fearing she'd hit a dead end, she filled the gas tank, then went into the station to pay. Two old-timers chewing tobacco played checkers behind the counter.

She rapped on the counter. "Excuse me, I need to pay. Fifteen dollars."

A gray-haired man ambled toward her, adjusting his wiry bifocals. "Thanks, hon."

Melissa nodded. "Listen, I'm looking for someone and wondered if you could help me."

"Do what I can. I know most people around here."

Early on, Melissa had fabricated a lie, that she was a long-lost friend of the Latone woman, but that hadn't worked. Maybe she'd invent another excuse. She introduced herself and learned the man's name was Homer Wilks. "I'm an insurance agent. I have a check for a woman named Candace Latone. For some reason, the printer blurred the address. Could you tell me where she lives?"

He scratched at the stubble on his chin. "Sure thing. Twenty-two Cypress Lane. Go past the bluff and turn left, can't miss it. She lives in a little cottage on the Wilmington River."

Melissa's heart fluttered. She thanked him, rushed to her car and drove toward the cottage. The island was fairly small, the lots filled with trees and well-tended flower beds, but as she veered onto Cypress, the beach cottages sprinkled along the streets appeared to be older and less kept. Palm trees swayed in the breeze, the telltale signs of age in the vacant weathered cabins for rent.

Seconds later, she stood at the doorway, inhaling the scents of the river and flowers on Candace's front porch, her courage waning as she imagined Candace Latone's reaction. What if she denied ever giving birth? What if she called the police?

Her pulse racing, she turned to leave, then pivoted around and faced the doorway. A strange thumping sound echoed from inside. Melissa paused and knocked again, waiting with bated breath. Another noise jarred her, like someone scrambling inside, then silence. She knocked again, tapping her foot up and down while she waited, her stomach jitterbugging as she scanned the cottage. Judging from the flower bed in front of the cottage and the row of tulips bordering the front lawn, her mother enjoyed gardening. What else did she like?

She knocked again, but still no answer. Had Candace Latone somehow discovered that she'd come looking for her and decided not to answer the door? Someone was definitely inside.

Melissa hadn't traveled this far to leave without a meeting.

Nerves jangling, she reached for the door and turned the knob. It twisted, and the door swung open, the torn screen slapping in the wind. The hair on the back of her neck prickled. Something didn't feel right. An odd odor permeated the air. A fishy smell—stale air? Blood?

A scent she recognized from old hospital rotations... death.

No, she was letting her imagination go crazy.

The air caught in her lungs. "Miss Latone? Are you here?" Darkness bathed the room, painting it in eerie shadows. The curtains covering the sliding-glass door hung open, the door stood ajar, the night breeze fluttering the sheers. Somewhere in the distance a bird cawed and another screeched in reply. "Is anybody home?"

She tiptoed past the tiny, dark kitchen nook, then around the corner. Her heart constricted. Dear God.

A frail-looking woman lay in a pool of blood on the floor, her eyes gaping open in deathly horror.

Chapter 4

When Eric returned to his cabin, he tried to access the hospital records, but stumbled on a roadblock with security. He'd have to ask Devlin if any of his contacts knew the system. Determined to learn all he could about the research facility, he logged on to the Internet and downloaded all the articles he could find on the companies housed at CIRP. He also earmarked any questionable government hot topics that might correlate between secretive projects on Nighthawk Island to see if he could uncover any possible nets that Hughes might hide beneath.

AIDS research and cloning topped the headlines, with news of successful animal cloning and the controversy over human cloning. Stem cell research was another controversial topic. And of course, chemical and germ warfare experiments.

He'd bet his last dollar the government was conducting biowarfare experiments on Nighthawk Island. Skimming the remainder of the articles, he noted some psychiatric studies under way as well: mind control, projects on treating autism, schizophrenia, bipolar disorder and various psychotic conditions. They had also experimented with a drug to enhance memory loss.

He'd been shocked when Devlin had described Denise Harley's Brainpower research. Of course, he'd read about genetic engineering in the news and shouldn't have been surprised at the scientist's efforts to expand it one step further and create the perfect child. Thankfully, Arnold Hughes would never learn that Simon, the baby Eric's brother and Alanna Hayes were raising as their own, was a product of the experiment *or* that Hughes had actually fathered the baby. If Hughes found out, he'd probably kidnap Simon from Alanna and his brother. Hughes was ruthless. There would be no witnesses left to tell the true story. Or to protect Simon.

He grimaced at the mere idea of using a child in an experiment. Couldn't parents accept their kids and love them for what they were? Did they have to have the perfect child?

Hell, your old man sure didn't think you were perfect.

Apparently, Melissa Fagan's hadn't, either. Had they given her up for adoption because of her seizure disorder, or for other reasons?

Melissa gasped, nausea rising to her throat at the sight of the woman's body. Was that Candace Latone? Had she finally located her mother, only to find her dead?

A trembling started deep within her. She had to get help, call someone.

She grabbed her cell phone. Her fingers shook as she dialed 911. "Hello...there's been a shooting."

"Ma'am, what's your name?"

"M-Melissa Fagan, hurry...there's blood, blood everywhere."

"Calm down, take a deep breath, I need an address. Tell me where you are."

Melissa's mind momentarily went blank. She staggered sideways, forcing her gaze away from Candace's bloody body. A sob built in her throat. There was no way the woman could still be alive....

"Ma'am? We need an address."

"Right...uh, Isle of Hope." What street was it? She couldn't think.

Wait. She'd been driving around. Tears dribbled down her cheeks. Her head was spinning. She'd stopped at the gas station...

Spying an envelope on the table, she flipped it over and read, "Candace Latone. Cypress Lane...22 Cypress Lane."

"We'll have an ambulance right there, ma'am. Are you hurt—"

The curtain fluttered. A footstep creaked on the floor behind her. Melissa swung around.

A shadow lunged toward her, then something slammed into her skull, and she fell into darkness.

Darkness fell early on the island, the gray cast covering the sky lowering the spring temperature and adding a chill that Eric found invigorating. Normally he enjoyed being alone, too, had found it peaceful to live in near isolation at the lake. Cain had called him moody.

Now those moods seemed even more acute.

Being alone simply felt lonely.

While he was recovering in the hospital, his brother had insisted the doctors send a counselor to talk to him, some pantywaist shrink who'd encouraged him to express his feelings and deal with residual anger from his youth and his accident. Eric had dismissed the man without even blinking, the black hole of despair dragging him into its clutches.

At the time, his life hadn't meant much to him.

Melissa Fagan's sultry smile floated in his mind, and his gut pinched.

Kissing her—now that would be living.

But he wouldn't be kissing her or doing anything else with her but therapy. Even if his scars didn't repulse her, which they probably would if he made an advance, he couldn't afford to get involved now. If he located Hughes, whoever was near him would be in danger.

He had a new purpose in life—a mission more personal than others, because Hughes had almost killed Eric and his brother.

He grunted and turned on the TV to distract himself. He'd never been much of a couch potato, and had grown even more restless with the mindless crap on the tube while he'd been forced to convalesce. But he kept up with the news.

"Ladies and gentlemen, we bring you this late-breaking story live."

Eric sat up straighter, eyes narrowing at the scene.

"Earlier this evening, a woman identified as Candace Latone was shot to death in her cottage on Isle of Hope." The camera panned the outside of the cottage, showing flowers and a neatly kept yard with an ambulance sitting in the driveway, its lights twirling. Police cars were parked at odd angles in the yard, a half-dozen spectators gathered. "Police are investigating the crime as we speak. A young woman discovered Miss Latone's body, although reports state that she did not see the killer. She was attacked from behind and suffered a mild concussion."

The camera zeroed in on the paramedics hauling a body bag from the scene, then swept to a gurney near the ambulance where paramedics attended the woman who'd found the body. Eric gripped the arms of his wheelchair, his heart pounding.

The woman was Melissa Fagan.

Melissa's head ached from the questions.

Detective Adam Black knelt beside her. A tough-looking female cop named Bernstein stood beside Black, eyeing Melissa as if she had murdered Candace Latone herself.

"Did you see anything?" Detective Black asked.

"No. The curtain fluttered, then I heard footsteps and someone attacked me from behind." She wrapped the blanket tighter around her shoulders.

"Was Miss Latone still alive when you arrived?" Bernstein asked.

"No... I don't think so." Visions of the splattered blood played before her, and she squeezed her eyes shut to block the images. "There was so much blood, and her eyes...they were wide open."

"Did you touch her?" Detective Black asked.

"No. I was in shock. Then I remember thinking I had to get help, and I reached for my phone."

"Did you touch anything else?" Black asked.

She strained to remember. "Just the door coming in. And...the floor when I fell. I think I hit the end table."

"Yes, with your head," he said gently. "You'll probably have a whopper headache for a while."

Melissa nodded. The police had taken photographs, the M.E. had completed a brief exam, and they'd carried Candace Latone's body to the ambulance. Her mother... or was she? Melissa hadn't even gotten to speak to her, to ask her the truth....

Detective Bernstein's voice turned cold. "What exactly was your relationship to Miss Latone?"

Startled, Melissa glanced away. The lights twirled against the dark sky. Voices hummed in the background. Neighbors had gathered to gawk and speculate. The old man from the gas station who'd given her directions stared at her through squinted eyes.

She cleared her throat, realizing she did look suspicious, and not liking it. "We didn't have one."

"You'd never met?" Bernstein asked.

"No."

Her dark eyebrows rose. "So, what were you doing here?"

Tears welled in Melissa's throat again, but she swallowed them, determined not to cry for a woman who'd abandoned her. But how should she answer the question?

The insurance story trembled on the tip of her tongue, but she couldn't lie to the police. A lie would only incriminate her more.

"Miss Fagan, what were you doing here?" Detective Black asked more gently.

She glanced up, willing them to understand. "I came to meet her. I...had reason to believe she was my m-mother."

Bernstein had been jotting notes in her notepad, but she paused. "Really? How interesting."

Melissa bit her lip, tasting blood and feeling sicker to her stomach by the minute. "I was born here in Savannah, but I was abandoned as a baby. A few months ago, I hired a private investigator to locate my birth parents."

"And he led you here?" Black asked.

"Yes."

Bernstein picked up the questioning. "Had you spoken with Miss Latone on the phone?"

"No."

"She wasn't expecting you?" Bernstein asked, her voice clipped.

"No." Melissa frowned. "At least I don't see how she could. I haven't confided my reasons for coming to Savannah to anyone." Except for Helen.

"How did you find Miss Latone's address?" Bernstein asked.

"A...nurse at the rehab center mentioned that Candace lived on the island. I stopped at the gas station for directions."

Bernstein clicked her pen, in and out, in and out. "Did you tell anyone that you thought Miss Latone was your mother?"

Melissa hesitated, the clicking sound grating on her nerves. "Actually, I did tell the nurse."

The clicking paused. "I thought you said you hadn't confided in anyone."

Melissa shrugged, growing dizzy from the inquisition. "I forgot."

Bernstein's incessant pen clicking began again. "What about the man at the gas station?"

She twisted the edges of the blanket, pulling it tighter as if the fabric could protect her from reality. "I... I said I was an insurance agent, that I came to give Candace a check."

Bernstein smirked. "So, you lied?"

Melissa glanced at the other cop for help, but his expression remained unreadable. "Yes, but…"

"If you lied then, why should we believe you now?"

Her temper flared. "You think I would walk into a woman's house, murder her, then stick around? I'd have to be pretty stupid to do that, wouldn't I, Detective Bernstein?"

"Maybe that was the plan. You thought your story would throw suspicion off of yourself."

They thought she was a cold-blooded killer?

"Young girl, abandoned as a baby, waited all these years to find her mother, then—" Bernstein snapped her fingers for emphasis "—wham, she confronts her, the woman denies she's her mother, and the girl loses her temper."

"That's not true."

Bernstein pushed her face toward Melissa, crowding her. "Maybe she ordered you to get lost, claimed she didn't want you then, and she didn't want you now."

"No, that's not what happened," Melissa cried.

"Why should we believe you?"

"Because I didn't kill her," Melissa said, hysteria rising. "I came here to talk to her, to meet her, that's all. I don't even own a gun."

"That can be checked out." Detective Black held up a warning hand when Bernstein started to pounce on her again. "Miss Fagan, where are you staying?"

"I work at the rehabilitation clinic at CIRP. I live in one of the employee cottages."

The odd look that flashed into Detective Black's eyes surprised her. "You're working at CIRP?"

"Yes. But I've only been there a few weeks." She clutched his arm. "Detective, is there any way you can keep my reasons for being here confidential? I don't want everyone to know that I thought Candace was my mother."

Bernstein resumed the pen clicking. "I doubt that, Miss Fagan. You've just given us a motive for murdering Miss Latone."

Eric's nerves were strung tight as he watched the remainder of the news. He recognized two of the cops on the scene, Detective Adam Black and Clayton Fox. Both had been involved with the investigation into CIRP. Black was partly responsible for uncovering the former CEO, Sol Santenelli and Arnold Hughes's original deception.

He had to see if Melissa was okay.

Outside, a spring breeze fluttered the tops of the palm trees and brought the scent of the ocean, along with a fine spray of salty water that brushed his face. He passed three cottages, then approached Melissa's and circled around to the front. He parked beneath the cluster of trees near her entrance and studied the constellations while he waited on her. When he was little, he'd enjoyed watching the stars, but his father had called him a sissy and had broken his telescope in one of his rages. Eric had given up star watching and childish dreams and turned serious.

Now he had to forget dreaming and focus on reality.

Silence hung in the thick, humid air. The ocean tides broke and crashed on the shore. Finally, a car engine cut into the tension, and Melissa's Camry roared up and screeched to a stop. She flicked off the headlights, then opened the car door, her face pale beneath the quarter moon. His gut clenched when he noticed the bruise on her forehead. She seemed unsteady as she walked up the pathway to the door.

"Melissa?"

She startled and jumped back, wide-eyed.

He silently cursed himself for scaring her. "I'm sorry, I didn't mean to frighten you."

She heaved a shaky breath, then fanned her face. "Eric, what are you doing here?"

"I saw the news." He steered the chair toward her. "Are you all right?"

Tears welled in her eyes. He wanted to reach out and touch her. But she stood a foot above him, and he was helpless to do anything but study her. "They said you were assaulted. Are you okay?"

She fumbled in her purse for her keys. "Yes… actually, no, I'm kind of shaken up." The keys rat- tled in her hands. She dropped them, picked them up and wrestled to insert the key in the door, but her hands were trembling so badly she couldn't manage the task.

He rolled forward and gently took them from her hands. "Here, let me help."

She relented, brushing a strand of hair from her face. He reached for the knob, but the door swung open. "You didn't lock it?"

Panic lit her eyes. "Yes… I did."

Protective instincts surfaced. He motioned for her to wait outside. "I'll check it out."

Melissa grabbed the back of his chair. "No, Eric, you can't go inside."

His jaw snapped tight as he realized her implication. *You're crippled. Helpless. How could you protect me when you can't even walk without assistance?*

Rage exploded inside him. If he couldn't protect a woman, what good was he?

"I said wait here." He hurled the chair forward, pausing to listen for intruders.

* * *

"Damn it, did you have to kill Candace Latone?" He tugged at his chin in agitation, screwed off the cap to his blood pressure medicine and downed a pill. He'd worked so hard all these years, things couldn't spiral out of control now.

The repercussions from Robert Latone would be harsh.

The other man wheezed over the line. "We can't take any chances. That Fagan woman is here, snooping into things."

"How much does she know?"

"I'm not sure. But she believes Candace was her mother."

"What? This is unreal." He raked a hand across his polished mahogany desk, sending papers scattering. Had Latone lied to him?

"Some Atlanta P.I. gave her Candace's name. He was investigating the research being done back then, too."

"What else does he know?"

"Don't worry about him, he's history."

"Make sure there's no connection." God, what a mess. "And don't get murder happy. The Feds are breathing down our necks already. We can't afford to bring any more suspicion to the center."

"Right. So, you want me to off the Fagan woman?"

"No. Not yet. Just watch her, and find out what she wants."

"And keep her from digging up secrets?"

"Exactly. I don't like her talking to those cops Black and Fox."

"Hey, they suspect she killed Candace. Maybe they'll take care of her for us, lock her up." He chuckled. "If not, maybe Candace's murder will scare her away."

He slammed down the phone. Maybe so.

But if not, well, he'd do whatever he had to do to protect the past.

But he had to wonder—had Latone lied to him?

If so, he'd be sorry....

Chapter 5

Melissa hesitated at the doorway. Even in her disoriented state, she'd insulted Eric Collier's male pride. Yet how could she allow him to enter a potentially threatening situation in his weakened condition, especially to protect her?

Even more unsettling, had someone been inside her cottage? And if so, why?

After the scene at Candace Latone's house, her imagination was running rampant, every horror movie she'd ever seen flitting into her mind. She removed her cell phone from her purse, ready to dial 911, then glanced in the corner, grabbed her umbrella for protection and tiptoed into the cabin. Eric had not bothered to turn on the light. He wheeled into the small den, glancing around the darkened interior, his movements deathly quiet for a man in a wheelchair. Her heartbeat thumped wildly in her chest as she inched up behind him.

He gestured toward the bedroom. His cabin must have been built on a similar plan, because he seemed to know the layout. The kitchen and dining nooks were connected to the small living room, creating an open space, with one bedroom and bath to the side.

She studied the room for anything amiss, and frowned. She hadn't brought very many personal things with her, and hadn't added a single item to make the place homey, choosing to keep the furniture that had come with the cottage. Not that she had any personal family photographs or collectibles to cart around, a sad testament to her lonely existence.

Besides, she'd intended to stay only long enough to get some answers.

Eric pointed to the desk in the corner near the sliding glass doors, and she noticed the drawer ajar. A few of her notes were scattered on the floor, the various files she'd collected from the private investigator tousled through as if someone had searched them.

Her pulse clamored. Someone *had* been here. But why would they be interested in her files?

Because they know why you're in Savannah, and they don't want you to learn the truth....

Dear Jesus. The answer hit her with the force of a fist, nearly robbing her breath. She clutched the wall for support. Eric caught her arm and motioned for her to leave, but she shook her head. He exhaled, then rolled into the bedroom doorway.

She stood behind him, eyeing the room. The navy comforter on the oak bed had been stripped, the closet door open, the meager contents of her wardrobe shuffled as if someone had scavenged through them. But whoever had broken in had already left.

Remembering the tiny handmade bonnet her mother

had left her, she raced past Eric to the nightstand where she kept it and threw open the drawer. The lid on the box had shifted. Relief spilled through her at the sight of the small cap. She pressed it to her cheek, the scent of the worn thread and baby softness reminding her of its preciousness.

Eric's hand gently touched hers. "Someone was in here."

She jerked her head up. "I know."

"Do you have any idea why?"

Candace Latone's bloody body flashed into her head. Even if Melissa hadn't shot the gun that had killed Candace, had her quest for the truth about her past caused her mother's death?

What kind of Pandora's box had she opened?

Eric realized Melissa saw him as handicapped, but he couldn't tolerate the fear in her pale green eyes or the pain etched on her beautiful face.

He had always been a sucker for a woman in trouble, and although Melissa was tougher than the abused women he'd helped in the past, she was definitely in trouble. At least he could be a friend to her.

She slumped down onto the bed.

He moved the chair closer to her, then tipped her chin up in his palm. "Melissa, talk to me. What's going on?"

She bit down on her lip, then squeezed the crocheted bonnet. "This...it's the only thing I have from my mother."

His gut pinched. Unable to admit he knew she'd been abandoned, he nodded, silently coaching her to continue.

"She dropped me off on the steps of a church when I was only a baby."

"And she left that cap with you?"

A small smile softened the tight lines of her mouth. "Silly for me to keep it, isn't it?"

Eric shook his head and gestured toward his gold cross. "My mother gave me this for my thirteenth birthday. She died not long after."

Melissa smiled, reached out and touched the cross.

He'd also kept the storybook his mother had read to him as a kid, *The Little Engine That Could*. God, how he'd loved that book, how he'd wanted to be that heroic little engine and carry his mother away from her mountain of troubles. But he'd failed and his mother had died.

He couldn't fail Melissa now.

"The woman that was murdered, was she your mother?" he asked quietly.

A small gasp escaped her. "How did you know?"

He shrugged. "Just putting two and two together."

She lowered her head again, a wealth of sadness in the movement. "I didn't even get to talk to her, to ask her." Her lower lip trembled. "She was d-dead when I arrived."

The tears overflowed then, gut-wrenching and honest. Eric had no choice. He pulled her into his arms and held her. Two lost souls clinging together as one for the moment.

"The police think I killed her." The admission gushed out, and Eric rocked her back and forth, soothing her with nonsensical words.

"They'll investigate, find out the truth." He stroked her hair, inhaling the sweet gardenlike fragrance of her shampoo.

"But what if they don't?" She raised her head, tears streaking her already pale cheeks. "And what if I am responsible?"

His chest ached for her. "You're not responsible."

She shook her head, her eyes wild with panic. "But what if I am? Do you really think it's a coincidence that she's lived here all this time, and the day I show up at her door, she's murdered?" She clutched his hands. "No wonder the police think I killed her."

He cupped her face in his hands, stroking his thumbs along her cheeks. "Shh. Everything's going to be all right."

"But how can it be?" she cried. "I came here looking for her. She died because of me."

"You can't be certain of that, Melissa."

"What other explanation could there be?" Her nails dug into his hands. "Just look around, Eric, someone broke in here and searched through the notes I'd gathered from the private investigator I hired. They wanted to see how much I knew about my mother."

"Maybe," he admitted. "I'm calling Seaside Security, Melissa, to tell them about the break-in. They'll change your locks."

"You think whoever broke in might come back?"

"It's possible, if they didn't find what they wanted tonight." She was shivering when he hung up. Eric pulled her into his arms again, stroking her hair and trying to soothe her.

Her deduction about the Latone woman's murder made sense. If the murderer thought Melissa had uncovered information that might expose him, she was definitely in danger herself.

And why had Candace Latone been murdered? Because of Melissa, or because Candace had been involved in some kind of experiment at the center? What kind of experiment? But why would someone come after her now, years later?

Had she been silenced because she knew something about Melissa's birth that would disrupt the lives of her blood relatives—maybe Melissa's father?

Melissa savored the feel of Eric's comforting arms, and for a brief few moments leaned into the hard wall of his chest. Closing her eyes, she blocked the images of Candace's eyes bulging in horror and the image of the hole in her chest. Though snatches of the red refused to fade, she inhaled, breathing in the menthol scent of Eric's aftershave and his masculine presence. She had been alone for so very long, had never had a father or any man to shelter her from the horrors of her own nightmarish past.

Unfortunately the nightmare had continued.

Could Eric really understand her feelings? How abandoned and alone she'd been all her life? He carried scars from the accident, but the man still emanated strength.

His arms tightened around her, and she felt a kiss brush her hair. Her stomach fluttered.

Then she angled her head to look up at him and saw a flicker of hunger in his dark brown eyes. Their gazes locked, and an attraction she could no longer deny obliterated the horror of the evening.

As if Eric read her mind, he caressed her cheek with his thumb, then slowly lowered his head a fraction of an inch. She could almost taste his desire, yet he paused as if seeking permission. Swept away by the moment and the feel of his thumb tantalizing her skin, she cupped his jaw in her hand and pulled him toward her. His lips touched hers with such gentle sweetness that she felt something deep inside her tug. Heat radiated through her, unleashing emotions she had never experienced.

The other men in her life had been aggressive. Cold. Had pushed for things she hadn't been ready to give.

Eric, on the other hand, ignited such a yearning in her that she craved more.

He deepened the kiss, and she succumbed, tasting his masculinity as he teased her lips apart and slipped his tongue inside. He threaded his fingers into her hair and she nibbled at his mouth. But the arms of his wheelchair cut into her side, bringing her back to reality.

She had always been alone, had never relied on anyone. She didn't know how to do so now.

Besides, Eric was a patient. Her job mandated she help him, not take advantage of his kindness.

And what about maintaining a professional relationship?

She ended the kiss slowly, the low moan he emitted making it more painful to pull away. She couldn't be his therapist and get involved with him. He was vulnerable, needy right now.

Besides, she had caused one woman's death. What if the killer came looking for her? She might unwillingly endanger Eric.

Summoning every vestige of restraint she possessed, she released him and stood, then walked to the bedroom doorway. "You'd better go, Eric."

He hesitated. "If that's what you want."

No, it wasn't what she wanted, but it had to be. "Yes, please. I...that shouldn't have happened."

The chair creaked across the floor toward her. Then he was beside her, looking up at her with passion-glazed eyes. And something else—a shadow of vulnerability.

"Because I'm like this?" Anger hardened his voice as he gestured down at his battered legs.

"Partly."

Hurt shadowed his face, a self-deprecating laugh following. "At least you're honest."

"Don't take it the wrong way, Eric." For goodness' sake, would she have allowed him to kiss her like that if she wasn't attracted to him? She hated to cause him further pain, but he had to understand they couldn't indulge in a relationship that had no future. She might be leaving soon, and when he learned to walk again, he would return to his life. "I'm supposed to be a professional, Eric." She inhaled sharply. "But if you want, I can get another therapist assigned to you."

"I don't want another therapist, Melissa. I want you."

A tingle traveled up her spine at his husky voice. But the security agency arrived, preventing any further discussion. Eric explained what had happened, then he took one last look at her and wheeled across the room. "Lock the doors. And call me if you need anything." Then he disappeared into the night, the sound of his wheelchair creaking across the pavement.

She pressed her fingers to her mouth, trying to get a grip so she could talk to the police. His parting words were imprinted in her brain just as his kiss had been imprinted on her lips.

Why had she met him now when they couldn't possibly have a relationship...?

Eric cursed himself the entire way back to his cottage. He shouldn't have kissed Melissa, shouldn't have taken advantage of the situation. Just because he was needy, and it had been forever since he'd touched a woman, and he had irrational, lustful thoughts of his therapist, didn't mean she viewed him in a sexual way.

He glared at his battered legs, a visible reminder of how little he had to offer.

Melissa Fagan was a beautiful woman. A whole woman who needed a whole man.

And even when he could walk, he hadn't been whole.

She'd been alone all her life. She certainly deserved to have a man who could give her everything, his body, his soul and a bright future.

Eric had lost all three.

Wheeling into his room, he still couldn't shake the worry. She had found a dead woman tonight, a woman she believed was her mother. Then someone had broken into her place.

Someone who knew she'd been searching for her parents.

But why kill Candace Latone?

He watched the evening news, but the police offered no more details on the Latone murder than they had earlier, although the camera panned to a live interview. Thankfully, they didn't mention the break-in at Melissa's.

"Mr. Latone," the reporter said. "I know you must be shocked to hear of your daughter's death."

"I'm devastated. She was my only child." Latone raised his chin, anger gleaming in the depths of his pain-filled eyes. "And I will make sure that whoever killed my daughter pays. Now—" his voice broke "—I'd like to be alone."

He hurried toward his limousine, and the camera zoomed back to the reporter. "That was Robert Latone, a foreign diplomat for the U.S. government, whose daughter was murdered tonight. If you have any information that might lead to the killer, phone your local police."

Eric frowned as he watched the limousine drive away. If Candace Latone was Melissa's mother, then

Robert Latone was her grandfather. Had he known about Melissa?

He phoned Luke Devlin. "It's Eric. What do you know about the Latone woman's murder?"

"Why are you interested?"

"Melissa Fagan, the woman who found the body, thinks Candace Latone was her birth mother."

A heartbeat of silence passed. "I see."

"Someone also broke into Melissa Fagan's cottage and searched through the files from the P.I."

"Interesting. Did she mention anything about her birth father?"

"No. But she blames herself for the Latone woman's death. And apparently, at least one of the cops who questioned her suspects she killed Candace."

"She does have motive."

"She's not a killer."

Devlin hissed into the silence. "Don't get involved with her, Eric. She might be a bigger part of this whole case than we thought."

"What do you mean? Is there something you're not telling me?"

Another hesitation. "No, but the coincidences are too strong. Anyone who knew Hughes or was at the center when he was employed has to be treated with suspicion. And Candace Latone's father, Jack Latone, has donated money to CIRP."

"Melissa didn't kill Candace Latone," Eric said again. "But she might be in danger."

"Right. Or she might be lying. Don't let a pretty face sucker punch you." Devlin whistled. "Use her, warm up to her, maybe she can help you gain access to the computer security system so we can hack into restricted files."

The idea of using Melissa sent a sour taste to Eric's mouth.

Devlin continued, oblivious, "I'll apprise the locals, Detectives Black and Fox, of the situation, and fill them in on your undercover role at CIRP. They both have vested interests in locating Hughes. Perhaps they'll know if there's a connection between Hughes and Candace Latone or her father."

"Right. And maybe Black and Fox will find evidence of the real killer," Eric added.

And something to exonerate Melissa.

Melissa checked the locks on the small cottage a half-dozen times. The headache that had been threatening all night had grown in intensity since Eric had left. She felt at least marginally safe while he'd been with her, but alone, the shadows screamed at her with self-incriminations, and flashes of blood red appeared before her eyes.

She needed sleep or she might have a seizure.

Restless, she swallowed one of the prescription pills the doctor had given her to help her relax at the onslaught of an episode, praying it would knock her out. Adding a cup of hot tea to the routine, she settled down in bed with a copy of a medical journal, hoping the newest techniques in rehabilitation for shoulder injuries might calm her.

But the words blurred on the page, and Eric's last comment reverberated in her mind.

When he had said he wanted her, had he meant as his therapist or did he mean he wanted *her*?

It doesn't matter. He's a patient. You cannot get involved with him. And if you did, and he was hurt, you'd never forgive yourself.

It's bad enough your search caused your mother's death....

The phone trilled, jarring her from the suffocating guilt. Half hoping it was Eric, but worried it might be that burly cop who'd all but accused her of killing Candace, she hesitated before answering. "Hello."

"Miss Fagan?"

The voice sounded muffled, distant. Not Eric. Maybe the cop?

"Yes? Who is this?"

"If you don't want to end up like Candace Latone, you'd better stop snooping around and leave town."

Melissa gasped. "Who is this?"

The phone clicked in response, then the line went dead, the beep of the dial tone blaring into the night.

Chapter 6

Eric woke feeling agitated, but eager for therapy.

Or maybe he was eager to see his therapist.

He dismissed the thought, reminding himself he had taken a step the day before. Today he would take another and another until he was free of that damn chair, and he could walk on his own two feet. His mobility meant he was closer to independence. To claiming back his life. To answers. To Hughes.

And to being able to protect Melissa.

After breakfast, he called Cain, as promised, to relay his progress. Cain was ecstatic.

"I never doubted you'd recover," Cain said. "But I hate that you've had to go through all this."

"How's Alanna and the baby?"

"Great. You should hear Simon, he's only a few months old and babbling like a toddler."

Eric laughed, his first true one in weeks. They had

suspected Simon had superior intelligence due to the experiment. It must be true.

"How about you, man? I know the therapy's tough."

Eric shrugged it off, and relayed the events about the Latone murder and Melissa.

"Keep your eyes and ears peeled," Cain said. "Devlin could be right. Melissa Fagan might be a trap."

"She's not," Eric said emphatically. "But I'll stay on my toes."

A tense silence stretched between them, but Eric chuckled. "It was a joke, bro. I'm really all right."

Cain sighed, still sounding worried, but Eric told him to kiss his new wife and baby for him, then hung up and headed to the rehab center. As soon as he spotted Melissa inside, his adrenaline kicked in, along with worry and a tingly sensation that he recognized as arousal. He hadn't experienced the feeling in such a long time, he'd almost forgotten how all-powerful sexual attraction could be.

He not only found Melissa physically desirable, but he admired her strength and tenacity in overcoming her own disability, and her pursuit of the truth about her ugly past.

There was no way she could have murdered Candace Latone.

A young woman who'd been alone all her life, who'd come seeking the truth about her mother, wouldn't have killed her only known parent without giving her the opportunity to forge a relationship.

But what if the Latone woman had flatly denied she was Melissa's mother? What if she'd denied wanting any part of her? Could she have driven Melissa to desperation?

Had he been snowed by the shadows of old hurts in her eyes?

No...

The cops had obviously jumped on that train of thought, looking for the easiest person to collar for the crime instead of delving deeper for a killer in disguise. He understood the art of deception.

He was a fake himself.

He couldn't even reveal his real name, or offer to help Melissa with the police. And he couldn't jeopardize the case by getting so sidetracked with her problems or his lust for her that he forgot the mission.

Could the two be connected in any way?

He had tossed the idea back and forth all night. As he approached Melissa, he channeled his energy into his physical regimen.

His job, his life, Melissa's life, might depend on his recovery.

Melissa hadn't slept at all the night before. The threatening phone call had played over and over in her mind, as had the images of Candace's dead body and the guilt that she had caused her own mother's death. And even when she'd reported the call, she'd sensed the police hadn't believed her.

If you don't want to end up like Candace Latone, you'd better stop snooping around and leave town.

She wasn't leaving. But what would she do if the killer attacked her? What didn't he want her to find? Her father?

Helen practically accosted her when she arrived. The nurse had watched the news and felt horrible, as if she thought she might be responsible for leading Melissa to Candace's house to kill her. Melissa had assured Helen that she wasn't a murderer, that she had desperately wanted to meet the woman who'd given her life and was crushed over being deprived of the opportunity.

"Good morning, Melissa."

She said goodbye to her other patient and turned toward Eric, bracing herself against a reaction. Memories of the kiss they'd shared the night before lingered in her mind.

From the way his dark eyes raked over her, he hadn't forgotten, either.

"Are you ready to get started?"

"Yes."

She nodded and they fell into their warm-up routine. More patients came in, working with Helen and two other therapists, while Nancy assisted. Melissa let the sight and sounds of the others distract her from indulging her fantasies of Eric, at the same time warning Eric not to overdo the workout. The small step the day before had fueled his determination and physical strength.

He was far more resilient and tougher than any of her former patients. Or any of the previous men in her life.

The night before, he'd been tender. Gentle. Understanding. He even knew about her condition and hadn't gone running....

He's not in your life, he's your patient.

Besides, what did she really know about the man and his former life? His chart stated that he owned a ranch in the North Georgia mountains, but he never spoke about it. And he didn't look like a rancher....

Questions and doubts assailed her as she coaxed him through the warm-up routine, punishing stretches and pressure exercises. When he gripped the bars, the veins in his arms bulged as they shook with the effort to stand

and move his feet forward, and she had to tear her eyes from his sexy physique.

Finally, after taking several steps on his own, Melissa insisted he rest. "You can try again later if you want, but you don't want to have a setback, do you?"

His mouth tightened. "No."

She patted his arm, aware the muscle flexed beneath her touch. "You worked hard today, you're making progress. You'll be walking with a cane in no time."

A long sigh escaped him, pent with frustration and acceptance. "You look tired. You didn't sleep?"

Odd, how she'd commented the same thing to him on several occasions. "I couldn't stop thinking about Candace."

Eric settled into his wheelchair and swiped at perspiration on his forehead. "And the intruder?"

She nodded, avoiding his eyes. "Are you ready for the whirlpool?"

Hoping to avoid any more questions, she stepped aside so he could wheel his way over, but he caught her hand. "Did something else happen last night, Melissa?"

Her fingers curled into a fist. "I…no."

"You're a terrible liar," he said in a low, almost intimate voice. "What is it?"

She bit down on her lip, remembering the sweet serenity of Eric's mouth upon hers. Heaven help her, but she craved that comfort again, that closeness.

"Tell me, Melissa."

"I…received a phone call."

"From whom?"

She shrugged, the fine hairs on the back of her neck prickling. "I don't know."

"What did the caller say, Melissa?"

She swallowed bile at the thought of the man's husky

threat. "He warned me to stop snooping around and leave town or else."

His dark eyes bored into hers. "Or else what?"

"Or else I'd end up like Candace."

A steely rage hardened Eric's mouth. Melissa had masked her fear with a brave face, but terror haunted her eyes. "Did you call the police?'

"Yes, but I'm not sure they believed me."

"What are you going to do?"

She tucked a strand of hair back into her ponytail. "I'm not running."

"Maybe you should."

She gestured toward the whirlpool. "I can't leave now, not without knowing who killed my mother and why."

"Let the police handle it, Melissa. You don't under-stand what you're up against." Or maybe she didn't care. He saw the desolation in her eyes and realized it was going to cause her to act recklessly.

"It's not your problem, Eric." She gripped his arm to help him stand, but he shook her hand away. "You need to focus on getting better. I can take care of my own problems."

He grabbed her hand. "What are you planning to do?"

She shrugged. "I told you it's not your problem."

"I'm making it my problem," he said in a deep voice. "Now, tell me your plans."

"I thought about going to Candace's father, but then he might not know Candace had a baby."

"True."

A moment's hesitation lapsed between them, then she finally replied, "I'd like to look inside Candace's house. Maybe there's something there that will give me insight into her life."

"And your own?"

"Yes…" She looked away. "I have to know about her family, the reason she gave me away. About my father."

The real reason she couldn't leave. Her need to investigate her parentage had driven her this far. It was an obsession that would keep driving her.

But would it drive her straight into her own grave?

Melissa checked her watch. "Now, Eric, relax in the whirlpool. I have another patient to see."

He glanced at the door and noticed a man in his midfifties wheeling toward her. The young candy striper had commented that the patient was a war vet who'd lost his leg to diabetes. Melissa was helping him learn to adjust to the prosthetic leg.

But Eric couldn't let her leave yet. "Promise me one thing."

"What?" She folded her arms across her chest, and he remembered the feel of her against his body. His sex hardened, began to ache. The sensations spurred his determination to walk even more. Her gaze caught his sudden arousal, and she shifted, ignoring his reaction, while he lowered himself into the water.

"Promise me that you won't go to the Latone woman's house by yourself."

"Eric—"

"Promise me," he insisted. "It's too dangerous, Melissa." He trapped her with his eyes. "Besides, if the police find you snooping alone, they might think you've returned to the scene of the crime to hide something from them."

He saw her waver, realize he was right. She finally

nodded, although her frown spoke volumes. "I'll see if Helen will ride out there with me."

"No. I'll go."

"Eric—"

"Don't insult me again by suggesting that I might not be able to help because I'm in this chair."

She opened her mouth to argue, but her next patient rolled toward her and prevented her reply.

Guilt niggled at Eric for misleading Melissa. He wanted to accompany her to protect her, but he also needed to wheedle any information out of her he could. If Candace Latone had been connected to CIRP or Hughes in any way, the connection might be hidden somewhere in the past she'd so obviously tried to bury.

How Melissa played into that was anybody's guess, but a few possibilities raced through his mind, none of which he hoped were true. All of which might prove dangerous to her.

By tagging along with her, he could ensure her safety and explore those possibilities.

His chat with Fox had proved enlightening, as well. Fox relayed the details of the memory transplant experiment the doctors had performed on him, and suggested that the center was working on other experimental brainwashing techniques, possibly in conjunction with the government. He suspected a contact in the FBI was overseeing the project with the intentions of using the techniques in warfare.

A very likely probability, Eric thought. But what exactly did the experiments entail?

He ate an early dinner at the cafeteria where he noticed Ian Hall, the new CEO, eating with Wallace

Thacker, the chemist who'd recently come on board at CIRP. One of the men might be Hughes. But which one?

So far Ian Hall had remained low-key, avoiding the press and extra media attention. He'd held one press conference that stated his mission for CIRP was to expunge the negative publicity surrounding the center and build it into the greatest research facility in the world. The reason he'd brought in Thacker. More renowned scientists from around the world would follow. A bone specialist named Steve Crayton had also been hired, but his age and body build didn't fit Hughes's profile.

Melissa met him just as he finished his coffee. "I'm going now."

"Don't you want to eat first?"

She flattened a hand over her stomach. "I'm not hungry. I'll grab something later."

He trailed her to the door.

"Eric, are you sure about this?"

He nodded. Hall was watching them, so Eric made a mental note to talk to the man the next day.

Melissa walked to the passenger side of her Camry and started to open the door, but he shook her hand off. "I can do it myself."

A small smile played on her mouth. "All right."

Using his upper-body strength, he hauled himself over to the seat, reached out and began to fold the chair. Melissa stood watching patiently, then stored it in the trunk of the car.

Leaving the confines of the center and the chair invigorated him. He almost felt normal. As if he was a man on a date with a beautiful woman for the night.

Until they turned onto the street leading to Candace Latone's house, and he saw the yellow crime-scene tape enveloping the house. Melissa's harsh intake of breath cemented reality.

This was not a date for either of them. He was on a mission, and she had come to learn about the woman who'd abandoned her shortly after her birth.

He couldn't forget it, either.

Nerves fluttered in Melissa's stomach as she parked the car and handed Eric the wheelchair. Thankfully, Candace's small cottage had been built on flat ground, eliminating the need for steps. Even though Eric was in a wheelchair, she felt safer simply having him along.

The man's voice from the phone call the night before echoed in her mind.

She would not allow him to scare her. And if her mother had been killed because of Melissa's search, she wanted the killer caught.

The sound of the ocean breaking on the shore filled the night, along with the scent of the marsh and Candace's flowers. Eric followed her to the door, waiting behind her.

"It's locked?" Eric asked.

Melissa jiggled the door and nodded. "I'll go around and check the back and windows."

"There's no need," Eric said. "I'm sure the police secured the premises when they left. Do you have a credit card?"

She nodded and removed a Visa card from her purse. Within seconds, he unlocked the door.

"We could get arrested for breaking and entering, Eric. And I am a suspect."

"That's true." He paused. "We don't have to go in."

"I know." She hesitated. "But I have to learn more about Candace." He offered no explanation about his breaking-in skills, either, and she quickly forgot the question when the scent of death assaulted her.

Melissa reached for the overhead light, but Eric shook his head. "It might arouse suspicion to the neighbors."

She nodded, and dropped her hand, scanning the small living area. Through the haze of filtered moonlight from the sliding-glass doors, she noticed fingerprint dust on the pine end table, saw the chalky line and tape marking the floor where Candace's body had been found. The furniture was sparse and simple. A dark green leather sofa, white-pine coffee table and end tables, fresh flowers in a crystal vase on the glass-top kitchen table in the corner eating nook. Flowers from Candace's own yard. They were already wilting.

She would take fresh flowers to her grave.

A small desk occupied the corner near the sliding-glass doors. On the opposite side, a narrow hall led to what she assumed was the bedroom and bath. Eric parked himself by the sofa and remained silent while she walked into the kitchen.

"I know it's silly," she said quietly as she rummaged through the cabinets, "but I want to see her dishes, her clothes, anything that might tell me something about her."

"It's not silly," Eric said, his voice slightly throaty. "Details reveal a lot about a person."

She removed a handcrafted colorful mug, then turned it over to study the bottom. "It has her initials carved on the bottom. I wonder if she made this herself."

"It's a possibility." Eric gestured toward a whimsical painting on the wall, a watercolor of the ocean and colorful sea creatures in a world of muted blues. "Her signature's on this painting, too."

"She was an artist." Melissa studied the painting. "She was actually pretty good. I wonder if she ever sold any of her work."

"You could check local galleries."

"Maybe I will." She glanced at the bedroom. "I'm going to look around in there."

He nodded. "I'll wait here."

She offered him a watery smile, grateful he understood that she needed some privacy, and walked into the bedroom. More paintings adorned the walls, some swatches of bright colors, full of animation and light. Others were dark, gray, moody shadows of another side of Candace that must have reflected her mental instability.

So far she'd seen no sign of her mother's needlework, that she might have crocheted the tiny cap that belonged to Melissa.

She opened the wooden chest at the foot of the bed and looked inside, hoping it held knitting yarn or crochet hooks and patterns, but linens filled the chest instead. Disappointed, she pivoted to the closet, opened the door and studied Candace's clothes. Like the paintings, her closet held a hodgepodge of bright colors and casual sundresses, capri pants and blouses, then a contrasting selection of dark, drab shirts and black slacks. A hatbox that had been pushed way back on the top shelf drew her eye, and she removed it, then sat on the edge of the corner rocker to survey the contents.

A handful of old letters, scribbled in near-illegible handwriting lay inside. Melissa felt as if she was violating Candace's privacy by touching them, but she couldn't stop herself.

Had the police searched these things? Read her letters?

She skimmed the first one.

Dear Baby,

I miss you so much. Today would have been your first birthday. I wonder if you're walking now, and talking, if you're calling another woman Mama. You're probably in a better place, but I miss you so. I had the nurse bring me a cupcake today with a candle in it, and I lit the candle and sang "Happy Birthday" to you, my angel. Then I closed my eyes and wished that I would see you again. Maybe one day soon, if I ever leave this place...

Love,
Your mama

Melissa swiped at the tears running down her cheeks. Had Candace written the letter to her?

And if she'd intended to find her baby when she was released from the hospital, why had she never followed through?

While Melissa looked around in the bedroom, Eric rolled over to the desk. Black and Fox had no doubt searched the contents, but he'd check it out himself in case they missed something.

The top drawer contained insurance papers, bills, all the mundane pieces of a person's life. The second drawer held colorful pens and stationery, along with a book on calligraphy. He shuffled through the third drawer, discovering several sketches of the ocean and sea creatures, then a box of old photos. A quick glance revealed pictures of seashells, birds, another slice of her artistic personality come alive.

No family or photos of a loving dad, a boyfriend or a baby.

He stuffed the box back into the drawer; then noticed a lone picture wedged between the back of the drawer and the edge of the desk.

Curious, he yanked the photo free and held it up to the light. The picture captured the image of five men standing side by side, all in front of the original Savannah Hospital twenty-plus years ago. Eric recognized Sol Santenelli and Arnold Hughes from the photos the Feds had shown him. The third man wore an army uniform. The fourth man resembled the current CEO of CIRP, although Hall supposedly had no former ties to Hughes.

Hall was definitely not Hughes resurfaced. But he had obviously known him.

The fifth man was Robert Latone, meaning Latone also had ties with Hughes early on.

He searched the desk again, and discovered a second photo trapped between the wooden edges. He released it, swallowing hard at the sight of Hughes and Candace Latone together, Hughes's arm draped affectionately around Candace's shoulders.

Candace had supposedly been involved in a research experiment at the center when she'd become pregnant. And she'd known Hughes. Had they been involved?

Could Hughes possibly be Melissa's father?

Chapter 7

Eric's imagination had run away with him. Melissa's father could have been any one of a hundred men. In order to pinpoint his identity, he'd have to investigate all the men Candace might have been involved with. And if she'd gotten pregnant through a sperm donor, as had Simon's surrogate mother, the possibilities were endless and would require DNA checking as well as an investigation into the experimental project at the time.

Which was an entirely different case.

Yet, if Melissa was Hughes's daughter, he could use her to get to Hughes....

No, he couldn't even contemplate such a possibility.

Melissa entered the room, the misery in her eyes wrenching his gut. She was an innocent in this situation, had searched for her mother only to find her dead. How would she feel about a cold-blooded murderer like Hughes fathering her?

Deciding to explore the possibility before turning her already fragile world upside down with his suspicions, he slid the picture he'd found in Candace's desk into his pocket.

Melissa cleared her throat. "You were looking through the desk?"

"Just trying to help."

She fidgeted with her fingers. "Did you find anything?"

He shook his head. "More art supplies. What about you?"

She nodded. "Some old letters."

"Did they confirm that Candace was your mother?"

Her lip trembled as she nodded. "Candace wrote them to her baby. She...missed me and wanted me back."

Eric's heart squeezed with compassion—and guilt over lying to her. He held out his hand to comfort her, but she shrugged it away. "Come on, let's get out of here."

He nodded and followed her to the car. If Candace was Melissa's mother, had she given her away out of choice or had someone forced her to?

Melissa's heart throbbed as she drove back to Skidaway Island. All her life she'd ached for her mother, wondered where she was and why she hadn't wanted her. Now, to realize her mother *had* wanted Melissa, had celebrated her birthdays, was a blessing. Yet it intensified the sadness.

She had been so close to meeting Candace, to being reunited. If she'd only arrived at the house a few minutes earlier, she might have been able to save Candace.

Eric laid a hand over hers. "Are you all right?"

No, she wasn't all right. "I…just need some time alone."

"I can understand that." Hadn't he wanted to shut himself away from everything and everyone after the explosion?

She parked in front of his cabin, then hopped out to retrieve his chair. He unfolded it, slid onto the seat, then looked up at her. "Are you sure you want to be alone? We could talk."

Determined not to break down and cry in front of him, she shook her head. "Thanks, but I'm pretty tired. And you need some rest, too."

His mouth tightened.

"Thanks for going with me, Eric. I appreciate it."

He nodded, but hesitated as if he wanted to say more. As if he wanted more.

She remembered the fiery kiss they'd shared the night before and craved another. But she felt so fragile and in need of comfort. If she relented to one kiss, she might lose control and succumb to more. Starting a relationship, even a short-lived one, definitely wouldn't be fair to Eric.

Besides, she couldn't allow herself to rely on anyone, especially a man with problems of his own. So, she said good-night, then climbed into her car alone.

When she pulled up to her cottage, a black limousine was parked in the driveway. For a moment, she remembered the threatening caller the night before. But if her visitor meant her harm, why arrive in something as conspicuous as a limousine?

Still, she removed her cell phone from her purse and held on to it as a safety net. The limo's door opened, a driver exited and opened the back door. An austere, tall, gray-haired man in a dark pin-striped suit emerged. He had a broad angular face with wide cheekbones and a neatly trimmed beard. His demeanor immediately suggested wealth and power. "Miss Fagan?"

She climbed out of the car, but remained in close proximity to the door. How had he known her name? "Yes."

"My name is Robert Latone. Are you the woman who discovered my daughter's body?"

Melissa swallowed. This man was Candace's father? That would make him her grandfather.

"Yes."

"May I come in and talk to you for a moment?"

Melissa's breath caught, but she nodded, then walked up the driveway and opened the door. The driver slid back into the car to wait, and Robert Latone followed her, his clipped steps on the sidewalk echoing like a soldier's measured pace.

When they entered, she gestured toward the sofa. He declined and shoved his hands into his trouser pockets. A play on power she assumed. She'd dealt with men and power issues in her foster-care homes before. She hadn't caved then, and she wouldn't now. Even if this man was her grandfather.

"Would you like some coffee? Tea?"

"No, thank you. This isn't exactly a social visit."

"I see." Animosity radiated from him in waves. She claimed a wing chair, forcing herself to make eye contact. Did he know she thought Candace was her mother?

"Tell me what you saw at my daughter's cottage."

"I already gave a full report to the police, Mr. Latone."

"You didn't see her killer?"

"No."

"What exactly did you see?"

"The door was open, so I went in. It was getting dark. I noticed the curtains fluttering in the breeze, the sliding-glass door was ajar. Then I saw m…her body." She paused, the images darting back in horrid snippets. "She was already dead."

"What did you do then?"

"I called 911, but someone attacked me from behind." She pressed a hand to her chest, the horror returning. "When I regained consciousness, the paramedics and police were there."

His thin lips creased downward. "My daughter didn't have many friends, Miss Fagan. How did you know her?"

Melissa twisted her hands in her lap, then realized he'd noticed and would read the movement as a sign of weakness, so she fisted them instead. "I didn't, we never met."

Surprise registered on his face a second before suspicion. "Then what were you doing at her house?"

She debated whether to tell him. But if she was his granddaughter, he might already know. And even if he did, he might not acknowledge her….

"I was abandoned when I was a baby, Mr. Latone. I came to Savannah in search of my mother."

Gray eyes bored into hers. "What does that have to do with my daughter?"

Melissa cleared her throat. "I hired a private investigator to find my birth parents. He told me that Candace was my mother."

Shock flared in his tightly reined jaw, then anger. "He was mistaken. My daughter never had a baby. I can have her medical records pulled to prove it." His voice turned hard, brittle. "And if you spread such ill rumors, I'll sue you for slander."

With one last warning look, he strode out the door, slamming it behind him. Melissa heard the soft purr of the limousine's engine, then shells spraying from the wheels as it disappeared into the night.

Had Candace not told her father about the baby, or was it possible that Candace hadn't delivered a child? Melissa had read the letters Candace had written. Unless, in her illness, Candace had invented the baby....

Had Robert Latone been telling the truth?

A soon as Eric returned to the cabin, he called Devlin and filled him in on the photograph.

"I'm sending our local contacts over to look at it," Devlin said. "Good work."

Eric hung up, a sour taste in his mouth. Good work—only he was keeping secrets from Melissa, secrets that involved her, secrets that might lead her to the answers she'd been seeking for years.

Unfortunately she might not like the answers.

Within the hour, Detectives Black and Fox arrived at his door.

"Agent Devlin said you found a photograph?" Black said without preamble.

"Yeah." Eric gestured for them to follow him to the living area. The layout mirrored Melissa's, the furniture utilitarian and sturdy, although his had been built with added handicapped accommodations.

He removed the photograph from the desk and handed it to Black. Fox sidled up to him so they could both study it.

"It's Hughes, Santenelli, Robert Latone, Candace Latone's father and the new CEO, Ian Hall. I'm not sure who the other man is," Eric said.

"Which means the new CEO is not Hughes," Fox said.

"It seems that way," Eric said.

"We'll see what we can find out on the other man," Black added.

"What do you know about Robert Latone?" Eric asked.

"He's a foreign diplomat," Black said. "So far, he's donated several million dollars to CIRP since its conception years ago."

"There's been speculation that he might be involved in espionage," Fox added.

Eric whistled through his teeth. "Do you have any idea what type of research experiment Candace Latone was involved in?"

"We're not sure, but there was some kind of scandal involving a fertility specialist," Black said. "He left the country before things were cleared up." Two fertility specialists had been involved in creating Simon.

"The psychological problems the Latone woman experienced might have been related to the experimental research," Fox added. "But details have been kept hush-hush."

Black narrowed his eyes, studying the photograph. "Wait a minute, are you thinking what I am?" He cut his gaze toward Eric. "You think there's a tie to the recent experiments with Project Simon?"

"How did you know about Simon?" Eric asked.

"Devlin filled us in," Fox said.

"Hughes can't find out about Simon," Eric said. "He'd ruin my brother's life as well as the baby's."

"You don't have to worry," Fox said. "The information goes no further than the three of us."

Eric nodded, still anxious.

"Do you think this all ties back to Melissa Fagan?" Black asked.

"I don't know." Eric scrubbed a hand over his face. "She was born at the center. And Candace and Hughes seem chummy in the photo."

Fox cleared his throat. "You think Hughes might be Melissa Fagan's father?"

Melissa was so shaken by Robert Latone's visit that she'd barely slept the night before. Candace would be buried today. Melissa had planned to attend. Now she didn't know what to do.

She grabbed a bagel and hurried to the rehab center, anxious to see Eric. Her therapy sessions would distract her from her problems, and she was excited by Eric's quick progress. Before the week ended, he'd be using a walker, maybe even a cane.

The sight of Eric's masculine body wheeling toward her sent heat exploding within her. Heat that had nothing to do with therapy sessions and work, but with the sexual chemistry brewing between them.

Even more unsettling, she felt safe with him. A feeling she had never experienced in her life, especially with a man.

"Good morning." She automatically assumed the pattern they'd established in the beginning for the warm-up stretching exercises. Eric was one step ahead of her, already propping his foot on the apparatus and flexing his calf. He seemed tense this morning.

"Did you have nightmares about the accident again last night?"

Eric shrugged. "I'm not sure if they'll ever go away."

She massaged his calf, then knelt and braced herself to help through the routine. "You want to talk about it?"

"Another man died in the accident," he said, his voice strained.

She hesitated. "A friend of yours?"

"Sort of. He was in trouble, I was trying to help him out."

"I'm sorry."

"It's not your fault."

But he blamed himself. She offered a feeble smile. "I know, but I'm still sorry. His death must haunt you." She coached him to the next level of the set. "You want to tell me how the accident happened?"

A mask slipped over his face, guarded, void of emotions. Or at least he wanted to hide them. But a deep pain settled in his eyes. "Maybe another time."

"All right."

"How about you?" he asked as she helped him stand and move to the bars. "Did you dream about your mother's murder?"

"No, but I didn't sleep, either." Melissa glanced down at his feet, urging him to take a step forward. "I had a visitor last night."

Eric gripped the bars and paused, searching her face. "The person who threatened you?"

She shook her head. "No, Robert Latone, Candace's father."

Eric remained still, waiting. "What did he want?"

"To find out if I'd seen anything that might help identify Candace's killer."

"Did he mention your relationship to Candace?"

She urged him to continue the drill, and he stepped forward. One step. Two steps. Three. Four. They were coming easier now, his brain and body beginning to heal and work together. "He denied that Candace had a child and threatened to sue me if I spread rumors."

Compassion softened Eric's expression, tightening the knot of unshed tears in Melissa's throat.

"Melissa, I'm sorry. But there are tests that can be run."

"Right." Melissa patted his hand, silently urging him through the workout. "I'll think about it. Although I doubt Robert Latone will cooperate. And if Candace's DNA has to be provided, he'll probably protest."

Eric nodded and they completed the session.

The young candy striper suddenly appeared. "Melissa, two police officers are in the office requesting to talk to you."

Melissa's breath caught. "All right, can you help Mr. Collier over to the whirlpool?"

"I can manage," Eric said in a gruff voice. He pushed Nancy's hands away when she reached out to offer assistance. Melissa smiled at his stubborn independence.

But nerves bunched in her stomach as she headed to the office. Had the police found her mother's murderer?

Or had they come to arrest her?

Eric had no idea why he'd confided in Melissa about the accident. He couldn't confess the truth, though, without revealing more about his identity and the reasons for being at CIRP.

He hated lying to her.

Ironic that after a lifetime of helping and protecting women, he now had to hide from the first woman he was interested in.

She couldn't be Hughes's daughter.

Maybe Latone was right. Maybe she wasn't Candace Latone's daughter, either.

And maybe you'll get married and ride away into the sunset on your ranch like they do in the movies.

He wiped his forehead with the gym towel, ignoring the candy striper who still couldn't bring herself to look at his ugly scars. Not that he blamed her. A pretty young girl like her should be protected from the grotesque violence of the world.

But no one had been there to protect Melissa.

Sliding himself from the chair, he braced his body using the rails and slowly lowered himself to the first step of the whirlpool. He eased into the water from there with no problem. He was getting stronger every day.

But would he be strong enough to protect Melissa if she needed him? What if the person who'd threatened her decided to carry out those threats?

Maybe he should try to convince her to drop the search for her parents, at least until he could finish the investigation, locate Hughes and lock him away. Then he'd help her.

He glanced toward the glass doors leading to the inner offices of the rehab center. Had the police caught her mother's killer?

Five minutes later, Melissa sat in the office, squeezing a tepid cup of hospital coffee between her hands, facing Detectives Black and Fox. Thankfully the gestapo-like Bernstein had not accompanied them.

"Miss Fagan, we need to ask you a few more questions." Black occupied the vinyl chair across from her, while Detective Fox stood, sipping a cup of coffee.

Something about Detective Black's tone triggered alarm in her belly. "Do I need a lawyer?"

He arched an eyebrow. "Not unless you have something to hide."

Her jaw tightened. "I told you I didn't kill Candace Latone. I'll do whatever I can to assist with the investigation."

"Good, we appreciate your cooperation," Black said.

Fox cleared his throat. "Miss Fagan, do you know Robert Latone?"

Melissa's head jerked up. "No. Well, not exactly."

The officers waited, and she clenched her hands to keep from fidgeting. "He showed up at my cottage last night. I've never met or talked to him before then."

"Why did he visit you?" Fox asked.

"To find out if I'd seen anything at Candace's house to help identify the killer."

They exchanged interested looks. "And how did you reply?"

"I gave him the same answer I gave you." Melissa took a sip of coffee and frowned at the bitterness.

"Did you confide your belief that Candace was your mother?" Black asked.

She chewed her lip. "Yes."

"How did he react?"

She sighed and rubbed her forehead, tension knotting her neck. "He denied that Candace had a child, then he warned me not to spread rumors."

The detective's expression remained unreadable, but questions rallied in her mind. What would Latone do if it were true? How far would he go to keep the truth from being revealed?

Black shuffled, stared at his boots, then back at her. "Miss Fagan, do you know a man named Larry Dormer?"

She glanced at him, then at Fox. "Yes, he's a private investigator. He lives in Atlanta."

"Did he give you the information about Candace being your mother?" Black asked.

"Yes. Why? What does he have to do with Candace's murder?"

Fox settled his foot on the edge of another chair, then

leaned forward, bracing his elbow on his knee. "When was the last time you saw him?"

Melissa swallowed, struggling to remember. "About three weeks ago, right before I moved here." Worry mushroomed inside. "Why?"

The two men traded speculative looks, then Black spoke in a low tone. "Because he was found murdered last night. And it looks like he's been dead for about three weeks."

Robert latone lit his cigar, poured himself a bourbon on the rocks and paced to the window of his study, the conversation with Melissa Fagan grating on his strained nerves.

If the Fagan woman exposed the past, she could destroy his life and his daughter's reputation.

He had built an empire for himself with money, power and contacts worldwide. His sole heir and the only person who'd ever mattered to him, Candace, was dead.

He could not lose anything else.

A low knock sounded on the polished mahogany door, then Edward Moor, his right-hand man and confidant, appeared. "Mr. Latone, the limousine is ready."

Robert downed the bourbon in one sip, grateful for the quick buzz of alcohol to dull the pain. Today was Candace's funeral.

He didn't know if he could stand to watch them put his baby in the ground.

Not that he hadn't lost her years ago, but he'd always maintained hope that the chasm between them would one day close and her vacuous behavior toward him would change. That he would have his real daughter back.

Now that would never happen.

"Mr. Latone?" Edward's low voice permeated the haze, and Latone moved across the room, smashing the cigar into the ashtray.

"Are you going to tell me about the meeting with that Fagan woman?" Edward said as they settled into the ride to the church for the funeral service.

Latone grunted. "She could be trouble."

Edward crossed his suited legs. "Elaborate."

"She claims she didn't see anything to help the police at Candace's house the night of the murder."

"That's too bad." Edward laid a hand over Robert's for a brief conciliatory moment, the black onyx inscripted ring shining in the sunlight. "Obviously you want her killer caught and punished."

Robert nodded. That went without saying.

"So who is this woman, and how did she know Candace?"

Robert stared into his friend's eyes. The secrets that lay between them were many, the cost of betrayal high if exposed. His fury was so strong he could barely contain his temper, but he controlled himself in order to test Edward's reaction. "She claims she's Candace's daughter."

Edward coughed, shock riding over his ruddy features. "But we handled that problem long ago." His hand shook as he lifted it and wiped perspiration from his forehead. "And we covered our tracks."

Robert gripped Edward's collar, tightening it across his throat. "You were in charge of the details," he growled. "You obviously talked to someone or left something uncovered."

Edward yanked at Robert's hands, his eyes bulging. "I swear I didn't, Robert. I don't know how she got any information…."

"I don't care how," Robert snapped. "I want this problem to go away. She can't ruin everything we've worked for. I won't allow it."

Edward nodded, heaving for air as Robert released him. Robert leaned back against the seat, his heart pounding as the church slipped into view. Edward understood him.

He'd take care of Melissa Fagan.

Chapter 8

Eric had showered and dressed, and was waiting for Melissa when she returned to the rehab center. The first thing he noticed was that she appeared pale and shaken. The second was that she headed in the opposite direction as if to avoid him.

What the hell had happened?

He fully expected her to have another patient after him, but she stopped and spoke to the older nurse, Helen, then strode toward the exit at a hurried pace. Eric cursed the fact that he couldn't walk and wheeled his chair across the facility, trying his damnedest to catch her. By the time he made it down the handicapped ramp, she'd reached her car.

"Melissa!"

She froze, then fumbled with her keys and opened the driver's side. He rolled toward her in double time, determined to find out what had upset her.

"Melissa, wait!" The engine rumbled to life, but he caught the door before it closed and she could switch gears. "Wait, what's wrong?"

She angled her face to look at him, and he saw tears glittering in her eyes. He gently brushed his hand across her cheek, and she fell forward against him, her body trembling.

"What happened?" he asked gruffly.

She sniffed and pressed a hand against his chest. "You shouldn't be near me."

He cupped her face in his hands and lifted her chin, forcing her to look into his eyes. "What are you talking about?"

"It's too dangerous, Eric, stay away from me," she cried. "Everyone's getting killed."

"Melissa, you aren't making sense. Tell me what happened."

Her lower lip wobbled. "The private investigator I hired to find my parents…he's dead."

Eric stifled a reaction. "When?"

"About three weeks ago." Her voice quavered. "Right after I left Atlanta."

Her hands clutched his, panic straining her features. "The police think I had something to do with it. Don't you see? That's why they were here today, to ask me when I last saw him."

"They can't believe you murdered the man," Eric said. Surely the cops were smarter than that. "You have no motive." Unless she'd wanted to cover her tracks. If she'd set out to kill Candace, which he didn't believe.

She shrugged, her hands tightening on his arms. "I'm not sure they're convinced of that. And even if they don't think I killed Mr. Dormer, he might have been murdered because of the information he provided me regarding my parents."

That theory made more sense. But why would someone go to such extremes to kill the private investigator?

Unless the killer thought the investigator knew more than he had told Melissa. But what exactly was the person hiding?

And if the private investigator's death was related to the Latone woman's murder and Melissa's investigation into her parentage, would she be next?

Melissa pulled away, composing herself. "Eric, I have to go. Thanks for listening, but you have to stay away from me. I don't want you hurt."

"I can take care of myself," Eric said between clenched teeth.

Her gaze fell to the wheelchair. It stood between them, a visible reminder that he was physically debilitated and needed therapy.

He dropped his hands. "You don't have to be alone anymore, Melissa."

Fear rippled through her, along with memories of her past. Wanting someone to help but having nowhere to turn. Running from one of her foster fathers. Being locked in a closet by another. But acceptance of her childhood had made her stronger. She wouldn't surrender to the fear now. "Yes, I have to be alone." She laid her palm against his cheek, a surge of warmth seeping through her, replacing the icy chill in her bones. "I appreciate your concern, but I'd never forgive myself if something happened to you, Eric." *Because I might be falling in love with you.*

No, she couldn't be in love.

She was attracted to Eric, but there was too much

chaos in her life for her to entertain feelings for this man. After everything he'd endured the past few months, he didn't deserve someone with ready-made problems.

Besides, she knew nothing about relationships. Nothing except saying goodbye.

And now, because of her search for her parents, her love might be fatal.

"I need to leave, Eric."

"Where are you going?"

She hesitated. This morning she hadn't decided whether or not to attend Candace's funeral. With the realization that Candace and the P.I. had both lost their lives because of her search, she had to attend. She needed the truth or their deaths would count for nothing. "I'm going to Candace Latone's funeral."

Eric nodded. "Then let me ride with you."

"No."

He clutched her hand. "You're not going alone. If I don't ride with you, I'll call a taxi and come by myself."

"But why? It might be dangerous."

"Shh." He kissed her hand. "Because I don't want you hurt, either."

Melissa swallowed, emotions welling in her throat. No one had ever said those words to her before.

Why would this man who'd barely survived a terrible explosion put his life on the line for her, when no one else, not even her own mother or father, had wanted her?

Guilt nagged at Eric as he rode with Melissa to the funeral. It was ironic. His entire life, he'd helped other women escape horrible family lives, yet this woman was trying to protect him, when he should be the protector.

Devlin's words reverberated in his brain. *Use her to get close to Hughes.*

He didn't like using people, especially innocent women. And Melissa was about as innocent as they came. Kind, caring, honest, compassionate. Alone.

All she'd wanted was to find the woman who'd given her birth and to understand why she'd been abandoned.

She knew nothing about Hughes, he was certain of it.

But unfortunately, she had walked into a bed of lies and danger she was not equipped to handle.

He cut his gaze toward her. Uncertainty plagued her features as she parked in front of the Savannah church. On the ride over, she'd stopped at a florist shop and bought a bouquet of fresh flowers. A goodbye offering for a woman she'd never met, a person who'd left her as a baby to fend for herself in the world.

Yet Melissa still cared about Candace, which proved she was a loving, forgiving woman.

Several cars lined the church parking lot, although it was by no means full, a sad testament to the life of the lady who lay inside in a casket ready to bid her final goodbye. Seconds later, more cars rolled in, all expensive makes and models. Affluent people emerged dressed in black, obviously friends of Robert Latone's who'd come to pay their respects and possibly win his favor. Eric wondered if any of them actually cared about the woman inside, then realized he was projecting his feelings about his own mother's death on the visitors, and remembering the near-empty church where they had held her service.

A service his own father had not attended.

Only Cain had stood beside him, fending off the concerned social worker and assuming the role of a father figure to Eric. He'd have to thank his brother the next time he talked to him. Eric had never appreciated how much Cain had sacrificed to take care of him. He'd been angry, hurt, confused—not an easy kid to parent.

But nobody had cared for Melissa.

He would be there for her now.

Eric placed a hand over hers, the flicker of heat igniting between them. "Are you sure you want to do this?"

She nodded and curled her fingers into his, her voice stronger now. "Yes, Eric. I have to learn the truth."

God, he felt for her. "Robert Latone will be here."

"I know." She squeezed his hand. "And I doubt he'll be very happy to see me."

Probably an understatement. "But you don't intend to let Latone intimidate you?"

"Whether Candace was my mother or not, I feel connected to her, Eric. There had to be a reason I was the one who discovered her body that night."

Eric remembered his father's abusive behavior. The unfairness of it all. "Sometimes there are no reasons, Melissa. Things just happen. People are in the wrong place at the wrong time."

"I still have to finish this." Melissa released his hand and closed her fingers around the flowers. "I have to know if Candace was my mother and if she died because of me."

"You think Robert Latone might have lied to you?"

"Maybe Candace never told him about the pregnancy. She could have hidden it, convinced a friend to drop me off at that church."

"That's true." He'd have to investigate the possibility. "But if he did know, and he's lying?"

"Then he might have forced Candace to give me away. Maybe exposing the truth will lead to Candace's killer."

Eric silently cursed as she exited the car. Melissa had raised some very good points. Whether or not this situation or her birth led to Arnold Hughes, he couldn't allow her to face Latone alone.

Because if she was right, and Latone was covering up his daughter's murder, then he would have no problem killing Melissa and covering up hers, as well.

Melissa slipped into the back of the church as quietly as possible, well aware Eric's chair squeaked slightly on the thick plush carpet. A hum of low whispers and greetings echoed from the pews as the visitors filled the rows, all well-dressed regal-looking men and women who were obviously friends of Robert Latone's. Had any of them been close to her mother, or even friends with her at all?

Robert Latone stood ramrod straight in the front row, shaking hands with a preacher clothed in a long robe. Melissa shivered, remembering the few times she'd attended church as a child. Her third foster father had been a self-proclaimed minister who preached hellfire and damnation and handled snakes. The experience had given her nightmares.

Later, as a college student, she'd visited the small chapel on campus and had felt solace in the quiet ceremonies and the softly spoken rituals of the Methodist congregation. Neither had compared to this ornate church with its stained-glass windows, carvings and decorative ten-foot ceilings.

Her gaze landed on the closed casket at the front of the church, pewter gray with a blanket of red roses. Red roses meant love—did Robert Latone really love his daughter?

The flower arrangement she'd bought seemed puny,

but she still wanted to offer it as a gesture of…of what? Love, respect? She had neither for the woman. Only a deep sadness and curiosity, and regret that she'd died, even pity that Candace had missed out on a relationship with her own daughter—if she had wanted one. Had she?

The preacher moved to the pulpit, an organist accompanied another woman singing "Amazing Grace." Melissa slid into the last pew, her stomach churning. Eric moved up beside her and collected her hands in his.

"Friends and family, we are here today to say a final farewell to one of our sisters, a kind woman who lived alone most of her life, who gave to her small community of friends and rarely bothered others. Candace saw life through an artist's eyes, using various venues to portray her inner emotions and views of the world surrounding her." The preacher's words about living alone could have described *her,* Melissa thought, wondering if she and Candace shared anything else in common. Melissa certainly wasn't artistic.

The next few minutes passed in a blur while the preacher read scripture from the Bible, then recited a eulogy that sounded practiced and aimed toward helping Robert Latone accept his daughter's rise into the kingdom of heaven. Another hymn ended the short unemotional service.

Melissa studied Candace's father, her gaze straying to the gray-haired gentleman sitting next to him. She'd seen him before but couldn't quite place where. She also recognized the old man who'd given her directions to Candace's cottage and a few of the neighbors who'd arrived on the scene after the murder.

Robert Latone bowed his head and pinched his fingers to the bridge of his nose, his face stoic as the ser-

vice ended, but his eyes remained dry. The other man
led him through the procession to the side door and the
guests followed accordingly.

There had been no open casket, no final moment for
Melissa to speak to the woman she believed had given
her birth. She wondered if Robert Latone had arranged a
private viewing earlier between himself and his daughter. According to the local paper, he'd opted to forgo a
traditional wake.

Melissa and Eric exited through the back, then fell
into step behind the people moving to the graveyard behind the church, a well-tended manicured cemetery on
the top of a hill. The sharp incline compounded Eric's
wheelchair maneuvers, and she reached for the chair
back to help him, but his fierce look dared her to insult
him by offering her assistance.

At the graveside service, Melissa hovered in the
throng of spectators while Robert Latone sat beneath
the tarp that protected him from the late-afternoon sunshine. Odd, there was no other family present. Robert
Latone might be a foreign diplomat and business ty-
coon, but either he had no other family or he'd distanced
himself from them.

Had he been close to Candace throughout the years?

A breeze stirred and rattled the surrounding trees,
scenting the air with the sweetness of the fresh flower
arrangements the attendants were placing around the
burial plot. Another Bible reading and prayer followed,
then guests lined up to offer condolences. Melissa hung
back. Latone's companion stared at her as if she'd in-
vaded a private family gathering.

Finally, the crowd dispersed, the funeral staff began
to shovel dirt onto the grave and Melissa forced her
feet to move forward. Her heart aching that she'd been

denied the opportunity to meet her mother, she knelt, whispered a silent goodbye and placed the flowers next to the grave.

Robert Latone's voice jerked her from her melancholy mood. "What are you doing here?"

She stood and faced him. "I came to pay my respects just like everyone else."

"You have no reason to be here."

Melissa gestured toward the parting crowd. "And all these people were her friends?"

He glared at her. "That's none of your business."

"Is there a problem, sir?" The gray-haired man who'd dogged Robert Latone all day approached her.

"No, Edward, I was just informing Miss Fagan that she doesn't belong here."

"He's right," the other man said. "This service is for friends and family only."

Melissa gave a sardonic laugh at his pointed remark. "And you don't think I'm family?"

"You're not," Robert Latone said.

"I have information which says otherwise," Melissa said.

"It's false information," Latone's watchdog said in a clipped voice. "Miss Latone never had children."

"And if she did, would you have recognized them?" Melissa asked, anger fueling her temper. "Or would you have forced her to get rid of her child so she wouldn't disgrace your reputation?"

Robert Latone's hand rose as if he might slap her. Eric's chair crunched gravel as he moved closer.

Edward's look turned lethal. "You should go now, Miss Fagan. Mr. Latone needs to grieve in peace."

Melissa shrugged his hand away. "I will find out the truth, Mr. Latone. No matter how much you attempt to hide it, secrets always have a way of coming out in the end."

Latone reached for her, but she strode away, her shoes kicking pebbles in her wake as Eric wheeled behind her.

Chapter 9

After she dropped Eric off at his cottage, Melissa's chest ached with emotion. She opened the car windows and drove along the island, inhaling the salty air and pungent smell of shrimp and the sea, willing away the feeling of doom. She had always been alone—nothing really had changed today.

Yet it had.

All her life, she'd thrived on the belief that one day she'd be reunited with her mother. Now, that hope had been buried with Candace Latone.

She parked at a low-hung cliff at the corner tip of Skidaway, climbed down the hill and walked along the shore, taking solace in the soft sand beneath her feet and the crunch of shells as she walked. The tides rolled and crashed against the rocks, mimicking her tumultuous feelings over lost chances and dreams. Wrapping her arms around herself, she faced the ocean, marveling at the vast expanse of the endless sea and finally giving in to the pain swelling inside her.

If she disappeared into the water, no one would ever know...no one would miss her or care. She was like a broken seashell that would be lost in the vastness forever.

She sucked in a harsh breath at the realization, remembering all the times she'd felt hopeless as a child. All the times she'd reminded herself to hold on, that one day her parents might find her. That they loved her and wanted her.

She no longer maintained that belief. Robert Latone had completely denied her relationship to Candace or him and wanted nothing to do with her.

Kicking off her shoes, she walked toward the edge of the ocean, the water lapping over her feet and washing back out to sea. White billowy clouds rolled above her in a clear blue sky. Suddenly an image of Eric's face floated unbidden to her mind.

He had been like a rock to her all day, sitting silently and offering support, hovering in the background as if he understood that she needed space and time alone, but also suggesting that he wanted to protect her.

She was in love with him.

She had no idea how to handle these new feelings. There was already so much turmoil in her life that she desperately wanted Eric to hold her, to comfort her, to kiss her again and make her forget the sorrows of the day.

But she was on her own.

Or maybe she wasn't. Maybe she should talk to Eric.

He could go with her to the island, talk to Candace's neighbors. She really didn't want to go back to the island alone.

* * *

Eric had been so furious with Robert Latone that he'd barely contained his rage. The fact that his physical limitations might prevent him from protecting Melissa had angered him even more.

But Melissa didn't deserve his wrath, not when her mother had just been buried and her grandfather had totally denied her existence. Did Robert Latone really think Candace hadn't given birth to a child, or was he trying to protect himself by covering up the fact that they'd both abandoned a baby? Was he worried about his reputation? His financial empire? Or some deeper secret being revealed?

Did he know the identity of the man who'd fathered Melissa?

Determined to unravel the truth, Eric spent the afternoon on the case. He needed fingerprints and DNA samples from the men he suspected might be Hughes. It would be tricky to obtain them without revealing himself though.

First, he paid a visit to Ian Hall, the new CEO of CIRP. Although the photo he'd discovered at Candace's suggested the improbability that Hall was Hughes, Eric had to make certain.

"I wanted to shake your hand and tell you how impressed I am with your center," Eric said.

"Thank you, Mr. Collier. We're proud of the facility and our staff." Hall's right eye twitched slightly as if he had a nervous tic. "I trust our staff is meeting your needs."

"Absolutely."

"You came here for physical therapy?" Hall asked.

"Yes, but I'm also scheduled for skin grafts. I needed time to heal first."

Hall nodded. "Our plastic surgeon, Crane, is top-notch."

"Yes, I've heard." He had given Clayton Fox a new face to fit his fake identity. Had he operated on Hughes, as well?

Eric glanced around the office, searching for a stray hair that might have fallen from Hall's jacket but saw none. He spotted the man's handkerchief and decided the Feds might be able to lift DNA from it.

Pretending interest in the diagram of the facility on the wall, he maneuvered his chair toward the desk. Hall followed, growing slightly agitated. "Do you have an interest in the center for some specific reason? Investment purposes maybe?"

"Perhaps."

"What exactly do you do, Mr. Collier?"

"I own a ranch in the North Georgia mountains. I'm planning a school for troubled teens and was curious about your counseling program. Perhaps I could talk to someone in the psychiatric department for a reference."

"Certainly." He scribbled a name on a business card and handed it to Eric. "Dennis Hopkins is phenomenal. He could definitely make some recommendations."

Eric intentionally dropped the card. While Hall bent to retrieve it, he swiped the handkerchief and stuffed it in his pocket.

"Thanks, Dr. Hall, you've been very helpful."

Hall followed him out, locking the door behind him. Eric wheeled back to his cottage and placed the card and handkerchief in a plastic bag to give to the authorities. He only hoped it provided them with some answers.

One more meeting with Dennis Hopkins. Maybe he'd surprise the man and show up unannounced. After all, if Hughes was hiding something, Eric didn't want to give him a chance to cover it up.

But as he stepped outside, he saw Melissa coming toward him.

"Dr. Hopkins, are you ready to begin with the patient?"

Hopkins glanced up from the file and nodded at the young nurse. So far, she'd expressed no personal interest in him, but that would change. If she didn't come around on her own, he'd have to do something. He'd wanted her the moment he laid eyes on her. Long auburn hair. Brown eyes. She was voluptuous, in spite of the fact that she camouflaged herself in those baggy uniforms. He wondered what she'd look like in an evening gown. Or naked.

"Dr. Hopkins?"

Damn. He wanted to play out the fantasy. "Give me five minutes. Go ahead and prep him."

"I think you may need to talk to him first. He's awfully agitated." She folded her hands across the clipboard, which she had nudged beneath her breasts.

Didn't she realize the movement only drew attention to her figure?

"All right. Go ahead and give him a dose of phenobarbital to calm him and I'll be right in."

She nodded, that mask of professionalism in place. He needed to work out how to push her romantic buttons. And if she rebuked him or didn't answer his needs, he'd turn her into putty in his hands.

He hurriedly skimmed the file, but the phone rang just as he stood. "Dr. Hopkins."

"Hopkins, listen, we've got trouble."

A curse word flew from his mouth. "What kind of trouble?"

"Someone's trying to hack into confidential files. The death of Robert Latone's daughter has drawn attention to the center. We can't let anyone find out what happened years ago."

It was always about protecting the past while he wanted to focus on the future. "Right."

"That new physical therapist, Melissa Fagan, the woman who found Candace's body, claims she's her daughter."

"Problematic."

"Word is that there may be a cop working undercover at the center, too."

"You think it's the Fagan woman?"

"We don't know yet. It could be another employee, hell, a janitor even. Or a patient. Keep your eyes and ears peeled."

"I will."

"And one more thing, hone up on those techniques. We may need to use them."

Hopkins grinned and thought of the unsuspecting guinea pig waiting in the other room. "Don't worry, I'm on it." He hung up and hurried toward the lab. The poor guy had no idea how the procedure would change him. Free will? Not with the new experimental drug, hypnosis and a little shock treatment.

Hell, the man would never know what happened. And if he didn't respond according to plan, he was dispensable, just like those three prisoners who'd traded early release time for their experimental services with that memory-altering drug. They were pawns in a very complicated, sophisticated, worldwide game of scientific chess.

A game Hopkins intended to win.

* * *

"What kind of game are you playing, lady?"

Melissa fought to keep her voice level and smiled at the older storekeeper, grateful Eric had agreed to accompany her to the island. Just having him waiting in the car made her feel safer. "I'm not playing games, Mr. Wilks. And I didn't hurt Candace Latone." She prayed he'd see her sincerity. "I simply wanted to talk to her, but she was dead when I arrived."

He smacked his dentures. "You didn't have an insurance check for her?"

Melissa hesitated, debating whether the truth would gain his compassion or incriminate her more. "No, I'm searching for my mother. I was born in Savannah and was given information that lead me here, to Candace Latone."

His expression softened slightly, then suspicion registered as if he realized the implications. "You were upset 'cause she gave you away?"

"No." She bit her lip. "Well, of course, I had mixed feelings, but I didn't come here to do her harm. You have to believe me, I simply wanted to meet her, to see if we had a chance at a relationship."

He fumbled with a stack of newspapers, shifting them as if he needed something to do. "You didn't ask her?"

"No." Melissa massaged her neck, the day's tension wearing on her. "I wish I'd had the chance. Now I'll never know."

He stared at her long and hard, then finally suggested, "You might want to talk to Louise Philigreen. She and Candace were friends. Candace kept mostly to herself, but Louise liked art and gardening so they visited sometimes."

Melissa thanked him and scribbled the directions, then hurried to the car. "I found a friend of Candace's," she said. "Maybe she can tell me something."

"I hope you find what you're looking for, Melissa."

She squeezed his hand, wondering why he looked so troubled. Five minutes later, she found the house. The spindly little fiftyish woman wore a big floppy sun hat and loose-fitting shift with tennis shoes and was watering her flower garden.

Melissa parked on the curb and climbed out. "Mrs. Philigreen?"

"Yes?" Louise smiled in welcome. "Samantha?"

Melissa frowned. "No, Ma'am, my name is Melissa Fagan."

"Oh...oh, dear." She raised the brim of her hat and squinted. "For a second there, I thought...well, never mind. What can I do for you?"

"Can we talk a few minutes?"

"Sure, hon, I love company. Samantha usually comes every day to visit. I don't know where she's been today."

"She sounds like a wonderful friend."

"Yes, actually she's my daughter. Would you like some lemonade?"

"No, thanks." Melissa gestured toward the mixture of spring flowers. "You have a beautiful flower garden."

"Thank you, I love to piddle. But Candace, she's the one with the green thumb." She bent to turn off the sprinkler hose and Melissa did it for her. "This morning, she told me she's entering her roses in the garden club fair," Louise tittered. "I've encouraged her to enter her roses for years."

Melissa glanced back at Eric and frowned. "Did you say you talked to her this morning?"

"Why, yes." She pressed a hand to her cheek. "We

had tea and this apple coffee cake that I bake sometimes. Would you like some, Samantha?" She noticed Eric. "Oh, and tell your young man to come in, too."

A blush heated Melissa's cheeks. Eric simply smiled at the woman, opened the door and maneuvered himself into his chair. Louise took Melissa by the arm and Eric followed. "I'm so glad you finally came. I've been looking for you all day."

Melissa's heart sank as they settled on the porch. "This may be a waste of time," she told Eric while Louise gathered refreshments.

"You never know," Eric said. "Maybe she can tell you something."

The woman tittered out, bringing cinnamon-raisin bread that had been store bought, not homemade apple cake.

"I'm so sorry, dear, I don't know what happened to the cake." Louise's voice quavered with agitation. "I guess Candace finished it off this morning. Have you seen her paintings?"

"Yes, a few," Melissa said.

"They are wonderful, aren't they?" She poured cold water in a mug over a tea bag. "Careful, don't burn yourself now."

Melissa nodded and accepted the cup, then handed one to Eric. "Thanks. Can you tell me anything else about Candace?"

"Well…" Louise sat down, and crossed her thin ankles. "She likes tulips and roses, and—what is that other flower?"

Sympathy filled Melissa. The woman obviously suffered from dementia.

"Did she ever talk about having children?" Melissa asked, hoping for a lucid moment.

Louise thumped her spoon on her cup. "I believe she had a boy. No...no, that was Inez that lives next door." Her soft green eyes met Melissa's. "I'm sorry, hon, what did you say your name was? You look so much like the baby girl I lost when I was young."

Melissa's heart stopped for a minute; could this woman be her mother instead of Candace?

No. Louise was simply confused.

"How did you lose your little girl?" Melissa asked.

"Oh, dear me, she drowned. It was so awful. I miss her so much..."

Eric reached out and gathered the woman's hand in between his. "I'm so sorry."

Her gaze met Eric's, tears brimming over. "You are such a nice gentleman. Thank you for coming."

Melissa was touched by Eric's sensitivity. She patted Louise's hand and thanked her, then they left.

"She was a sweet lady," she said in the car. "I almost wish..."

"That she was your mother."

She nodded. "I think I'll go back and visit her anyway. She seems lonely."

Eric turned brooding eyes toward the window, and Melissa frowned. What had she said or done that had upset him?

Eric gripped the seat, wanting to reach out and touch Melissa. To comfort her and reassure her that one day she'd find her family. But how could he do that when he suspected Hughes might be her father? When he was supposed to be using her?

And that poor woman, Louise...seeing her had only made him wonder what his own mother might have looked like now if she had lived.

Melissa pulled up to his cabin, and he reached for

his wheelchair. The fact that he needed it was a bitter reminder of why he had to finish the job.

Hughes had to pay.

He just hated that Melissa might be hurt in the process.

But he wasn't the only one Hughes had hurt. And he had to put a stop to it.

Melissa let Eric out at his cabin and drove to hers, tension knotting her neck. Why had Eric grown so sullen?

Wearily, she dragged herself inside. No sooner had she closed the door when a knock sounded. Maybe it was Eric coming back. Maybe he'd open up and tell her what was wrong.

Instead of Eric though, the man who'd acted as Robert Latone's watchdog at the funeral stood at the door. "Miss Fagan, we need to talk."

Melissa pressed her mouth into a tight line. "What about?"

"About you."

"Mr...?"

"Moor. I'm Robert Latone's personal assistant."

"I see. Well, Mr. Moor, unless you have information regarding my mother, then we have nothing to say to one another."

"You're wrong about that. Mr. Latone has suffered enough the last few days." He shouldered his way inside, and Melissa gasped, panic needling her. "He doesn't need you making false accusations about being his granddaughter or slandering his daughter's name by insisting she gave birth to an illegitimate child. Let Candace rest in peace."

"I want her to rest," Melissa said. "But I also want her killer caught."

"Good, then let us handle things." His hand shifted to the inside of his suit jacket pocket. Melissa backed up. Did he have a gun?

He removed a checkbook instead. "How much will it take for you to leave town and drop this matter?"

It was after five by the time Eric arrived at Hopkins's office. A bulky man with tribal tattoos snaking up and down his arms exited the doctor's office as Eric entered. The man's expression was blank, his entire demeanor strange. What kind of treatment had he come for?

"Can I help you?" a young blond nurse asked from the receptionist's desk.

"Yes, I need to talk to Dr. Hopkins."

"I'm sorry, but he can't see you today. Is this for a consultation?"

"Yes, I've been suffering post-traumatic stress disorder relating to my accident," Eric said by way of a cover.

Shouting echoed from down the hall. Eric turned in the direction of the sound, curious.

"That's one of Dr. Hopkins's patients," she explained. "The poor man's psychotic, gets volatile at times." She sputtered a nervous laugh as the shouting grew louder, the patient's voice rising in hysteria.

"Listen, Mr. Collier, let me put you down for an appointment. I need to go help Dr. Hopkins."

"Sure." She squeezed him in for a brief consultation for the following week, and he wheeled toward the door, grateful she didn't wait for him to leave before she raced down the hall to assist with the patient.

Eric wheeled back in, opened the office door and scanned the room, searching for something that might offer Hopkins's DNA. He found a pen on the desk, dropped it in the bag he'd brought and slid it beneath him. At least he could get the man's prints. Eyeing the computer and the files on the desk, he noticed the initials GS=nB-2, but the patient's voice grew quiet and he was afraid the nurse would return any minute.

Cursing the confines of his limited mobility, he wheeled out of the office and into the hallway. Outside, he breathed in the fresh air and glanced up at the building, wondering about Hopkins's therapy techniques. The research notes he'd read about earlier work mentioned special drugs being tested on patients, prisoners who'd traded early-release time to serve as guinea pigs. Had Hopkins continued the unethical procedures? What exactly did GS=nB-2 stand for?

Anxious for the fingerprint results, as soon as he returned to his cottage, he phoned Detective Black. A half hour later, Black and Fox arrived to claim the items.

"We'll get them to Devlin," Black said. "Good work."

"I have a meeting with Dr. Hopkins next week, maybe I can find out more." He explained about the file. "I don't know what the initials GS=nB2 mean, but it could be important."

"We'll check into it," Black said. "Have you learned anything from the Fagan woman?"

"She didn't kill Candace Latone."

"She tell you about the P.I.?" Fox asked.

"Yes, and I'm afraid Melissa's in danger."

Black and Fox exchanged concerned looks. "Be careful," Black warned.

"I can take care of myself," Eric grunted. "Robert Latone claims his daughter never had a child. We need to know if he's lying."

"We're on him," Black said. "And his hound dog,

Edward Moor. The Feds have suspected Latone of espionage for years, but haven't pinpointed any concrete evidence."

"Keep looking," Eric said.

"And you hang with the Fagan woman," Fox said. "She might be our ticket to Hughes."

Eric silently balked, although he knew they were right.

He still didn't have to like it.

They let themselves out, and he splashed cold water on his face, then grabbed his new cane. Maybe he'd visit Melissa tonight, and talk. After burying her mother today, she might need company.

Even if she said she wanted to be alone, he knew all about self-imposed exile. And he refused to allow her to give in to it.

"I think you'd better leave." Melissa gestured toward the cottage door, livid.

Edward Moor settled his intimidating stare on Melissa's face. "Don't be stupid, Miss Fagan. You have nothing to substantiate your claims. And I'm aware of your financial situation, you can use the money."

"I'm not interested in your money," Melissa said. "I came to Savannah for the truth, not to blackmail Mr. Latone."

His eyebrow arch said otherwise. "Mr. Latone would appreciate it if you left town. Soon."

Melissa folded her arms across her chest. "I can't do that."

"You can't or you won't?"

"Both. In case you haven't read the papers, I discovered Candace's body, so that makes me a material witness in a crime. I've been told not to leave Savannah."

"But you said you saw nothing."

"I didn't see anything, but the police still want me for questioning."

A sly grin lit his eyes. "Or they suspect you killed Candace out of revenge because you believe she abandoned you?"

"She did."

He scribbled an amount on the check, then shoved it toward Melissa. "Take this and keep your mouth shut. Or you might end up in jail for killing Candace. Mr. Latone would like to see the murderer caught."

Melissa glanced at the check and stifled a gasp. One million dollars.

If they intended to pay her that much, they definitely had something to hide. She accepted the check, then tore it into shreds, pushed the man out of the entryway and slammed the door in his face.

Furious and frustrated, she stripped off her clothes and climbed in the shower, wanting to wash away the ugliness of the day. Moor and his bribe repulsed her.

She needed to calm herself and sleep. Forget that he had darkened her door with the insinuation that she had sought out Candace for money, or that she would settle for a bribe in place of the truth.

How could Robert Latone care for that man and not his own grandchild?

Had he treated Candace in such a vile manner? If so, she could understand the woman falling for any man who offered the love her father had withheld from her.

She soaped herself and shampooed her hair, closing her eyes as the hot water beat a soothing pattern down her body. The soap bubbles slithered to the floor and swirled around her, the comforting task slowly washing away her anxiety. The soapy scent reminded her of

Eric fresh from the shower after his therapy session, the scent triggering memories of his gentle comforting touches today and the kiss they'd shared.

She desperately wanted more. Wanted him to hold her tonight and erase the pain and emptiness of knowing that her hopes of having a mother had died with Candace. Images of Eric's large hands running over her body taunted her, and a titillating sensation stole through her body. What would it feel like for Eric to stroke her naked skin? To kiss and tease her in all those secret places that no other man had ever touched?

Wild sensations spiraled through her at the sheer thought. She turned off the water, toweled off and pulled on a terry-cloth robe. The soft fabric reminded her of the baby blanket one of her foster mothers had given her.

Another had taken it away, saying she was too old to cling to such nonsense.

If she ever had a child, she would never say such harsh things.

She dragged a brush through her long hair, combing out the tangles, then faced herself in the mirror and stared at her reflection. Why had her parents been unable to love her?

Why had anyone since?

She opened the medicine chest and reached for her medication, but a screeching sound startled her, and she hesitated to listen. The whisper of the wind? A tree branch scraping the window?

It sounded again, low and eerie. Her senses sprang to full alert, and she listened at the door. Nothing.

Still, caution interceded as she remembered the events of the past few days, and she slowly inched open the door, squinting through the dimly lit interior. Nothing. Certain her imagination was overreacting again, she stepped into the hall, but a large hand grabbed her around the waist, and another one settled over her mouth.

Melissa tried to scream, raised her leg to kick backward in a defensive move she'd learned when she was young, but her attacker knocked her in the head.

They both crumbled to the floor in a tangle of fists and fighting.

Chapter 10

Melissa scrambled sideways, but the man's fist rammed into her chest, and she gasped. Pain sliced through her rib cage and cut off her oxygen. He flipped her to her stomach, jerked her arms behind her and twisted them upward, grinding her face into the floor. A needle jabbed her arm. Then the metallic taste of blood filled her mouth, and dizziness blurred her vision.

The phone trilled, over and over, and the message machine clicked on. "Hi, Melissa, it's Eric. I'm on my way. See you in a few minutes."

Tears dribbled down her face, the salty taste mingling with the blood as Eric's face flashed into her mind. She was losing consciousness.

And she had one last regret. She wished she'd made love to him before she died.

* * *

Before Eric could make it out the door, Cain called and then Luke Devlin.

"I talked to Black and received the fingerprints. Thanks, Collier."

"Tell me about this Dr. Hopkins."

"He's been working on hypnosis techniques with patients during therapy. Word is he might be involved in a special project for the government—GS–B2. Government-sanctioned brainwashing experiments."

"Great. I'm supposed to see him next week."

"Be careful," Devlin warned. "If he suspects the real reason you're there, you might end up a guinea pig."

Eric's fingers tightened around the handset. Old distrust issues rose to haunt him. Eric had always seen the grays, never trusted anyone but his brother. Now he'd been forced to rely on Devlin and two local cops he'd met days ago. He didn't like it.

"What's happening with the Fagan woman?"

"She went to Candace Latone's funeral today. Latone wasn't happy to see her. He denied Candace had a child." He sighed and massaged a cramp in his upper thigh. "He's either in the dark about the baby Candace delivered or he's hiding something."

"Interesting, considering his donations to CIRP. I've been doing some background research."

"Anything new?"

"Apparently, doctors at the hospital ran a special fertility clinic back in the eighties. They were also researching a new birth control pill and experimenting with fertility drugs. Candace was in one of the experiments, but I'm not sure which."

"Do you know who fathered her baby?"

"Everything points to Hughes. He had some kind of God complex, I guess. Figured his sperm was superior to others." A sardonic chuckle escaped him. "Or maybe at that point in his career, he wasn't bold enough to involve outsiders in his experiments."

"Did he have a personal relationship with Candace?"

"It's too early to tell, but my sources believe he did. Even if he didn't, though, if Candace received the fertility treatments, Hughes was likely the father."

"Why would a single woman like her take fertility treatments?"

"To antagonize her father."

Eric let the comment stand. Had Candace gotten pregnant as a rebellious statement against Robert Latone? "An affair with Hughes would serve the same purpose and be even more personal. Get back at her daddy by screwing his friend."

"Right. Or maybe she was looking for a father figure and Hughes provided it."

"And he gladly took advantage of the fact." Eric's opinion of the man dropped ever lower on the scale of humanity. "God, I want to catch this bastard."

"I'm glad to hear you say that." Devlin paused. "You realize we finally have the perfect way to draw out Hughes."

Damn it. He was going to suggest Eric use Melissa as bait to trap Hughes. Eric did not want to tell Melissa her father was a monster, or lie to her and use her. "Hey, I want Hughes as bad as you do, but I refuse to put Melissa in the middle...."

"Think about it," Devlin said in a low voice. "We could finally arrest Hughes for all the lives he's hurt and still might hurt."

Eric remembered Cain and Alanna and little baby Simon. Hughes definitely posed a threat to his family. What should he do?

Melissa stirred, disoriented and gasping for air. She'd been bound and gagged and was trapped somewhere underground. The smell of damp earth assaulted her.

Where was she? A cave? A cellar? A basement? Was she still at CIRP?

The floor rocked beneath her, and for a moment she thought she was on a boat. Then the movement settled. The rocking motion was her own head spinning from the drugs. She dug downward with her elbows to lift herself but tasted dirt.

Fear snaked through her, claustrophobia mounting. Had her attacker buried her alive?

Panic stabbed at her, destroying rational thought. She struggled against the heavy ropes. Skin scraped and blood trickled down her hands. She didn't care. She had to free herself. Claw her way out of this hell-hole. Scream for help.

Where was Eric? Was he close by? Had he returned in time to see the man who'd assaulted her drag her off?

The cloying odor of rotting foliage and a dead animal permeated her nostrils. She bit the inside of her cheek, nausea rising. A dead mouse. A rat. If there was one, there would be others. All sorts of bugs and creatures lived underground, ready to feed off her.

Stop panicking. Breathe slowly so you don't waste oxygen.

She tried to scoot downward to acclimate herself. The area was tight, only a few feet, like a basement crawl space. She rolled to her back, fighting the pain from her bruised ribs, but dizziness swept over her again.

A sob escaped, and she twisted onto her side, rocking herself back and forth. Terror overcame her. No one would ever find her here.

If only she'd taken a chance on Eric, if only she'd told him how she felt…but now he would never know. And she would die alone just as she'd lived all her life.

Eric propped the cane on his lap and wheeled along the path that paralleled the ocean, hoping the fresh salty air would clear his head. He desperately wanted to see Melissa tonight, but his need for her company had nothing to do with the case.

He did not want to use her or confess his suspicions about her father. She had received a devastating blow in finding her mother dead, and then having her grandfather deny her existence. How would she react if she learned she might be the daughter of a mad scientist who had killed innocent people and tried to shape others' lives with his twisted research and need for power?

The waves crashed against the rocks, a seagull swooped low on the sandy shore below to search for crumbs. A lone fisherman stood casting out his line. A patient, most likely. Eric had enjoyed fishing on the lake back home. When he'd invented the story about building a ranch for troubled teens, he'd realized it wasn't a bad idea. Maybe when he finished this mission, he'd draw up a plan. What would Melissa think of the idea?

The lake on his property could provide fishing for the kids and other recreational activities, the horses would offer the opportunity to ride, as well as work for the boys, and the on-site counselors would guide them back on track.

His emotions calmer, he headed toward Melissa's cabin. Tonight he would simply talk to her, offer her a shoulder if she needed one. Tomorrow he'd figure out a way to draw out Hughes without Melissa's involvement.

He wheeled across the quadrangle that separated the patient housing from employee cottages, frowning when he noticed her door ajar. Remembering the earlier break-in, he approached with caution. His pulse accelerated when he rolled inside the doorway and spotted a lamp shattered on the floor. Magazines had been scattered, and the coffee table sat sideways as if it had been kicked or moved. A damp towel lay on the carpet near the bathroom in a puddle. All signs of a scuffle.

"Melissa?" An eerie silence pervaded the room. "Melissa?"

No answer.

The first strains of panic wove through his system as he wheeled through the rest of the cottage. No Melissa. He raced back to the living area and scanned the room for any indication of where she might be. Her purse mocked him from the kitchen counter. Her car had been parked outside. She hadn't driven anywhere.

And judging from the strewn items on the floor, she hadn't left willingly.

Had Hughes discovered her identity and kidnapped her? Had Latone or one of his cronies decided to stop her from asking questions?

Had the killer who'd murdered Candace attacked Melissa?

He reached for the phone, his pulse pounding. Damn it, the line had been cut.

He slammed it down and raced outside. Thank God he'd brought his cell phone. He called the locals.

"We're on our way," Fox said.

Eric hung up, his fear intensifying, his frustration mounting. He had to do something.

Minutes could cost Melissa her life.

A noise rattled the brush. Footsteps maybe? He paused and listened. Nothing.

The wind howled off the ocean, the onset of a spring storm brewing in the distance. The temperature had dropped with the cloud cover, adding a chill to the air. Could Melissa have escaped her attacker? If so, she might be outside, running for her life. Where would she go? To him? Down to the water?

He scanned the pavement for footprints, anything to indicate where her attacker might have taken her, and noticed the grass had been flattened to the right. Something had been dragged over it.

A body maybe.

Praying he wasn't too late, he steered off the paved path onto the grassy area and followed the indented grass blades. Footprints that looked as if they'd been made by running shoes marred the dry ground, and a few fibers—terry cloth maybe? a bathrobe?—dotted the grass.

He wheeled faster, searching the area for someplace the perpetrator might have taken Melissa. Another patch of land next to one of the storage buildings that looked recently disturbed. Was she inside the building? He wheeled closer and checked the door, but it was padlocked from the outside. No windows. Damn.

He rolled around the outside perimeter, listening for signs of someone trapped inside, but heard nothing.

He contemplated giving up, when he noticed a small patch of land covering a storage door that led to a crawl space. Had the center built an underground shelter in case of a nuclear attack or some kind of chemical or biological spillover from Nighthawk Island?

He paused and listened. The wind howled again, but below its whine, he detected another sound. Scratching beneath the ground. A few white fibers lay in the grass nearby. Could Melissa be down in that hole?

Was she alive? Hurt?

He cursed his legs as he fought to free himself from the chair. Finally he managed to support himself with the cane and took two steps toward the covering. Slowly lowering himself, he crawled the rest of the way, then lay on his belly and pulled at the circular concrete covering. His muscles strained as he moved it aside. Darkness filled the mouth of the opening, a rancid smell escaping.

"Melissa?" He leaned farther into the opening and yelled her name again. "Melissa, are you there?"

Nothing.

"Melissa?" He leaned farther into the hole, searching for light, walls, anything to orient him. A scratching sound rose from the depths of the darkness.

Bracing himself on his hands and knees, he swung his body around and slid himself down into the opening, clawing at the sides and steps built into the wall. Using his upper body to support most of his weight, he moved down the steps, his weakened legs trembling as he descended. He half dragged himself the rest of the way. His hands dug at the dirt walls. His fingers bled from the jagged rocks he met on the way. Finally, he dropped to the floor and scrambled through the darkness toward the sound of the scratching. A sliver of light radiated from the mouth of the tunnel. Then he saw a body.

"Melissa?"

She lay facedown, her arms bound behind her, a gag around her mouth. One foot twitched back and forth. Her toe was bloody where she'd been trying to scratch the ground.

At least she was alive.

Emotions clogged his throat as he slid on his belly the remaining few feet to her. The hole was obviously the end of a tunnel, maybe an emergency escape from the storage building. His hands shaking, he lifted her in his lap and turned her over. She was limp, her eyes glassy, her breathing so shallow it was barely audible. Pushing dirt-covered hair from her face, he untied the gag to make breathing easier, and checked her for injuries. Blood seeped from a gash on the back of her head and another on her forehead.

"Melissa, talk to me, honey, wake up and look at me."

She lay motionless in his arms though, her body icy cold, sending another bout of fear through him. Had she been drugged?

He remembered her seizure disorder, grabbed his cell phone and punched in Fox's number.

"We're on the island now."

"I found her," Eric said in a gruff voice. "Get an ambulance, she's in trouble." He gave Fox directions to the building, then hung up and rocked Melissa back and forth to comfort her.

Chapter 11

"Shh, Melissa, be strong, baby, you have to be all right." A siren wailed close by and roared up to the cottage. Black appeared first, his head in the mouth of the opening.

"Collier?"

"Yeah, we're down here."

"How's she doing?"

"She's unconscious. I…her body's cold and clammy, eyes are dilated." He wiped her damp forehead with his palm.

"We'll get a crime team to check her place," Black called. "How the hell did you wind up in there?"

"I crawled down to find Melissa."

"It's a miracle you didn't kill yourself. Hold on, we'll have you out in a minute."

Damn it, Eric thought. If he had full function of his limbs, he'd already have rescued Melissa himself. "She has some kind of seizure disorder, Black. I think she takes regular medication, we'll need the name of the meds for the hospital."

Fox's voice echoed to him, "I'll look for it in the cottage. The ambulance is pulling in now."

The siren wailed closer. Seconds later, he heard Black directing the paramedics to the tunnel. One rescue worker descended the steps, then rushed over, knelt and took Melissa's vitals. He yelled them up to the other paramedic. "We need a stretcher board down here. We'll lift her out."

He glanced at Eric. "Are you all right, sir? Do you have injuries?"

"I'm fine, just take care of her." He felt helpless as he watched the men work to save Melissa. They secured her to the stretcher, and with Black's help lifted her through the opening. The first paramedic returned to assist him.

"I can hang on to a rope if you can haul me up," he said between clenched teeth.

The paramedic nodded, and Eric crawled over and grabbed the end of the rope. Thank God he'd continued to lift weights and maintain his upper-body strength. He needed it now more than ever.

By the time Black helped him up, he'd grabbed his cane, and hobbled over to Melissa, the paramedics had started an IV. Fox raced back from the cottage with a bottle of prescription pills and handed them to the paramedics. They called the E.R. for instructions.

"We're ready to transport her." The first paramedic turned to Eric. "We need to check you out, sir."

"I wasn't hurt tonight," Eric said, hating his obvious physical problems. "But I'm going with you."

The paramedics traded questioning looks with the detectives, then one of them nodded.

"We'll search the cottage for evidence of her attacker," Black said.

"You'd better find him," Eric growled as he allowed the paramedic to help him into the ambulance. "The SOB has to pay."

"Is our problem extinguished?"

"Not exactly." He scrubbed a hand over his sweating face, cursing aloud. "I planned to finish her off at her cottage, but that damn crippled guy called. He was on his way. I put her in the crawl space so I wouldn't get caught. I thought she'd suffocate there or I could go back later and complete the assignment, but Collier found her."

"Who is this Collier? What does he know?"

"I'm not sure. He's a patient, Melissa Fagan is his physical therapist."

"Hmm. Find out more on the man."

"Right."

"Do I need to take care of the Fagan problem myself?"

He rolled a cigarette between his fingers, yanked out a match, but decided to wait until the paramedics and cops left the vicinity before he lit up. "No, I can do it." He had been trained well. The mission was part of his initiation; he had to complete it, live up to the symbols tattooed on his arms. The scent of the kill taunted him. He could taste the blood, death.

And he knew exactly where to finish the job—at the hospital, right under all the unsuspecting noses.

Melissa felt as if she was drifting through a haze of never-ending darkness. She swam through the murky water, but the undertow dragged her deeper into the abyss, pulling at her legs and arms. Unknown terrors waited for her as she traveled deeper, a thick quicksand-like marsh sucking her underneath its muddy, brown folds. She couldn't see. She couldn't breathe.

She couldn't fight it.

After the pain, the darkness, there had to be a light. Peace. Freedom. She ached to find it.

"Pulse is weak and thready, she's not breathing! We're losing her!"

Voices echoed through the haze. Distant, far away. The droning of other noises interceded. A wailing sound like a siren. Then she was moving again, plowing through the water. Thick weeds and underbrush battered her body and gouged her skin like talons. Something hard slammed against her chest, and she bucked upward. A puff of air sifted through the concentrated quicksand, exploding into her mouth and lungs.

"Fight it, Melissa, fight it."

Fingers yanked at her, trying to pull her back through the murkiness, but a whirlwind sucked her the other way. "Come on, breathe, damn it!"

A coldness settled around her, chilling her to the bone. Numbness slowly seeped through her, obliterating the pain. She was floating. She welcomed the lifeless sensation, wanted to escape the suffocating darkness where she was all alone.

"Don't you dare give up, Melissa," the voice whispered. "You're not alone. Do you hear me, you're not alone. I'm here."

But she was alone. The floating felt so peaceful....

"Melissa, I care about you, please, don't give up. Come back to me."

She began to spin in circles, weaving through the

darkness, around and around. The pain was back, pricking at her skin, the air thick with death, the light…

"I'm here, Melissa, hold my hand and fight." Her hand moved upward, pressed against something coarse, damp. A face, tears.

Eric. He was calling her name, dragging her from the well of darkness.

"I need you, Melissa. I've never said that to anyone but my brother, but I need you. Please don't leave me here alone."

The pain receded, faded to a dull droning ache. Light burst through the gray. A soft halo of someone's face.

Eric's.

She wiggled her fingers in an attempt to squeeze his hand, but she was so weak, she didn't know if he could feel it.

Eric cradled Melissa's hand in his, pressing it against his cheek. He lowered his head, emotions battling to the surface. He couldn't lose her. A flutter of her fingers, and he jerked his head up.

"She's breathing on her own again," the paramedic said.

Relief surged through him.

He stroked her cheek. "Melissa, hang in there, you hear me. You're strong, you're going to be all right."

Her squeeze felt stronger this time, and he finally released the breath he'd been holding. The ambulance barreled into the hospital parking lot, and the paramedics catapulted into motion, barking details of her condition to the doctors and nurses waiting to greet them.

The second paramedic helped Eric from the ambulance. His legs felt unsteady as the man assisted him in, and brought him a wheelchair. Now his adrenaline surge had petered off, the familiar ache of his injuries had returned.

But at least he had been able to save Melissa.

They rushed her into the E.R., and he wheeled into the waiting room, for the first time since his accident, craving the sweet relief of nicotine.

He felt so damn helpless.

Black and Fox were investigating Melissa's cabin for evidence and the doctors were taking care of Melissa. What the hell could he do but wait?

The familiar scents of the hospital bombarded him, reminding him of his long stint in the burn ward. Cain must have been out of his mind when he'd thought Eric had died in the explosion. His brother had thrown himself into saving Alanna and Simon as a favor to Eric, but thankfully, Cain had found love in the process. His brother deserved it.

He punched in Cain's number. Alanna answered on the third ring. "Hello."

"Alanna, it's Eric."

"Eric, we were just talking about you. How are things at CIRP?"

"That's why I'm calling. Can I speak to Cain?"

"Sure." She sounded worried but she called Cain to the phone. His brother cooed to baby Simon, then said hello.

"What's wrong, Eric? Are you in trouble?"

He explained about the incident with Melissa. "I don't want her to die," Eric admitted in a gruff voice. "And Devlin wants me to use Melissa to bait Hughes."

Cain hesitated. "You're falling for her, aren't you?"

Eric scrubbed a hand over his face. "I don't know. I...but I don't want anything bad to happen to her."

Cain chuckled. "You always were a sucker for a

woman in trouble." Cain whispered something to Alanna. "Then again, I guess I should be grateful. I would never have met Alanna or Simon if you weren't such a good-hearted bastard."

"I'm not good-hearted," Eric growled.

Cain snorted in disbelief. "Do you want me to come to Savannah? Say the word, and I'm there."

"No. You need to stay with your family."

Family…the one thing they'd both lost early on.

"Do what you think is right," Cain said. "But be careful, Eric. And call me if you need me."

Eric hung up, feeling marginally better. He was glad Cain had a new family. But what about him? Did he deserve to have a woman in his life?

Or was he destined to live his life alone?

He glanced down at his scarred body. Would any woman be able to accept him the way he was now? Would Melissa…

He wanted to touch her, taste her, tell her the truth.

But she would hate him when she learned he had lied about his identity.

"Mr. Collier?"

Eric jerked his head up, shocked to find the CEO of CIRP, Ian Hall, standing in front of him. "What are you doing here?"

Hall dug his hands into the pockets of his suit pants. "I heard one of our employees was hurt and had to be admitted."

Eric bottled his volatile emotions. "*Hurt* isn't exactly the right word. Melissa Fagan was assaulted, bound and gagged and left to die in some underground crawl space next to one of the storage buildings."

"My God." A concerned frown creased the skin between Hall's eyes as he dropped into a chair beside Eric. "How is her condition?"

"I don't know. I'm waiting to hear now."

Hall raked a hand through his neatly clipped hair. "Do the police have any idea who attacked her or why?"

"The police are searching her cottage for evidence now."

"Was there a robbery?"

"No sign of one."

"I'll alert Seaside Security to watch for outsiders, beef up security and put a special guard on Miss Fagan's place."

"What if it wasn't an outsider?"

Hall's face blanched. "What are you suggesting, Mr. Collier?"

"That someone on the staff might be involved."

"That's ridiculous." Hall reached for his cell phone. "By the way, what exactly is your relationship to Miss Fagan?"

"She's my therapist," Eric said, refusing to elaborate.

A doctor approached then and Hall stood. Eric gripped the wheelchair arm. "How is she?"

"We've stabilized her for now. The drugs, coupled with the blow to the head, triggered a seizure, but she should be all right by tomorrow." He folded his hands in front of him. "We need to keep her overnight for observation."

Eric nodded. "Of course."

"Good work, Dr. Curry." Hall shook the middle-aged doctor's hand. "And please call me if there are any changes in her condition. I want to know immediately."

"I certainly will."

Hall turned, offered his hand and Eric accepted it. "I heard you made a pretty heroic rescue, Mr. Collier.

As the director of CIRP, I want to extend my thanks. We value each of our employees and patients here." He dropped his hand. "And please let me know if you see something suspicious or if Miss Fagan has information about her attacker. I'm sure Seaside Security will do whatever it can to find the person and see justice served."

Eric watched Hall walk away. He had said all the right things, made all the right moves.

Was he on the level, or was he hiding something?

An hour later, they had finally settled Melissa into a private room. Eric had phoned Black to relay her condition and to ask if they'd discovered anything. The police didn't have the results of the fingerprint tests, but they had bagged a stray hair, which they were testing for DNA.

Shanika, a kind African-American nurse, strode in, introduced herself and patted his arm. He figured he looked pathetic, all dirty and exhausted, parked beside Melissa's bed, but he didn't care.

"You can stay with her, but don't expect her to wake up before morning. She's weak and suffered a trauma." The nurse took Melissa's vitals and recorded them on her chart. "Fatigue also follows this type of seizure, along with a depressed mood. Both will fade, but she needs rest and time to recover."

Eric nodded. He was a patient man. He wasn't going anywhere. He'd give her all the time in the world to recover. In the meantime, he'd do his damnedest to keep her safe.

Shanika graced him with an understanding smile, then left the room. Eric wheeled closer to Melissa and cradled her hand in his, rubbing her fingers between his to warm her. The other hand was hooked to an IV, the constant drip a reminder that she'd nearly died earlier. Bruises marked her forehead, and a scrape on her cheek testified to the brutality of the crime.

He hated men who used physical force on women, and had vowed he would never raise his hand to a female or child.

But now he wanted to kill the bastard who'd hurt her.

Trying to tamp his anger, he kissed her fingers one by one, then pressed them against his cheek. Her eyelids fluttered. For a second, he thought he'd imagined it, but then they fluttered once more, opening partway. Her eyes seemed unfocused, and she blinked, as if searching through the haze of drugs and pain.

"I'm right here, Melissa, you're going to be all right."

A frown pulled at her mouth and she tried to speak, but no sound came out. She wrestled beneath the covers though, as if struggling with her assailant.

"Shh, don't talk now. Just rest." He stroked her hands again. "Tomorrow will be soon enough for you to tell me what happened. Tonight, rest, concentrate on getting better."

Her eyes fluttered again, then closed, and her breathing became more even, but her body jerked once more, a moan rumbling from deep within her.

Her anguish tore him in two, but he continued to hold her hand and to whisper nonsensical comforting words until she finally settled into a deep peaceful sleep.

Damn it, he didn't think that Collier guy was ever going to leave the woman's side. He must be some kind of desperate. Of course, after looking at the man, no doubt he'd be hot to trot for anything with two legs that smiled at him.

He checked his watch. Two-thirty. Finally the man wheeled his chair from the room and headed down the hall. But he still had to get rid of the security guard plastered to the woman's door.

He had a plan. Had been trained well for his mission.

Slipping down the hall and around the corner, he spied the storage room. Inside were the janitor's cleaning chemicals. With a gloved hand, he read the contents. Just as he thought. Volatile as hell.

Stifling a laugh, he sprinkled the chemicals on the cleaning rags, dumped them in a big garbage bin in the small room, then dropped a lit match into the center. The flame ignited, caught the chemicals and began smoldering,

Covering his face with a surgical mask to match his scrubs, he slipped out of the room before the smoke curled through the doorway. He moved down the hall unnoticed, then waited in the corridor across from his victim's room until a nurse noticed the string of smoke.

"Fire!" She waved her arms to attract someone's attention.

Another nurse ran up, someone shouted at the security guard, and the guard jogged down the hall to help.

He chuckled beneath the mask. So easy.

Flexing his hand beneath his lab coat, he reached inside for the hypodermic and slid soundlessly into Melissa Fagan's room. She was sleeping like a baby, already so exhausted from their earlier jaunt that she didn't even stir. Damn. It really was more fun when they put up a fight.

Still, he had to finish her off tonight.

He raised the needle, injected the drug into her IV, turned and walked from the room. She would be dead before morning. Before anyone discovered she'd been given the wrong combination of drugs.

And no one would ever know the real reason—or who had killed her.

Chapter 12

Eric had almost reached the elevator when the smoke alarm sounded. He'd intended to get some fresh air, then return and sit by Melissa's side for the night, but he spun the wheelchair around and raced back down the hall. No way could he leave Melissa if a fire had broken out. He searched the corridors, his suspicious nature surfacing. What better diversion for a personal attack on a patient than a fire?

Heart beating double time, he rounded the corner and nearly crashed into a young orderly.

"Sir, can't you hear the alarm? This isn't a drill, you have to evacuate now."

Eric shrugged off his concern. "I can't leave, not until I know my friend is okay."

"Look, buddy, it'll be hard enough to get patients out if we need to, much less the visitors, especially handicapped ones."

Fury balled in Eric's stomach. "Let me worry about myself. Now, take your hands off the chair, or I'll do it for you."

The young man jumped back, and Eric wheeled down the hallway toward Melissa's room, bypassing a doctor and nurse in earnest conversation, then a surgeon, who cut his eyes toward Eric, his steps clipped, his attention returning to the file in his hands.

The nurses' station was empty, the crew gathered down the hall near a storage closet where the fire had apparently broken out. He scanned the hallway by Melissa's room, but the security guard had left his post to check on the source of the fire.

Livid at the man's incompetency, Eric approached the hospital room. Fear for Melissa tightened his gut as he opened the door.

She lay still in the bed, her breathing a series of hard rasps. He glanced at the IV, remembered the surgeon rushing down the hall, and panic slammed into him.

He turned and called into the hallway, "Help, room 111! Emergency!"

Without waiting further, he ripped the IV from Melissa's arm and yelled for help again. Shanika rushed in, saw Melissa's agitated breathing and ran to the door.

"We need a crash cart stat!"

Eric cradled Melissa's hand. "Hang on, honey, help is on the way. Don't give up."

Seconds later, a team of nurses and doctors ran in, and Eric moved aside while they treated her. Once she resumed breathing, he was banned to the waiting room, so he phoned Detective Black and filled him in.

"I want one of your guys here," Eric said. "That Seaside Security guard left her alone."

"A rookie mistake," Black said.

"Yeah, one that almost cost Melissa her life." Eric blew into his balled fist to release his pent-up frustration. "I don't trust CIRP's security. For all we know, Hughes, or whoever is involved in this conspiracy, has the security team in his pocket."

"You're probably right," Black said. "I'll assign someone immediately."

It galled Eric that he'd had to ask for help. He thanked Black and hung up, then rolled back to Melissa's room. He had almost lost her twice today.

He wouldn't let it happen again. He only hoped that when Melissa woke, she could tell them something concrete to lead them to her attacker.

Melissa stirred from a troubled sleep, her body languid and heavy. She struggled to open her eyes, finally forcing them partway open, only to look through a foggy haze. Where was she? What had happened? Why did she feel so exhausted and drained and ...confused?

Memories crashed back. The shower...someone had attacked her, she'd been tied and gagged and left in a cave to die. The claustrophobia—she couldn't breathe. She had to claw her way out. Then voices. Eric beside her. Lifting her, murmuring sweet loving words, whispering that she wasn't alone. The darkness, then the brilliant white light had beckoned her, but he had called her back.

Emotions welled inside her. Where was she now?

The whine of an IV drip and another sound—snoring—drifted through her consciousness. She twisted sideways. Eric's dark head lay facedown on the edge of her bed. His hands were curled around her free one, and he'd fallen asleep. He had stayed with her all night.

"Eric?" It hurt to talk, her mouth was so dry, like cotton.

He jerked his head up, the remnants of sleep and fatigue lining his handsome face.

Love for Eric swelled in her chest.

But what could she do about it? Someone was trying to kill her. She couldn't put him in danger.

If your father is trying to keep you from finding him, maybe you don't want to know who he is.

"Melissa, thank God, you're finally awake." Worry deepened his gruff voice.

"How..." She paused and wet her parched lips. "How long have I been here?"

"Since last night." A small smile tugged at his lips. "But it feels like days."

"You stayed all night?"

He nodded, lifted her hand and planted a kiss in her palm. "I promised you I wouldn't leave you alone."

"You always keep your promises?"

His eyes clouded. "I do my best."

She felt such a connection with him that it frightened her. What had she done to deserve his kindness? And how would he react if she confessed that she was falling in love with him?

"You should be at your place resting. And your therapy—"

"Don't worry about me, Melissa." He brushed her hair away from her forehead. "You need to take care of yourself."

She shrugged and angled her head down to study their hands. The nightmare from the evening before flashed into her mind again. She'd had a seizure, she was certain of it. That accounted for part of her fatigue. She didn't want to be weak, to appear helpless in front of Eric.

"You rescued me?"

He released a self-deprecating laugh. "I had some help."

"But you climbed down in that hole to save me." Her gaze met his again. "Your legs?"

"They're fine," Eric said, denying the mutinous throbbing that had taken root in the wee hours of the morning.

"You need to stretch, go to the rehab center, have Helen work the muscles—"

"Shh." He pressed a finger to her lips. "I told you to stop worrying about me."

"Promise me you will, Eric. I don't want you to have a setback."

He didn't want that, either. He'd progressed too far. "All right, I promise."

A knock sounded at the door, then Detective Black poked his head in, and glanced from Melissa to Eric. "If it's all right, I'd like to ask you some questions, Miss Fagan."

She nodded, residual fear resurfacing. But she had to talk to the police sometime. She might as well get it over with.

Eric forced himself to give Melissa some space while Black questioned her. Or maybe he needed space or he'd cling to her like a lovesick puppy.

Hearing the details of Melissa's ordeal only fueled his fury more. He stared out the window, watching each nurse and doctor who entered and exited the building, his distrust growing like a cold virus. Someone had disguised himself as a surgeon, slipped into Melissa's room and tried to kill her.

Was it someone who worked at CIRP? Robert Latone or one of his hired guns?

"Did you see the man's face?" Black asked.

"No." Melissa's voice was fading by the minute. "He grabbed me from behind. We struggled, I kicked him, but he hit me. I must have blacked out."

"And when you woke up?"

"I was tied, already in that...that hole."

"Did he say anything while he was attacking you? Did you recognize his voice?"

"No." She paused. "I... I remember the message machine clicking on...it was Eric saying he was coming over."

Black sighed. "He probably dragged you to the crawl space so Eric wouldn't catch him."

"Or he would have killed me then," Melissa said, echoing Eric's own thoughts.

Black gave a clipped nod.

"Eric saved my life." Melissa's voice dropped even lower.

Thank God, Eric thought. He'd catch the man who'd tried to kill her if it was the last thing he ever did.

Melissa finally persuaded Eric to rest, but he had only agreed after Detective Black had assigned one of his men to guard her door.

The next morning, when she was released, she felt like a prisoner in her cottage, the guard a visual reminder that someone had actually attempted to kill her.

After showering and dressing, she poured herself a cup of coffee. Should she forget her search and return to Atlanta? Two people had already died because of her, and she had almost lost her own life. If Eric hadn't rescued her...

She did not want him hurt because of her.

The letters she'd brought with her from Candace's house mocked her from her bedside table. Although she'd read them already, maybe she'd missed something that might clue her in to her father's identity.

Dear Baby,

I miss you so much. Every time I see a young mother pushing a stroller at the mall or running along the beach collecting seashells with their toddler, my heart squeezes into a gigantic knot. They say pain becomes more bearable as time passes, but each day I only miss you more.

Today, I painted an ocean scene and added a sand castle, one I wish we could build together. I imagine your face lit up with animation, your eyes bright with laughter. Your skin would be turning pink, so I coat you with sunscreen and tie a bonnet around your head to protect your delicate face.

I picture what you look like in my mind. You would be two years old today. Do you have my wiry hair and artistic eye? Or did you inherit your father's straight locks and detail-oriented mind?

Wherever you are, sweetheart, know that Mommy loves you. Maybe someday I'll get to hold you in my arms again.

Love,
Your mama

Melissa pressed the letter to her chest. Candace had loved her and wanted her. But she'd given her away and pined for her afterward.

Melissa could not return to Atlanta without knowing the truth about why she'd given her away or who had killed her.

Eric's face flashed into her mind. Tonight she'd tell him they couldn't see each other again.

She'd do anything to protect him.

In spite of losing a night's sleep, Eric felt surprisingly strong. Adrenaline surged through him as he worked through his therapy. Although he didn't enjoy the session with Helen near as much as he enjoyed working with Melissa, she seemed kind and allowed him to increase his routine.

"Are you sure you're ready to lose the chair?" Helen asked.

"Yes, ma'am. I'm tired of being confined." Besides, he'd taken steps with Melissa, then the night she was attacked.

"Don't overdo, Mr. Collier."

"I won't. Melissa warned me about a setback."

"Dear, I hope that girl's doing okay." Helen's forehead furrowed. "I can't believe someone assaulted her right on CIRP's property."

He wondered if Melissa had confided her reasons for being in Savannah to Helen. "You've worked here a long time, haven't you?"

Helen nodded. "When it was just a plain hospital with a few research labs."

"You knew Arnold Hughes?"

"Not personally." Helen shifted her plump body, looking uncomfortable with Eric's question. "Why all the interest in the center?"

"Curiosity. Too much time on my hands, I suppose, so I've been reading."

She nodded. "There's Mr. Stinson, let me get him started while you finish those reps."

"Sure." He pumped the weight with his leg, glancing sideways as she hurried to greet the war veteran. His craggy features looked tired and frustrated. Eric had never been a religious person, having lost his faith the day he and Cain had discovered his mother's suicide, but today he thanked the heavens the doctors had been able to save his legs.

He finished the weight lifting, then practiced walking with the support of the bars, increasing his speed and control daily. A session in the whirlpool relaxed his muscles later, then he showered and headed over to see Melissa. He allowed himself to use the chair on the way to her place, but he carried his cane.

Tonight he planned to walk in to see her and surprise her. He couldn't wait to see her face.

Melissa rationalized her dismal mood as an after-effect of her seizure, but her quest for her parents and the recent attacks on her life complicated things more. And then there were her feelings for Eric, feelings she'd never had for another man...

She needed to take a long walk along the beach, to think and put her life in perspective, but she no longer felt free to do so. Danger lurked in every shadow and corner.

And walking with a guard didn't seem conducive to soul-searching.

A knock sounded at the door and she started, stuffing the last of Candace's letters into her bedside table. Assuming it was the officer stationed outside the cottage, she hurried to answer it, but found Eric on her doorstep.

"Hi."

She drank in his features, reminding herself she had to end this maddening flirtation, or whatever they were doing. "Hi."

"Can I come in?"

"Actually, I was going for a walk on the beach."

His dark eyebrow raised, and he glanced at the officer. "That sounds good. Let's go."

"But…"

"You're not going alone." Eric gestured toward the cop. "It's him or me."

No choice. "All right." She slipped on a windbreaker, then stepped outside and began to follow the paved path to the shore. Eric followed, filling the silence with chitchat about his therapy session with Helen.

"She's been very nice to me," Melissa said. Barring the time she'd asked about the labor/delivery unit.

"It's easy to be nice to you, Melissa."

Her heart lurched. They'd reached the sand and she turned to Eric. It would be difficult to maneuver the chair down the beach. "I won't go far."

"I'm going with you."

She started to shake her head, but he pushed himself up, then gripped the cane and took a step toward her.

"Eric—"

"I'm improving," he said. "Not ready to jog yet, but I can manage a short walk."

Assuring herself it would be therapeutic for both of them, she allowed him to join her, but mentally gauged the distance. "You've made amazing progress, Eric."

"I have a great physical therapist."

His husky voice massaged her frayed nerve endings, igniting desire and other emotions she didn't want to deal with. They walked several feet in silence, the salty breeze lifting her hair, the scent of the ocean and sound of the waves crashing on the shore soothing her.

"It's really beautiful here," Melissa said. She sat down on the edge of a huge boulder to give Eric a rest, and stared out at the vast sea.

Eric leaned against the rock and nodded, but he wasn't looking at the ocean. His gaze warmed her face. "So are you."

Her breath caught when she turned and saw the hunger flaring in his eyes. Then, he raised his hand, slid it behind her neck and lowered his mouth to hers. She hesitated a fraction of a second, but the moment his lips dampened her own, she was lost in the sweet bliss of his caress.

Eric couldn't help himself. Ever since he'd found Melissa unconscious in that damn hole, he'd wanted to hold her and kiss her. He had almost lost her twice, he needed reassurance that she was here, in his arms, alive.

She tasted like sweet berries and desire, a heady mixture that immediately sent a bolt of longing through him. He threaded his fingers into her silky hair, desperate to obliterate the image of her near death.

He wanted her. Ached to make her his.

A low moan escaped her lips, heightening his hunger even more. He teased her lips apart with his tongue and probed the warm recesses of her mouth, seeking, yearning, exploring, telling her silently how he wanted to love her. She clutched his arms, her breathing ragged as he lowered his mouth and kissed her neck, planting teasing tongue brushes all along her neck as his hands stroked her back, then moved to her waist. She groaned again and moved against him. He slid his hands beneath her jacket to cup the plump mounds of her breasts in his hands.

He wanted more.

She was fire in his hands, a literal flame that had caught, ready to burn out of control. He wanted to extinguish her desire by tearing off her clothes and thrusting himself inside her, but reined in his animalistic urges and slowed the pace to prolong the pleasure.

The wind whispered around them, the surf playing a symphonic love song as he lifted his hands to her face. "Melissa, I... I want to make love to you."

Her passion-glazed eyes fixed on his face for a fraction of a second before reality intervened. That moment of hesitation cost him, he realized, but he couldn't regret giving her the choice.

"I...no, Eric, we can't do this."

"Why? Because I'm your patient."

She dropped her head forward. "Partly."

"Then Helen can continue my therapy."

Her gaze shot up to his. "No...there's more."

"You mean there's another man?"

She shook her head, obviously collecting her thoughts. "I...we can't. I mean, I like you, Eric, and you've been kind to me—"

"Kind?" His voice hardened. "I don't want your pity, Melissa."

She chewed on her bottom lip, and bolted to her feet. "I'm sorry, then, because that's all I have to give."

Eric jerked back, her words hitting him with more force than any physical punch could have caused. Then she turned and ran back up the beach, leaving him to hobble after her, with his heart in his throat.

* * *

Robert Iatone peeled the end off the cigar wrapper, raked his hand through his clipped hair and frowned at the headlines as he read silently to himself.

*Local Physical Therapist Attacked
on CIRP Premises*

Attacker unknown, but police are investigating the matter and hope to apprehend the assailant. Ian Hall, CEO of CIRP, claims he is cooperating fully with the police and will provide extra security until the matter is solved.

The maid knocked on his office door. "Mr. Latone, two detectives are here to speak to you."

Robert barked a sarcastic laugh. What had taken them so long?

A broad-shouldered man with dark hair that needed trimming, and another brown-haired detective he recognized from the publicity about the failed memory transplant experiment, appeared.

The one called Black introduced them both. "Mr. Latone, we need to ask you some questions."

"Certainly, gentlemen." He gestured toward the leather wing chairs opposite his desk. "I hope you're here to tell me you've arrested the person responsible for my daughter's murder."

The detectives exchanged odd looks. "We're working on it," Black said.

"Actually, we need to ask you about Melissa Fagan."

Ah, he figured. "Yes, the young woman who found Candace's body. Does she have more information?"

"Not exactly. In fact—" Fox nodded toward the paper on Robert's desk "—you read that she was assaulted."

"Yes. Do you think this attack has something to do with Candace's murder?"

"It's possible the killer thinks she knows something and intends to silence her."

Robert inhaled a drag from the cigar. "Then shouldn't you be out looking for him?"

"We have people investigating it as we speak," Fox said.

"Good, the SOB needs to be behind bars."

Black cleared his throat. "Melissa Fagan claims she has information indicating she was Candace's daughter, but it's our understanding that you disagree."

Robert leveled a suspicious look at Black. "I see, and you think that I'd kill this woman because of her misguided ramblings."

"She has admitted that she received a threatening phone call warning her to leave town, and that you were not very cordial."

He stood. "I believe this conversation is over, gentlemen. The next time you want to ask me questions, contact me first so I can have my lawyer present."

Black and Fox both nodded. Robert waited until they had cleared the room and were outside before he called Moor. "Edward, the cops were just here. They think I tried to kill Melissa Fagan to keep her from poking into the past."

He snuffed out the cigar. "Now, if they question you next, remember—you're my alibi."

Chapter 13

Melissa stewed all night over the way she'd handled Eric. She hadn't wanted to hurt him, she'd only meant to protect him. Yet the anguish she'd seen in his eyes at her comment haunted her. He hadn't deserved to be treated so poorly, not when he'd risked his life or more injuries to save her from that awful burial spot where the madman had left her.

She desperately wanted to talk to him, to apologize and declare her love, and see if he might reciprocate the feeling. Yet to keep him safe, she needed to relinquish her search for her parents.

Did it really matter who they were? She'd begun to wonder....

After all, Eric was here now. Eric hadn't abandoned her. He had pushed his own battered body beyond its limits to save her life.

Confused and aching from wanting him, she braced

herself for their morning session. But when she arrived, he was already working with Helen. She paused and savored the sight, then walked over to the weight set.

"Thanks, Helen, I can take it from here."

"There's no need," Eric said in a flat voice. "Helen and I are working fine together."

Helen gave her a perplexed look. "Mr. Stinson wanted to come in early today. He didn't seem pleased with me yesterday, so maybe it's best you take him…"

She let the sentence trail off. Melissa glanced at Eric, but he kept his back to her and continued the weight lifting. Feeling bereft, as if she'd lost something more valuable than she'd first realized, she tackled her patient.

"Hi, Mr. Stinson, I'm sorry I was out yesterday."

He scowled. "Helen said someone assaulted you? Did they find the guy?"

"No, not yet." She assisted while he tried to stand, using the prosthetic leg. "But I'm sure they will."

"I hope so, Melissa. I'd hate to see anything happen to you." His gaze seemed to be probing. "I bet your folks are worried sick."

"My parents have been gone a long time." Melissa patted his arm, encouraging him to stand. She glanced back at Eric, aching all over for him, once again considering her options.

Maybe she should renounce her search. After all, if her father had murdered her mother, and would rather kill her than reveal her existence, did she really want to meet him?

Eric poured all his anger and energy into his therapy session, determined to reach his optimum physical level so he could complete this job and get the hell out of Savannah.

Whether Melissa wanted him or not, he had to protect her and arrest the man who'd tried to kill her.

But he didn't want her pity.

Her reply reverberated in his head, "That's all I have to give."

Sheer pain radiated through him, along with humiliation. Why had he believed she might want a man like him?

Because for a few minutes, she'd certainly responded as if she had....

He dismissed the mesmerizing hold she had on his body and mind, showered and returned to his cabin, then phoned Black to see if they had any leads on Hughes or Melissa's attacker.

"Nothing so far," Black said, "but we did receive fingerprint results on the CEO and that scientist, Hopkins. Apparently they're who they claim to be."

"Then neither one of the men are Hughes?"

"It appears that way, unless someone planted fake prints and covered themselves in the database."

"Is that possible?"

"Anything's possible with today's technology, but duplicity to that extent would require an insider's assistance."

Damn.

"I'd say we keep looking. Is there anyone else at CIRP who fits Hughes's profile?"

"I'll check again," Eric said. "Maybe I missed someone." He rubbed his forehead. "How about the fifth man in the photo? Did you ever find him?"

"Records say he's dead. He was killed in combat."

Eric sighed. They were no closer to finding the answers than they were when he'd first come there.

And now, he had to worry about Melissa....

* * *

"Damn it, I thought you killed the Fagan woman."

"I tried." He muttered a string of obscenities. "But that Collier man came to the rescue again. Who the hell is he?"

"He's working with the damn cops," the man barked. "His name is not Collier, but Caldwell."

"Caldwell?"

"Yes, the brother of the man who helped that pediatric nurse disappear with Project Simon."

"Hell, he was supposed to be dead, too."

"Someone screwed up. He almost died in that explosion, but now he's here for physical therapy working undercover. And if we don't do something, he might expose us all."

A cold chill skated up his spine. They couldn't let that happen. Not now, not when they'd just gotten more money for their research. Not when they had their own inside man at the FBI helping to ease the path for their success.

"I'll take care of both of them."

"Yeah?" A bark of disbelief followed. "Then do it right this time or I'm replacing you."

He shuddered. He knew what that meant.

Fail and die.

He wasn't ready for the end just yet, but Caldwell and Melissa Fagan had better be.

After his session, Eric reviewed the employee list at CIRP once again. Another name caught his attention— Wallace Thacker, a chemist who'd recently transferred from the research center in Oakland, Tennessee—the facility that Cole Turner had supposedly transferred from.

Of course, Cole had been Clayton Fox, and the identity a bogus one that had been invented to give Clay a past to fit his new name and face.

Frank Chadburn, the director of that center, had also disappeared after the memory transplant experiment had been revealed.

Where was he now?

And what kind of story could Eric use to meet the chemist?

If you confided in Melissa, she might be able to help you gain access to confidential files.

No. He would not use her, especially after the way she'd dismissed him the day before.

Frustrated, he phoned Devlin to discuss a plan of action, but the agent didn't answer, so Eric left a message, grabbed his cell phone and cane and decided to take a walk. He'd make sure the guard was still posted at Melissa's.

Needing fresh air, he took the path along the beach, remembering the last time he'd walked along the shore with Melissa. The wind whistled behind him, the salty spray wetting his face with a fine mist. He felt the sting bite his cheek, then realized the sting hadn't originated from the wind, but a bullet had just grazed his face. His instincts kicking in, he pivoted to search for the shooter. In the distance on a cliff at the heart of Serpent's Cove, he spotted a man in dark clothing. The shooter fired again, this bullet zinging an inch from Eric's chest.

Eric began to run, dodging the gunfire, stumbling across the sand with his weakened legs....

Melissa was walking back to her cottage when she spotted Eric scrambling up the embankment from the beach. What was going on? Why wouldn't he take the level path? And where was his wheelchair?

She launched into a run, forgetting about the guard. "Eric!"

The young rookie, Dothan, grabbed her arm to stop her. "Ma'am, wait."

"It's my patient, I have to see what's wrong."

Dothan nodded. "Then I'll go with you."

He followed her to the edge. Eric was struggling up the hill, his feet slipping in the sand and overgrown sea oats.

When he noticed Melissa, his eyes widened in alarm. "Melissa, get out of here!"

"Why?" She reached for his hand to help him, but he shrugged away her offer. He was only two feet from her, yet he refused to let her help him.

"I said, get out of here. There's a shooter on the cliff behind me!"

Melissa gasped and spotted a dark dot disappearing into the distance.

She turned to the guard. "Call someone to catch that man!"

Dothan phoned in, while Eric crested the hill. Melissa immediately clutched his arm. "Are you all right?" Blood dotted his cheek. She raised a hand to wipe it away and check his wound.

"It's only a graze. Come on, let's go inside." Eric ushered her toward her cottage, leaning on his cane.

She slid her arm beneath his waist to give him added support, but he backed away. "I can do it," he growled.

"Just shut up and let's go," she said, refusing to let him push her away.

They hurried down the path, the guard behind them,

his gun drawn as he canvassed the area for another attacker. Melissa unlocked the door, her heart pounding as they fell inside. Eric's breathing was erratic, and he favored his good leg, but at least he was alive.

She flung herself at him, checking his face and chest for injuries. "My God, Eric, he almost shot you."

"I'm fine."

Tears burned her eyes as she threw her arms around him. "But you could have died."

He trapped her hands, clutching them between his own. "He didn't shoot me, Melissa. It's all right."

Hysteria bubbled inside her. "But I thought if we weren't together, you'd be safe. Don't you see, I thought..." She released his hands, paced across the small living area, running her fingers through her hair, her panic wild. "I wanted to protect you, but he's after you anyway. Who's doing this?"

When she paused, Eric was watching her with an intense darkness in his eyes. "Is that the reason you pushed me away? To protect me?"

Melissa realized she'd revealed herself, but the guard knocked, and Eric let him in.

"Did they catch him?" Eric asked.

Dothan shook his head. "Sorry, he escaped."

Eric nodded. "Thanks." His gaze shot back to Melissa, then to the rookie. "I'm going to stay awhile, why don't you take a break. Go for dinner."

Dothan gestured toward Melissa. "Is that all right with you, ma'am?"

"Yes, yes, of course."

Dothan excused himself, and Melissa wrapped her arms around her waist. Did she dare admit the truth to Eric and see where things led them?

* * *

Eric had bottled any hope that Melissa might have feelings for him, but when she'd hugged him moments ago, she hadn't acted like a woman who pitied him.

But he didn't want her guilt, either.

Eric had to know, then he'd move on. "Did you send me away the other night to protect me, or because you don't want me?"

Her gaze met his, emotions softening her eyes. He had his answer.

"I don't want your guilt, or pity," he said to clarify. "And I won't take advantage of you because you're frightened."

"I am scared," Melissa said in a low voice. "I'm scared of losing you, Eric."

His breath hitched in his throat. He'd never imagined wanting a woman the way he craved Melissa. And he'd certainly never allowed himself to believe she'd love him back, especially with his scarred body.

Then she was in his arms, hugging and holding him, and kissing him with all the fervor of a woman who had truly wanted a man for a long time. Eric cupped her face in his hands and kissed her tenderly. The flame of hunger was lit, the heat intensifying with each nibble and caress. She met his tongue thrust for thrust, seeking, yearning, silently telling him she liked his touch.

He was glad to oblige.

His soul had been dark and empty for so long that he welcomed the light. She offered it in the sweet moan that escaped her mouth as he threaded his fingers through the silky tresses of her hair. Their lips tangled and met, while her hands clutched at his arms, then skated over his back. His body hardened, the tantalizing feel of her breasts against his chest creating a slow torture inside him that ignited his arousal to a painful peak.

She surprised him by pulling back slightly and extending her hand. His breath rasped out, and he stared at her hand for a moment, then lifted her chin to look into her eyes. "Are you sure?"

A sultry smile played on her lips. "Oh, yeah, I'm sure. I want you, Eric, in my arms, in my bed, beside me."

A balloon of joy exploded in his chest, and he nodded, then followed her to the bedroom. A lamp lit the room, bathing it in a soft glow, but he flicked it off, letting the moonlight spilling through the window paint the room in a more romantic glow.

She stroked her fingers along his jaw in an erotic game that stirred his senses even more, and he kissed her again, then slowly lowered his hands to cup her breasts. They were full and heavy, hot beneath his hands as he massaged the weight. A throaty groan escaped him as he imagined baring them for his sight.

A shy look passed in her eyes that teased him even more.

"You're beautiful, Melissa. I... I wanted you the first time I saw you."

"I wanted you, too," she admitted. "But I thought it would be wrong."

"Sometimes breaking the rules is right." Grateful for the condom he kept in his wallet, he gently lifted her shirt over her head, his heart thumping as her breasts spilled over the lacy edge of a pale pink bra. Would her nipples be that pale or would they be darker, rose-tipped like the lipstick she wore?

He was dying to know, aching to feel her bare skin against his, to plunge inside her and claim her as his.

"I want to kiss you all over." He lowered his head and tasted the swell of her breasts, then lower to suck her nipples through the bra. She writhed against him, clinging to his arms to keep her balance, and he tugged the fabric down, teasing her body with his tongue and teeth. Hunger flared hotter inside him, his sex swelling and jutting toward her.

She sighed and dug her fingernails in his arms while he stripped her bra, then slipped her loose skirt to the floor. Pale pink bikini panties arched high on her slender thighs taunted him, the wisp of dark hair beneath almost sending him over the edge.

Then she pushed at his shirt, unbuttoning the first, then second button, and he stilled for the first time since he'd entered, his first signs of doubt creeping into his mind.

Melissa realized Eric's moment of hesitation but refused to allow him to hold back because of his scars. "I don't see them when I look at you," she whispered in his ear. "I see a handsome, strong man." She traced her tongue along his ear. "A man that I love."

Eric's hands cupped her face. "I… Melissa…"

"Shh, you don't have to say it back," Melissa whispered. "But I had to tell you."

He looked moved by her words as he claimed her mouth again, this kiss long and slow, tender and passionate all at the same time. Inflamed by his strength, she savored the feel of his arms around her and tugged off his shirt, running her hands over his bare back.

"You feel so wonderful, Eric."

He dropped a kiss into her hair. "Melissa, do you have any idea how much I want to make love to you?"

She smiled and kissed him. "I feel the same way."

He chuckled, and gently eased her down on the bed.

But she raised herself on her knees and began to kiss his chest, tracing each scar gently with her finger, then her lips. "Tell me if I hurt you."

He cradled her head in his hands, closing his eyes and letting her heavenly touch erase the pain. "You can't." He rasped out a breath when she licked his nipple. "You won't hurt me."

Melissa prayed Eric was right. But she couldn't think of the danger right now, only that Eric might have died earlier, and she might never have had the chance to lie in his arms. She might never have made love to him.

And she desperately wanted that tonight. Wanted him to be her first.

And her last.

But she wouldn't ask for promises....

"Enough." His husky voice triggered a flood of yearning in her belly.

With a wicked gleam in his eyes, he pushed her back on the bed and kissed her again, this time hungrily, as if there would be no tomorrow. Another kiss and his hand unclasped her bra. He lowered his head and stared at her bare breasts with an almost reverent expression in his eyes. She shivered, her nipples aching pinpoints begging for his mouth.

Finally, he traced his tongue over each turgid peak and sucked them into his mouth, his greedy gulps of pleasure igniting tingling sensations through her body.

Eric fed her desires with his heady, throaty moans.

She ached to claw his back but remembered his tender skin, and restrained her urges, instead pouring them into the sounds she emitted and a desperate cry for release as sensations built within her. His fingers danced down her belly, followed by his tongue, and when he dipped them inside her panties, skimming them along her heat, she thought she might die.

Ripple after ripple of pleasure soared through her as he gently stroked her inner thighs, then slid down her body and placed his tongue to the sensitive skin between her legs. His breath caressed her heat while his tongue tortured her with teasing delicious strokes. And when he tasted her, she bucked upward, crying out his name in euphoric release.

Emotions welled inside Eric like a tidal wave as Melissa's body convulsed in his arms. She tasted like fire and sweetness, her declaration of love completely stunning him.

No one had ever loved him before except his brother.

Aching for fulfillment, he wrestled the condom from his wallet, pulled it over his length, rose above her and braced his arms by her sides, then teased her legs farther apart with his good leg and slid his erection against her heat. She whimpered and lifted her hips, begging him to enter her, and he thrust inside with a moan.

Her tightness surprised him.

Her virginity shocked him.

"Melissa…" He stilled, but she pressed her hands to his cheeks and dragged his mouth toward hers.

"Please, Eric, I have to have you."

Heaven sent down a shooting star that obliterated any misgivings. He knew he should mouth loving words back, but he was so humbled by her offering, he could only kiss her, thrusting his tongue deep into her mouth as he thrust his sex into her welcoming heat. He hesitated, giving her time to adjust to his size, but she moaned and moved below him, pulling him deeper and deeper inside her until he'd filled her to the core.

Unable to control his fierce longing for another moment, he began to pump inside her, in and out, teasing her to the edge of another orgasm and himself to insanity.

"I do love you, Eric," she whispered as release swept her into a trembling mass.

He fell into the vortex with her, soaring, soaring, soaring....

Eric cradled Melissa in his arms, the titillating sensations still rippling through him. He'd never experienced such intensity with a woman, such closeness. He wanted to wrap her in his arms and keep the two of them buried in this warm cocoon of bliss forever.

But they had to talk. He should say something, confess his feelings, only they were so new and foreign to him, his emotions so raw that his voice refused to cooperate. He had been so angry and confused and lost when his mother died, and after the explosion. He'd thought he was meant to protect others, to get revenge. Never had he considered that he might have a normal life, a woman to love him....

He wanted that normal life. He wanted to be with Melissa forever.

She gently traced a finger over his chest and his heart swelled with such longing that he cleared his throat to tell her, but a knock sounded at the door. Damn it, he didn't want to answer.

But what if the police had found the shooter? What if they had the break in the case and he could put it to rest, lock Hughes away and start looking toward a future?

Melissa sighed as the knocking grew louder. "I should get it, I guess."

He shook his head. "No, stay here. I'll go."

She bit down on her lip, but relented. He stood, dragged on his jeans and shirt, grabbed his cane, then headed to the living area, closing the bedroom door to give her privacy. He hurriedly buttoned his shirt, not ready to share his newfound relationship with the guard.

But Special Agent Devlin stood on the other side, looking harried and in a rush. "We have to talk."

Eric jammed his hands in his pockets. "What are you doing here?"

"Black filled me in on the shooting. Listen, Eric, we need to move on this investigation."

"Why?"

"Word is that Hughes has not only resurfaced but that he has scientists working on brainwashing techniques."

"You knew that all along."

"Yes, but we think he's using unsuspecting patients as guinea pigs. And we're almost certain Hughes is Melissa Fagan's father."

Eric's stomach knotted. "How can you be sure?"

Devlin's moment of hesitation sparked Eric's suspicion. "You knew before. That's why you sent me here, arranged to have me work with Melissa." Anger tightened his throat. "You set me up, didn't you?"

Guilt flashed in Devlin's eyes for a millisecond before he masked it.

"We had no way of being sure you'd actually meet her, but I did some checking when you mentioned you had, and we finally hacked into the old files." Devlin's voice was level. "Believe it or not, Hughes was actually listed on the birth certificate of the baby Candace Latone delivered."

Eric let that fact sink in. What would Melissa think? How would she react if she learned her father was a monster? He had to protect her from the truth. "So, Robert Latone lied about his daughter having a child?"

"He not only lied, he personally dropped the baby at the church."

The door squeaked open, and Melissa stepped into the entryway. Eric's pulse clamored at the yellowish tint to her pallor. Apparently, she'd been listening to their conversation.

Just how much had she heard?

Chapter 14

A cold numbness enveloped Melissa as she stared at the man who had taken her in his arms and joined his body with hers, the man she had proclaimed that she loved.

He obviously wasn't the man she believed him to be. And his heart had not been in the joining.

Who was he?

"What's going on?" she asked in a surprisingly calm voice. Her body was trembling from the inside out, still adjusting from lying sated in Eric's arms to the shock of betrayal.

His dark eyes flickered downward in avoidance. Regret. Guilt.

The suited man with dark blond hair started to speak, but Eric threw up a hand. "Let me explain."

Melissa folded her arms across her waist, wishing she'd had the good sense to dress instead of slipping on her robe. She felt raw, exposed. Vulnerable. And she hated it.

"This is Special Agent Luke Devlin, Melissa, he's with the FBI."

She swallowed hard. "And you are?"

His gaze met hers. "Eric Caldwell."

A knot of pain clogged her throat. "So you lied about your name?"

He gave a clipped nod. "But there are reasons."

She cut a sharp gaze toward the federal agent, then back at Eric, a sickening thought emerging. "You're an FBI agent?"

Eric shook his head. "Not exactly." He scrubbed his hand through his hair, eliciting memories of when he'd run his hands through her own. Nausea climbed to her throat. "I... I have been working with them. So have Detectives Black and Fox."

"I don't understand. To find Candace's murderer?" Had Eric suspected her as the killer? Had he cozied up to her to find out?

"Yes, and to investigate CIRP."

"We have reason to believe Arnold Hughes has resurfaced," Agent Devlin interjected.

Melissa pieced together the remnants of the conversation she'd overheard, the truth dawning in all its ugly details. "And you think he's my father?" She pierced Eric with a cold look. "That's the reason you warmed up to me, to find him?"

Eric's silence said it all. The closeness she'd felt earlier disintegrated, the pain of his lie engulfing her.

"Why do you want him so badly?" she asked, her voice a mere whisper.

"You've heard about the things he did," Devlin answered. "He's responsible for the loss of several people's lives, unethical experiments, using prisoners as human guinea pigs. He ordered memory transplant experiments to be performed on Detective Fox. Who knows what other twisted games he has in the works."

"And he might have killed Candace Latone," Eric added in a gruff voice.

She met Eric's haunted gaze, her breath locked in her chest as she read between the lines. There was something he wasn't telling her, something more personal. His hand brushed his hair back, revealing the scar on his forehead, and she realized the truth. "Your accident?"

"It wasn't an accident." He closed his eyes, the bleakness she'd seen before returning when he opened them. "I was trying to help one of his nurses escape from Nighthawk Island. She was rescuing a baby his scientists had involved in an experiment."

"A baby? Oh my God." Her legs collapsed. Eric reached for her, but she pushed his hands away and staggered to the couch. Her head spinning, she dropped it forward into her hands and sucked in air, ordering herself not to pass out.

Hughes, a madman with no scruples, was her father? He had killed countless people, played with their lives, tried to kill Eric. And he might have murdered Candace?

Why? Because he thought Candace might reveal that Hughes was Melissa's father?

Had her own father tried to kill her?

A chill engulfed her. Eric had known the truth about Hughes all along.

Worse, he had never cared for her. He'd only used her to find Hughes for his own vengeful purposes.

And being the lost desperate-for-love soul she'd been,

she'd played right into his hands like a puppet on a string.

She'd not only offered him her love, she'd given him her virginity.

Eric despised the look of anguish and betrayal in Melissa's eyes. If only he'd told her he loved her, confided the truth earlier, maybe she'd understand. He could have cushioned the blow.

He wanted to take her in his arms and make her understand, but Devlin's condemning look halted his confession.

He knew Eric had crossed the line, had slept with her.

And Eric could not let his personal feelings compromise the mission.

"We have reason to believe Robert Latone is working with Hughes," Devlin said, breaking into his confused thoughts. "And we think Hughes is overseeing brainwashing experiments on psychiatric patients without their knowledge. He's not only training them as spies and hit men for the government, but also for his own purposes."

"You think one of them was the shooter who fired at me from the cliff?"

Devlin nodded. "We also have reason to believe he might be planning to leave the country soon."

"How do you know all this?" Eric asked.

"I can't reveal my source's name, it's too dangerous, but the information is reliable."

Melissa toyed with her robe belt. "How...was my mother involved with Hughes?"

"There were experiments with infertility drugs in place at the time, as well as various birth control pills and in vitro fertilization," Devlin explained. "We believe Candace had an affair with Hughes, and that she took an experimental form of birth control pill. We also believe she experienced an adverse reaction to the drug."

"It caused her mental problems," Melissa filled in.

Devlin shrugged. "It's possible."

"Do you think it was passed to me, that the drug might have caused my seizures?"

"It might have been a side effect, yes."

Melissa rubbed her forehead, a headache pinching. "You think Hughes and Robert Latone conspired to kill me because they were afraid I'd figure out what they'd done to Candace?"

Eric stared at her, seeing the horror in her eyes. Not only had her father and grandfather abandoned her, now they'd killed her mother and tried to murder her. The depth of their evil was almost impossible to comprehend, even for a jaded man like himself who'd seen terrible things parents inflicted on their children.

"Our theory is that Hughes and Latone have been working together."

"But why would Robert Latone want to keep the drug's problems quiet if the drug affected his daughter adversely?" Melissa asked.

Eric cleared his throat. "Money. If he'd funded the experimental project, he'd want to keep it quiet."

"Even at the expense of his daughter's health?"

"We're talking millions. We think they'd already sold the pill to some foreign countries, and if word had leaked that the drug had adverse reactions, the deal would have been killed," Devlin continued.

"It's also possible that Hughes doesn't know you are his daughter," Eric said quietly. "Latone could have forced Candace to give you up without telling the father."

"That would be another reason Latone would want you dead. If he kept your identity from Hughes all these years, chances are Hughes would retaliate against him. Of all people, Latone knows how ruthless Hughes can be."

Melissa knotted her hands together, her mind reeling. Her father, her grandfather, both despicable men. Poor Candace… "How do you plan to catch Hughes?"

Devlin telegraphed his silent suggestion to Eric, but Eric shook his head.

"What?" Melissa asked, confused. "Can't you drag Robert Latone in and force him to talk?"

"We've questioned him, but he lawyered up."

Melissa saw the awkward look pass between the men again and put two and two together. She wanted this to end so she could return to Atlanta. And Hughes and Latone should pay for what they had done to her mother. "I could help trap Hughes."

Eric stalked toward her, arms crossed. "Absolutely not."

Melissa squared her shoulders, refusing to back down. "You have nothing to say about it."

"It's too dangerous, Melissa. We'll find another way."

"You lied to me, Eric, why should I listen to you now?"

His mask slipped slightly, raw emotion darkening his eyes. "Because I refuse to let you act as bait for a madman." He curled his fingers around her wrist, then lowered his voice. "I care about you, Melissa. I don't want you in danger."

"It's too late for that." She hesitated, hating the crack

in her voice. "Besides, if you cared so much, you would have been honest."

"Damn it, Melissa, you can't do this."

"I don't need your permission." She turned to the federal agent, her resolve in place. If these men thought she'd crumble, they were wrong. She'd been on her own, survived foster care and her teenage years alone. She would survive this, too.

"Agent Devlin, tell me what to do."

A steely rage blazed through Eric as Devlin detailed the plan. Melissa hadn't looked at him once. She'd drawn a curtain over her emotions and shut him out.

He recognized the signs because he'd used the same coping skill countless times in his own life.

The fact that he had hurt her badly enough to send her back into that isolated darkness made him feel lower than he'd ever felt.

"I'll leak the story to the press," Devlin explained. "Say the police questioned you regarding Candace Latone's murder, and you admitted that you were searching for your parents, Candace Latone and Arnold Hughes. With all the publicity about CIRP in the past, the story should make front page."

"And how will we arrange for him to meet me?"

"Oh, he'll come looking," Devlin said. "And we'll be ready."

"You never make a mistake, do you?" Eric glared at the agent, remembering other missions gone awry, the reason he'd taken the law into his own hands a few times. The reason he'd been protecting that witness in the Bronsky case.

He wanted to protect Melissa now.

Because he'd fallen in love.

Unfortunately, she was barreling forward, putting her own life on the line because he'd hurt her.

God, what a mess.

"We'll have plenty of backup," Devlin said. "In fact, I'll guard you personally, Miss Fagan."

Melissa exhaled. "Then let's do it."

Devlin nodded.

"I'll be with her at all times," Eric said.

"No." Melissa's condemning look cut him to the quick. "One agent will be enough."

"I'm not leaving you alone," Eric said. He directed his next comment to Devlin. "And if you don't agree with that, she's out of this completely."

Devlin frowned. "Are you sure you're up to it, Caldwell?"

Anger flared inside Eric. Another agent would be stronger, more agile. "Yes," he said anyway. "I started this investigation and I'm seeing it through."

"The story should run tomorrow," Devlin said.

Melissa nodded.

Devlin yanked Eric's arm, pulling him outside. "You need to let us handle things from here on out."

Eric pried the agent's fingers from his arm. "You think I can't take care of myself if it gets rough?"

"I think you're too damn involved with the woman." Devlin scraped his hair back from his forehead. "It's obvious you slept with her."

Eric gritted his teeth, ready to deny it.

"You're not objective, man, and she sure as hell isn't objective where you're concerned." He lowered his voice, his tone lethal. "Her safety is my priority."

"It had better be." For a brief second, Eric vacillated, though, wondered if Devlin was right about his ability to protect Melissa. What if someone attacked her, and he failed to fight them off? What if he let her down and he lost her forever?

His mother's bloody body flashed into his mind.

No, Melissa was nothing like his mother. She was a fighter, she was tough and strong, and he would give his life to protect her.

He didn't trust anyone else to keep her safe.

Robert latone accepted coffee from his maid, claimed his usual chair on the veranda and unfolded the morning paper. His gaze landed on the headlines, and his chest spasmed. Dear God in heaven, he couldn't believe the Fagan woman had talked to the press. And to publicly claim Candace her mother and Hughes her father—was she on a suicide mission?

Fury rattling his movements, he jerked up and stalked inside. Moor marched through the front door, his face livid, before Robert could even call him.

"Have you seen the paper?" Moor asked.

"Hell, yes." Robert slapped it on the cherry table-top. "I thought you were handling the Fagan woman."

"I tried." Moor wiped sweat from his graying eye-brow.

"What are we going to do now?" Robert shrieked. "If Hughes reads this, he'll be all over my ass."

Moor's fingers trembled as he spread his palms on top of the article. "I'll think of something, Robert. Don't worry. No one will ever find out the truth."

"Talk to Hopkins."

Moor's pallor had turned a chalky gray. "I'm on it."

"Right away," Latone hissed. "And don't screw up this time. We can't let this go any further."

Moor unpocketed his cell phone and began to punch

in numbers. "Hopkins, meet me at the marina in half an hour. I have a job for you."

Latone jabbed in numbers on his own phone. He had to make arrangements to leave the country. It was bad enough the police suspected him of killing his own daughter. When Hughes read the article, he would think Robert had betrayed him.

And he didn't intend to take the repercussions of Hughes's wrath.

"Melissa fagan, please."

Melissa's fingers tightened around the handset. Eric lifted his head from where he'd been reading notes on Hughes from Devlin's ongoing file. "This is she."

"Do you really want to meet your father?"

She swallowed hard, motioning at Eric to trace the call.

"Then come to the marina. Tonight. Midnight." His heavy breathing wheezed over the line. "And come alone, Melissa."

"Who—" Melissa's voice broke at the sound of the dial tone.

Devlin shook his head. "Not enough time to get a trace."

Eric muttered a curse. Melissa ignored him. He didn't like the setup, had tried to persuade her to back out, but Melissa refused to be a quitter.

Besides, she wanted this quest for her parents to be over. Every second in proximity with Eric made his deception even more painful.

"What did the caller want?" Eric asked.

"He said if I wanted to meet my father to come to the marina tonight at midnight."

Devlin nodded. "This could be the break we've been waiting for."

And the day she'd anticipated forever—meeting her father.

Only, instead of walking into his loving arms, she might be walking into a trap.

And instead of finding a loving father, she would be looking at the face of the man who'd killed her mother, and wanted her buried in the ground beside Candace.

Trepidation filled Eric as they drove to the marina. He had worked out all morning, strengthening his arms and legs, and channeling his energy so he would be able to help tonight. He couldn't fail Melissa, not any more than he already had.

When they caught Hughes, he'd rectify his past mistakes with Melissa. He had no idea how, but he'd find some way to convince her that he loved her.

She looked frail and strong at the same time as she braced herself for the confrontation he knew would follow. If the meeting turned out to be a trap, they were prepared. Devlin had stationed two other agents around the marina, patrolling the area in advance, one disguised as a fisherman, another a local tourist.

A spring thunderstorm loomed on the horizon, thunderclouds obliterating the stars and adding an even more ominous feel to the gloomy atmosphere. The sound of docked boats rocking in the increasingly turbulent water mingled with the occasional whine of a motor. Eric hung back, hidden in the shadows of a cruiser, his senses charged.

Melissa's shoes clicked on the boardwalk as she paced to the end of the dock and stared out at the water.

A ten-foot cruiser coasted by. Odd for it to be out this time of night.

It had to be the caller.

Eric stepped forward to warn Melissa, but the boat coasted to a stop, and Devlin waved him to hold off. Eric was too far away, Devlin even farther. Where were the two other agents?

Suddenly gunfire rang out, and all hell broke loose behind him. He pivoted and saw the first agent go down in a bloody heap. The fisherman/agent was nowhere to be seen. Devlin fired his gun, warding off the shooter, while Eric hobbled down the dock as fast as his cane would allow him.

A man grabbed Melissa, but she swung her fists at him. Another appeared out of nowhere and assaulted Eric, bringing him down with a whack on the back of the head. More gunfire pinged behind him. He clawed at the wooden slats to right himself, but a karate punch to his lower back and a blow to his ribs knocked the air from his lungs. Then something hard connected with his head. The blunt end of a gun.

Melissa screamed, her voice fading into the darkness as Eric lost consciousness.

Chapter 15

Melissa stirred, her vision blurring as she struggled to discern what had happened on the dock. A rocking motion spiked nausea, the sound of a motor humming from above alerting her to the fact that she was on a boat. She turned her head, squinting through the darkness. She was in a small berth on the bottom level. Her arms and legs were bound, but her captors hadn't gagged her, which either meant that they hadn't expected her to regain consciousness or they were so far away from shore no one would hear if she screamed.

She fought hopelessness. The room faded, then cleared again, and she spotted Eric on the floor in the corner. He lay sideways, blood trickling from his head, his face ghostly white.

Please don't let him be dead.

She shifted and scooted across the floor, each movement causing her stomach to capitulate. "Eric." She finally reached him, and nudged him with her foot. "Eric, wake up."

He stirred slightly, and she nudged him again. "Eric, wake up, tell me you're all right."

A moan rumbled from his chest, and he slowly opened his eyes. He looked disoriented as he lifted his head. Blood trickled from his forehead down his jaw.

"Are you okay?" Melissa whispered.

He nodded. "What about you?"

"Yes, but we have to get out of here."

He glanced around the cabin. "Do you know where they're taking us?"

"No."

"Did you see Hughes?"

"No, some guy grabbed me and knocked me out, but he was too young to be Hughes."

"Hired help," Eric growled. "I'm sorry, Melissa. I never should have let you go through with this."

"I made my own choice, Eric."

"But I should have protected you." He dropped his head forward, his voice anguished. "My mother... I couldn't protect her, and now you."

Melissa had no idea what he meant about his mother, but explanations had to wait. They needed to escape. "Do you think you can untie me?"

He nodded. "Roll over, put your back to me."

She did as he said, and he flipped himself over, so his own bound hands could reach hers. For the next several minutes, they lay in tense silence as Eric struggled to unravel the thick knots.

"Damn it, I need a knife." He glanced around the cabin, but barring a small foldout sofa-type bed, it appeared empty. Shifting again, he tried the knots once more.

"Tell me what you meant about your mother," Melissa whispered in an attempt to fill the dreadful silence.

"My father, he abused her," Eric said in a voice that echoed with old pain. "She finally gave up one day and killed herself."

"She left you and your brother alone to face him?"

Eric stilled for a moment. "Yeah. I always blamed myself, though. I've been helping women escape situations like that for years through an underground service. That's the reason my brother's wife, Alanna, came to me when she and baby Simon were in trouble."

So the job on his patient file was bogus. "Do you work for an agency?"

"No, I'm on my own."

She closed her eyes, letting the truth wash over her. He wasn't a cop or a federal agent, but a really good guy. No wonder she had connected with him. And fallen in love.

Still, he'd used her and lied to her. And he hadn't once mentioned loving her in return.

Even if he had feelings for her, would he blame her for what her father had done to him?

Eric had almost gotten the first knot untangled, when the boat slowed and the motor died. They had docked. He hoped Devlin or one of the other agents had survived and followed them. It might be their only chance to get out of this alive.

The door swung open, and a beefy man sporting tattoos up and down his arms entered, a Glock in his hand—the man he'd seen leaving Hopkins's office.

Melissa tensed and curled closer to him, but the man jerked Eric upright. His bad leg buckled, and he fought through the pain, but the man kicked the back of Eric's kneecap, and he nearly crumpled.

"Stop it!" Melissa cried.

"It's time," the man mumbled.

Eric offered Melissa a silent look, telling her he would be all right, but the man pressed the gun to his head, then dragged him out the door.

Melissa's terrified cries rang through the thin doorway as the man hauled him up the steps. Seconds later, the sound of a hawk soaring above made him jerk his head up, and he scanned the area. He was on Nighthawk Island.

He had no idea who had kidnapped them, but he doubted he would leave the island alive.

Why were they separating him and Melissa? Why not kill them together?

His captor shoved him into a dark sedan and slammed the door. Five minutes later, the car stopped, and he was dragged into a lab. The building was small, with several other labs along the hall, all sterile and functional with Restricted warning signs. One sign noted possible biohazard materials, another germ warfare. The lab was filled with petri dishes and appeared to be a hot room for growing germs.

The man shoved him onto a gurney, then a doctor garbed in sterile attire, mask and gloves included, moved above him, a hypodermic in hand. Hopkins?

"Now we'll find out how strong your willpower is, Mr. Caldwell. See if you can resist our techniques."

Eric recognized Hopkins's voice.

"What are you planning to do to me?" Eric asked.

"Brainwash you to do our dirty work." Hopkins laughed. "Then our hands will be clean."

Eric had to escape. He fought against the ropes, then

bucked upward, trying to knock the needle from the doctor's hand, but the beefy man who'd dragged him in pounced on his throbbing leg. Another man restrained his arms, and the doctor fed him the shot.

Melissa curled into a ball, hopelessness engulfing her. Eric was gone. They'd taken him at gunpoint hours ago.

He was probably dead.

The anguish that consumed her was overwhelming.

You have to fight back. You've been on your own before, you can do it again.

Yet the thought of going on, knowing Eric had been murdered, nearly paralyzed her.

The boat rocked and swayed where they'd docked. Why hadn't they come to kill her yet? Was Hughes behind the kidnapping, or had someone intervened to keep her from knowing his identity? The man who'd dragged Eric from the cabin was obviously a hired gun. Had he murdered her mother?

The door swung open and fear knifed through her.

She was shocked to see Eric at the door.

Relief made her giddy, but evaporated when she spoke his name and he didn't respond. His eyes were glazed, his pupils dilated, his posture stiff as if he hadn't heard her. She glanced behind him, searching for the gun man, but saw no one.

"Eric, hurry, untie me."

He didn't acknowledge her plea. Instead, he continued to stare into empty space, like a robot.

"Hurry, before they come back."

He stalked toward her. Then he jerked her up by her bound arms and began to drag her up the steps. Fear replaced her earlier relief.

"Eric, what are you doing? Talk to me!" Panic made her words shrill. "Stop it, Eric, you're hurting me. Tell me what's going on."

He gripped her arm tighter, then dragged her off the boat. Her toes scattered broken shells in the path. Darkness shrouded the island, and a screeching sound echoed in the distance as if a wild animal had cornered its prey.

Melissa understood the feeling.

She cringed at the vacant look in Eric's eyes. He'd obviously been drugged, but what else had they done to him?

Had the scientists destroyed Eric's memory as they had done to that cop?

"Walk ahead." His command sounded harsh, his voice deeper than Eric's as he pushed her forward. She stumbled, her bound legs making it impossible to walk.

"Untie me, Eric, and we can run."

He hauled her forward, then shoved her through the underbrush until they reached a clearing on the cliff.

"Eric, you're scaring me. What's going on? What did they do to you?"

He stared straight ahead, his mouth a flat line. Finally he spoke, his tone lethal. "You have to die."

Fear chilled Melissa's spine. The scientists had hypnotized him. She had to bring him back, to save him. Both of them.

He pulled out a gun, and she froze. She was going to die.

And whoever had drugged Eric had somehow convinced him to do the killing.

But how? Why?

To frame him...

"Eric, you don't want to hurt me." She struggled to maintain a calm voice, afraid a panicked cry might trigger whatever hypnotic suggestion they'd given him. It had to be a hypnotic suggestion, that was the only explanation that made sense.

But she didn't think a person could be hypnotized against his will.

He aimed the gun at her. "It will be over soon."

Melissa shivered. He spoke in a monotone, like someone programmed to kill her. Was that part of the research on Nighthawk Island? Were the scientists hypnotizing, brainwashing men to be trained assassins, to kill on demand?

She had to jar him from this trance. "Eric, you don't want to do this," she said softly. "You know you don't. You're a good man, a protector. Remember, you wanted to save your mother from pain, but you couldn't." She inhaled. "You helped all those other women escape their abusive husbands and boyfriends. You could never hurt a woman."

His jaw tightened, his eyes flickering, as if her words had registered on some distant plane.

"You have a brother, Cain, you told me about him and his wife. And they have a son, Simon, isn't that his name?" She was grasping now, determined to reach him. "You came to CIRP to find Arnold Hughes and make him pay for hurting other people because you're not evil like them. You can't hurt anyone, you protect and save others. You helped me."

His hand shook slightly, the gun wobbling.

"Remember me, I'm Melissa. We worked together to teach you to walk again. And now you don't need the wheelchair anymore. We made love the other night, Eric. I lay in your arms and you held me and we kissed…."

He blinked, his eyes flittering sideways, his body wavering.

"Remember how sweet it was, Eric. I whispered that I love you, then we made slow beautiful love together in my cottage. It was tender and passionate, and we wanted the night to last forever."

The gun lowered slightly and hope dawned, featherlight but alive.

"I kissed your scars, made them disappear, because when I'm with you, I don't see them, I see only a strong man who's always protected the weaker ones around him. You tried to rescue your mother, your clients and me. You didn't want me to set a trap for Hughes because you wanted to keep me safe, Eric, not hurt me." She inched forward, although she couldn't walk more than baby steps.

"You told me you care about me, and you wanted to keep me from being hurt again. I am safe, Eric, safe when I'm in your arms."

His hand trembled, the mask on his face slipping. She had him, she just had to keep talking.

But a man appeared in the background, hidden in the shadows.

"Shoot her, Caldwell. You've been trained to be a killer, now carry out your orders."

Melissa's heart sank as he raised the gun and aimed.

"You're a killer, you've been trained to shoot." Eric heard the words. They were true.

He had killed before. Memories of a car explosion splintered through his brain. A man begging for his help, for mercy. Eric watching him die.

And then there were fights. His own father. Other

men. Holding a gun on someone. His brother, the cops, hounding at the door to stop him.

"Eric, please, hear me now, it's Melissa. I love you, you don't want to hurt me."

"Do it, Caldwell. You have a job to do. Finish it."

Yes, he had a job to do. The reason he'd come to this island. To get revenge. He had to complete the mission.

He angled the gun, aimed.

"Eric, think about your mother. What would she want you to do? Think about Cain, his wife. We could have that, too. A family."

The voice—Melissa? She sounded so familiar. He knew her....

No, he had lost her. He had done something bad to her, she hated him.

"Kill her. Go ahead and shoot," the man ordered.

"You're not a killer. You're a protector, a savior," Melissa whispered. "You aren't bad like them, Eric. Don't let them win."

He walked both sides of the law. And he had used his fists before on another man....

"You're good, Eric. That's the reason I fell in love with you." Melissa's whispers called to him, reaching through the murky haze to his soul. "I want us to be together."

"She's lying, Caldwell. Do it. Do it now."

"No, Eric... I love you."

Eric's hand trembled, but he aimed the gun, pressed the trigger and fired.

Melissa dropped to the ground, the sound of gunfire rippling through the air, stealing her breath. For a split second, she thought she'd been shot, then realized that Eric had pivoted when he fired and hit the man behind him. She tasted dirt and tried to stand, but her chin scraped the ground with her feeble attempt. A helicopter roared above and descended into the clearing. Two men rushed through the underbrush. Eric seemed transfixed, his gaze focused on the bleeding man on the ground.

"Eric, hurry, untie me!"

He suddenly spun around, saw her and started toward her, but another gunshot rang out and his body jolted, then hit the dirt.

"No!"

"Melissa!" He barely raised his head, his voice a raspy whisper.

Two men stalked toward Melissa, jerked her up and dragged her toward a dark sedan that appeared from nowhere.

She screamed for Eric, but another man emerged from the sedan.

"Miss Fagan?"

She gulped, shocked. She recognized him from the center. "What? Who are you?"

"I'm Arnold Hughes. I need to know if you're really my daughter."

Chapter 16

Pain needled Eric's side where the bullet had pierced him, but he rolled sideways and sat up. Dear God, he'd almost killed Melissa.

He pressed his hand to stem the blood and searched the space to find her.

A dark sedan had driven up, a driver stood beside the vehicle and another man—Stinson, the war vet with the artificial leg—faced Melissa. What the hell was going on?

He quickly checked behind him. Hopkins was still down.

The sound of another chopper spun above him, and the trees and dirt rustled with its landing.

"Melissa!"

Stinson grabbed her arm and shoved her into the sedan. Eric vaulted upward and stood, blood dripping down his side, but his bad leg buckled, throbbing where his attacker had kicked it earlier. Damn it. He would never make it.

Through the clearing, voices sounded, and Detectives Black and Fox jogged toward them, weapons drawn. Devlin approached, too, his wounded arm in a sling. Two other agents circled the vehicle.

"It's over," Devlin shouted to the driver. "Put your hands up and surrender."

Stinson gripped the car door and glanced at Eric, then Devlin and the surrounding cops and agents, his expression grim. "Hold your fire."

Devlin trained his weapon on Stinson, a heartbeat of silence following. But Stinson shocked everyone by raising his hands and surrendering without a fight. "You can take me in, but don't shoot. I don't want Melissa harmed."

Eric frowned and hobbled closer while Devlin handcuffed Stinson and his driver. Black radioed for a stretcher for Hopkins.

Melissa climbed from the car, and Eric met her gaze.

Guilt slammed into him as he remembered holding a gun on her. Her face looked pained, but she started toward him. "Eric?"

He held his side, his emotions torn. He wanted to drag her into his arms and make sure she was all right. But how could she forgive him for almost killing her?

"What's Stinson got to do with this?" he asked.

She bit down on her lip. "He claims he's Arnold Hughes. He wanted to know if he's my father."

Melissa recognized the anguish in Eric's eyes and understood he blamed himself for what had happened earlier. Her own head was spinning from the ordeal and from shock at learning the man she'd been helping with therapy was actually Arnold Hughes.

She reached out to Eric, but he drew back. Detective Black approached him. "We need to get you to the hospital."

Eric nodded. "Hopkins?"

"He'll make it. I can't wait to interrogate him and Stinson, though."

Eric frowned, his body growing weaker. Fox met Melissa and guided her to the helicopter, and a few minutes later, they were in the air.

"We need to stop his bleeding," Melissa said.

Black found some bandages and gauze from the emergency kit. "Here, will this work?"

Melissa nodded, removed the items and tore his shirt. Eric froze, riddled with pain and shame. He didn't deserve her care.

She pressed gauze to his wound, then applied pressure to stem the bleeding, and wrapped his side with bandages, her gaze meeting his. "You saved my life," she whispered.

He shook his head, hating himself. "I almost killed you."

"You were brainwashed, Eric. You didn't kill me, because you couldn't. You shot Hopkins instead."

Eric closed his eyes, wanting to believe her, but images of the fear in Melissa's eyes when he had pointed the gun at her face haunted him. He'd been violent. Evil. Out of control.

People could fight hypnosis, brainwashing, if they were strong. Hopkins never could have forced him to be a killer if he didn't already possess an inherent dark side.

The images would stay with him forever.

"I want testing done," he heard Melissa say to Detective Black. "I have to know if Mr. Stinson is Arnold Hughes, and if he's my real father."

"We'll run tests right away," Black assured her.

Eric grimaced as he realized their mistake—they had searched all of CIRP's personnel records, but it had never occurred to him or the other agents that Hughes might be at the center as a patient. And Stinson was the name of the war veteran in the picture, the missing man.

Fox cleared his throat. "We're also bringing in Robert Latone and his friend, Edward Moor, for further questioning."

"Who killed Candace?" Melissa asked.

"Don't worry, Miss Fagan," Black assured her. "Now that we have Hughes in custody, we'll get the rest of the answers."

Melissa paced the waiting room while Eric was in surgery. He had looked so desolate and alone when they'd wheeled him into the E.R., so distant. As if he'd already decided to end their relationship.

She pieced together her own emotions. He had lied to her and used her when he'd first come to CIRP, and she'd been hurt. But he'd had good reasons. Hughes had caused the explosion that had killed Eric's witness and nearly killed him.

But how did Dr. Hopkins play into it all? Why would he brainwash Eric to kill her?

Eric…admittedly he had frightened her. But he hadn't hurt her. Could he move past the incident on the island and possibly love her?

"Miss Fagan?"

Melissa startled and turned to see a tall dark-haired man and a woman holding a baby. "Yes?"

"I'm Cain Caldwell, Eric's brother." Cain gestured toward the woman. "This is my wife, Alanna, and our son, Simon."

Melissa smiled. "Yes, Eric told me all about you."

Cain's eyebrows rose. "Really?"

"Yes." She played with the baby's hand. "Hey, Simon, your uncle is so proud of you." One day she'd like to have a little boy of her own. Maybe one who looked like Eric.

"Yeah, Simon's pretty special." Cain grinned, the goofy proud look of a father. "How's my brother?"

"He's in surgery now. The bullet pierced his abdomen."

"How about you?" Alanna asked softly.

Melissa shrugged. "Shaken, but okay." She glanced back to Cain. "Did you know the reason Eric was here?"

"Yes, although I was against Eric working undercover," Cain admitted. "But my brother can be pretty damn stubborn."

"That stubborn nature helped him learn to walk again, it should get him through surgery, too," Melissa said. Although, it might prevent him from forgiving himself.

Alanna jiggled the baby on her hip. "You want to fill us in on what happened?"

Melissa folded her arms across her stomach and relayed the ordeal. "Eric blames himself for the brainwashing," Melissa said. She gave his brother a pleading look. "But he wouldn't hurt me," she said, staring down at her knotted hands. "He couldn't, he's too much of a protector."

Alanna curved a comforting arm around Melissa.

"Let's just hope we can convince him of that," Cain said.

The doctor appeared in the doorway. "Miss Fagan?"

"Yes." She gestured toward Cain and his wife and introduced them.

"How's my brother?" Cain asked.

"Mr. Caldwell came through surgery fine. He'll need some time to recover, but he'll be all right."

He would be physically, but what about his mental and emotional state?

When she and Cain and Alanna entered the room to see him a few minutes later, her fears were confirmed. Eric refused to look at her.

And the soul-deep anguish and loneliness she'd seen in him when they'd first met had returned.

The next two days were torture for Eric. Not only did his side throb like the devil, but so did his leg. And he missed Melissa.

She had stopped by to visit, but he had refused to see her. How could he look into her eyes after almost killing her? She deserved a good strong, whole man, not a scarred one who possessed a dangerous side.

"You're crazy," Cain told him. "That woman loves you."

"Let it go," Eric told his brother. "I'm not interested."

"Then why the hell do you look like you lost your best friend?" Cain asked.

Alanna rocked Simon in her arms. "I may be new to the family, Eric, but you deserve some happiness for a change."

"That's right," Cain said. "You've served your penance for Mom's death."

"This has nothing to do with her." In fact, he'd realized how much stronger Melissa was than their mother.

She had been weak, even selfish in giving up, in leaving her boys alone to fend for themselves.

Melissa never gave up—she was a fighter.

"Go after her," Cain said.

"Just drive me to the station," Eric said. "I want to be there when they interrogate Latone and Moor." The Feds had caught Latone and Moor trying to escape the country the night before. Hughes had given in to a DNA test and they were waiting for results. So far, Hughes had admitted to his other crimes, and that he had overseen the brainwashing experiments. The police had also found the tattooed man who'd been brainwashed and had him in custody.

Cain shook his head, a disgusted look on his face, but he and Eric headed outside, then Cain drove him.

"Shouldn't Melissa be here?" Cain asked as they seated themselves in the interrogation room.

"Let's see what we find," Eric said, determined to cushion the blow for her.

He cornered Devlin before they started. "How did Hopkins and his men know who we were and where we were meeting Hughes?"

"We have a leak in the FBI. We don't know who yet, but someone is working both sides, us and CIRP." Devlin excused himself to meet with Latone and Moor.

Eric frowned, wondering who the FBI mole might be. Devlin would pursue the matter later. He and Cain watched behind a two-way glass window as Devlin, Black and Fox began questioning. Latone looked haggard, Moor worried.

Devlin leaned his hands on the scarred wooden table. "Latone, why did you try to kill Melissa Fagan?"

Latone glanced at his lawyer, then spoke, "I didn't."

"We believe otherwise, Latone. We think you didn't want people to know she was your granddaughter, so you tried to kill her."

"As I explained before, Miss Fagan has no biological relationship to me."

"Hughes admitted that he got your daughter pregnant."

The door opened and Arnold Hughes walked in, a little unsteady with his new leg, but he still had a commanding presence about him. "That's right, but you claimed she lost our baby." Hughes's tone sounded ominous. "Did you give our child away, Robert?"

Latone looked truly nervous for the first time. Moor shifted in his seat, remaining tight-lipped.

"I told you the truth," Latone said. "Candace lost the baby. Melissa Fagan is not your child."

A rap sounded on the door, a uniformed officer came in, handed Devlin a paper, and left. Devlin read it, then stared at Hughes. "His story checks out, Hughes. Melissa Fagan is not your daughter. She's also not Candace Latone's child."

Eric gripped the window edge in shock. If Candace Latone wasn't Melissa's mother, who had given birth to her?

Hughes sank into one of the hardback chairs. "So, she's really not my daughter? I thought after all these years…maybe…"

Latone fisted his hands on the table. "Did you kill Candace, Arnold?"

Hughes shook his head. "No, why would I?"

Latone spun toward Moor, accusation in his eyes. "It was you, wasn't it?" His face turned ashen. "You killed my daughter."

Moor glared at Latone. "I was trying to protect you, Robert. Candace was nothing but a sick tramp, a black hole of need, and a detriment to you all these years."

"I loved my daughter," Latone said, his temper rising. "She was not a danger to me."

"What if she had spilled the truth?" Moor stood and paced, furious. "I was trying to protect you. When that Fagan woman came asking questions, I was afraid Candace would expose the truth. Then your reputation, your career, everything we've worked for all these years would be ruined."

Latone vaulted across the table and attacked Moor, trying to choke him. Black and Fox dragged them apart and thrust them back into the chairs.

"So, you killed Candace?" Devlin said to Moor.

Moor nodded, rubbing his neck. "For him."

"I never asked you to kill my own daughter."

"No, but you did ask me to assume responsibility for keeping your reputation intact, and just as always, you left the dirty details up to me." He shrugged. "This time was no different."

Devlin interrupted before the situation became more volatile. "Latone, you dropped Melissa off at the church, didn't you?"

Latone nodded.

"So, if Melissa Fagan wasn't Candace's child, who were her parents, and why did you abandon her at the church?" Black asked.

Latone's lawyer shot him a warning look, but Latone seemed to realize all was lost. He wiped sweat from his forehead. "The night Candace's baby died, she was so distraught. She...wasn't herself, she had an emotional imbalance, all because she had a reaction to those experimental birth control pills. The pills caused the baby to have birth defects."

"The reason I spearheaded research to improve intelligence in infants," Hughes said.

To create the perfect child. Project Simon. Eric grimaced and glanced at Cain.

"But Candace was beyond reason. She was so upset, she was out of her mind," Latone said. "In the middle of the night, she kidnapped a newborn from the nursery."

"Melissa Fagan?" Devlin asked.

Latone nodded, looking miserable. "When I found out, I figured if the police discovered what she'd done, they'd arrest her and lock her up for life."

"So, you took the baby to a church and abandoned her instead of returning her to her parents?"

"What else could I have done?" Latone bellowed. "If I'd carried her back to the hospital, I would have had to explain. Candace was *my* baby, I felt responsible, I had to protect her."

Eric's heart pounded. He wanted to tear the man apart limb by limb. He had essentially destroyed Melissa's life to protect his sick daughter and his own reputation.

"But Candace never forgave me. She got it in her head that Melissa was really hers, and she...she was never the same."

The room grew quiet as the revelations registered.

Finally, Devlin directed his comments to Moor, "So, you arranged with Dr. Hopkins to brainwash a hired man to kill Candace, then Melissa?"

Moor nodded and glanced at Latone, but Latone gave him a bitter unforgiving look.

Eric's jaw tightened. The pieces had all come together. Latone, Moor, Hughes, Hopkins—they would all pay for their crimes.

But Melissa had suffered because of all of them. Who were her parents?

Chapter 17

Melissa had spent the longest three days of her life waiting for answers. She wanted closure about Candace's murder and her parents.

But more than that, she wanted Eric.

Would he ever change his mind and see her? Could he forgive her for her father's crimes against him? Or would he always remind him of Hughes and the explosion?

Maybe he doesn't love you.

If so, she needed to accept the truth and move on. Maybe return to Atlanta. Although she enjoyed her work at CIRP, she didn't belong here, not after all the bad memories....

She poured herself a cup of coffee, brushed through her hair, preparing to go to work, when a knock sounded. Hope that it might be Eric flickered through her.

She hurried and answered the door, a smile of relief

coming when she actually saw him on her doorstep. He still looked serious, haunted, a little leaner from his surgery, but so handsome that her heart swelled with love.

"Can I come in, Melissa? We have to talk."

"Yes." Talk would be good, at least a start.

He followed her to the living area, his limp pronounced.

"You need to continue therapy."

"I will." He waited until she sat on the sofa, then claimed the chair opposite her. "I have some news about the case."

Nerves fluttered in her stomach. "You found out who killed Candace?"

"Yes." Eric leaned his elbows on his knees. "Edward Moor, Robert Latone's assistant. Apparently, he thought he was protecting Latone from his own daughter."

"Did Robert Latone know what Mr. Moor had done?"

Eric shook his head no. "But Latone wanted the two of us out of the picture."

"We were getting too close to the truth?"

"Exactly." Eric sighed. "Hughes was working with Dr. Hopkins on brainwashing experiments, so Moor contacted him, and Hopkins hypnotized this thug to be his hired gun."

"So they would have an alibi?"

"Exactly. Meanwhile, Hughes assumed the identity of an old war buddy. If we'd checked the patient files, we might have made the connection earlier. But there's more." Eric glanced up into her eyes for the first time. "Latone wanted to protect Candace, so he gave you away, but Candace Latone is not your mother."

Melissa gasped. "What?"

Eric gave her a somber look. "Apparently, Candace lost her own baby in childbirth. The baby had birth defects due to the experimental drugs Hughes had given her. Candace was so distraught and inconsolable that she kidnapped a newborn from the nursery."

"The newborn…" Her voice faded. "It was me?"

Eric nodded. "When Latone discovered the kidnapping, he didn't want the police to arrest Candace, so he carried you to the church and left you."

Melissa rubbed her forehead, seeing the events and the way they'd played out. "Instead of returning me to my real parents."

"Yes."

So selfish. So many people hurt, lives changed. "And my real parents, then, who are they?"

"Your mother is waiting outside."

"What?"

"I found her for you, Melissa. It's a present to make up for—"

"You don't have anything to make up for, Eric."

"Then call it my goodbye gift." He stood then, bent and kissed her lips, and limped to the door. She sat in stunned silence as he walked out, struggling to comprehend all that had happened.

Who was her mother? Louise? The woman who'd been so confused…

A second later, Helen, the nurse she'd been working with at the hospital, appeared in the doorway. She looked hesitant, shaken, emotional.

Melissa stared at her in shock. "Helen?"

Helen's eyes filled with tears. "Melissa… I… I can't believe this, but Mr. Caldwell, he found proof. You're… I'm…you're my baby."

"How?" Melissa's throat closed. "Are you sure?"

"I thought…you were kidnapped, but… I was told

you were a boy. I've looked for you for all these years, but I've been searching for a son."

"A son?"

"Yes." Helen swiped at her eyes. "When you mentioned you were looking for your parents, it never occurred to me that you could be my child."

"And that's the reason you acted so oddly when I asked about the labor and delivery wing."

"I couldn't talk about it," Helen admitted. "It was just too hard. I...wanted a baby so badly." She hugged her stomach. "The night they told me you'd been kidnapped, I wanted to die."

Melissa pressed her hand to her mouth. "My father?"

Tears flowed down Helen's cheeks. "He died before you were born. I had to go on alone, and there were times...times I didn't think I'd survive."

Melissa took a step forward. "I know... I felt the same way." But she had to be sure, she'd thought Candace was her mother. "Wait here just a minute." She ran to the bedroom and retrieved the tiny crocheted bonnet from the keepsake box, then returned with it pressed lovingly in her hands.

"Oh, my heavens." Helen's face paled as she spotted the cap. "You kept it... I made that with my own hands...."

Melissa enveloped Helen into a hug and sagged against her, both dissolving into tears of joy. Neither one of them would ever have to be alone again.

After all these years and nearly getting killed, she had finally come home.

There was only one thing missing... Eric.

Three weeks later, Eric sat on the boat dock behind his cabin on Lake Lanier, the slow lull of the water against the embankment soothing his agitated mind. He had spent the past few weeks recovering and trying to put the past behind him.

But he couldn't forget Melissa.

Sweet, strong, gutsy Melissa who had challenged him to walk, who had kissed his scars and confessed that she loved him, who had given him her virginity and hope when he thought he had none left for his life.

Every whisper of the wind brought memories of her strength and courage. Every night he lay awake, imagining her in his arms. Wishing he'd been good enough for her, courageous enough to be the kind of man to fulfill her dreams.

At least she had her mother now—the family she had always wanted.

And he had Cain and Alanna and Simon.

So why did he still feel lonely?

A car engine purred in the distance, and he pivoted, fishing line in hand. Cain and Alanna had been checking on him regularly. Devlin had even offered him a job, but Eric had declined, the ranch idea growing in his mind.

A familiar Camry pulled into his driveway, and he tensed. Melissa?

Was something wrong?

He held his breath as she exited the car and glanced around. Then she spotted him on the dock and strode toward him. His hands tightened around the fishing pole.

"Eric?"

She looked more beautiful now, rested, a soft pink rosiness to her cheeks that hadn't been there before. And she was smiling. Tentative, but a real smile. God, she looked gorgeous in that slinky sundress with her long hair spilling across her shoulders and the wind kissing her cheeks. He wanted to kiss her....

"Melissa, what are you doing here?"

"I had to see you."

"Is something wrong?"

"Yes."

"Your mother? Did things not work out?"

"No, Helen is fine." Melissa smiled. "Thank you for finding her, she's the family I never had."

"I'm glad. I want you to be happy."

"I am. Except there's still something missing."

His heart pounded, and he started to stand, but she dropped to the dock beside him, letting her feet dangle over the edge of the water. "I have to ask you something."

"What?" Anything. He'd do anything for her.

"Do you blame me for the things Hughes did?"

He grunted in shock. "Of course not. Why would I?"

She shrugged. "Is there someone else?"

"Excuse me?"

"Another woman?" She gestured toward the cabin. "Here, in Atlanta, is there another girl in your life?"

He was so starved for her, he studied her face, memorized her eyes. "No, there's no one else." Didn't she know there never had been?

She bit down on her bottom lip, then turned toward him, her eyes full of emotion. "Then why can't you love me?"

A raspy breath escaped him. She had been so honest with him, so giving, had helped him through so much. Cain said he was a fool for not pursuing a relationship with her.

"Is it because you want to be single? Do you like your single life?"

"Uh, no." He hated it. The empty bed. The TV dinners. The quiet. Whereas once the lake felt peaceful, now it felt lonely.

She pressed her hand over her heart. "Then is something wrong with me?"

"How can you ask that?" He couldn't resist. She looked so vulnerable, soft, delicious. "You're the most perfect woman I've ever known, Melissa."

She wet her lips. "Then why? Is it because of my seizures?"

"No. Hell no." He cleared his throat, studied his fingernails. "You deserve someone better than me, someone stronger, whole." Anger churned through him, and he stood, hating that his leg still hadn't completely healed, and he had to grab the post to support himself. "I'm broken down."

She stood, her voice husky. "Eric, you are the most stubborn man I've ever met. But I love you, and I want you." Tears laced her voice. "Don't make me beg."

He clutched her arms, aching to drag her to him. "You don't have to beg."

"Do you love me? Yes or no?" She stared him straight in the eyes. "Say no, on your mother's cross, and I'll walk away and never bother you again."

She would always bother him, haunting his memories with her tenderness and strength. His chest squeezed, his throat closed. He glanced down at the cross that had become a symbol for so much in his life. For his mother's dreams, his own hopes.

He couldn't lie.

And he didn't want Melissa to walk away and never come back. He wanted her to stay, to kiss his scars, to hold him all through the night. And he wanted to do the same for her. "I…"

"Yes or no, Eric?"

He closed his eyes. He wanted her as his wife. "Yes."

"Yes, what?" she whispered.

"Yes, I love you." The admission liberated him, opened up the dark vortex in his soul and filled it with sunshine. He opened his eyes, and caught her smiling.

Once he'd said the words, they kept spilling out. "I love you, Melissa, I love you with all my heart."

She laughed, and he clinched his arms around her waist and spun her around, a giddy feeling bursting inside him. Then he raised his head and shouted it to the wind and the sky. "I love Melissa Fagan. I love you, love you, love you!"

Melissa looped her arms around his neck, cradled his face in her hands and pressed her mouth to his. "So, show me, lover boy."

And he did.

He spread a blanket on the grass beneath a shady oak, stripped her clothes and made slow, sweet love to her until the sun faded into the night, and she promised to be his wife.

* * * * *

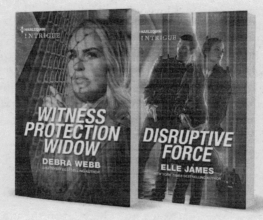

He'd recognize that voice anywhere, even though he'd
heard it live and in person just a few times and never
so…forceful. He believed her, but he had no intention
of letting her off the hook so easily.

He raised his hands. "I'm LAPD Detective
Jake McAllister. Are you all right?"

A sudden gust of wind carried her sigh down the trail
toward him.

"It…it's Kyra Chase. I'm sorry. I'm putting away my
weapon."

Lowering his hands, he said, "Is it okay for me to
move now?"

"Of course. I didn't realize… I thought you were…"

"The killer coming back to his dump site?" He flicked on the flashlight in his hand and continued down the trail, his shoes scuffing over dirt and pebbles. "He wouldn't do that—at least not so soon after the kill."

When he got within two feet of her, he skimmed the beam over her body, her dark clothing swallowing up the light until it reached her blond hair. "I didn't mean to scare you, but what are you doing here?"

"Probably the same thing you are." She hung on to the strap of her purse, her hand inches from the gun pocket.

"I'm the lead detective on the case, and I'm doing some follow-up investigation."

"Believe it or not, Detective, I have my own prep work that I like to do before meeting a victim's family. I want to have as much information as possible when talking to them. I'm sure you can understand that."

"Sure, I can. And call me Jake."

Don't miss
The Setup *by Carol Ericson,*
available April 2021 wherever
Harlequin Intrigue books and ebooks are sold.

Harlequin.com

Love Harlequin romance?

DISCOVER.

Be the first to find out about promotions,
news and exclusive content!

Facebook.com/HarlequinBooks

Twitter.com/HarlequinBooks

Instagram.com/HarlequinBooks

Pinterest.com/HarlequinBooks

YouTube.com/HarlequinBooks

ReaderService.com

EXPLORE.

Sign up for the Harlequin e-newsletter and
download a free book from any series at
TryHarlequin.com

CONNECT.

Join our Harlequin community to
share your thoughts and connect
with other romance readers!
Facebook.com/groups/HarlequinConnection

HSOCIAL2021

HARLEQUIN

Heartfelt or thrilling, passionate or uplifting—Harlequin is more than just happily-ever-after.

With twelve different series to choose from and new books available every month, you are sure to find stories that will move you, uplift you, inspire and delight you.

HNEWS2021